This marvellous collection of twentieth-century tales — many from the 1920s and 1930s, the heyday of the ghost story — includes work by some thirty women writers. All of them demonstrate a subtle power to delight and chill at the same time as they explore those ghostly margins of the supernatural which are part of private experience as well as of popular tradition.

Absorbing, entertaining, deliciously unnerving, the collection is an important addition to women's literary heritage. It is also an irresistible read for those with a taste for being spooked.

Richard Dalby is a literary researcher and bibliographer whose published works include several anthologies of ghost stories: *The Sorceress in Stained Glass*, *The Best Ghost Stories of H. Russell Wakefield*, *Dracula's Brood*, *Ghosts and Scholars* and *The Virago Book of Victorian Ghost Stories*. He lives in North Yorkshire.

Jennifer Uglow has published *George Eliot*, a study of the author's life and works (Virago 1987) and is editorial director of the Hogarth Press in London.

THE VIRAGO BOOK OF

GHOST STORIES

THE TWENTIETH CENTURY

EDITED BY
RICHARD DALBY

WITH AN INTRODUCTION BY
JENNIFER UGLOW

Published by VIRAGO PRESS Limited 1990
20−23 Mandela Street, Camden Town, London NW1 OHQ

First published in Great Britain by VIRAGO PRESS 1988

British Library Cataloguing in Publication Data
The Virago Book of Ghost Stories.
Vol. 1: Twentieth century
1. Ghost stories, English
2. English fiction − Women authors
I. Dalby, Richard
823′.01′08375   PR1309.G5
ISBN 0-86068-810-0

Typeset by Goodfellow & Egan, Cambridge
Printed by Cox and Wyman Ltd, Reading, Berks

CONTENTS

CONTENTS

PREFACE

'MY "attitude" towards ghost stories is one of enthralling interest and admiration if they are well told. I regard the ghost story as a perfectly legitimate form of art, and at the same time as the most difficult. Ghosts have their own atmosphere and their own reality, they have also their setting in the everyday reality we know; the story-teller is handling two realities at the same time . . .' – MAY SINCLAIR, *Bookman*, 1923

Since the early days of the sublime Gothic terrors of Ann Radcliffe, Clara Reeve and Mary Shelley, women have produced many of the finest ghost stories ever written. This has been acknowledged by connoisseurs of the genre, from M. R. James to Roald Dahl, but never properly reflected in anthologies, where often ninety per cent of the stories are by men.

The present collection seeks to remedy that situation.

This is an anthology of stories from the twentieth century. Its companion volume, *The Virago Book of Victorian Ghost Stories*, to be published in 1988, will include Elizabeth Gaskell, Mary Braddon, Mrs Oliphant, Rhoda Broughton, Mary E. Wilkins, Willa Cather and many more. The wealth of ghost stories in the twentieth century is such that, due to limitations of space, some writers have had to be excluded, among them Joan Aiken, Christine Brooke-Rose, A. S. Byatt, Clotilde Graves, Elizabeth Fancett, and Margaret Irwin. I have tried to make my selection as varied and representative as possible, ranging from the end of the Edwardian era to the 1980s, and including both writers famous in the genre and others who experimented successfully, but rarely, with the form. The stories are arranged in chronological order, so the reader can easily perceive how the form of the ghost story has developed over the past seventy-five years. The early tales, especially those from the pre-war 'Golden Age' of the ghost story, have a timeless quality which makes them easily accessible to the modern reader. All are examples of fine, imaginative story-telling with a supreme command of the supernatural.

Richard Dalby

ACKNOWLEDGEMENTS

Permission to reproduce the following stories has kindly been granted by the following: 'The Token', May Sinclair, copyright May Sinclair 1923, by Curtis Brown Ltd, London; 'The Shadowy Third', Ellen Glasgow, copyright 1923 by Doubleday & Company, Inc., renewed 1951 by First and Merchants National PPJK of Richmond by the Richmond SPCA and by Harcourt Brace Jovanovich Inc., USA; 'The Haunted Saucepan', Margery Lawrence, from *Nights of the Round Table*, 1926, by David Higham Associates Ltd, London; 'The Amorous Ghost', Enid Bagnold, by the Executors of Enid Bagnold; 'The Accident' and 'A Persistent Woman', Marjorie Bowen, by Hilary Long; 'The Waiting-Room', Phyllis Bottome, from *Strange Fruit*, 1928, by David Higham Associates Ltd, London; 'Sophy Mason Comes Back', E. M. Delafield, by Rosamund Dashwood; 'The Doll's House', Hester Gorst, copyright Hester Gorst 1933, by the author; 'The Night Nurse's Story', Edith Olivier, by John Johnson Ltd, London; 'The Follower', Lady Cynthia Asquith, by the Executors of Lady Cynthia Asquith; 'Roaring Tower', Stella Gibbons, copyright Stella Gibbons 1937, by the author; 'The Happy Autumn Fields', Elizabeth Bowen, copyright Elizabeth Bowen 1944, by Curtis Brown Ltd, London and by Alfred A. Knopf Inc, USA; 'The Empty Schoolroom', Pamela Hansford Johnson, by Curtis Brown Ltd, London, on behalf of the Executors of Pamela Hansford Johnson; 'Three Miles Up', Elizabeth Jane Howard, copyright Elizabeth Jane Howard 1951, by the author; 'Whitewash', Rose Macaulay, copyright the Estate of Rose Macaulay 1952, by A. D. Peters Ltd, London; 'Poor Girl', Elizabeth Taylor, by A. M. Heath Ltd, London; 'On No Account, My Love', Elizabeth Jenkins, copyright Elizabeth Jenkins 1955, by the author; 'The Mistress in Black', Rosemary Timperley, copyright © Rosemary Timperley 1969, by the author; 'A Curious Experience', Norah Lofts, copyright © Norah Lofts 1971, by Curtis Brown Ltd, London, on behalf of the Estate; 'Breakages', Fay Weldon, copyright © Fay Weldon 1975, by the author and Hodder & Stoughton Ltd, London and Antony Sheil Associates Ltd, London; 'Dual Control', Elizabeth Walter, from *Dead Woman*, Copyright © Elizabeth Walter 1975, by the author.

'Lady with Unicorn', Sara Maitland, copyright © Sara Maitland 1987; 'Diamond Jim', Lisa St Aubin de Terán, copyright © Lisa St Aubin de Terán 1987; 'Ashputtle', Angela Carter, copyright © Angela Carter 1987.

Every effort has been made to trace copyright holders in all copyright material in this book. The editor regrets if there has been oversight and suggests the publisher is contacted in any such event.

INTRODUCTION

NOTHING compares with the pleasurable shiver and the shudder and the lingering awe aroused by a really good ghost story. We love to be scared, yet know that we are safe – to close the book and take comfort in the outlines of a familiar room. Yet somehow, as waking from a dream, that room will not be quite the same: the ordinary has become infected by the strange, brushed by the wings of the unknown. In this collection, as you will discover, even a saucepan can hide a spectre.

But are women's ghosts different from men's ghosts? In fiction at least, many aficionados can find no difference. Richard Dalby, a powerful authority, would claim that if one reads the excellent ghost story, without knowing the sex of the author, it is often virtually impossible to guess correctly; when Elizabeth Jane Howard and Robert Aickman wrote *We Are For the Dark*, three tales each, nearly everyone attributed their pieces wrongly. So, in compiling this anthology, he has merely picked some of the best modern stories, which just happen to be by women.

Ghost stories, however, often turn out to be more than games, and burying myself enjoyably in these ghoulish tales, I am haunted (in more ways than one) by the way in which the wraiths seem to emanate from women's lives, from their longings, their anger, their fears and their struggles. Women bring to their writing the qualities of their particular experience, their history of living on the margins. Until recently, although generations have relished their stories, this contribution has been neglected. A 'great tradition' of supernatural writing descends from Walpole to Poe and Hawthorne, Stevenson and Kipling, Le Fanu and Henry James, M. R. James and Arthur Machen. Histories of the genre often leave the women, rivals of these masters, invisible and silent. Yet they have been there since the beginning. Mrs Radcliffe, whose *Mysteries of Udolpho* was published in 1794 in the flowering of the Gothic, herald of the modern fantastic, was the first to pin down the subtle difference between terror and horror, in 1826:

They must be men of very cold imaginations with whom certainty is more terrible than surmise. Terror and horror are so far opposite, that the first expands the soul, and wakens the faculties to a higher degree of life; the other contracts, freezes and nearly annihilates them.

And eight years earlier the mechanical but soul-filled creation of Franken-stein had already leapt from the mind of the nineteen-year-old Mary Shelley, to wander through the frozen wastes towards our future. Women writers have always starred in the form, as they have in other varieties of fiction. The good women writers of ghost stories are so many, in fact, that they have spilled over a single volume and it has proved necessary to divide them, beginning with those nearest in time (don't worry – more are to come!). And even now there are others we would like to include who are left out in the cold, crying, like their own ghosts, to be given space and made visible again.

Many of their tales first appeared in magazines, now yellowing in cupboards, if not lost forever, or in annuals and anthologies which endured for a season and are long out of print. One of the joys of this volume is that it brings into focus several women who have made the form peculiarly their own: Cynthia Asquith, responsible for the influential *Ghost Books* of the 1920s and '50s; Margery Lambe, queen of the long-forgotten mystery magazines; Eleanor Scott, author of the sought-after collection, *Randall's Round*; Hester Gorst, now in her hundredth year, as adept at evoking a spook as her great-aunt Mrs Gaskell; Rosemary Timperley, one of the finest contemporary ghost-story writers. Some of the other contributors – Edith Nesbit, Mary Webb, Elizabeth Bowen, Fay Weldon, Angela Carter – have always been drawn to those shifting realms where a breath of the fantastic dislocates everyday life. But the roll-call also includes names associated with quite different kinds of writing – Edith Wharton, E. M. Delafield, Winifred Holtby, Pamela Hansford Johnson, Rose Macaulay, Elizabeth Taylor, Norah Lofts. They, too, call up spirits into worlds coloured by their own special qualities: their comic realism, their acute perception of character, their politics, their sense of the exotic.

While these are all twentieth-century stories, one is struck by how curiously old they feel, as if they were looking over their shoulder into a distant age. This is partly inherent in the subject; ghosts arise out of the past, of a person, a place, a society. It is partly to do with cultural history, for writers often invoke ancient forms. Angela Carter looks back to the oral folk-tale, Sara Maitland to the iconography of medieval tapestry, Winifred Holtby to the classical satire of misrule where the eruption of another world hilariously reveals the idiocy of this one. Even where there is no formal debt, authors are archaeologists digging back in time. Some, like E. M. Delafield, peel off the layers of time gradually, following the ghost's track backwards from a recent appearance, through gossip and hearsay, to original documents where it speaks in its own words, long written and unread. Others spring time open like Pandora's box, unleashing the restless spirit of letters and faded photographs. 'You've got some good morbid stuff in this box, Mary,' says the down-to-earth Travis in Elizabeth Bowen's 'The Happy Autumn Fields'. Elizabeth Taylor even offers us a ghost from the future: time becomes one-dimensional, the past flowing on within the present like a cold current beneath the surface of a mighty stream.

The old-fashioned feeling is also related to the development of the genre itself. The modern ghost story, in its short form, really began in the 1820s and reached a peak in later nineteenth-century journals, like Dickens' *Household Words*. As historians of the form such as Julia Briggs have argued, the appeal of the supernatural coincided, perhaps not by chance, with a widespread loss of religious belief, and with the rapid spread of industrialisation. Both pressures may have created a need to recall older, magical spirits which promised the existence of another world, even if a rather uncomfortable one. This was one of the arguments of Freud in his 1919 essay on 'The Uncanny'.

The popularity of ghost stories endured to the end of the 1930s and then died away, with the magazines they had flourished in, after the Second World War. Today there is a resurgence of interest in the form. Maybe our own time, in which people refer to Victorian values, is still more bereft of a certain cosmology than the Victorians themselves; quantum physics, psychoanalysis, a new surrealism in art, literature and film, linguistic analysis, have leap-frogged each other to shake and question neatly ordered assumptions of reality. The 'real' has come to seem distinctly unreal. As long ago as 1952, in her introduction to *The Second Ghost Book*, Elizabeth Bowen drew attention to the way modern ghosts were happily making themselves at home:

The universal battiness of our century looks like providing them with a propitious climate – hitherto confined to antique manors, castles, graveyards, cross-roads, yew walks, cloisters, cliff-edges, moors or city backwaters, they may now roam at will. They do well in flats and are villa-dwellers. They know how to curdle electric light, chill off heating, or de-condition air. Long ago they captured railway trains and installed themselves in liners' luxury cabins; now telephones, motors, planes and radio wave-lengths offer them self-expression. The advance of psychology has gone their way; the guilt-complex is their especial friend.

Freud had also seen the literature of the uncanny as a vehicle for projection of repressed desires. But if, since then (or since Henry James' *The Turn of the Screw*) our ghosts seem to lurk in the mind rather than clanking their chains in predictable dungeons, they are still remarkably powerful and not at all willing to be pinned down. It is noticeable how often, in occult tales by women, the ghosts and those who see them resent the subtle labels of psychiatry. Cynthia Asquith's heroine (faced by a supposed psychiatrist wearing a black mask and ominously called 'Dr Stone'!) speaks for many when she says, 'It would not be easy to tell him of her fantastic experiences – "hallucinations" her own doctor insisted on calling them.' The denial of madness and dreaming plays an important part in winning over the reader, whose suspension of disbelief is even more necessary than for fiction as a whole (which in its essence conjures beings out of nothing). In ghost stories the impossible must be accepted as fact. We *have* to trust that authority of personal experience to which Edith Nesbit's narrator ingenuously appeals when she says, 'I do not know how to weave a plot, nor how to embroider it. These things happened. I have no skill to add to what happened; nor is any adding of mine needed.' In this collection the resistance to accusations of make-believe is, however, more than a literary device, for it reminds us how often the subversive energy and aberrant behaviour of women themselves have been held down by the language of madness, sickness, 'nerves' and irrationality.

Can one tell from these stories what women are most haunted by? Well, they are the fears that stalk all women, not brought to life, but summoned up in their shimmering, insistent half-life. Even a simple tale of menace, skilfully told, can take the breath away by its profound suggestiveness. Women readers of Asquith's 'The Follower' will recognise her dread at once: the loafer in the street, the pursuing footsteps, the panic which makes one unable to walk alone, the exposing, assaulting gaze, the 'lashless eyes that searched me like unshaded lights'. Gradually this sexual terror, too easily written off as paranoia, spreads outwards to implicate men in general, who mask under benign exteriors an urge to destroy the women who trust them – to take away their freedom, their mobility, their children, their life. And, almost without admitting it, this is what the sufferer herself knows:

In the violent distaste I felt for him there was a faint element of – shall I say sub-sub-conscious recognition? – as though he reminded me of something I had once dreamt or imagined.

Again and again, with almost shocking repetitiveness, the stories attack the symbolic and actual domination of the father, the husband, the lover, the doctor, the cruel emperor – the men of power. At times there is no escaping the role of victim, but at others the tables are turned. The she-devil, in Fay Weldon's gloriously comic story, is let loose at last; the persecuted, in Ellen Glasgow's darker tale, turns on the tormentor. Vengeance is ours:

Something – it may have been, as the world believes, a misstep in the dimness, or it may have been, as I am ready to bear witness, an invisible judgement – something had killed him at the very moment when he most wanted to live.

Superficially these retributive endings reinstate the accepted moral order and the female anger which fuels revenge is cloaked by conventions of poetic justice. But we feel the heat, as well as the ghostly chill.

A different energy which burns in women's ghost stories is that of female desire and its more 'feminine' but equally consuming counterpart, the hunger for love. Its desperate force is often perceived as a threat by men and feared by women themselves, but its strength can be conveyed by the lightest touch: Elizabeth Bagnold's 'The Amorous Ghost' and Elizabeth Jane Howard's 'Three Miles Up' wickedly suggest the comedy of male fantasies or the danger of falling for the perfect women; real *femme fatales*. And Edith Wharton, in a brilliant story with echoes of *Dorian Gray*, shows how a man's complacent self-esteem, which rejects the irritating dependency of both women and men, can corrode the inner soul. But other writers concentrate on the women themselves, facing the fire directly. The way a surge of desire can fill the world and isolate those possessed is dazzlingly conveyed in the stories of Elizabeth Bowen, Stella Gibbons and Elizabeth Taylor.

Such stunning sensuality is unusual; more often yearning slides silently into despair. Indeed, it is astonishing how many of these tales are stories of unrequited love. Sometimes the love itself is unconventional, unspoken, even taboo; the closeness of sisters, the love of one woman for another whose husband does not understand her, the furious jealousy of a man whose friend is about to marry, the physical attraction which pulses between a governess and her seven-year-old pupil. But in every case the ghost of passion craves a response, it cannot bear to remain unseen and unfulfilled. Like Cathy, crying at the window in *Wuthering Heights*, it pleads to be reunited with the object of its love. And although there are stories where the breach is healed, like 'The Token' and 'The Waiting-Room' there are others, such as 'Miss de Mannering of Asham' and the grimly powerful 'Sophy Mason Comes Back', which dwell on the consequences of lonely lives shattered by reckless love; women betrayed, abandoned, pregnant, always alone. At the heart of their plight beats a still more terrible fear, the unendurable loss of a child. 'Oh my baby', cries one spectre, 'if I could have seen him smile.' 'You look kind. I wonder if you could have seen my little girl?' whispers another. Grief is compounded by guilt and remorse and by complex feelings about childbirth itself. The horror of a child's death, the ultimate violation of maternity, has always reverberated through women's writing about the supernatural, and the theme takes us back again to Mary Shelley who dreamt of her dead baby and went on to give imaginative birth to an immortal monster. In this context Angela Carter has (as so often) created a rarity – the nurturing ghost whose mothering power, as well as her vengefulness, extends beyond the grave.

The knot of female fears clustering around vulnerability and marginality, sex and childbirth, love and jealousy, intensifies the loneliness which marks all ghost stories, whether by men or women. Often we encounter a deprivation of tenderness which creates an unending spiral, making its victims cruel until their cruelty finds victims who, in turn, come back as ghosts to torment their tormentors. The diabolical, in its modern form, is a death of the heart which renders the world absurd and meaningless. Only a great gesture of pity, even self-pity, can release the beast within.

Supernatural fictions, like dreams, carry us to the borderlines of existence, beyond our own reflections in the mirror, down tunnels with no light at the end, up winding stairs we have never seen before, through doors we would rather not open. Their settings are often familiar to the point of cliché – the lonely house on the moors, the villa left empty for years, the garden with its dried-up fountain whose motto, half-overgrown with moss, reads 'Time flieth, hope dieth'. In ghost stories beds give no rest and houses are no longer homes; we are at risk where we should be most secure. Housework itself, as Norah Lofts wryly reminds us (and some of us don't need reminding) can come to haunt the unwary. In a profound and powerful way, buildings, however normal they look, become shells imbued with disembodied passions, a point neatly symbolised in Hester Gorst's story where an evil doll's house makes the narrator brood, with hideous irony, on the independent existence of the subconscious: 'Can jealousy, love, hatred be hidden from their possessor, yet leave their atmosphere in some place where they have lived?' This model, like all the other houses, is the architecture of the mind itself.

And beyond the house lies . . . what? It may be a twilit Gothic scene with dark avenues of trees, or a busy modern street. For ghosts carry their own space with them, and, as one of them discovers to her own amazement, they can even be sat upon by stout German ladies in pavement cafés. But, although the scenery through which ghosts move may look substantial, there is always a suspicion that it might suddenly fade into nothingness, poking doubt at the realism of fiction itself. Many women in this anthology equal the most famous men in their evocation of atmosphere. Some of their settings take us out of our element altogether, into the currents which swirl around Rose Macaulay's Capri where the waves lisp in terror in the caves, or into the amorphous mud, mist and marshes of Elizabeth Jane Howard's fenland canals, the sedgy lake where no bird sings and where 'the light drained out of the sky into the water and slowly drowned there'. A classic example of a dissolving world is the double landscape of Elizabeth Bowen's superb story. The happy autumn fields of the title glow with the valedictory sunshine of a golden past which makes the hills flow together 'so that not a ripple showed where the girls lived', while the narrator dreams in blitz-torn London where 'the environment's being in semi-ruin struck her less than its being some sort of device, a trap; and she rejoiced, if anything, at its decrepitude'. But which is the trap – the past or the present?

Into these transitional landscapes and treacherous dwellings march a series of innocents quite unaware of what they are about to meet. Be warned –

getting a house for a snip or taking a holiday is just as dangerous as visiting a graveyard at midnight. Some people are traditionally receptive; servants, Celts, children and adolescents, or teachers and nurses whose work makes them sensitive to the shifting frontiers between child and adult, sickness and health, life and death. But most of the men and women who see ghosts are practical, often comical figures who can carry the reader's scepticism with them into the story. An added pleasure of these particular stories are the sly, affectionate pictures of 'real' women like the sturdy suffragette Annis Breck whose friends – '(who were not many and were all women) generally spoke with respect of her Sound Good Sense, her Practical Ability and her Capabilities'. Their feet are usually solidly on the ground, and often those feet are pretty solid themselves – if a little sprained – like the ankle of Dorothy Broster's Flora Halkett, the matronly thriller writer who rests her swollen limb on an embroidered footstool as she reaches out for her Britannia-metal teapot with repoussé roses. The only villainies Miss Halkett has met so far are those of the printer whose proofs have made her 'banker' into a 'baker' and invented 'a man of noble *berth* – as if it were a matter of a state-cabin'. "'I'm not sure," she admits, with commendable candour, "that my particular brand of story could happen anywhere!"'. But we, of course, know better.

What these rational creatures are about to see, in Henry James' famous phrase, is 'the other side of the tapestry', the untidy side of life which sensible people prefer to forget or at least to keep hidden. Coming from this other side – whether they are to be hated, pitied or welcomed – ghosts are always to be feared. There is danger in crossing these boundaries as Elizabeth Jenkins' stern, caring spirit points out in 'On No Account, My Love'. The ghosts rise up, like guilty consciences, unfettered by place or time, without warning and apparently without reason, or so their victims feel:

What makes it so much more terrible is that there was no reason why it should happen, it was as if the earth had opened suddenly and showed a chasm down which we must fall.

The sudden fracture of the normal, combined with the fact that these spectres return, after all, from the regions of death, creates a breathtaking apprehension. The numbing sense of loss and loneliness they carry with them would be too much to bear were it not, oddly enough, for the formal trickery of the ghost story itself. Fictional spirits, unlike random apparitions, need to have motives and goals to drive on their narratives and the reader has to discover them. So, as in detective stories (which also contain and defuse the fear of anarchy and irrationality), the reader, guided by what H. P. Lovecraft called 'the author's knowing wink', hurries to turn the page and find out, not 'whodunnit' but why they are doing it, and what will happen. The bizarre climax, the sudden cry, the final twist of plot take us back with a gasp into the 'real' world. This is why comedy is not alien to the ghost story but almost essential. Laughter is the ultimate shock absorber.

The shocks, surprises and delights of this collection are infinitely varied. And although they have made me look into the blackness from which the spirits emerge, I have relished every story and am sure that all their readers will be gripped to the very last line. But as you enjoy them remember, women, – they are our ghosts, and we will probably never escape them.

Jennifer Uglow, Canterbury, 1987

Edith Wharton

THE EYES

I

WE had been put in the mood for ghosts, that evening, after an excellent dinner at our old friend Culwin's, by a tale of Fred Murchard's – the narrative of a strange personal visitation.

Seen through the haze of our cigars, and by the drowsy gleam of a coal fire, Culwin's library, with its oak walls and dark old bindings, made a good setting for such avocations; and ghostly experiences at first hand being, after Murchard's opening, the only kind acceptable to us, we proceeded to take stock of our group and tax each member for a contribution. There were eight of us, and seven contrived, in a manner more or less adequate, to fulfil the condition imposed. It surprised us all to find that we could muster such a show of supernatural impressions, for none of us, excepting Murchard himself and young Phil Frenham – whose story was the slightest of the lot – had the habit of sending our souls into the invisible. So that, on the whole, we had every reason to be proud of our seven 'exhibits', and none of us would have dreamed of expecting an eighth from our host.

Our old friend, Mr Andrew Culwin, who had sat back in his arm-chair, listening and blinking through the smoke circles with the cheerful tolerance of a wise old idol, was not the kind of man likely to be favoured with such contacts, though he had imagination enough to enjoy, without envying, the superior privileges of his guests. By age and by education he belonged to the stout Positivist tradition, and his habit of thought had been formed in the days of the epic struggle between physics and metaphysics. But he had been, then and always, essentially a spectator, a humorous detached observer of the immense muddled variety show of life, slipping out of his seat now and then for a brief dip into the convivialities at the back of the house, but never, as far as one knew, showing the least desire to jump on the stage and do a 'turn'.

Among his contemporaries there lingered a vague tradition of his having, at a remote period, and in the romantic clime, been wounded in a duel; but this legend no more tallied with what we younger men knew of his character than my mother's assertion that he had once been 'a charming little man with nice eyes' corresponded to any possible reconstitution of his physiognomy.

'He never can have looked like anything but a bundle of sticks,' Murchard had once said of him. 'Or a phosphorescent log, rather,' someone else amended; and we recognized the happiness of this description of his small squat trunk, with the red blink of the eyes in a face like mottled bark. He had always been possessed of a leisure which he had nursed and protected, instead of squandering it in vain activities. His carefully guarded hours had been devoted to the cultivation of a fine intelligence and a few judiciously chosen habits; and none of the disturbances common to human experience seemed to have crossed his sky. Nevertheless, his dispassionate survey of the universe had not raised his opinion of that costly experiment, and his study of the human race seemed to have resulted in the conclusion that all men were superfluous, and women necessary only because someone had to do the cooking. On the importance of this point his convictions were absolute, and gastronomy was the only science which he revered as a dogma. It must be owned that his little dinners were a strong argument in favour of this view, besides being a reason – though not the main one – for the fidelity of his friends.

Mentally he exercised a hospitality less seductive but no less stimulating. His mind was like a forum, or some open meeting-place for the exchange of ideas; somewhat cold and draughty, but light, spacious, and orderly – a kind of academic grove from which all the leaves have fallen. In this privileged area a dozen of us were wont to stretch our muscles and expand our lungs; and, as if to prolong as much as possible the tradition of what we felt to be a vanishing institution, one or two neophytes were now and then added to our band.

Young Phil Frenham was the last, and the most interesting, of these recruits, and a good example of Murchard's somewhat morbid assertion that our old friend 'liked 'em juicy'. It was indeed a fact that Culwin, for all his dryness specially tasted the lyric qualities in youth. As he was far too good an Epicurean to nip the flowers of soul which he gathered for his garden, his friendship was not a disintegrating influence: on the contrary, it forced the young idea to robuster bloom. And in Phil Frenham he had a good subject for experimentation. The boy was really intelligent, and the soundness of his nature was like the pure paste under a fine glaze. Culwin had fished him out of a fog of family dullness, and pulled him up to a peak in Darien; and the adventure hadn't hurt him a bit. Indeed, the skill with which Culwin had contrived to stimulate his curiosities without robbing them of their bloom of awe seemed to me a sufficient answer to Murchard's ogreish metaphor. There was nothing hectic in Frenham's efflorescence, and his old friend had not laid even a finger-tip on the sacred stupidities. One wanted no better proof of that than the fact that Frenham still reverenced them in Culwin.

'There's a side of him you fellows don't see. I believe that story about the duel!' he declared; and it was of the very essence of this belief that it should impel him – just as our little party was dispersing – to turn back to our host with the joking demand: 'And now you've got to tell us about *your* ghost!'

The outer door had closed on Murchard and the others; only Frenham and I remained; and the devoted servant who presided over Culwin's destinies, having brought a fresh supply of soda-water, had been laconically ordered to bed.

Culwin's sociability was a night-blooming flower, and we knew that he expected the nucleus of his group to tighten around him after midnight. But Frenham's appeal seemed to disconcert him comically, and he rose from the chair in which he had just reseated himself after his farewells in the hall.

'*My* ghost? Do you suppose I'm fool enough to go to the expense of keeping one of my own, when there are so many charming ones in my friends' closets? Take another cigar,' he said, revolving toward me with a laugh.

Frenham laughed, too, pulling up his slender height before the chimney-piece as he turned to face his short bristling friend.

'Oh,' he said, 'you'd never be content to share if you met one you really liked.'

Culwin had dropped back into his arm-chair, his head embedded in the hollow of worn leather, his little eyes glimmering over a fresh cigar.

'Liked – *liked!* Good Lord!' he growled.

'Ah, you *have*, then!' Frenham pounced on him in the same instant, with a side-glance of victory at me; but Culwin cowered gnome-like among his cushions, dissembling himself in a protective cloud of smoke.

'What's the use of denying it? You've seen everything, so of course you've seen a ghost!' his young friend persisted, talking intrepidly into the cloud. 'Or, if you haven't seen one, it's only because you've seen two!'

The form of the challenge seemed to strike our host. He shot his head out of the mist with a queer tortoise-like motion he sometimes had, and blinked approvingly at Frenham.

'That's it,' he flung at us on a shrill jerk of laughter; 'it's only because I've seen two!'

The words were so unexpected that they dropped down and down into a deep silence, while we continued to stare at each other over Culwin's head, and Culwin stared at his ghosts. At length Frenham, without speaking, threw himself into the chair on the other side of the hearth, and leaned forward with his listening smile. . . .

II

'Oh, of course they're not show ghosts – a collector wouldn't think anything of them . . . Don't let me raise your hopes . . . their one merit is their numerical strength: the exceptional fact of there being *two*. But, as against this, I'm bound to admit that at any moment I could probably have exorcised them both by asking my doctor for a prescription, or my oculist for a pair of spectacles. Only, as I never could make up my mind whether to go to the doctor or the oculist – whether I was afflicted by an optical or a digestive delusion – I left them to pursue their interesting double life, though at times they made mine exceedingly uncomfortable . . .

'Yes – uncomfortable; and you know how I hate to be uncomfortable! But it was part of my stupid pride, when the thing began, not to admit that I could be disturbed by the trifling matter of seeing two –

'And then I'd no reason, really, to suppose I was ill. As far as I knew I was simply bored – horribly bored. But it was part of my boredom – I remember – that I was feeling so uncommonly well, and didn't know how on earth to work off my surplus energy. I had come back from a long journey – down in South America and Mexico – and had settled down for the winter near New York, with an old aunt who had known Washington Irving and corresponded with N. P. Willis. She lived, not far from Irvington, in a damp Gothic villa, overhung by Norway spruces, and looking exactly like a memorial emblem done in hair. Her personal appearance was in keeping with this image, and her own hair – of which there was little left – might have been sacrificed to the manufacture of the emblem.

'I had just reached the end of an agitated year, with considerable arrears to make up in money and emotion; and theoretically it seemed as though my aunt's mild hospitality would be as beneficial to my nerves as to my purse. But the deuce of it was that, as soon as I felt myself safe and sheltered, my energy began to revive; and how was I to work it off inside of a memorial emblem? I had, at that time, the illusion that sustained intellectual effort could engage any man's whole activity; and I decided to write a great book – I forget about what. My aunt, impressed by my plan, gave up to me her Gothic library, filled with classics bound in black cloth and daguerreotypes of faded celebrities; and I sat down at my desk to win myself a place among their number. And to facilitate my task she lent me a cousin to copy my manuscript.

'The cousin was a nice girl, and I had an idea that a nice girl was just what I needed to restore my faith in human nature, and principally in myself. She was neither beautiful nor intelligent – poor Alice Nowell! – but it interested me to see any woman content to be so uninteresting, and I wanted to find out the secret of her content. In doing this I handled it rather rashly, and put it out of joint – oh, just for a moment! There's no fatuity in telling you this, for the poor girl had never seen anyone but cousins . . .

'Well, I was sorry for what I'd done, of course, and confoundedly bothered as to how I should put it straight. She was staying in the house, and one evening, after my aunt had gone to bed, she came down to the library to fetch a book she'd mislaid, like any artless heroine, on the shelves behind us. She was pink-nosed and flustered, and it suddenly occurrred to me that her hair, though it was fairly thick and pretty, would look exactly like my aunt's when she grew older. I was glad I had noticed this, for it made it easier for me to decide to do what was right; and when I had found the book she hadn't lost I told her I was leaving for Europe that week.

'Europe was terribly far off in those days, and Alice knew at once what I meant. She didn't take it in the least as I'd expected – it would have been easier if she had. She held her book very tight, and turned away a moment to wind up the lamp on my desk – it had a ground glass shade with vine leaves, and glass drops around the edge, I remember. Then she came back, held out her hand, and said: "Good-bye". And as she said it she looked straight at me and kissed me. I had never felt anything so fresh and shy and brave as her kiss. It was worse than any reproach, and it made me ashamed to deserve a reproach from her. I said to myself: "I'll marry her, and when my aunt dies she'll leave us this house, and I'll sit here at the desk and go on with my book; and Alice will sit over there with her embroidery and look at me as she's looking now. And life will go on like that for any number of years." The prospect frightened me a little, but at the time it didn't frighten me as much as doing anything to hurt her; and ten minutes later she had my seal ring on her finger, and my promise that when I went abroad she should go with me.

'You'll wonder why I'm enlarging on this incident. It's because the evening on which it took place was the very evening on which I first saw the queer sight I've spoken of. Being at that time an ardent believer in a necessary sequence between cause and effect, I naturally tried to trace some kind of link between what had just happened to me in my aunt's library, and what was to happen a few hours later on the same night; and so the coincidence between the two events always remained in my mind.

'I went up to bed with rather a heavy heart, for I was bowed under the weight of the first good action I had ever consciously committed; and young as I was, I saw the gravity of my situation. Don't imagine from this that I had hitherto been an instrument of destruction. I had been merely a harmless young man, who had followed his bent and declined all collaboration with Providence. Now I had suddenly undertaken to promote the moral order of the world, and I felt a good deal like the trustful spectator who had given his gold watch to the conjuror, and doesn't know in what shape he'll get it back when the trick is over . . . Still, a glow of self-righteousness tempered my fears, and I said to myself as I undressed that when I'd got used to being good it probably wouldn't make me as nervous as it did at the start. And by the time I was in bed, and had blown out my candle, I felt that I really *was* getting used to it, and that, as far as I'd got, it was not unlike sinking down into one of my aunt's very softest wool mattresses.

'I closed my eyes on this image, and when I opened them it must have been a good deal later, for my room had grown cold, and intensely still. I was waked by the queer feeling we all know – the feeling that there was something in the room that hadn't been there when I fell asleep. I sat up and strained my eyes into the darkness. The room was pitch black, and at first I saw nothing, but gradually a vague glimmer at the foot of the bed turned into two eyes staring back at me. I couldn't distinguish the features attached to them, but as I looked the eyes grew more and more distinct; they gave out a light of their own.

'The sensation of being thus gazed at was far from pleasant, and you might suppose that my first impulse would have been to jump out of bed and hurl myself on the invisible figure attached to the eyes. But it wasn't – my impulse was simply to lie still . . . I can't say whether this was due to an immediate sense of the uncanny nature of the apparition – to the certainty that if I did jump out of bed I should hurl myself on nothing – or merely to the benumbing effect of the eyes themselves. They were the very worst eyes I've ever seen: a man's, yes – but what a man! My first thought was that he must be frightfully old. The orbits were sunk, and the thick red-lined lids hung over the eyeballs like blinds of which the cords are broken. One lid drooped a little lower than the other, with the effect of a crooked leer; and between these folds of flesh, with their scant bristle of lashes, the eyes themselves, small glassy discs with an agate-like rim, looked like sea-pebbles in the grip of a starfish.

'But the age of the eyes was not the most unpleasant thing about them. What turned me sick was their expression of vicious security. I don't know how else to describe the fact that they seemed to belong to a man who had done a lot of harm in his life, but had always kept just inside the danger lines. They were not the eyes of a coward, but of someone much too clever to take risks; and my gorge rose at their look of base astuteness. Yet even that wasn't the worst; for as we continued to scan each other I saw in them a tinge of derision, and felt myself to be its object.

'At that I was seized by an impulse of rage that jerked me to my feet and pitched me straight at the unseen figure. But, of course, there wasn't any figure there, and my fists struck at emptiness. Ashamed and cold, I groped about for a match and lit the candles. The room looked just as usual – as I had known it would; and I crawled back to bed, and blew out the lights.

'As soon as the room was dark again the eyes reappeared; and I now applied myself to explaining them on scientific principles. At first I thought the illusion might have been caused by the glow of the last embers in the chimney; but the fireplace was on the other side of my bed, and so placed that the fire could not be reflected in my toilet glass, which was the only mirror in the room. Then it struck me that I might have been tricked by the reflection of the embers in some polished bit of wood or metal; and though I couldn't discover any object of the sort in my line of vision, I got up again, groped my way to the hearth, and covered what was left of the fire. But as soon as I was back in bed, the eyes were back at its foot.

'They were an hallucination, then. That was plain. But the fact that they were not due to any external dupery didn't make them a bit pleasanter. For if they were a projection of my inner consciousness, what the deuce was the matter with that organ? I had gone deeply enough into the mystery of morbid pathological states to picture the conditions under which an exploring mind might lay itself open to such a midnight admonition; but I couldn't fit it to my present case. I had never felt more normal, mentally and physically; and the only unusual fact in my situation – that of having assured the happiness of an amiable girl – did not seem a kind to summon unclean spirits about my pillow. But there were the eyes still looking at me . . .

'I shut mine, and tried to evoke a vision of Alice Nowell's. They were not remarkable eyes, but they were as wholesome as fresh water, and if she had had more imagination – or longer lashes – their expression might have been interesting. As it was, they did not prove very efficacious, and in a few moments I perceived that they had mysteriously changed into the eyes at the foot of the bed. It exasperated me more to feel these glaring at me through my shut lids than to see them, and I opened my eyes again and looked straight into their hateful stare . . .

'And so it went on all night. I can't tell you what that night was like, nor how long it lasted. Have you ever lain in bed, hopelessly wide awake, and tried to keep your eyes shut, knowing that if you opened 'em you'd see something you dreaded and loathed? It sounds easy, but it's devilish hard. Those eyes hung there and drew me. I had the *vertige de l'abîme*, and their red lids were the edge of my abyss . . . I had known nervous hours before: hours when I'd felt the wind of danger in my neck; but never this kind of strain. It wasn't that the eyes were awful; they hadn't the majesty of the powers of darkness. But they had – how shall I say? – a physical effect that was the equivalent of a bad smell: their look left a smear like a snail's. And I didn't see what business they had with me, anyhow – and I stared and stared, trying to find out . . .

'I don't know what effect they were trying to produce; but the effect they *did* produce was that of making me pack my portmanteau and bolt to town early next morning. I left a note for my aunt, explaining that I was ill and had gone to see my doctor; and as a matter of fact I did feel uncommonly ill – the night seemed to have pumped all the blood out of me. But when I reached town I didn't go to the doctor's. I went to a friend's rooms, and threw myself on a bed, and slept for ten heavenly hours. When I woke it was the middle of the night, and I turned cold at the thought of what might be waiting for me. I sat up, shaking, and stared into the darkness; but there wasn't a break in its blessed surface, and when I saw that the eyes were not there I dropped back into another long sleep.

'I had left no word for Alice when I fled, because I meant to go back the next morning. But the next morning I was too exhausted to stir. As the day went on, the exhaustion increased, instead of wearing off like the fatigue left by an ordinary night of insomnia: the effect of the eyes seemed to be cumulative, and the thought of seeing them again grew intolerable. For two days I fought my dread; and on the third evening I pulled myself together and decided to go back the next morning. I felt a good deal happier as soon as I'd decided, for I knew that my abrupt disappearance, and the strangeness of my not writing, must have been very distressing to poor Alice. I went to bed with an easy mind, and I fell asleep at once; but in the middle of the night I woke, and there were the eyes . . .

'Well, I simply couldn't face them; and instead of going back to my aunt's, I bundled a few things into a trunk and jumped aboard the first steamer for England. I was so dead tired when I got on board that I crawled straight into my berth, and slept most of the way over; and I can't tell you the bliss it was to wake from those long dreamless stretches and look fearlessly into the dark, *knowing* that I shouldn't see the eyes . . .

'I stayed abroad for a year, and then I stayed for another; and during that time I never had a glimpse of them. That was enough reason for prolonging my stay if I'd been on a desert island. Another was, of course, that I had perfectly come to see, on the voyage over, the complete impossibility of marrying Alice Nowell. The fact that I had been so slow in making this discovery annoyed me, and made me want to avoid explanations. The bliss of escaping at one stroke from the eyes, and from this other embarrassment, gave my freedom an extraordinary zest; and the longer I savoured it the better I liked its taste.

'The eyes had burned such a hole in my consciousness that for a long time I went on puzzling over the nature of the apparition, and wondering if it would ever come back. But as time passed I lost this dread, and retained only the precision of the image. Then that faded in its turn.

'The second year found me settled in Rome, where I was planning, I believe, to write another great book – a definitive work on Etruscan influences in Italian art. At any rate, I'd found some pretext of the kind for taking a sunny apartment in the Piazza di Spagna and dabbling about in the Forum; and there, one morning, a charming youth came to me. As he stood there in the warm light, slender and smooth and hyacinthine, he might have stepped from a ruined altar – one to Antinous, say; but he'd come instead from New York, with a letter from (of all people) Alice Nowell. The letter – the first I'd had from her since our break – was simply a line introducing her young cousin, Gilbert Noyes, and appealing to me to befriend him. It appeared, poor lad, that he "had talent", and "wanted to write"; and, an obdurate family having insisted that his calligraphy should take the form of double entry, Alice had intervened to win him six months' respite, during which he was to travel abroad on a meagre pittance, and somehow prove his ability to increase it by his pen. The quaint conditions of the test struck me first: it seemed about as conclusive as a medieval "ordeal". Then I was touched by her having sent him to me. I had always wanted to do her some service, to justify myself in my own eyes rather than hers; and here was a beautiful occasion.

'I imagine it's safe to lay down the general principle that predestined geniuses don't, as a rule, appear before one in the spring sunshine of the Forum looking like one of its banished gods. At any rate, poor Noyes wasn't a predestined genius. But he *was* beautiful to see, and charming as a comrade. It was only when he began to talk literature that my heart failed me. I knew all the symptoms so well – the things he had "in him", and the things outside him that impinged! There's the real test, after all. It was always – punctually, inevitably, with the inexorableness of a mechanical law – it was *always* the wrong thing that struck him. I grew to find a certain fascination in deciding in advance exactly which wrong thing he'd select; and I acquired an astonishing skill at the game . . .

'The worst of it was that his *bêtise* wasn't of the too obvious sort. Ladies who met him at picnics thought him intellectual; and even at dinners he passed for clever. I, who had him under the microscope, fancied now and then that he might develop some kind of a slim talent, something that he could make "do" and be happy on; and wasn't that, after all, what I was concerned with? He was so charming – he continued to be so charming – that he called forth all my charity in support of this argument; and for the first few months I really believed there was a chance for him . . .

'Those months were delightful. Noyes was constantly with me, and the more I saw of him the better I liked him. His stupidity was a natural grace – it was as beautiful, really, as his eyelashes. And he was so gay, so affectionate, and so happy with me, that telling him the truth would have been about as pleasant as slitting the throat of some gentle animal. At first I used to wonder what had put into that radiant head the detestable delusion that it held a brain. Then I began to see it was simply protective mimicry – an instinctive ruse to get away from family and life and an office desk. Not that Gilbert didn't – dear lad! – believe in himself. There wasn't a trace of hypocrisy in him. He was sure that his "call" was irresistible, while to me it was the saving grace of the situation that it *wasn't*, and that a little money, a little leisure, a little pleasure, would have turned him into an inoffensive idler. Unluckily, however, there was no hope of money, and with the alternative of the office desk before him, he couldn't postpone his attempt at literature. The stuff he turned out was deplorable, and I see now that I knew it from the first. Still, the absurdity of deciding a man's whole future on a first trial seemed to justify me in withholding my verdict, and perhaps even in encouraging him a little, on the ground that the human plant generally needs warmth to flower.

'At any rate, I proceeded on that principle, and carried it to the point of getting his term of probation extended. When I left Rome he went with me, and we idled away a delicious summer between Capri and Venice. I said to myself: "If he has anything in him, it will come out now"; and it *did*. He was never more enchanting and enchanted. There were moments of our pilgrimage when beauty born of murmuring sound seemed actually to pass into his face – but only to issue forth in a flood of the palest ink . . .

'Well, the time came to turn off the tap; and I knew there was no hand but mine to do it. We were back in Rome, and I had taken him to stay with me, not wanting him to be alone in his *pension* when he had to face the necessity of renouncing his ambition. I hadn't, of course, relied solely on my own judgement in deciding to advise him to drop literature. I had sent his stuff to various people – editors and critics – and they had always sent it back with the same chilling lack of comment. Really there was nothing on earth to say –

'I confess I never felt more shabbily than I did on the day when I decided to have it out with Gilbert. It was not well enough to tell myself that it was my duty to knock the poor boy's hopes into splinters – but I'd like to know what act of gratuitous cruelty hasn't been justified on that plea? I've always shrunk from usurping the functions of Providence, and when I have to exercise them I decidedly prefer that it shouldn't be on an errand of destruction. Besides, in the last issue, who was I to decide, even after a year's trial, if poor Gilbert had it in him or not?

'The more I looked at the part I'd resolved to play, the less I liked it; and I liked it still less when Gilbert sat opposite me, with his head thrown back in the lamplight, just as Phil's is now . . . . I'd been going over his last manuscript, and he knew it, and he knew that his future hung on my verdict – we'd tacitly agreed to that. The manuscript lay between us, on my table – a novel, his first novel, if you please! – and he reached over and laid his hand on it, and looked up at me with all his life in the look.

'I stood up and cleared my throat, trying to keep my eyes away from his face and on the manuscript.

"'The fact is, my dear Gilbert," I began –

'I saw him turn pale, but he was up and facing me in an instant.

"'Oh, look here, don't take on so, my dear fellow! I'm not so awfully cut up as all that!" His hands were on my shoulders, and he was laughing down on me from his full height, with a kind of mortally stricken gaiety that drove the knife into my side.

'He was too brutally brave for me to keep up any humbug about my duty. And it came over me suddenly how I should hurt others in hurting him: myself first, since sending him home meant losing him; but more particularly poor Alice Nowell, to whom I had so longed to prove my good faith and my desire to serve her. It really seemed like failing her twice to fail Gilbert –

'But my intuition was like one of those lightning flashes that encircle the whole horizon, and in the same instant I saw what I might be letting myself in for if I didn't tell the truth. I said to myself: "I shall have him for life" – and I'd never yet seen anyone, man or woman, whom I was quite sure of wanting on those terms. Well, this impulse of egotism decided me. I was ashamed of it, and to get away from it I took a leap that landed me straight in Gilbert's arms.

"'The thing's all right, and you're all wrong!" I shouted up at him; and as he hugged me, and I laughed and shook in his clutch, I had for a minute the sense of self-complacency that is supposed to attend the footsteps of the just. Hang it all, making people happy *has* its charms –

'Gilbert, of course, was for celebrating his emancipation in some spectacular manner; but I sent him away alone to explode his emotions, and I went to bed to sleep off mine. As I undressed I began to wonder what their aftertaste would be – so many of the finest don't keep. Still, I wasn't sorry, and I meant to empty the bottle, even if it *did* turn a trifle flat.

'After I got in bed I lay for a long time smiling at the memory of his eyes – his blissful eyes . . . Then I fell asleep, and when I woke the room was deathly cold, and I sat up with a jerk – and there were *the other eyes* . . .

'It was three years since I'd seen them, but I'd thought of them so often that I fancied they could never take me unawares again. Now, with their red sneer on me, I knew that I had really believed they would come back, and that I was as defenceless as ever against them . . . As before, it was the insane irrelevance of their coming that made it so horrible. What the deuce were they after, to leap out at me at such a time? I had lived more or less carelessly in the years since I'd seen them, though my worst indiscretions were not dark enough to invite the searchings of their infernal glare; but at this particular moment I was really in what might have been called a state of grace; and I can't tell you how the fact added to their horror . . .

'But it's not enough to say they were as bad as before: they were worse. Worse by just so much as I'd learned of life in the interval, by all the damnable implications my wider experience read into them. I saw now what I hadn't seen before: that they were eyes which had grown hideous gradually, which had built up their baseness coralwise, bit by bit, out of a series of small turpitudes slowly accumulated through the industrious years. Yes – it came to me that what made them so bad was that they'd grown bad so slowly . . .

'There they hung in the darkness, their swollen lids dropped across the little watery bulbs rolling loose in the orbits, and the puff of flesh making a muddy shadow underneath – and as their stare moved with my movements, there came over me a sense of their tacit complicity, of a deep hidden understanding between us that was worse than the first shock of their strangeness. Not that I understood them; but that they made it so clear that some day I should . . . Yes, that was the worst part of it, decidedly; and it was the feeling that became stronger each time they came back . . .

'For they got into the damnable habit of coming back. They reminded me of vampires with a taste for young flesh, they seemed so to gloat over the taste of a good conscience. Every night for a month they came to claim their morsel of mine: since I'd made Gilbert happy they simply wouldn't loosen their fangs. The coincidence almost made me hate him, poor lad, fortuitous as I felt it to be. I puzzled over it a good deal, but I couldn't find any hint of an explanation except in the chance of his association with Alice Nowell. But then the eyes had let up on me that moment I had abandoned her, so they could hardly be the emissaries of a woman scorned, even if one could have pictured poor Alice charging such spirits to avenge her. That set me thinking, and I began to wonder if they would let up on me if I abandoned Gilbert. The temptation was insidious, and I had to stiffen myself against it; but really, dear boy! he was too charming to be sacrificed to such demons. And so, after all, I never found out what they wanted . . . .'

III

The fire crumbled, sending up a flash which threw into relief the narrator's gnarled face under its grey-black stubble. Pressed into the hollow of the chair-back, it stood out an instant like an intaglio of yellowish red-veined stone, with spots of enamel for the eyes; then the fire sank and it became once more a dim Rembrandtish blur.

Phil Frenham, sitting in a low chair on the opposite side of the hearth, one long arm propped on the table behind him, one hand supporting his thrown-back head, and his eyes fixed on his old friend's face, had not moved since the tale began. He continued to maintain his silent immobility after Culwin had ceased to speak, and it was I who, with a vague sense of disappointment at the sudden drop of the story, finally asked: 'But how long did you keep on seeing them?'

Culwin, so sunk into his chair that he seemed like a heap of his own empty clothes, stirred a little, as if in surprise at my question. He appeared to have half-forgotten what he had been telling us.

'How long? Oh, off and on all that winter. It was infernal. I never got used to them. I grew really ill.'

Frenham shifted his attitude, and as he did so his elbow struck against a small mirror in a bronze frame standing on the table behind him. He turned and changed its angle slightly; then he resumed his former attitude, his dark head thrown back on his lifted palm, his eyes intent on Culwin's face. Something in his silent gaze embarrassed me, and as if to divert attention from it I pressed on with another question:

'And you never tried sacrificing Noyes?'

'Oh, no. The fact is I didn't have to. He did it for me, poor boy!'

'Did it for you? How do you mean?'

'He wore me out – wore everybody out. He kept on pouring out his lamentable twaddle, and hawking it up and down the place till he became a thing of terror. I tried to wean him from writing – oh, ever so gently, you understand, by throwing him with agreeable people, giving him a chance to make himself felt, to come to a sense of what he *really* had to give. I'd foreseen this solution from the beginning – felt sure that, once the first ardour of authorship was quenched, he'd drop into his place as a charming parasitic thing, the kind of chronic Cherubino for whom, in old societies, there's always a seat at table, and a shelter behind the ladies' skirts. I saw him take his place as "the poet": the poet who doesn't write. One knows the type in every drawing-room. Living in that way doesn't cost much – I'd worked it all out in my mind, and felt sure that, with a little help, he could manage it for the next few years; and meanwhile he'd be sure to marry. I saw him married to a widow, rather older, with a good cook and a well-run house. And I actually had my eye on the widow. . . . Meanwhile I did everything to help the transition – lent him money to ease his conscience, introduced him to pretty women to make him forget his vows. But nothing would do him: he had but one idea in his beautiful obstinate head. He wanted the laurel and not the rose, and he kept on repeating Gautier's axiom, and battering and filing at his limp prose till he'd spread it out over Lord knows how many hundred pages. Now and then he would send a barrelful to a publisher, and of course it would always come back.

'At first it didn't matter – he thought he was "misunderstood". He took the attitudes of genius, and whenever an opus came home he wrote another to keep it company. Then he had a reaction of despair, and accused me of deceiving him, and Lord knows what. I got angry at that, and told him it was he who had deceived himself. He'd come to me determined to write, and I'd done my best to help him. That was the extent of my offence, and I'd done it for his cousin's sake, not his.

'That seemed to strike home, and he didn't answer for a minute. Then he said: "My time's up and my money's up. What do you think I'd better do?"

'"I think you'd better not be an ass," I said.

'"What do you mean by being an ass?" he asked.

'I took a letter from my desk and held it out to him.

'"I mean refusing this offer of Mrs Ellinger's: to be her secretary at a salary of five thousand dollars. There may be a lot more in it than that.'

'He flung out his hand with a violence that struck the letter from mine. "Oh, I know well enough what's in it!" he said, red to the roots of his hair.

'"And what's the answer, if you know?" I asked.

'He made none at the minute, but turned away slowly to the door. There, with his hand on the threshold, he stopped to say, almost under his breath: "Then you really think my stuff's no good?"

'I was tired and exasperated, and I laughed. I don't defend my laugh – it was in wretched taste. But I must plead in extenuation that the boy was a fool, and that I'd done my best for him – I really had.

'He went out of the room, shutting the door quietly after him. That afternoon I left for Frascati, where I'd promised to spend the Sunday with some friends. I was glad to escape from Gilbert, and by the same token, as I learned that night, I had also escaped from the eyes. I dropped into the same lethargic sleep that had come to me before when I left off seeing them; and when I woke the next morning, in my peaceful room above the ilexes, I felt the utter weariness and deep relief that always followed on that sleep. I put in two blessed nights at Frascati, and when I got back to my rooms in Rome I found that Gilbert had gone . . . Oh, nothing tragic had happened – the episode never rose to *that*. He'd simply packed his manuscripts and left for America – for his family and the Wall Street desk. He left a decent enough note to tell me of his decision, and behaved altogether, in the circumstances, as little like a fool as it's possible for a fool to behave . . .'

IV

Culwin paused again, and Frenham still sat motionless, the dusky contour of his young head reflected in the mirror at his back.

'And what became of Noyes afterward?' I finally asked, still disquieted by a sense of incompleteness, by the need of some connecting thread between the parallel lines of the tale.

Culwin twitched his shoulders. 'Oh, nothing became of him – because he became nothing. There could be no question of "becoming" about it. He vegetated in an office, I believe, and finally got a clerkship in a consulate, and married drearily in China. I saw him once in Hong Kong, years afterward. He was fat and hadn't shaved. I was told he drank. He didn't recognize me.'

'And the eyes?' I asked, after another pause which Frenham's continued silence made oppressive.

Culwin, stroking his chin, blinked at me meditatively through the shadows. 'I never saw them after my last talk with Gilbert. Put two and two together if you can. For my part, I haven't found the link.'

He rose, his hands in his pockets, and walked stiffly over to the table on which reviving drinks had been set out.

'You must be parched after this dry tale. Here, help yourself, my dear fellow. Here, Phil –' He turned back to the hearth.

Frenham made no response to his host's hospitable summons. He still sat in his low chair without moving, but, as Culwin advanced toward him, their eyes met in a long look; after which the young man, turning suddenly, flung his arms across the table behind him, and dropped his face upon them.

Culwin, at the unexpected gesture, stopped short, a flush on his face.

'Phil – what the deuce! Why, have the eyes scared *you*? My dear boy – my dear fellow – I never had such a tribute to my literary ability, never!'

He broke into a chuckle at the thought, and halted on the hearthrug, his hands still in his pockets, gazing down at the youth's bowed head. Then, as Frenham still made no answer, he moved a step or two nearer.

'Cheer up, my dear Phil! It's been years since I've seen them – apparently I've done nothing lately bad enough to call them out of chaos. Unless my present evocation of them has made *you* see them, which would be their worst stroke yet!'

His bantering appeal quivered off into an uneasy laugh, and he moved still nearer, bending over Frenham, and laying his gouty hands on the lad's shoulders.

'Phil, my dear boy, really – what's the matter? Why don't you answer? *Have* you seen the eyes?'

Frenham's face was still hidden, and from where I stood behind Culwin I saw the latter, as if under the rebuff of this unaccountable attitude, draw back slowly from his friend. As he did so, the light of the lamp on the table fell full on his congested face, and I caught its reflection in the mirror behind Frenham's head.

Culwin saw the reflection also. He paused, his face level with the mirror, as if scarcely recognizing the countenance in it as his own. But as he looked his expression gradually changed, and for an appreciable space of time he and the image in the glass confronted each other with a glare of slowly gathering hate. Then Culwin let go of Frenham's shoulders, and drew back a step . . . Frenham, his face still hidden, did not stir.

E. Nesbit

THE VIOLET CAR

DO you know the downs – the wide windy spaces, the rounded shoulders of the hills leaned against the sky, the hollows where farms and homesteads nestle sheltered, with trees round them pressed close and tight as a carnation in a button-hole? On long summer days it is good to lie on the downs, between short turf and pale, clear sky, to smell the wild thyme, and hear the tiny tinkle of the sheep-bells and the song of the skylark. But on winter evenings when the wind is waking up to its work, spitting rain in your eyes, beating the poor, naked trees and shaking the dusk across the hills like a grey pall, then it is better to be by a warm fireside, in one of the farms that lie lonely where shelter is, and oppose their windows glowing with candle light and firelight to the deepening darkness, as faith holds up its love-lamp in the night of sin and sorrow that is life.

I am unaccustomed to literary effort – and I feel that I shall not say what I have to say, or that it will convince you, unless I say it very plainly. I thought I could adorn my story with pleasant words, prettily arranged. But as I pause to think of what really happened, I see that the plainest words will be the best. I do not know how to weave a plot, nor how to embroider it. It is best not to try. These things happened. I have no skill to add to what happened; nor is any adding of mine needed.

I am a nurse – and I was sent for to go to Charlestown – a mental case. It was November – and the fog was thick in London, so that my cab went at a foot's pace, so I missed the train by which I should have gone. I sent a telegram to Charlestown, and waited in the dismal waiting room at London Bridge. The time was passed for me by a little child. Its mother, a widow, seemed too crushed to be able to respond to its quick questionings. She answered briefly, and not, as it seemed, to the child's satisfaction. The child itself presently seemed to perceive that its mother was not, so to speak, available. It leaned back on the wide, dusty seat and yawned. I caught its eye, and smiled. It would not smile, but it looked. I took out of my bag a silk purse, bright with beads and steel tassels, and turned it over and over. Presently, the child slid along the seat and said, 'Let me' – After that all was easy. The mother sat with eyes closed. When I rose to go, she opened them and thanked me. The child, clinging, kissed me. Later, I saw them get into a first-class carriage in my train. My ticket was a third-class one.

I expected, of course, that there would be a conveyance of some sort to meet me at the station – but there was nothing. Nor was there a cab or a fly to be seen. It was by this time nearly dark, and the wind was driving the rain almost horizontally along the unfrequented road that lay beyond the door of the station. I looked out, forlorn and perplexed.

'Haven't you engaged a carriage?' It was the widow lady who spoke.

I explained.

'My motor will be here directly,' she said, 'you'll let me drive you? Where is it you are going?'

'Charlestown,' I said, and as I said it, I was aware of a very odd change in her face. A faint change, but quite unmistakable.

'Why do you look like that?' I asked her bluntly. And, of course, she said, 'Like what?'

'There's nothing wrong with the house?' I said, for that, I found, was what I had taken that faint change to signify; and I was very young, and one has heard tales. 'No reason why I shouldn't go there, I mean?'

'No – oh no –' she glanced out through the rain, and I knew as well as though she had told me that there was a reason why *she* should not wish to go there.

'Don't trouble,' I said, 'it's very kind of you – but it's probably out of your way and . . .'

'Oh – but I'll take you – of *course* I'll take you,' she said, and the child said 'Mother, here comes the car.'

And come it did, though neither of us heard it till the child had spoken. I know nothing of motor cars, and I don't know the names of any of the parts of them. This was like a brougham – only you got in at the back, as you do in a waggonette; the seats were in the corners, and when the door was shut there was a little seat that pulled up, and the child sat on it between us. And it moved like magic – or like a dream of a train.

We drove quickly through the dark – I could hear the wind screaming, and the wild dashing of the rain against the windows, even through the whirring of the machinery. One could see nothing of the country – only the black night, and the shafts of light from the lamps in front.

After, as it seemed, a very long time, the chauffeur got down and opened a gate. We went through it, and after that the road was very much rougher. We were quite silent in the car, and the child had fallen asleep.

We stopped, and the car stood pulsating as though it were out of breath, while the chauffeur hauled down my box. It was so dark that I could not see the shape of the house, only the lights in the downstairs windows, and the low-walled front garden faintly revealed by their light and the light of the motor lamps. Yet I felt that it was a fair-sized house, that it was surrounded by big trees, and that there was a pond or river close by. In daylight next day I found that all this was so. I have never been able to tell how I knew it that first night, in the dark, but I did know it. Perhaps there was something in the way the rain fell on the trees and on the water. I don't know.

The chauffeur took my box up a stone path, whereon I got out, and said my good-byes and thanks.

'Don't wait, please, don't,' I said. 'I'm all right now. Thank you a thousand times!'

The car, however, stood pulsating till I had reached the doorstep, then it caught its breath, as it were, throbbed more loudly, turned, and went.

And still the door had not opened. I felt for the knocker, and rapped smartly. Inside the door I was sure I heard whispering. The car light was fast diminishing to a little distant star, and its panting sounded now hardly at all. When it ceased to sound at all, the place was quiet as death. The lights glowed redly from curtained windows, but there was no other sign of life. I wished I had not been in such a hurry to part from my escort, from human companionship, and from the great, solid, competent presence of the motor car.

I knocked again, and this time I followed the knock by a shout.

'Hello!' I cried. 'Let me in. I'm the nurse!'

There was a pause, such a pause as would allow time for whisperers to exchange glances on the other side of a door.

Then a bolt ground back, a key turned, and the doorway framed no longer cold, wet wood, but light and a welcoming warmth – and faces.

'Come in, oh, come in,' said a voice, a woman's voice, and the voice of a man said: 'We didn't know there was anyone there.'

And I had shaken the very door with my knockings!

I went in, blinking at the light, and the man called a servant, and between them they carried my box upstairs.

The woman took my arm and led me into a low, square room, pleasant, homely, and comfortable, with solid mid-Victorian comfort – the kind that expressed itself in rep and mahogany. In the lamplight I turned to look at her. She was small and thin, her hair, her face, and her hands were of the same tint of greyish yellow.

'Mrs Eldridge?' I asked.

'Yes,' said she, very softly. 'Oh! I am so glad you've come. I hope you won't be dull here. I hope you'll stay. I hope I shall be able to make you comfortable.'

She had a gentle, urgent way of speaking that was very winning.

'I'm sure I shall be very comfortable,' I said; 'but it's I that am to take care of you. Have you been ill long?'

'It's not me that's ill, really,' she said, 'it's him—'

Now, it was Mr Robert Eldridge who had written to engage me to attend on his wife, who was, he said, slightly deranged.

'I see,' said I. One must never contradict them, it only aggravates their disorder.

'The reason . . .' she was beginning, when his foot sounded on the stairs, and she fluttered off to get candles and hot water.

He came in and shut the door. A fair, bearded, elderly man, quite ordinary.

'You'll take care of her,' he said. 'I don't want her to get talking to people. She fancies things.'

'What form do the illusions take?' I asked, prosaically.

'She thinks I'm mad,' he said, with a short laugh.

'It's a very usual form. Is that all?'

'It's about enough. And she can't hear things that I can hear, see things that I can see, and she can't smell things. By the way, you didn't see or hear anything of a motor as you came up, did you?'

'I came up *in* a motor car,' I said shortly. 'You never sent to meet me, and a lady gave me a lift.' I was going to explain about my missing the earlier train, when I found that he was not listening to me. He was watching the door. When his wife came in, with a steaming jug in one hand and a flat candlestick in the other, he went towards her, and whispered eagerly. The only words I caught were: 'She came in a real motor.'

Apparently, to these simple people a motor was as great a novelty as to me. My telegram, by the way, was delivered next morning.

They were very kind to me; they treated me as an honoured guest. When the rain stopped, as it did late the next day, and I was able to go out, I found that Charlestown was a farm, a large farm, but even to my inexperienced eyes, it seemed neglected and unprosperous. There was absolutely nothing for me to do but to follow Mrs Eldridge, helping her where I could in her household duties, and to sit with her while she sewed in the homely parlour. When I had been in the house a few days, I began to put together the little things that I had noticed singly, and the life at the farm seemed suddenly to come into focus, as strange surroundings do after a while.

I found that I had noticed that Mr and Mrs Eldridge were very fond of each other, and that it was a fondness, and their way of shewing it was a way that told that they had known sorrow, and had borne it together. That she shewed no sign of mental derangement, save in the persistent belief of hers that *he* was deranged. That the morning found them fairly cheerful; that after the early dinner they seemed to grow more and more depressed; that after the 'early cup of tea' – that is just as dusk was falling – they always went for a walk together. That they never asked me to join them in this walk, and that it always took the same direction – across the downs towards the sea. That they always returned from this walk pale and dejected; that she sometimes cried afterwards alone in their bedroom, while he was shut up in the little room they called the office, where he did his accounts, and paid his men's wages, and where his hunting-crops and guns were kept. After supper, which was early, they always made an effort to be cheerful. I knew that this effort was for my sake, and I knew that each of them thought it was good for the other to make it.

Just as I had known before they shewed it to me that Charlestown was surrounded by big trees and had a great pond beside it, so I knew, and in as inexplicable a way, that with these two fear lived. It looked at me out of their eyes. And I knew, too, that this fear was not her fear. I had not been two days in the place before I found that I was beginning to be fond of them both. They were so kind, so gentle, so ordinary, so homely – the kind of people who ought not to have known the name of fear – the kind of people to whom all honest, simple joys should have come by right, and no sorrows but such as come to us all, the death of old friends, and the slow changes of advancing years.

They seemed to belong to the land – to the downs, and the copses, and the old pastures, and the lessening cornfields. I found myself wishing that I, too, belonged to these, that I had been born a farmer's daughter. All the stress and struggle of cram and exam, of school, and college and hospital, seemed so loud and futile, compared with these open secrets of the down life. And I felt this the more, as more and more I felt that I must leave it all – that there was, honestly, no work for me here such as for good or ill I had been trained to do.

'I ought not to stay,' I said to her one afternoon, as we stood at the open door. It was February now, and the snowdrops were thick in tufts beside the flagged path. 'You are quite well.'

'I am,' she said.

'You are quite well, both of you,' I said. 'I oughtn't to be taking your money and doing nothing for it.'

'You're doing everything,' she said; 'you don't know how much you're doing.'

'We had a daughter of our own once,' she added vaguely, and then, after a very long pause, she said very quietly and distinctly:

'He has never been the same since.'

'How not the same?' I asked, turning my face up to the thin February sunshine.

She tapped her wrinkled, yellow-grey forehead, as country people do.

'Not right here,' she said.

'How?' I asked. 'Dear Mrs Eldridge, tell me; perhaps I could help somehow.'

Her voice was so sane, so sweet. It had come to this with me, that I did not know which of those two was the one who needed my help.

'He sees things that no one else sees, and hears things no one else hears, and smells things that you can't smell if you're standing there beside him.'

I remembered with a sudden smile his words to me on the morning of my arrival:

'She can't see, or hear, or smell.'

And once more I wondered to which of the two I owed my service.

'Have you any idea why?' I asked. She caught at my arm.

'It was after our Bessie died,' she said – 'the very day she was buried. The motor that killed her – they said it was an accident – it was on the Brighton Road. It was a violet colour. They go into mourning for Queens with violet, don't they?' she added; 'and my Bessie, she was a Queen. So the motor was violet: That was all right, wasn't it?'

I told myself now that I saw that the woman was not normal, and I saw why. It was grief that had turned her brain. There must have been some change in my look, though I ought to have known better, for she said suddenly, 'No. I'll not tell you any more.'

And then he came out. He never left me alone with her for very long. Nor did she ever leave him for very long alone with me.

I did not intend to spy upon them, though I am not sure that my position as nurse to one mentally afflicted would not have justified such spying. But I did not spy. It was chance. I had been to the village to get some blue sewing silk for a blouse I was making, and there was a royal sunset which tempted me to prolong my walk. That was how I found myself on the high downs where they slope to the broken edge of England – the sheer, white cliffs against which the English Channel beats for ever. The furze was in flower, and the skylarks were singing, and my thoughts were with my own life, my own hopes and dreams. So I found that I had struck a road, without knowing when I had struck it. I followed it towards the sea, and quite soon it ceased to be a road, and merged in the pathless turf as a stream sometimes disappears in sand. There was nothing but turf and furze bushes, the song of the skylarks, and beyond the slope that ended at the cliff's edge, the booming of the sea. I turned back, following the road, which defined itelf again a few yards back, and presently sank to a lane, deep-banked and bordered with brown hedge stuff. It was there that I came upon them in the dusk. And I heard their voices before I saw them, and before it was possible for them to see me. It was her voice that I heard first.

'No, no, no, no, no,' it said.

'I tell you yes,' that was his voice; 'there – can't you hear it, that panting sound – right away – away? It must be at the very edge of the cliff.'

'There's nothing, dearie,' she said, 'indeed there's nothing.'

'You're deaf – and blind – stand back I tell you, it's close upon us.'

I came round the corner of the lane then, and as I came, I saw him catch her arm and throw her against the hedge – violently, as though the danger he feared were indeed close upon them. I stopped behind the turn of the hedge and stepped back. They had not seen me. Her eyes were on his face, and they held a world of pity, love, agony – his face was set in a mask of terror, and his eyes moved quickly as though they followed down the lane the swift passage of something – something that neither she nor I could see. Next moment he was cowering, pressing his body into the hedge – his face hidden in his hands, and his whole body trembling so that I could see it, even from where I was a dozen yards away, through the light screen of the over-grown hedge.

'And the smell of it!' – he said, 'do you mean to tell me you can't smell it?'

She had her arms round him.

'Come home, dearie,' she said. 'Come home! It's all your fancy – come home with your old wife that loves you.'

They went home.

Next day I asked her to come to my room to look at the new blue blouse. When I had shown it to her I told her, what I had seen and heard yesterday in the lane.

'And now I know,' I said, 'which of you it is that wants care.'

To my amazement she said very eagerly, 'Which?'

'Why, he – of course' – I told her, 'there was nothing there.'

She sat down in the chintz covered armchair by the window, and broke into wild weeping. I stood by her and soothed her as well as I could.

'It's a comfort to know,' she said at last, 'I haven't known what to believe. Many a time, lately, I've wondered whether after all it could be me that was mad, like he said. And there was nothing there? There always *was* nothing there – and it's on him the judgement, not on me. On him. Well, that's something to be thankful for.'

So her tears, I told myself, had been more of relief at her own escape. I looked at her with distaste, and forgot that I had been fond of her. So that her next words cut me like little knives.

'It's bad enough for him as it is,' she said, 'but it's nothing to what it would be for him, if I was really to go off my head and him left to think he'd brought it on me. You see, now I can look after him the same as I've always done. It's only once in the day it comes over him. He couldn't bear it, if it was all the time – like it'll be for me now. It's much better it should be him – I'm better able to bear it than he is.'

I kissed her then and put my arms round her, and said, 'Tell me what it is that frightens him so – and it's every day, you say?'

'Yes – ever since . . . I'll tell you. It's a sort of comfort to speak out. It was a violet-coloured car that killed our Bessie. You know our girl that I've told you about. And it's a violet-coloured car that he thinks he sees – every day up there in the lane. And he says he hears it, and that he smells the smell of the machinery – the stuff they put in it – you know.'

'Petrol?'

'Yes, and you can *see* he hears it, and you can *see* he sees it. It haunts him, as if it was a ghost. You see, it was he that picked her up after the violet car went over her. It was that that turned him. I only saw her as he carried her in, in his arms – and then he'd covered her face. But he saw her just as they'd left her, lying in the dust . . . you could see the place on the road where it happened for days and days.'

'Didn't they come back?'

'Oh yes . . . they came back. But Bessie didn't come back. But there was a judgement on them. The very night of the funeral, that violet car went over the cliff – dashed to pieces – every soul in it. That was the man's widow that drove you home the first night.'

'I wonder she uses a car after that,' I said – I wanted something common-place to say.

'Oh,' said Mrs Eldridge, 'it's all what you're used to. We don't stop walking because our girl was killed on the road. Motoring comes as natural to them as walking to us. There's my old man calling – poor old dear. He wants me to go out with him.'

She went, all in a hurry, and in her hurry slipped on the stairs and twisted her ankle. It all happened in a minute and it was a bad sprain.

When I had bound it up, and she was on the sofa, she looked at him, standing as if he were undecided, staring out of the window, with his cap in his hand. And she looked at me.

'Mr Eldridge mustn't miss his walk,' she said. 'You go with him, my dear. A breath of air will do you good.'

So I went, understanding as well as though he had told me, that he did not want me with him, and that he was afraid to go alone, and that he yet had to go.

We went up the lane in silence. At that corner he stopped suddenly, caught my arm, and dragged me back. His eyes followed something that I could not see. Then he exhaled a held breath, and said, 'I thought I heard a motor coming.' He had found it hard to control his terror, and I saw beads of sweat on his forehead and temples. Then we went back to the house.

The sprain was a bad one. Mrs Eldridge had to rest, and again next day it was I who went with him to the corner of the lane.

This time he could not, or did not try to, conceal what he felt. 'There – listen!' he said. 'Surely you can hear it?'

I heard nothing.

'Stand back,' he cried shrilly, suddenly, and we stood back close against the hedge.

Again the eyes followed something invisible to me, and again the held breath exhaled.

'It will kill me one of these days,' he said, 'and I don't know that I care how soon – if it wasn't for her.'

'Tell me,' I said, full of that importance, that conscious competence, that one feels in the presence of other people's troubles. He looked at me.

'I will tell you, by God,' he said. 'I couldn't tell *her*. Young lady, I've gone so far as wishing myself a Roman, for the sake of a priest to tell it to. But I can tell *you*, without losing my soul more than it's lost already. Did you ever hear tell of a violet car that got smashed up – went over the cliff?'

'Yes,' I said. 'Yes.'

'The man that killed my girl was new to the place. And he hadn't any eyes – or ears – or he'd have known me, seeing we'd been face to face at the inquest. And you'd have thought he'd have stayed at home that one day, with the blinds drawn down. But not he. He was swirling and swivelling all about the country in his cursed violet car, the very time we were burying her. And at dusk – there was a mist coming up – he comes up behind me in this very lane, and I stood back, and he pulls up, and he calls out, with his damned lights full in my face: '"Can you tell me the way to Hexham, my man?" says he.

'I'd have liked to shew him the way to hell. And that was the way for me, not him. I don't know how I came to do it. I didn't mean to do it. I didn't think I was going to – and before I knew anything, I'd said it. "Straight ahead," I said; "keep straight ahead." Then the motor-thing panted, chuckled, and he was off. I ran after him to try to stop him – but what's the use of running after these motor-devils? And he kept straight on. And every day since then, every dear day, the car comes by, the violet car that nobody can see but me – and it keeps straight on.'

'You ought to go away,' I said, speaking as I had been trained to speak. 'You fancy these things. You probably fancied the whole thing. I don't suppose you ever *did* tell the violet car to go straight ahead. I expect it was all imagination, and the shock of your poor daughter's death. You ought to go right away.'

'I can't,' he said earnestly. 'If I did, some one else would see the car. You see, somebody *has* to see it every day as long as I live. If it wasn't me, it would be someone else. And I'm the only person who *deserves* to see it. I wouldn't like any one else to see it – it's too horrible. *It's* much more horrible than you think,' he added slowly.

I asked him, walking beside him down the quiet lane, what it was that was so horrible about the violet car. I think I quite expected him to say that it was splashed with his daughter's blood . . . What he did say was, 'It's too horrible to tell you,' and he shuddered.

I was young then, and youth always thinks it can move mountains. I persuaded myself that I could cure him of his delusion by attacking – not the main fort – that is always, to begin with, impregnable, but one, so to speak, of the outworks. I set myself to persuade him not to go to that corner in the lane, at that hour in the afternoon.

'But if I don't, someone else will see it.'

'There'll be nobody there *to* see it,' I said briskly.

'Someone will be there. Mark my words, someone will be there – and then they'll know.'

'Then I'll be the someone,' I said. 'Come – you stay at home with your wife, and *I'll* go – and if I see it I'll promise to tell you, and if I don't – well, then I will be able to go away with a clear conscience.'

'A clear conscience,' he repeated.

I argued with him in every moment when it was possible to catch him alone. I put all my will and all my energy into my persuasions. Suddenly, like a door that you've been trying to open, and that has resisted every key till the last one, he gave way. Yes – I should go to the lane. And he would not go.

I went.

Being, as I said before, a novice in the writing of stories, I perhaps haven't made you understand that it was quite hard for me to go – that I felt myself at once a coward and a heroine. This business of an imaginary motor that only one poor old farmer could see, probably appears to you quite commonplace and ordinary. It was not so with me. You see, the idea of this thing had dominated my life for weeks and months, had dominated it even before I knew the nature of the domination. It was this that was the fear that I had known to walk with these two people, the fear that shared their bed and board, that lay down and rose up with them. The old man's fear of this and his fear of his fear. And the old man was terribly convincing. When one talked with him, it was quite difficult to believe that he was mad, and that there wasn't, and couldn't be, a mysteriously horrible motor that was visible to him, and invisible to other people. And when he said that, if he were not in the lane, someone else would see it – it was easy to say 'Nonsense,' but to think 'Nonsense' was not so easy, and to *feel* 'Nonsense' quite oddly difficult.

I walked up and down the lane in the dusk, wishing not to wonder what might be the hidden horror in the violet car. I would not let blood into my thoughts. I was not going to be fooled by thought transference, or any of those transcendental follies. I was not going to be hypnotised into seeing things.

I walked up the lane – I had promised him to stand near that corner for five minutes, and I stood there in the deepening dusk, looking up towards the downs and the sea. There were pale stars. Everything was very still. Five minutes is a long time. I held my watch in my hand. Four – four and a quarter – four and a half. Five. I turned instantly. And then I saw that *he* had followed me – he was standing a dozen yards away – and his face was turned from me. It was turned towards a motor car that shot up the lane. It came very swiftly, and before it came to where he was, I knew that it was very horrible. I crushed myself back into the crackling bare hedge, as I should have done to leave room for the passage of a real car – though I knew that this one was not real. It looked real – but I knew it was not.

As it neared him, he started back, then suddenly he cried out. I heard him. 'No, no, no, no – no more, no more,' was what he cried, with that he flung himself down on the road in front of the car, and its great tyres passed over him. Then the car shot past me and I saw what the full horror of it was. There was no blood – that was not the horror. The colour of it was, as she had said, violet.

I got to him and got his head up. He was dead. I was quite calm and collected now, and felt that to be so was extremely creditable to me. I went to a cottage where a labourer was having tea – he got some men and a hurdle.

When I had told his wife, the first intelligible thing she said was: 'It's better for him. Whatever he did he's paid for now –' So it looks as though she had known – or guessed – more than he thought.

I stayed with her till her death. She did not live long.

You think perhaps that the old man was knocked down and killed by a real motor, which happened to come that way of all ways, at that hour of all hours, and happened to be, of all colours, violet. Well, a real motor leaves its mark on you where it kills you, doesn't it? But when I lifted up that old man's head from the road, there was no mark on him, no blood – no broken bones – his hair was not disordered, nor his dress. I tell you there was not even a speck of mud on him, except where he had touched the road in falling. There were no tyre-marks in the mud.

The motor car that killed him came and went like a shadow. As he threw himself down, it swerved a little so that both its wheels should go over him.

He died, the doctor said, of heart failure. I am the only person to know that he was killed by a violet car, which, having killed him, went noiselessly away towards the sea. And that car was empty – there was no one in it. It was just a violet car that moved along the lanes swiftly and silently, and was empty.

Henrietta D. Everett

THE CRIMSON BLIND

I

RONALD McEwan, aged sixteen, was invited to spend a vacation fortnight at his uncle's rectory. Possibly some qualms of conscience had tardily spurred the Rev. Sylvanus Applegarth to offer this hospitality, aware that he had in the past neglected his dead sister's son. Also, with a view to the future, it might be well for Ronald to make acquaintance with his own two lads, now holidaying from English public schools.

Mr Applegarth was a gentleman and a scholar, one who loved above all things leisure and a quiet house: he retained a curate at his own expense to run matters parochial in Swanmere, and buried himself among his books. The holidays were seasons of trial to him on each of the three yearly occasions, and it would not be much worse, so he reflected, to have three hobbledehoy lads romping about the place, and clumping up and down stairs with heavy boots, when it was inevitable he must have two.

The young Applegarths were not ill-natured lads, but they were somewhat disposed to make a butt of the shy Scottish cousin, who was midway between them in age, and had had a different upbringing and schooling from themselves. Ronald found it advisable to listen much and say little, not airing his own opinions unless they were directly challenged. But in one direction he had been outspoken, afterwards wishing devoutly he had held his tongue. Spooks were under discussion, and it was discovered – a source of fiendish glee to the allied brothers – that Ronald believed in ghosts, as he preferred more respectfully to term them, and also in such marvels as death-warnings, wraiths, and second-sight.

'That comes of being a Highlander,' said Jack the elder. 'Superstition is a taint that gets into the blood, and so is born with you. But I'll wager anything you have no valid reason for believing. The best evidence is only second-hand; most of it third or fourth hand, if as near. You have never seen a ghost yourself?'

'No,' acknowledged Ronald somewhat sourly, for he had been more than sufficiently badgered. 'But I've spoken with those that have.'

'Would you like to see one? Now give a straight answer for once' – and Jack winked at his brother.

'I wouldn't mind.' Then, more stoutly: 'Yes, I would like – if I'd the chance.'

'I think we can give you a chance of seeing something, if not exactly a ghost. We've got no Highland castles to trot out, but there's a house here in Swanmere that is said to be haunted. Just the thing for you to investigate, now you are on the spot. Will you take it on?'

It would have been fatal to say no, and give these cousins the opening to post him as a coward. Ronald gave again the grudging admission that he 'wouldn't mind.' And then, being Sunday morning, the lads said they would take him round that way after church, and he should have a look at the window which had earned a bad repute. Then they might find out who had the keys in charge, if he felt inclined to pass a night within.

'I suppose, as neither of you believe, you would not be afraid to sleep there?' said Ronald, addressing the two.

'Certainly we would not be *afraid*.' Jack was speech-valiant at least. 'As we believe there is nothing in it but a sham, like all the other tales.'

Alfred, the younger boy, did not contradict his brother, but it might have been noticed that he kept silence.

'Then I'll do what you do.' This was Ronald's ultimatum. 'If you two choose to sleep in the haunted house, I'll sleep there too.'

But, as the event fell out, the Applegarths did not push matters to the point of borrowing keys from the house-agent and camping out rolled in blankets on the bare floors – an attractive picture Jack went on to draw of the venture to which Ronald stood committed. After the morning service the three lads walked some half mile beyond the village in the direction of the seashore. Here the houses were few and far between, but two or three villas were in course of building, and other plots beyond them were placarded as for sale. Swanmere was 'rising' – in other words, in process of being spoiled. Niched in between two of these plots was an empty house to let, well placed in being set some way back from the high road, within the privacy of thick shrubberies, and screened at the back by a belt of forest trees.

A desirable residence, one would have said at a first glance, but closer acquaintance was apt to induce a change of mind. The iron gates of the drive were fastened with padlock and chain, but the young Applegarths effected an entrance by vaulting over the palings at the side. Everywhere was to be seen the encroachment and overgrowth of long neglect: weeds knee-high, and branches pushing themselves across the side-paths, though the carriage approach had been kept clear. The main entrance was at the side, and in front bowed windows, on two floors, were closely shuttered within, and grimed with dirt without.

The boys pushed their way round to the back, where the kitchen offices were enclosed by a yard. But midway between the better and the inferior part of the house a large flat window on the first floor overlooked the flower-garden and shrubbery. This window was not shuttered, but was completely screened by a wide blind of faded red, drawn down to meet the sill. Jack pointed to it.

'That is where the ghost shows – not every night, but sometimes. Maybe you'll have to watch for a whole week before there is anything to see. But, if rumour says true, you will be repaid in the end. Whatever the appearance may be.'

Ronald thought he saw a wink pass between the brothers. He was to be hoaxed in some way; of that he felt assured.

'I'll go, if we three go together, you and Alfred and I. If there is a real ghost to be seen, you shall see it too. What is it said to be like?'

'A light comes behind the red blind, and some people see a figure, or the shadow of a figure, in the room. Perhaps it is according to the open eye, some less and some more. You may see more still, being Highland born and bred. Very well, as you make it a condition, we will go together.'

'To-night?'

'Better not to-night. There's evening church and supper, and the governor might not like it, being Sunday. We will go to-morrow. That will serve as well for you.'

The fake, whatever it might be, could not be prepared in time for that first evening, Ronald reflected. He was quite unbelieving about the red blind and the light, but firm in his resolve. If he was to be trotted out to see a ghost, the Applegarth cousins should go too. It was a matter of indifference to him which night was chosen for the expedition, so Monday was agreed upon, the trio to set out at midnight, when all respectable inhabitants of Swanmere should be in their beds.

When Monday night came, the sky was clear and starlit, but it was the dark of the moon. One of the lads possessed an electric torch, which Jack put in his pocket. And when it came to the point, it appeared that only Jack was going with him. Alfred, according to his brother, had developed a sore throat, and Mrs Dawson, the housekeeper, was putting him on a poultice which had to be applied in bed.

So it was the younger Applegarth who had been chosen to play the ghost, Ronald instantly concluded: he had no faith at all in the poultice, or in Mrs Dawson's application of it, though he remembered Alfred had complained of the soreness of his throat more than once during the day.

There was little interchange of words between the two lads as they went. Ronald was inwardly resentful, and Jack seemed to have some private thoughts which amused him, for he smiled to himself in the darkness. Arrived at the Portsmouth road, they got over the fence at the same place as before;

and now Jack's torch was of use, as they pushed their way through the tangled garden to the spot determined on as likely to afford the best view of the window with the crimson blind. Neither blind nor window could now be distinguished; the house reared itself before them a silhouette of blacker darkness, against that other darkness of the night.

'We can sit on this bench while we wait,' and young Applegarth flashed his torch on a rustic structure, set beneath overshadowing trees. 'I propose to time ourselves and give an hour to the watch. Then, if you have seen nothing, we can come away and return another night. For myself, sceptic as I am, I don't expect to see.'

He could hardly be more sceptical than Ronald felt at the moment. Certain that a trick was about to be played on him, all his senses had been on the alert from the moment they left the road, and he felt sure that as they plunged through the wilderness of shrubbery he had heard another footstep following. He did not refuse to seat himself on the bench, but he took care to have the bole of the tree immediately at his back, as some protection from assault in the rear.

Some five or six minutes went by, and he was paying little attention to the house, but much to certain rustling noises in the shrubbery behind them, when Jack Applegarth exclaimed in an altered voice: 'By Jove, there *is* a light there after all!' and he became aware that the broad parallelogram of the window was now faintly illuminated behind the crimson blind, sufficiently to show its shape and size, and also the colour of the screen. Could young Alfred have found some means of entrance, and set up a lighted candle in the room? – but somehow he doubted whether, without his brother to back him, the boy would have ventured into the ghostly house alone. The fake he anticipated was of a different sort to this.

As the boys watched, the light grew stronger, glowing through the blind; the lamp within that room must have been a strong one of many candle-power. Then a shadow became visible as if cast by some person moving to and fro in front of the light; this was faint at first, but gradually it increased in intensity, and presently came close to the window, pulling the blind aside to look out.

This was so ordinary an action that it did not suggest the supernatural. A moment later, however, the whole framework of the window seemed to give way and fall outwards with a crash of breaking glass. The figure now showed clearly defined, standing outside on the sill with the red illumination behind; but its pause there was one only of seconds before it leaped to the ground and came rushing towards them; a figure so far in ghostly likeness that it appeared to be clad in white. Following the crash of glass came other sounds, a pistol-shot and a scream, but the rush of the flying figure was unaccompanied by noise. It passed close to the bench where they were seated, and young Applegarth grasped Ronald's arm in a terror well-acted if unreal.

'Come away,' he said thickly. 'I've had enough of this. Come away.'

The light behind the blind was dying out, and presently the window was again in darkness, but these spectators did not stay to see. Jack Applegarth dragged Ronald back towards the road, and the younger lad broke from the bushes and followed them, sobbing in what seemed to be real affright, and with a white bundle hugged in his arms. They climbed the palings and went pelting home, and not till the distance was half accomplished did any one of them speak. Then Ronald had the first word:

'Why, Alfred, I thought you were in bed. I hope your throat will not suffer through coming out to trick me with a sham ghost. I made sure all along that was what you and Jack would do.'

Alfred hugged tighter the bundle he was carrying: did he fear it would be snatched off him and displayed? – it looked exceedingly like a white sheet.

'I had nothing to do with *that thing*,' he blurted out between chattering teeth. 'I don't know what it was, or where it came from. But I swear I'll never go near the blamed place again, either by night or by day!'

II

Whether there was any natural explanation of what they had seen, Ronald never knew. His visit to his Applegarth relatives was drawing to a close, and, shortly after, the old Rector died suddenly during the service in church. The home was broken up, the two schoolboy cousins had their way to make in the world, and, whether ill or well made, this history knows them no more. And between the just concluded chapter, and this which is now begun, must be set an interval of twenty years.

Ronald had done well for himself in the meantime. He had become an alert, hard-headed business man, a good deal detached from the softer side of life, for which, he told himself, there would be time and to spare by-and-by. But now, at thirty-six there began to be a different telling. He could afford to keep a wife in comfort, and it seemed to him that the time for choice had come.

This does not pretend to be a love-story, so it will only briefly chronicle that it was the business of wife-selection which took Ronald again to Swanmere. He happened to act as best man at his friend Parkinson's wedding, and one of the bridesmaids seemed to him an unusually attractive girl, happy herself, and likely to make others happy, which is better than mere beauty. Probably he let fall a wish that he might see Lilian again; anyway, some time later, he was invited to run down and pay a weekend visit to the newly married pair, when Lilian was at the same time expected to stay. And, as it happened, the Peregrine Parkinsons had settled at Swanmere.

'Do you know this place at all?' queried Mrs Parkinson, who was meeting him at the station with the small pony-carriage, of which, and of her skill as a whip, she was inordinately proud.

'I was here once before, many years ago,' was Ronald's answer. 'I was only a schoolboy in those days, visiting an old uncle, who then was rector of the parish. Swanmere seems to have grown a good deal bigger than I remember it, or else my recollection is at fault.'

'Oh yes, it has grown; places do grow, don't they? There was a great deal of new building before the War – villas you know, and that style; but 1914 stopped everything. Peregrine and I were fortunate in meeting with an older house, in a quite delightful well-grown garden. Oh no, not old enough to be inconvenient, and it has been brought up-to-date for us. We were lucky to get it, I can assure you: it is so difficult in these days to find anything moderate-sized. They are snapped up directly they are vacant; the demand is so much in excess of the supply.'

Ronald did not recognize the direction taken, even when the pony willingly turned in at an open pair of iron gates, which he had last seen chained and padlocked – or, if not these gates, their predecessors, as gates have a way of perishing in untended years. All was trim within, pruned and swept and gravelled, and the garden a riot of colour with its summer flowers. But the front of the house, with double bows carried up to the first floor, did strike a chord of association. 'I wonder!' he said to himself, and then the wonder was negatived. 'No, it isn't possible; it would be too odd a coincidence.' And upon this he dismissed the thought from his mind.

It did not return during the evening, not even when he went up – in a hurry, and at the last moment – to dress for dinner in the bedroom allotted to him: a spacious and well-appointed one, where his port-manteau had been unpacked and habiliments laid out. After dinner there was the diversion of some good music; Mrs Parkinson played and Lilian sang. The Swanmere experience of twenty years ago was quite out of mind when he retired for the night; pleasanter thoughts had pushed it into the background and held the stage. But the recollection was vaguely renewed last thing, when he drew aside the curtains and opened the window, noting its unusual square shape, divided into three uprights, two of which opened casement fashion.

It was the only window in the room, but so wide that it nearly filled the outer wall. Certainly its shape recalled the window of twenty years ago which was screened by a crimson blind, and his watch in the garden with Jack Applegarth. He was never likely to forget that night, though he was far from sure whether the ghost was ghost indeed, or a sham faked by the Applegarth boys for his discomfiture. Probably these suburban villas were built all upon one plan, and an older foundation had set the note of fashion for those that followed. He never knew the name or number of the haunted house, or locality, except that it was entered from the Portsmouth road, so in that way he could not identify it. And again he dismissed the idea, and addressed himself to sleep.

Neither this recollection nor the dawning love interest was potent to keep him awake. He slept well the early part of the night, and did not wake till morning was brightening in the east. Then, as he opened his eyes and turned to face the light, he saw, and was astonished seeing, that the window was covered with a crimson blind, drawn down from top to sill.

He could have declared that nothing of the sort was in place there overnight. The drawn-back curtains had revealed a quite ordinary green venetian, which he had raised till it clicked into stoppage at its height. To all outward seeming this was a material blind, swaying in the air of the open casement, and with no light behind it but that of the summer dawn. And yet, for all that, he lay staring at it with nerves on edge, and hammering pulses which beat thickly in his ears and throat: something within him recognized the nature of the appearance and responded with agitation, despite the scepticism of the outward man. That was a bird's song vocal outside, wheels went by in the road, the ordinary world was astir. He would rise and assure himself that the blind was a mundane affair, palpable to touch; it had of course slipped down in the night owing to a loosened cord, and was hung within the other.

And then he discovered that his limbs were powerless: it was as if invisible bands restrained him. He writhed against them in vain, and in the end, despite those rapid pulses of the affrighted heart, he fell suddenly into trance or sleep.

He had had a seizure of nightmare, he concluded when he awoke later, with the servant knocking at the door to bring in tea and shaving-water, and the open window cheerful and unscreened, letting in the summer air.

His first act was to examine the window-frame, but – of course, as he told himself – there was no crimson blind, nothing but the green venetian, and the curtains drawing on their rod. He had dreamt the whole thing, on the suggestion of that memory of a schoolboy visit long ago.

He was well assured of the folly of it all, and yet he had again and again to reason the thing out, and repeat that it was folly – himself in colloquy with himself. This was still more necessary when in the course of the morning he strolled out into the garden and round the shrubbery paths. Though the wild growth of long ago had been pruned back and certain changes made, he had no difficulty in finding the spot – what he thought the spot – where he and Jack Applegarth had watched. There was still a rustic seat under the trees, full in view of the square window of his room where the red blind no longer was displayed. He sat down to light a cigarette, and presently his host appeared, pipe in mouth, and joined him on the bench in the shade.

'You have a nice place here,' Ronald said, by way of opening conversation.

'Yes,' Parkinson agreed. 'I like it, and Cecilia likes it, and in every way it suits us well. Convenient for business you know, and not too pretentious for young beginners. We both fell in love with it at first sight. But I heard something the other day' (poking with his knife at a pipe which declined to draw), 'something that rather disturbed me. Not that I believe it, you know; I'm not that sort. I only hope and trust that no busybody will consider it his or her duty to inform Cecilia.'

'What did you hear?'

'Why, some fools were saying the house used to be haunted, and that was the reason why it stood long unlet and fell into bad repair. Stories of that sort are always put about when a place happens to be nobody's fancy, whether the real drawback is rats or drains, or somebody wanting to keep it vacant for interests of their own. As you know. In this case I should say it was the latter. Because the man told me lights were seen when the place was shut up and empty. A thieves' dumping ground, no doubt. Or possibly coiners.'

This in pauses, between whiffs of the pipe. Parkinson ended:

'I don't want Cecilia to know. She is fond of the place, and I wouldn't like her to be nervous or upset.'

'Couldn't you warn the man?'

'I did that. But there are other men who know. And, what is worse, women. You know what women's tongues are. Especially when they think they have got hold of something spicey. Or what will annoy somebody else!'

'Why not tell your wife yourself, and trust to her good sense not to mind. Better for her to learn it so, than by chance whispers from a stranger. She won't like it if she thinks you were aware, and kept it up your sleeve.'

But Parkinson shook his head. Fond as he was of his Cecilia, perhaps his opinion of her good sense had not been heightened by the experience of four or five months of marriage. And Ronald checked his own impulse to communicate the history of that former episode, together with the odd dream – if it was a dream – which visited him the night before. But he had found out one thing: now it was beyond doubt. This smartly done-up villa with its modern improvements was identical with the closed and neglected house of long ago.

That day was Saturday. He had been invited to stay over the weekend, so there were two more nights that he was bound to spend at the villa. He did not enjoy the anticipation of those nights, though some slight uneasiness would cheaply purchase the intermediate day to be spent with Lilian. And what harm could any ghost do him, and what did it matter whether the window was covered with a crimson blind, or a white or a green!

It mattered little when regarded in the day, but during the watches of the night such affairs take on a different complexion, though Ronald McEwan was no coward. He woke earlier on this second night, woke to be aware of a faint illumination in the room, and of – he thought after, though it was hardly realized at the time – the instantaneous glimpse of a figure crossing from wall to wall. One thing he did distinctly see: over the window there hung again – the crimson blind! Then in the space of half a dozen heart-beats the faint light faded out, and the room was left in darkness.

This time the paralysis of the night before did not recur. He had been careful to place within reach at the bedside the means of striking a light, and presently his candle showed the window unscreened and open, and the door locked as he left it overnight. He did not extinguish that candle, but let it burn down in the socket; and he was not again disturbed.

During Sunday he debated with himself the question to speak or not to speak. That spare room might next be occupied by someone to whom the terror of such a visitation would be harmful; and yet, he supposed, all turned on whether or not the occupier was gifted (or shall we say cursed?) with the open eye. He felt thankful he had been quartered there and not Lilian. Finally he resolved that Parkinson must be warned, but not till he himself was on the point of leaving – not till he had passed a third night in the haunted room, disturbed or not disturbed. And, after all, what had he to allege against it in this later time? Could a room be haunted by the apparition of a crimson blind?

Saturday had been brilliantly fine throughout, but Sunday dawned upon unsettled weather, and a wet gale rushing over from the not distant sea. He went to rest that night resolved to keep a light burning through the dark hours, but found it necessary to shut the window on account of the driven storm. He strove to reason himself into indifference and so prepare for sleep, which visited him sooner than he expected, and for a while was profound. It was somewhere between two and three o'clock when he started up, broad awake on the instant, with the consciousness of something wrong.

It was not the moderate light of his candle which now illuminated the room, but the fierce glow of mounting flames, though he could not see whence they proceeded. The red blind hung again over the window, but that was a negligible matter: some carelessness of his had set the Parkinsons' house on fire, and he must give the alarm. He struggled up in bed, only to find he was not alone. There at the bed-foot stood gazing at him a man, a stranger, plainly seen in the glare of light. A man haggard of countenance, with the look of a soul that despaired; clad in white or light-coloured garments, possibly a sleeping-suit.

Ronald believed he made an attempt to speak to this creature, to ask who he was and what he was doing there, but whether he really achieved articulate words he does not know. For the space of perhaps a minute the two stared at each other, the man in the flesh and he who was flesh no more; then the latter sprang to the window, standing on the low sill, and tore aside the crimson blind. There was a great crash of glass like that other crash he remembered, a cry from below in the garden, and a report like a pistol-shot; the figure had disappeared, leaping through the broken gap. Then all was still and the room in darkness; those fierce flames were suddenly extinguished, and his own candle had gone out.

He groped for the matches and struck a light. The red blind had disappeared from the window, there was no broken glass and no fire, and everything remained as he had left it overnight.

No one else appeared to have heard that shot and cry in the dead middle of the night. After breakfast he took Parkinson into confidence, who heard the story gloomily enough, plainly discomforted though unwilling to believe.

'You have been right to tell me, my dear fellow, and I am sure you think you experienced all these impossible things. But look at probability. Those Applegarth boys hoaxed you years ago, the impression dwelt on your mind, and was revived by discovering this house to be the same. Such was the simple cause of your visions; any doctor would tell you so. As for my own action, I don't see clear. It is a horribly awkward affair, and we have been to no end of expense settling in. Cecilia likes the place, and it suits her. So long as she does not know −!'

'Look here, Parkinson. There is one thing I think I may ask − suggest, at least. You have another spare bedroom. Don't put any other guest where I have been sleeping. Couldn't you make it a store-room − box-room − anything that is not used at night?'

Parkinson still was doubtful: he shook his head.

'Not without an explanation to Cecilia. She happens to be particularly *gone* on that room on account of the big window. It was just a toss-up that she didn't put Lilian there, and you in the other. And − if in time to come a nursery should be needed, that is the room on which she has her eye. She would never consent to give it up for a glory-hole or a store-room without a strong reason − a very strong reason indeed.'

Ronald could do no more: his friend was warned, the responsibility was no longer his. It was some comfort to know that Lilian was leaving two days later, going on to another visit, and the fatal house did not seem to have affected her up to now.

After this, a couple of months went by, during which the Parkinsons made no sign, and he for his part kept his lips entirely sealed about his experiences at Swanmere. It might be, as Jack Applegarth said long before, his Highland blood which rendered him vulnerable to uncanny influences, and the Parkinsons and their Southern friends might remain entirely immune. But at the end of two months he received the following letter:

DEAR OLD CHUM,

It is all up with us here, and I think you will wish to know how it came about. I am trying to sub-let Ashcroft, and hope to find somebody fool enough to take it. I haven't a fault to find with the place, neither of us have seen or heard a thing, and really it seems absurd. The servants picked up some gossip about the haunting, and then one of them was scared – by her own shadow, I expect, and promptly had hysterics. After that, all three of them went to Cecilia in a body, and said they were willing to forfeit their wages, and sorry to cause us inconvenience, but nothing would induce them to stop on in a haunted house – not if we paid them hundreds – and they must leave at once. Then I had to have it out with Cecilia, and she was not pleased to have been kept in the dark. She says I hoodwinked her – but if I did, it was for her own good; and when we took the place, I had not the least idea. Of course she could not stay when the servants cleared out – and nor could I; so she has gone to her mother's, and I am at the hotel – with everyone asking questions, which I can assure you is not pleasant. I shall take jolly good care not to be trapped a second time into a place where ghosts are on the loose.

There is one thing that may interest you, as it seems to throw light on your experience. The house was built by a doctor who took in lunatic patients – harmless ones they were supposed to be, and he was properly certificated and all that: there was no humbug about it that I know. One man who was thought quite a mild case suddenly became violent. He locked himself into his room and set it on fire, and then smashed a window – I believe it was *that* window – and jumped out. It was only from the first floor, but he was so badly injured that he died: a good riddance of bad rubbish, I should say. I don't know anything about a red blind or a pistol-shot: those matters seem to have been embroidered on. But the coincidence is an odd one, I allow.

We were pleased to hear of your engagement to Lilian, and I send you both congratulations and good wishes, in which Cecilia would join if here. I suppose you will soon be Benedick the married man.

Yours ever,
PEREGRINE PARKINSON

THE TOKEN

I

I HAVE only known one absolutely adorable woman, and that was my brother's wife, Cicely Dunbar.

Sisters-in-law do not, I think, invariably adore each other, and I am aware that my chief merit in Cicely's eyes was that I am Donald's sister; but for me there was no question of extraneous quality – it was all pure Cicely.

And how Donald – But then, like all the Dunbars, Donald suffers from being Scottish, so that, if he has a feeling, he makes it a point of honour to pretend he hasn't it. I daresay he let himself go a bit during his courtship, when he was not, strictly speaking, himself; but after he had once married her I think he would have died rather than have told Cicely in so many words that he loved her. And Cicely wanted to be told. You say she ought to have known without telling? You don't know Donald. You can't conceive the perverse ingenuity he could put into hiding his affection. He has that peculiar temper – I think it's Scottish – that delights in snubbing and fault-finding and defeating expectation. If he knows you want him to do a thing, that alone is reason enough with Donald for not doing it. And my sister, who was as transparent as white crystal, was never able to conceal a want. So that Donald could, as we said, 'have' her at every turn.

And, then, I don't think my brother really knew how ill she was. He didn't want to know. Besides, he was so wrapt up in trying to finish his 'Development of Social Economics' (which, by the way, he hasn't finished yet) that he had no eyes to see what we all saw: that, the way her poor little heart was going, Cicely couldn't have very long to live.

Of course he understood that this was why, in those last months, they had to have separate rooms. And this in the first year of their marriage when he was still violently in love with her. I keep those two facts firmly in my mind when I try to excuse Donald; for it was the main cause of that unkindness and perversity which I find it so hard to forgive. Even now, when I think how he used to discharge it on the poor little thing, as if it had been her fault, I have to remind myself that the lamb's innocence made her a little trying.

She couldn't understand why Donald didn't want to have her with him in his library any more while he read or wrote. It seemed to her sheer cruelty to shut her out now when she was ill, seeing that, before she was ill, she had always had her chair by the fireplace, where she would sit over her book or her embroidery for hours without speaking, hardly daring to breathe lest she should interrupt him. Now was the time, she thought, when she might expect a little indulgence.

Do you suppose that Donald would give his feelings as an explanation? Not he. They were *his feelings*, and he wouldn't talk about them; and he never explained anything you didn't understand.

That – her wanting to sit with him in the library – was what they had the awful quarrel about, the day before she died; that and the paper-weight, the precious paper-weight that he wouldn't let anybody touch because George Meredith had given it him. It was a brass block, surmounted by a white alabaster Buddha painted and gilt. And it had an inscription: *To Donald Dunbar, from George Meredith. In Affectionate Regard*.

My brother was extremely attached to this paper-weight, partly, I'm afraid, because it proclaimed his intimacy with the great man. For this reason it was known in the family ironically as the Token.

It stood on Donald's writing-table at his elbow, so near the ink-pot that the white Buddha had received a splash or two. And this evening Cicely had come in to us in the library, and had annoyed Donald by staying in it when he wanted her to go. She had taken up the Token, and was cleaning it to give herself a pretext.

She died after the quarrel they had then.

It began by Donald shouting at her.

'What are you doing with that paper-weight?'

'Only getting the ink off.'

I can see her now, the darling. She had wetted the corner of her handkerchief with her little pink tongue and was rubbing the Buddha. Her hands had begun to tremble when he shouted.

'Put it down, can't you? I've told you not to touch my things.'

'*You* inked him,' she said. She was giving one last rub as he rose, threatening. 'Put – it – down.'

And, poor child, she did put it down. Indeed, she dropped it at his feet.

'Oh!' she cried out, and stooped quickly and picked it up. Her large tear-glassed eyes glanced at him, frightened.

'He isn't broken.'

'No thanks to you,' he growled.

'You beast! You know I'd die rather than break anything you care about.'

'It'll be broken some day, if you *will* come meddling.'

I couldn't bear it. I said, 'You mustn't yell at her like that. You know she can't stand it. You'll make her ill again.'

That sobered him for a moment.

'I'm sorry,' he said; but he made it sound as if he wasn't.

'If you're sorry,' she persisted, 'you might let me stay with you. I'll be as quiet as a mouse.'

'No; I don't want you – I can't work with you in the room.'

'You can work with Helen.'

'You're not Helen.'

'He only means he's not in love with *me*, dear.'

'He means I'm no use to him. I know I'm not. I can't even sit on his manuscripts and keep them down. He cares more for that damned paper-weight than he does for me.'

'Well – George Meredith gave it me.'

'And nobody gave you me. I gave myself.'

That worked up his devil again. He *had* to torment her.

'It can't have cost you much,' he said. 'And I may remind you that the paper-weight has *some* intrinsic value.'

With that he left her.

'What's he gone out for?' she asked me.

'Because he's ashamed of himself, I suppose,' I said. 'Oh, Cicely, why *will* you answer him? You know what he is.'

'No!' she said passionately – 'that's what I don't know. I never have known.'

'At least you know he's in love with you.'

'He has a queer way of showing it, then. He never does anything but stamp and shout and find fault with me – all about an old paper-weight!'

She was caressing it as she spoke, stroking the alabaster Buddha as if it had been a live thing.

'His poor Buddha. Do you think it'll break if I stroke it? Better not . . . Honestly, Helen, I'd rather die than hurt anything he really cared for. Yet look how he hurts me.'

'Some men *must* hurt the things they care for.'

'I wouldn't mind his hurting, if only I knew he cared. Helen – I'd give anything to know.'

'I think you might know.'

'I don't! I don't!'

'Well, you'll know some day.'

'Never! He won't tell me.'

'He's Scotch, my dear. It would kill him to tell you.'

'Then how'm I to know! If I died to-morrow I should die not knowing.'

And that night, not knowing, she died.

She died because she had never really known.

II

We never talked about her. It was not my brother's way. Words hurt him, to speak or to hear them.

He had become more morose than ever, but less irritable, the source of his irritation being gone. Though he plunged into work as another man might have plunged into dissipation, to drown the thought of her, you could see that he had no longer any interest in it; he no longer loved it. He attacked it with a fury that had more hate in it than love. He would spend the greater part of the day and the long evenings shut up in his library, only going out for a short walk an hour before dinner. You could see that soon all spontaneous impulses would be checked in him and he would become the creature of habit and routine.

I tried to rouse him, to shake him up out of his deadly groove; but it was no use. The first effort – for he did make efforts – exhausted him, and he sank back into it again.

But he liked to have me with him; and all the time that I could spare from my housekeeping and gardening I spent in the library. I think he didn't like to be left alone there in the place where they had the quarrel that killed her; and I noticed that the cause of it, the Token, had disappeared from his table.

And all her things, everything that could remind him of her, had been put away. It was the dead burying its dead.

Only the chair she had loved remained in its place by the side of the hearth – *her* chair, if you could call it hers when she wasn't allowed to sit in it. It was always empty, for by tacit consent we both avoided it.

We would sit there for hours at a time without speaking, while he worked and I read or sewed. I never dared to ask him whether he sometimes had, as I had, the sense of Cicely's presence there, in that room which she had so longed to enter, from which she had been so cruelly shut out. You couldn't tell what he felt or didn't feel. My brother's face was a heavy, sombre mask; his back, bent over the writing-table, a wall behind which he hid himself.

You must know that twice in my life I have more than *felt* these presences; I have seen them. This may be because I am on both sides a Highland Celt, and my mother had the same uncanny gift. I had never spoken of these appearances to Donald because he would have put it all down to what he calls my hysterical fancy. And I am sure that if he ever felt or saw anything himself he would never own it.

I ought to explain that each time the vision was premonitory of a death (in Cicely's case I had no such warning), and each time it only lasted for a second; also that, though I am certain I was wide awake each time, it is open to anybody to say I was asleep and dreamed it. The queer thing was that I was neither frightened nor surprised.

And so I was neither surprised nor frightened now, the first evening that I saw her.

It was in the early autumn twilight, about six o'clock. I was sitting in my place in front of the fireplace; Donald was in his armchair on my left, smoking a pipe, as usual, before the lamplight drove him out of doors into the dark.

I had had so strong a sense of Cicely's being there in the room that I felt nothing but a sudden sacred pang that was half joy when I looked up and saw her sitting in her chair on my right.

The phantasm was perfect and vivid, as if it had been flesh and blood. I should have thought that it was Cicely herself if I hadn't known that she was dead. She wasn't looking at me; her face was turned to Donald with that longing, wondering look it used to have, searching his face for the secret that he kept from her.

I looked at Donald. His chin was sunk a little, the pipe drooping from the corner of his mouth. He was heavy, absorbed in his smoking. It was clear that he did not see what I saw.

And whereas those other phantasms that I told you about disappeared at once, *this* lasted some little time, and always with its eyes fixed on Donald. It even lasted while Donald stirred, while he stooped forward, knocking the ashes out of his pipe against the hob, while he sighed, stretched himself, turned, and left the room. Then, as the door shut behind him, the whole figure went out suddenly – not flickering, but like a light you switch off.

I saw it again the next evening and the next, at the same time and in the same place, and with the same look turned towards Donald. And again I was sure that he did not see it. But I thought, from his uneasy sighing and stretching, that he had some sense of something there.

No; I was not frightened. I was glad. You see, I loved Cicely. I remember thinking, 'At last, at last, you poor darling, you've got in. And you can stay as long as you like now. He can't turn you away.'

The first few times I saw her just as I have said. I would look up and find the phantasm there, sitting in her chair. And it would disappear suddenly when Donald left the room. Then I knew I was alone.

But as I grew used to its presence, or perhaps as it grew used to mine and found out that I was not afraid of it, that indeed I loved to have it there, it came, I think, to trust me, so that I was made aware of all its movements. I would see it coming across the room from the doorway, making straight for its desired place, and settling in a little curled-up posture of satisfaction, appeased, as if it had expected opposition that it no longer found. Yet that it was not happy, I could still see by its look at Donald. *That* never changed. It was as uncertain of him now as she had been in her lifetime.

Up till now, the sixth or seventh time I had seen it, I had no clue to the secret of its appearance; and its movements seemed to me mysterious and without purpose. Only two things were clear: it was Donald that it came for – the instant he went it disappeared; and I never once saw it when I was alone. And always it chose this room and this hour before the lights came, when he sat doing nothing. It was clear also that he never saw it.

But that it was there with him sometimes when I was not I knew; for, more than once, things on Donald's writing-table, books or papers, would be moved out of their places, though never beyond reach; and he would ask me whether I had touched them.

'Either you lie,' he would say, 'or I'm mistaken. I could have sworn I put those notes on the *left*-hand side; and they aren't there now.'

And once – that was wonderful – I saw, yes, I *saw* her come and push the lost thing under his hand. And all he said was, 'Well, I'm – I could have sworn –'

For whether it had gained a sense of security, or whether its purpose was now finally fixed, it began to move regularly about the room, and its movements had evidently a reason and an aim.

It was looking for something.

One evening we were all there in our places, Donald silent in his chair and I in mine, and it seated in its attitude of wonder and of waiting, when suddenly I saw Donald looking at me.

'Helen,' he said, 'what are you staring for like that?'

I started. I had forgotten that the direction of my eyes would be bound, sooner or later, to betray me.

I heard myself stammer, 'W – w – was I staring?'

'Yes. I wish you wouldn't.'

I knew what he meant. He didn't want me to keep on looking at that chair; he didn't want to know that I was thinking of her. I bent my head closer over my sewing, so that I no longer had the phantasm in sight.

It was then I was aware that it had risen and was crossing the hearthrug. It stopped at Donald's knees, and stood there, gazing at him with a look so intent and fixed that I could not doubt that this had some significance. I saw it put out its hand and touch him; and, though Donald sighed and shifted his position, I could tell that he had neither seen nor felt anything.

It turned to me then – and this was the first time it had given any sign that it was conscious of my presence – it turned on me a look of supplication, such supplication as I had seen on my sister's face in her lifetime, when she could do nothing with him and implored me to intercede. At the same time three words formed themselves in my brain with a sudden, quick impulsion, as if I had heard them cried.

'Speak to him – speak to him!'

I knew now what it wanted. It was trying to make itself seen by him, to make itself felt, and it was in anguish at finding that it could not. It knew then that I saw it, and the idea had come to it that it could make use of me to get through to him. I think I must have guessed even then what it had come for.

I said, 'You asked me what I was staring at, and I lied. I was looking at Cicely's chair.'

I saw him wince at the name.

'Because,' I went on, 'I don't know how *you* feel, but I always feel as if she were there.'

He said nothing; but he got up, as though to shake off the oppression of the memory I had evoked, and stood leaning on the chimney-piece with his back to me.

The phantasm retreated to its place, where it kept its eyes fixed on him as before.

I was determined to break down his defences, to make him say something it might hear, give some sign that it would understand.

'Donald, do you think it's a good thing, a *kind* thing, never to talk about her?'

'Kind? Kind to whom?'

'To yourself, first of all.'

'You can leave me out of it.'

'To me, then.'

'What's it got to do with you?' His voice was as hard and cutting as he could make it.

'Everything,' I said. 'You forget, I loved her.'

He was silent. He did at least respect my love for her.

'But that wasn't what she wanted.'

That hurt him. I could feel him stiffen under it.

'You see, Donald,' I persisted, '*I* like thinking about her.'

It was cruel of me; but I *had* to break him.

'You can think as much as you like,' he said, 'provided you stop talking.'

'All the same, it's as bad for you,' I said, 'as it is for me, not talking.'

'I don't care if it is bad for me. I *can't* talk about her, Helen. I don't want to.'

'How do you know,' I said, 'it isn't bad for *her*?'

'For *her*?'

I could see I had roused him.

'Yes. If she really is there, all the time.'

'How d'you mean, *there*?'

'Here – in this room. I tell you I can't get over that feeling that she's here.'

'Oh, feel, feel,' he said; 'but don't talk to me about it!'

And he left the room, flinging himself out in anger. And instantly her flame went out.

I thought, 'How he must have hurt her!' It was the old thing over again: I trying to break him down, to make him show her; he beating us both off, punishing us both. You see, I knew now what she had come back for: she had come back to find out whether he loved her. With a longing unquenched by death, she had come back for certainty. And now, as always, my clumsy interference had only made him more hard, more obstinate. I thought, 'If only he could see her! But as long as he beats her off he never will.'

Still, if I could once get him to believe that she was there –

I made up my mind that the next time I saw the phantasm I would tell him.

The next evening and the next its chair was empty, and I judged that it was keeping away, hurt by what it had heard the last time.

But the third evening we were hardly seated before I saw it.

It was sitting up, alert and observant, not staring at Donald as it used to, but looking round the room, as if searching for something that it missed.

'Donald,' I said, 'if I told you that Cicely is in the room now, I suppose you wouldn't believe me?'

'Is it likely?'

'No. All the same, I see her as plainly as I see you.'

The phantasm rose and moved to his side.

'She's standing close beside you.'

And now it moved and went to the writing-table. I turned and followed its movements. It slid its open hands over the table, touching everything, unmistakably feeling for something it believed to be there.

I went on. 'She's at the writing-table now. She's looking for something.'

It stood back, baffled and distressed. Then suddenly it began opening and shutting the drawers, without a sound, searching each one in turn.

I said, 'Oh, she's trying the drawers now!'

Donald stood up. He was not looking at the place where it was. He was looking hard at me, in anxiety and a sort of fright. I suppose that was why he remained unaware of the opening and shutting of the drawers.

It continued its desperate searching.

The bottom drawer stuck fast. I saw it pull and shake it, and stand back again, baffled.

'It's locked,' I said.

'What's locked?'

'That bottom drawer.'

'Nonsense! It's nothing of the kind.'

'It is, I tell you. Give me the key. Oh, Donald, give it me!'

He shrugged his shoulders; but all the same he felt in his pockets for the key, which he gave me with a little teasing gesture, as if he humoured a child.

I unlocked the drawer, pulled it out to its full length, and there, thrust away at the back, out of sight, I found the Token.

I had not seen it since the day of Cicely's death.

'Who put it there?' I asked.

'I did.'

'Well, that's what she was looking for,' I said.

I held out the Token to him on the palm of my hand, as if it were the proof that I had seen her.

'Helen,' he said gravely, 'I think you must be ill.'

'You think so? I'm not so ill that I don't know what you put it away for,' I said. 'It was because she thought you cared for it more than you did for her.'

'You can remind me of that? There must be something very badly wrong with you, Helen,' he said.

'Perhaps. Perhaps I only want to know what *she* wanted . . . You *did* care for her, Donald?'

I couldn't see the phantasm now, but I could feel it, close, close, vibrating, palpitating, as I drove him.

'Care?' he cried. 'I was mad with caring for her! And she knew it.'

'She didn't. She wouldn't be here now if she knew.'

At that he turned from me to his station by the chimney-piece. I followed him there.

'What are you going to do about it?' I said.

'Do about it?'

'What are you going to do with this?'

I thrust the Token close towards him. He drew back, staring at it with a look of concentrated hate and loathing.

'Do with it?' he said. 'The damned thing killed her! This is what I'm going to do with it –'

He snatched it from my hand and hurled it with all his force against the bars of the grate. The Buddha fell, broken to bits, among the ashes.

Then I heard him give a short, groaning cry. He stepped forward, opening his arms, and I saw the phantasm slide between them. For a second it stood there, folded to his breast; then suddenly, before our eyes, it collapsed in a shining heap, a flicker of light on the floor, at his feet.

Then that went out too.

III

I never saw it again.

Neither did my brother. But I didn't know this till some time afterwards; for, somehow, we hadn't cared to speak about it. And in the end it was he who spoke first.

We were sitting together in that room, one evening in November, when he said, suddenly and irrelevantly:

'Helen – do you never see her now?'

'No,' I said – 'Never!'

'Do you think, then, she doesn't come?'

'Why should she?' I said. 'She found what she came for. She knows what she wanted to know.'

'And that – was what?'

'Why, that you loved her.'

His eyes had a queer, submissive, wistful look.

'You think that was why she came back?' he said.

Ellen Glasgow

THE SHADOWY THIRD

WHEN the call came I remember that I turned from the telephone in a romantic flutter. Though I had spoken only once to the great surgeon, Roland Maradick, I felt on that December afternoon that to speak to him only once – to watch him in the operating-room for a single hour – was an adventure which drained the color and the excitement from the rest of life. After all these years of work on typhoid and pneumonia cases, I can still feel the delicious tremor of my young pulses; I can still see the winter sunshine slanting through the hospital windows over the white uniforms of the nurses.

'He didn't mention me by name. Can there be a mistake?' I stood, incredulous yet ecstatic, before the superintendent of the hospital.

'No, there isn't a mistake. I was talking to him before you came down.' Miss Hemphill's strong face softened while she looked at me. She was a big, resolute woman, a distant Canadian relative of my mother's, and the kind of nurse I had discovered in the month since I had come up from Richmond, that Northern hospital boards, if not Northern patients, appear instinctively to select. From the first, in spite of her hardness, she had taken a liking – I hesitate to use the word 'fancy' for a preference so impersonal – to her Virginia cousin. After all, it isn't every Southern nurse, just out of training, who can boast a kinswoman in the superintendent of a New York hospital.

'And he made you understand positively that he meant me?' The thing was so wonderful that I simply couldn't believe it.

'He asked particularly for the nurse who was with Miss Hudson last week when he operated. I think he didn't even remember that you had a name. When I asked if he meant Miss Randolph, he repeated that he wanted the nurse who had been with Miss Hudson. She was small, he said, and cheerful-looking. This, of course, might apply to one or two of the others, but none of these was with Miss Hudson.'

'Then I suppose it is really true?' My pulses were tingling. 'And I am to be there at six o'clock?'

'Not a minute later. The day nurse goes off duty at that hour, and Mrs Maradick is never left by herself for an instant.'

'It is her mind, isn't it? And that makes it all the stranger that he should select me, for I have had so few mental cases.'

'So few cases of any kind,' Miss Hemphill was smiling, and when she smiled I wondered if the other nurses would know her. 'By the time you have gone through the treadmill in New York, Margaret, you will have lost a good many things besides your inexperience. I wonder how long you will keep your sympathy and your imagination? After all, wouldn't you have made a better novelist than a nurse?'

'I can't help putting myself into my cases. I suppose one ought not to?'

'It isn't a question of what one ought to do, but of what one must. When you are drained of every bit of sympathy and enthusiasm, and have got nothing in return for it, not even thanks, you will understand why I try to keep you from wasting yourself.'

'But surely in a case like this – for Doctor Maradick?'

'Oh, well, of course – for Doctor Maradick.' She must have seen that I implored her confidence, for, after a minute, she let fall carelessly a gleam of light on the situation: 'It is a very sad case when you think what a charming man and a great surgeon Doctor Maradick is.'

Above the starched collar of my uniform I felt the blood leap in bounds to my cheeks. 'I have spoken to him only once,' I murmured, 'but he is charming, and so kind and handsome, isn't he?'

'His patients adore him.'

'Oh, yes, I've seen that. Everyone hangs on his visits.'

Like the patients and the other nurses, I also had come by delightful, if imperceptible, degrees to hang on the daily visits of Doctor Maradick. He was, I suppose, born to be a hero to women. From my first day in his hospital, from the moment when I watched, through closed shutters, while he stepped out of his car, I have never doubted that he was assigned to the great part in the play. If I had been ignorant of his spell – of the charm he exercised over his hospital – I should have felt it in the waiting hush, like a drawn breath, which followed his ring at the door and preceded his imperious footstep on the stairs. My first impression of him, even after the terrible events of the next year, records a memory that is both careless and splendid. At that moment, when, gazing through the chinks in the shutters, I watched him, in his coat of dark fur, cross the pavement over the pale streaks of sunshine, I knew beyond any doubt – I knew with a sort of infallible prescience – that my fate was irretrievably bound up with his in the future. I knew this, I repeat, though Miss Hemphill would still insist that my foreknowledge was merely a sentimental gleaning from indiscriminate novels. But it wasn't only first love, impressionable as my kinswoman believed me to be. It wasn't only the way he looked. Even more than his appearance – more than the shining dark of his eyes, the silvery brown of his hair, the dusky glow in his face – even more than his charm and his magnificence, I think, the beauty and sympathy in his voice won my heart. It was a voice, I heard someone say afterwards, that ought always to speak poetry.

So you will see why – if you do not understand at the beginning, I can never hope to make you believe impossible things! – so you will see why I accepted the call when it came as an imperative summons. I couldn't have stayed away after he sent for me. However much I may have tried not to go, I know that in the end I must have gone. In those days, while I was still hoping to write novels, I used to talk a great deal about 'destiny' (I have learned since then how silly all such talk is), and I suppose it was my 'destiny' to be caught in the web of Roland Maradick's personality. But I am not the first nurse to grow love-sick about a doctor who never gave her a thought.

'I am glad you got the call, Margaret. It may mean a great deal to you. Only try not to be too emotional.' I remember that Miss Hemphill was holding a bit of rose-geranium in her hand while she spoke – one of the patients had given it to her from a pot she kept in her room – and the scent of the flower is still in my nostrils – or my memory. Since then – oh, long since then – I have wondered if she also had been caught in the web.

'I wish I knew more about the case.' I was pressing for light. 'Have you ever seen Mrs Maradick?'

'Oh, dear, yes. They have been married only a little over a year, and in the beginning she used to come sometimes to the hospital and wait outside while the doctor made his visits. She was a very sweet-looking woman then – not exactly pretty, but fair and slight, with the loveliest smile, I think, I have ever seen. In those first months she was so much in love that we used to laugh about it among ourselves. To see her face light up when the doctor came out of the hospital and crossed the pavement to his car was as good as a play. We never tired of watching her – I wasn't superintendent then, so I had more time to look out of the window while I was on day duty. Once or twice she brought her little girl in to see one of the patients. The child was so much like her that you would have known them anywhere for mother and daughter.'

I had heard that Mrs Maradick was a widow, with one child, when she first met the doctor, and I asked now, still seeking an illumination I had not found, 'There was a great deal of money, wasn't there?'

'A great fortune. If she hadn't been so attractive, people would have said, I suppose, that Doctor Maradick married her for her money. Only,' she appeared to make an effort of memory, 'I believe I've heard somehow that it was all left in trust away from Mrs Maradick if she married again. I can't, to save my life, remember just how it was; but it was a queer will, I know, and

Mrs Maradick wasn't to come into the money unless the child didn't live to grow up. The pity of it –'

A young nurse came into the office to ask for something – the keys, I think, of the operating-room, and Miss Hemphill broke off inconclusively as she hurried out of the door. I was sorry that she left off just when she did. Poor Mrs Maradick! Perhaps I was too emotional, but even before I saw her I had begun to feel her pathos and her strangeness.

My preparations took only a few minutes. In those days I always kept a suitcase packed and ready for sudden calls; and it was not yet six o'clock when I turned from Tenth Street into Fifth Avenue, and stopped for a minute, before ascending the steps, to look at the house in which Doctor Maradick lived. A fine rain was falling, and I remember thinking, as I turned the corner, how depressing the weather must be for Mrs Maradick. It was an old house, with damp-looking walls (though that may have been because of the rain) and a spindle-shaped iron railing which ran up the stone steps to the black door, where I noticed a dim flicker through the old-fashioned fanlight. Afterwards I discovered that Mrs Maradick had been born in the house – her maiden name was Calloran – and that she had never wanted to live anywhere else. She was a woman – this I found out when I knew her better – of strong attachments to both persons and places; and though Doctor Maradick had tried to persuade her to move uptown after her marriage, she had clung, against his wishes, to the old house in lower Fifth Avenue. I dare say she was obstinate about it in spite of her gentleness and her passion for the doctor. Those sweet, soft women, especially when they have always been rich, are sometimes amazingly obstinate. I have nursed so many of them since – women with strong affections and weak intellects – that I have come to recognize the type as soon as I set eyes upon it.

My ring at the bell was answered after a little delay, and when I entered the house I saw that the hall was quite dark except for the waning glow from an open fire which burned in the library. When I gave my name, and added that I was the night nurse, the servant appeared to think my humble presence unworthy of illumination. He was an old negro butler, inherited perhaps from Mrs Maradick's mother, who, I learned afterwards, was from South Carolina; and while he passed me on his way up the staircase, I heard him vaguely muttering that he 'wa'n't gwinter tu'n on dem lights twel de chile had done playin'.'

To the right of the hall, the soft glow drew me into the library, and crossing the threshold timidly, I stooped to dry my wet coat by the fire. As I bent there, meaning to start up at the first sound of a footstep, I thought how cozy the room was after the damp walls outside to which some bared creepers were clinging; and I was watching the strange shapes and patterns the firelight made on the old Persian rug, when the lamps of a slowly turning motor flashed on me through the white shades at the window. Still dazzled by the glare, I looked round in the dimness and saw a child's ball of red and blue rubber roll towards me out of the gloom of the adjoining room. A moment later, while I made a vain attempt to capture the toy as it spun past me, a little girl darted airily, with peculiar lightness and grace, through the doorway, and stopped quickly, as if in surprise at the sight of a stranger. She was a small child – so small and slight that her footsteps made no sound on the polished floor of the threshold; and I remember thinking while I looked at her that she had the gravest and sweetest face I had ever seen. She couldn't – I decided this afterwards – have been more than six or seven years old, yet she stood there with a curious prim dignity, like the dignity of an elderly person, and gazed up at me with enigmatical eyes. She was dressed in Scotch plaid, with a bit of red ribbon in her hair, which was cut in a fringe over her forehead and hung very straight to her shoulders. Charming as she was, from her uncurled brown hair to the white socks and black slippers on her little feet, I recall most vividly the singular look in her eyes, which appeared in the shifting light to be of an indeterminate color. For the odd thing about this look was that it was not the look of childhood at all. It was the look of profound experience, of bitter knowledge.

'Have you come for your ball?' I asked; but while the friendly question was still on my lips, I heard the servant returning. In my confusion I made a second ineffectual grasp at the plaything, which had rolled away from me into the dusk of the drawing-room. Then, as I raised my head, I saw that the child also had slipped from the rooms; and without looking after her I followed the old negro into the pleasant study above, where the great surgeon awaited me.

Ten years ago, before hard nursing had taken so much out of me, I blushed very easily, and I was aware at the moment when I crossed Doctor Maradick's study that my cheeks were the color of peonies. Of course, I was a fool – no one knows this better than I do – but I had never been alone, even for an instant, with him before, and the man was more than a hero to me, he was – there isn't any reason now why I should blush over the confession – almost a god. At that age I was mad about the wonders of surgery, and Roland Maradick in the operating-room was magician enough to have turned an older and more sensible head than mine. Added to his great reputation and his marvelous skill, he was, I am sure of this, the most splendid-looking man, even at forty-five, that one could imagine. Had he been ungracious – had he been positively rude to me, I should still have adored him; but when he held out his hand, and greeted me in the charming way he had with women, I felt that I would have died for him. It is no wonder that a saying went about the hospital that every woman he operated on fell in love with him. As for the nurses – well, there wasn't a single one of them who had escaped his spell – not even Miss Hemphill, who could have been scarcely a day under fifty.

'I am glad you could come, Miss Randolph. You were with Miss Hudson last week when I operated?'

I bowed. To save my life I couldn't have spoken without blushing the redder.

'I noticed your bright face at the time. Brightness I think, is what Mrs Maradick needs. She finds her day nurse depressing.' His eyes rested so kindly upon me that I have suspected since that he was not entirely unaware of my worship. It was a small thing, heaven knows, to flatter his vanity – a nurse just out of a training school – but to some men no tribute is too insignificant to give pleasure.

'You will do your best, I am sure.' He hesitated an instant – just long enough for me to perceive the anxiety beneath the genial smile on his face – and then added gravely, 'We wish to avoid, if possible, having to send her away.'

I could only murmur in response, and after a few carefully chosen words about his wife's illness, he rang the bell and directed the maid to take me upstairs to my room. Not until I was ascending the stairs to the third story did it occur to me that he had really told me nothing. I was as perplexed about the nature of Mrs Maradick's malady as I had been when I entered the house.

I found my room pleasant enough. It had been arranged – at Doctor Maradick's request, I think – that I was to sleep in the house, and after my austere little bed at the hospital, I was agreeably surprised by the cheerful look of the apartment into which the maid led me. The walls were papered in roses, and there were curtains of flowered chintz at the window, which looked down on a small formal garden at the rear of the house. This the maid told me, for it was too dark for me to distinguish more than a marble fountain and a fir-tree, which looked old, though I afterwards learned that it was replanted almost every season.

In ten minutes I had slipped into my uniform and was ready to go to my patient; but for some reason – to this day I have never found out what it was that turned her against me at the start – Mrs Maradick refused to receive me. While I stood outside her door I heard the day nurse trying to persuade her to let me come in. It wasn't any use, however, and in the end I was obliged to go back to my room and wait until the poor lady got over her whim and consented to see me. That was long after dinner – it must have been nearer eleven than ten o'clock – and Miss Peterson was quite worn out by the time she came for me.

'I'm afraid you'll have a bad night,' she said as we went downstairs together. That was her way, I soon saw, to expect the worst of everything and everybody.

'Does she often keep you up like this?'

'Oh, no, she is usually very considerate. I never knew a sweeter character. But she still has this hallucination –'

Here again, as in the scene with Doctor Maradick, I felt that the explanation had only deepened the mystery. Mrs Maradick's hallucination, whatever form it assumed, was evidently a subject for evasion and subterfuge in the household. It was on the tip of my tongue to ask, 'What is her hallucination?' – but before I could get the words past my lips we had reached Mrs Maradick's door, and Miss Peterson motioned me to be silent. As the door opened a little way to admit me, I saw that Mrs Maradick was already in bed, and that the lights were out except for a night-lamp burning on a candle-stand beside a book and a carafe of water.

'I won't go in with you,' said Miss Peterson in a whisper; and I was on the point of stepping over the threshold when I saw the little girl, in the dress of Scotch plaid, slip by me from the dusk of the room into the electric light of the hall. She held a doll in her arms, and as she went by she dropped a doll's work-basket in the doorway. Miss Peterson must have picked up the toy, for when I turned in a minute to look for it I found that it was gone. I remember thinking that it was late for a child to be up – she looked delicate, too – but, after all it was no business of mine, and four years in the hospital had taught me never to meddle in things that do not concern me. There is nothing a nurse learns quicker than not to try to put the world to rights in a day.

When I crossed the floor to the chair by Mrs Maradick's bed, she turned over on her side and looked at me with the sweetest and saddest smile.

'You are the night nurse,' she said in a gentle voice; and from the moment she spoke I knew that there was nothing hysterical or violent about her mania – or hallucination, as they called it. 'They told me your name, but I have forgotten it.'

'Randolph – Margaret Randolph.' I liked her from the start, and I think she must have seen it.

'You look very young, Miss Randolph.'

'I am twenty-two, but I suppose I don't look quite my age. People usually think I am younger.'

For a minute she was silent, and while I settled myself in the chair by the bed, I thought how strikingly she resembled the little girl I had seen first in the afternoon, and then leaving her room a few moments before. They had the same small, heart-shaped faces, colored ever so faintly; the same straight, soft hair, between brown and flaxen; and the same large, grave eyes, set very far apart under arched eyebrows. What surprised me most, however, was that they both looked at me with that enigmatical and vaguely wondering expression – only in Mrs Maradick's face the vagueness seemed to change now and then to a definite fear – a flash, I had almost said, of startled horror.

I sat quite still in my chair, and until the time came for Mrs Maradick to take her medicine not a word passed between us. Then, when I bent over her with the glass in my hand, she raised her head from the pillow and said in a whisper of suppressed intensity:

'You look kind. I wonder if you could have seen my little girl?'

As I slipped my arm under the pillow I tried to smile cheerfully down on her. 'Yes, I've seen her twice. I'd know her anywhere by her likeness to you.'

A glow shone in her eyes, and I thought how pretty she must have been before illness took the life and animation out of her features. 'Then I know you're good.' Her voice was so strained and low that I could barely hear it. 'If you weren't good you couldn't have seen her.'

I thought this queer enough, but all I answered was, 'She looked delicate to be sitting up so late.'

A quiver passed over her thin features, and for a minute I thought she was going to burst into tears. As she had taken the medicine, I put the glass back on the candle-stand, and bending over the bed, smoothed the straight brown hair, which was as fine and soft as spun silk, back from her forehead. There was something about her – I don't know what it was – that made you love her as soon as she looked at you.

'She always had that light and airy way, though she was never sick a day in her life,' she answered calmly after a pause. Then, groping for my hand, she whispered passionately, 'You must not tell him – you must not tell any one that you have seen her!'

'I must not tell any one?' Again I had the impression that had come to me first in Doctor Maradick's study, and afterwards with Miss Peterson on the staircase, that I was seeking a gleam of light in the midst of obscurity.

'Are you sure there isn't any one listening – that there isn't any one at the door?' she asked, pushing aside my arm and raising herself on the pillows.

'Quite, quite sure. They have put out the lights in the hall.'

'And you will not tell him? Promise me that you will not tell him.' The startled horror flashed from the vague wonder of her expression. 'He doesn't like her to come back, because he killed her.'

'Because he killed her!' Then it was that light burst on me in a blaze. So this was Mrs Maradick's hallucination! She believed that her child was dead – the little girl I had seen with my own eyes leaving her room; and she believed that her husband – the great surgeon we worshipped in the hospital – had murdered her. No wonder they veiled the dreadful obsession in mystery! No wonder that even Miss Peterson had not dared to drag the horrid thing out into the light! It was the kind of hallucination one simply couldn't stand having to face.

'There is no use telling people things that nobody believes,' she resumed slowly, still holding my hand in a grasp that would have hurt me if her fingers had not been so fragile. 'Nobody believes that he killed her. Nobody believes that she comes back every day to the house. Nobody believes – and yet you saw her –'

'Yes, I saw her – but why should your husband have killed her?' I spoke soothingly, as one would speak to a person who was quite mad. Yet she was not mad, I could have sworn this while I looked at her.

For a moment she moaned inarticulately, as if the horror of her thoughts were too great to pass into speech. Then she flung out her thin, bare arm with a wild gesture.

'Because he never loved me!' she said. 'He never loved me!'

'But he married you,' I urged gently while I stroked her hair. 'If he hadn't loved you, why should he have married you?'

'He wanted the money – my little girl's money. It all goes to him when I die.'

'But he is rich himself. He must make a fortune from his profession.'

'It isn't enough. He wanted millions.' She had grown stern and tragic. 'No, he never loved me. He loved someone else from the beginning – before I knew him.'

It was quite useless, I saw, to reason with her. If she wasn't mad, she was in a state of terror and despondency so black that it had almost crossed the border-line into madness. I thought once that I would go upstairs and bring the child down from her nursery; but, after a moment's hesitation, I realized that Miss Peterson and Doctor Maradick must have long ago tried all these measures. Clearly, there was nothing to do except soothe and quiet her as much as I could; and this I did until she dropped into a light sleep which lasted well into the morning.

By seven o'clock I was worn out – not from work but from the strain on my sympathy – and I was glad, indeed, when one of the maids came in to bring me an early cup of coffee. Mrs Maradick was still sleeping – it was a mixture of bromide and chloral I had given her – and she did not wake until Miss Peterson came on duty an hour or two later. Then, when I went downstairs, I found the dining-room deserted except for the old housekeeper, who was looking over the silver. Doctor Maradick, she explained to me presently, had his breakfast served in the morning -room on the other side of the house.

'And the little girl? Does she take her meals in the nursery?'

She threw me a startled glance. Was it, I questioned afterwards, one of distrust or apprehension?

'There isn't any little girl. Haven't you heard?'

'Heard? No. Why, I saw her only yesterday.' The look she gave me – I was sure of it now – was full of alarm.

'The little girl – she was the sweetest child I ever saw – died just two months ago of pneumonia.'

'But she couldn't have died.' I was a fool to let this out, but the shock had completely unnerved me. 'I tell you I saw her yesterday.'

The alarm in her face deepened. 'That is Mrs Maradick's trouble. She believes that she still sees her.'

'But don't you see her?' I drove the question home bluntly.

'No.' She set her lips tightly. 'I never see anything.'

So I had been wrong, after all, and the explanation, when it came, only accentuated the terror. The child was dead – she had died of pneumonia two months ago – and yet I had seen her, with my own eyes, playing ball in the library; I had seen her slipping out of her mother's room, with her doll in her arms.

'Is there another child in the house? Could there be a child belonging to one of the servants?' A gleam had shot through the fog in which I was groping.

'No, there isn't any other. The Doctor tried bringing one once, but it threw the poor lady into such a state she almost died of it. Besides, there wouldn't be any other child as quiet and sweet-looking as Dorothea. To see her skipping along in her dress of Scotch plaid used to make me think of a fairy, though they say that fairies wear nothing but white or green.'

'Has any one else seen her – the child, I mean – any of the servants?'

'Only old Gabriel, the colored butler, who came with Mrs Maradick's mother from South Carolina. I've heard that negroes often have a kind of second sight – though I don't know that that is just what you would call it. But they seem to believe in the supernatural by instinct, and Gabriel is so old and dotty – he does no work except answer the door-bell and clean the silver – that nobody pays much attention to anything that he sees –'

'Is the child's nursery kept as it used to be?'

'Oh no. The doctor had all the toys sent to the children's hospital. That was a great grief to Mrs Maradick; but Doctor Brandon thought, and all the nurses agreed with him, that it was best for her not to be allowed to keep the room as it was when Dorothea was living.'

'Dorothea? Was that the child's name?'

'Yes, it means the gift of God, doesn't it? She was named after the mother of Mrs Maradick's first husband, Mr Ballard. He was the grave, quiet kind – not the least like the doctor.'

I wondered if the other dreadful obsession of Mrs Maradick's had drifted down through the nurses or the servants to the housekeeper; but she said nothing about it, and since she was, I suspected, a garrulous person, I thought it wiser to assume that the gossip had not reached her.

A little later, when breakfast was over and I had not yet gone upstairs to my room, I had my first interview with Doctor Brandon, the famous alienist who was in charge of the case. I had never seen him before, but from the first moment that I looked at him I took his measure almost by intuition. He was, I suppose, honest enough – I have always granted him that, bitterly as I have felt towards him. It wasn't his fault that he lacked red blood in his brain, or that he had formed the habit, from long association with abnormal phenomena, of regarding all life as a disease. He was the sort of physician – every nurse will understand what I mean – who deals instinctively with groups instead of with individuals. He was long and solemn and very round in the face; and I hadn't talked to him ten minutes before I knew he had been educated in Germany, and that he had learned over there to treat every emotion as a pathological manifestation. I used to wonder what he got out of life – what any one got out of life who had analysed away everything except the bare structure.

When I reached my room at last, I was so tired that I could barely remember either the questions Doctor Brandon had asked or the directions he had given me. I fell asleep, I know, almost as soon as my head touched the pillow; and the maid who came to inquire if I wanted luncheon decided to let me finish my nap. In the afternoon, when she returned with a cup of tea, she found me still heavy and drowsy. Though I was used to night nursing, I felt as if I had danced from sunset to daybreak. It was fortunate, I reflected, while I drank my tea, that every case didn't wear on one's sympathies as acutely as Mrs Maradick's hallucination had worn on mine.

Through the day I did not see Doctor Maradick; but at seven o'clock when I came up from early dinner on my way to take the place of Miss Peterson, who had kept on duty an hour later than usual, he met me in the hall and asked me to come into his study. I thought him handsomer than ever in his evening clothes, with a white flower in his buttonhole. He was going to some public dinner, the housekeeper told me, but then, he was always going somewhere. I believe he didn't dine at home a single evening that winter.

'Did Mrs Maradick have a good night?' He had closed the door after us, and turning now with the question, he smiled kindly, as if he wished to put me at ease in the beginning.

'She slept very well after she took the medicine. I gave her that at eleven o'clock.'

For a minute he regarded me silently, and I was aware that his personality –

his charm – was focused upon me. It was almost as if I stood in the center of converging rays of light, so vivid was my impression of him.

'Did she allude in any way to her – to her hallucination?' he asked.

How the warning reached me – what invisible waves of sense-perception transmitted the message – I have never known; but while I stood there, facing the splendor of the doctor's presence, every intuition cautioned me that the time had come when I must take sides in the household. While I stayed there I must stand either with Mrs Maradick or against her.

'She talked quite rationally,' I replied after a moment.

'What did she say?'

'She told me how she was feeling, that she missed her child, and that she walked a little every day about her room.'

His face changed – how I could not at first determine.

'Have you seen Doctor Brandon?'

'He came this morning to give me his directions.'

'He thought her less well today. He has advised me to send her to Rosedale.'

I have never, even in secret, tried to account for Doctor Maradick. He may have been sincere. I tell only what I know – not what I believe or imagine – and the human is sometimes as inscrutable, and inexplicable, as the supernatural.

While he watched me I was conscious of an inner struggle, as if opposing angels warred somewhere in the depths of my being. When at last I made my decision, I was acting less from reason, I knew, than in obedience to the pressure of some secret current of thought. Heaven knows, even then, the man held me captive while I defied him.

'Doctor Maradick,' I lifted my eyes for the first time frankly to his, 'I believe that your wife is as sane as I am – or as you are.'

He started. 'Then she did not talk freely to you?'

'She may be mistaken, unstrung, piteously distressed in mind' – I brought this out with emphasis – 'but she is not – I am willing to stake my future on it – a fit subject for an asylum. It would be foolish – it would be cruel – to send her to Rosedale.'

'Cruel, you say?' A troubled look crossed his face, and his voice grew very gentle. 'You do not imagine that I could be cruel to her?'

'No, I do not think that.' My voice also had softened.

'We will let things go on as they are. Perhaps Doctor Brandon may have some other suggestion to make.' He drew out his watch and compared it with the clock – nervously, I observed, as if his action were a screen for his discomfiture or perplexity. 'I must be going now. We will speak of this again in the morning.'

But in the morning we did not speak of it, and during the month that I nursed Mrs Maradick I was not called again into her husband's study. When I met him in the hall or on the staircase, which was seldom, he was as charming as ever; yet, in spite of his courtesy, I had a persistent feeling that he had taken my measure on that evening, and that he had no further use for me.

As the days went by Mrs Maradick seemed to grow stronger. Never, after our first night together, had she mentioned the child to me; never had she alluded by so much as a word to her dreadful charge against her husband. She was like any woman recovering from a great sorrow, except that she was sweeter and gentler. It is no wonder that everyone who came near her loved her; for there was a loveliness about her like the mystery of light, not of darkness. She was, I have always thought, as much of an angel as it is possible for a woman to be on this earth. And yet, angelic as she was, there were times when it seemed to me that she both hated and feared her husband. Though he never entered her room while I was there, and I never heard his name on her lips until an hour before the end, still I could tell by the look of terror in her face whenever his step passed down the hall that her very soul shivered at his approach.

During the whole month I did not see the child again, though one night, when I came suddenly into Mrs Maradick's room, I found a little garden, such as children make out of pebbles and bits of box, on the window-sill. I did not mention it to Mrs Maradick, and a little later, as the maid lowered the shades, I noticed that the garden had vanished. Since then I have often wondered if the child were invisible only to the rest of us, and if her mother still saw her. But there was no way of finding out except by questioning, and Mrs Maradick was so well and patient that I hadn't the heart to question. Things couldn't have been better with her than they were, and I was beginning to tell myself that she might soon go out for an airing, when the end came so suddenly.

It was a mild January day – the kind of day that brings the foretaste of spring in the middle of winter, and when I came downstairs in the afternoon, I stopped a minute by the window at the end of the hall to look down on the box maze in the garden. There was an old fountain, bearing two laughing boys in marble, in the center of the graveled walk, and the water, which had been turned on that morning for Mrs Maradick's pleasure, sparkled now like silver as the sunlight splashed over it. I had never before felt the air quite so soft and spring-like in January; and I thought, as I gazed down on the garden, that it would be a good idea for Mrs Maradick to go out and bask for an hour or so in the sunshine. It seemed strange to me that she was never allowed to get any fresh air except the air that came through her window.

When I went into her room, however, I found that she had no wish to go out. She was sitting, wrapped in shawls, by the open window, which looked down on the fountain; and as I entered she glanced up from a little book she was reading. A pot of daffodils stood on the window-sill – she was very fond of flowers and we tried always to keep some growing in her room.

'Do you know what I am reading, Miss Randolph?' she asked in her soft voice; and she read aloud a verse while I went over to the candle-stand to measure out a dose of medicine.

'"If thou hast two loaves of bread, sell one and buy daffodils, for bread nourisheth the body, but daffodils delight the soul." That is very beautiful, don't you think so?'

I said, 'Yes,' that it was beautiful; and then I asked her if she wouldn't go downstairs and walk about in the garden.

'He wouldn't like it,' she answered; and it was the first time she had mentioned her husband to me since the night I came to her. 'He doesn't want me to go out.'

I tried to laugh her out of the idea; but it was no use, and after a few minutes I gave up and began talking of other things. Even then it did not occur to me that her fear of Doctor Maradick was anything but a fancy. I could see, of course, that she wasn't out of her head; but sane persons, I knew, sometimes have unaccountable prejudices, and I accepted her dislike as a mere whim or aversion. I did not understand then and – I may as well confess this before the end comes – I do not understand any better today. I am writing down the things I actually saw, and I repeat that I have never had the slightest twist in the direction of the miraculous.

The afternoon slipped away while we talked – she talked brightly when any subject came up that interested her – and it was the last hour of day – that grave, still hour when the movement of life seems to droop and falter for a few precious minutes – that brought us the thing I had dreaded silently since my first night in the house. I remember that I had risen to close the window, and was leaning out for a breath of the mild air, when there was the sound of steps, consciously softened, in the hall outside, and Doctor Brandon's usual knock fell on my ears. Then, before I could cross the room, the door opened, and the doctor entered with Miss Peterson. The day nurse, I knew, was a stupid woman; but she had never appeared to me so stupid, so armored and encased in her professional manner, as she did at that moment.

'I am glad to see that you are taking the air.' As Doctor Brandon came over to the window, I wondered maliciously what devil of contradictions had made him a distinguished specialist in nervous diseases.

'Who was the other doctor you brought this morning?' asked Mrs Maradick gravely; and that was all I ever heard about the visit of the second alienist.

'Someone who is anxious to cure you.' He dropped into a chair beside her and patted her hand with his long, pale fingers. 'We are so anxious to cure you that we want to send you away to the country for a fortnight or so. Miss Peterson has come to help you to get ready, and I've kept my car waiting for you. There couldn't be a nicer day for a trip, could there?'

The moment had come at last. I knew at once what he meant, and so did Mrs Maradick. A wave of color flowed and ebbed in her thin cheeks, and I felt her body quiver when I moved from the window and put my arms on her shoulders. I was aware again, as I had been aware that evening in Doctor Maradick's study, of a current of thought that beat from the air around into my brain. Though it cost me my career as a nurse and my reputation for sanity, I knew that I must obey that invisible warning.

'You are going to take me to an asylum,' said Mrs Maradick.

He made some foolish denial or evasion; but before he had finished I turned from Mrs Maradick and faced him impulsively. In a nurse this was flagrant rebellion, and I realised that the act wrecked my professional future. Yet I did not care – I did not hesitate. Something stronger than I was driving me on.

'Doctor Brandon,' I said, 'I beg you – I implore you to wait until tomorrow. There are things I must tell you.'

A queer look came into his face, and I understood, even in my excitement, that he was mentally deciding in which group he should place me – to which class of morbid manifestations I must belong.

'Very well, very well, we will hear everything,' he replied soothingly; but I saw him glance at Miss Peterson, and she went over to the wardrobe for Mrs Maradick's fur coat and hat.

Suddenly, without warning, Mrs Maradick threw the shawls away from her, and stood up. 'If you send me away,' she said, 'I shall never come back. I shall never live to come back.'

The gray of twilight was just beginning, and while she stood there, in the dusk of the room, her face shone out as pale and flower-like as the daffodils on the window-sill. 'I cannot go away!' she cried in a sharper voice. 'I cannot go away from my child!'

I saw her face clearly; I heard her voice; and then – the horror of the scene sweeps back over me! – I saw the door open slowly and the little girl run across the room to her mother. I saw the child lift her little arms, and I saw the mother stoop and gather her to her bosom. So closely locked were they in that passionate embrace that their forms seemed to mingle in the gloom that enveloped them.

'After this can you doubt?' I threw out the words almost savagely – and then, when I turned from the mother and child to Doctor Brandon and Miss

Peterson, I knew breathlessly – oh, there was a shock in the discovery! – that they were blind to the child. Their blank faces revealed the consternation of ignorance, not of conviction. They had seen nothing except the vacant arms of the mother and the swift, erratic gesture with which she stooped to embrace some invisible presence. Only my vision – and I have asked myself since if the power of sympathy enabled me to penetrate the web of material fact and see the spiritual form of the child – only my vision was not blinded by the clay through which I looked.

'After this can you doubt?' Doctor Brandon had flung my words back to me. Was it his fault, poor man, if life had granted him only the eyes of flesh? Was it his fault if he could see only half of the thing there before him?

But they couldn't see, and since they couldn't see I realised that it was useless to tell them. Within an hour they took Mrs Maradick to the asylum; and she went quietly, though when the time came for parting from me she showed some faint trace of feeling. I remember that at the last, while we stood on the pavement, she lifted her black veil, which she wore for the child, and said: 'Stay with her, Miss Randolph, as long as you can. I shall never come back.'

Then she got into the car and was driven off, while I stood looking after her with a sob in my throat. Dreadful as I felt it to be, I didn't, of course, realize the full horror of it, or I couldn't have stood there quietly on the pavement. I didn't realise it, indeed, until several months afterwards when word came that she had died in the asylum. I never knew what her illness was, though I vaguely recall that something was said about 'heart failure' – a loose enough term. My own belief is that she died simply of the terror of life.

To my surprise Doctor Maradick asked me to stay on as his office nurse after his wife went to Rosedale; and when the news of her death came there was no suggestion of my leaving. I don't know to this day why he wanted me in the house. Perhaps he thought I should have less opportunity to gossip if I stayed under his roof; perhaps he still wished to test the power of his charm over me. His vanity was incredible in so great a man. I have seen him flush with pleasure when people turned to look at him in the street, and I know that he was not above playing on the sentimental weakness of his patients. But he was magnificent, heaven knows! Few men, I imagine, have been the objects of so many foolish infatuations.

The next summer Doctor Maradick went abroad for two months, and while he was away I took my vacation in Virginia. When we came back the work was heavier than ever – his reputation by this time was tremendous – and my days were so crowded with appointments, and hurried flittings to emergency cases, that I had scarcely a minute left in which to remember poor Mrs Maradick. Since the afternoon when she went to the asylum the child had not been in the house; and at last I was beginning to persuade myself that the little figure had been an optical illusion – the effect of shifting lights in the gloom of the old rooms – not the apparition I had once believed it to be. It does not take long for a phantom to fade from the memory – especially when one leads the active and methodical life I was forced into that winter. Perhaps – who knows? – (I remember telling myself) the doctors may have been right, after all, and the poor lady may have actually been out of her mind. With this view of the past, my judgement of Doctor Maradick insensibly altered. It ended, I think, in my acquitting him altogether. And then, just as he stood clear and splendid in my verdict of him, the reversal came so precipitately that I grow breathless now whenever I try to live it over again. The violence of the next turn in affairs left me, I often fancy, with a perpetual dizziness of the imagination.

It was in May that we heard of Mrs Maradick's death, and exactly a year later, on a mild and fragrant afternoon, when the daffodils were blooming in patches around the old fountain in the garden, the housekeeper came into the office, where I lingered over some accounts, to bring me news of the doctor's approaching marriage.

'It is no more than we might have expected,' she concluded rationally. 'The house must be lonely for him – he is such a sociable man. But I can't help feeling,' she brought out slowly after a pause in which I felt a shiver pass over me, 'I can't help feeling that it is hard for that other woman to have all the money poor Mrs Maradick's first husband left her.'

'There is a great deal of money, then?' I asked curiously.

'A great deal.' She waved her hand, as if words were futile to express the sum. 'Millions and millions!'

'They will give up this house, of course?'

'That's done already, my dear. There won't be a brick left of it by this time next year. It's to be pulled down and an apartment-house built on the ground.'

Again the shiver passed over me. I couldn't bear to think of Mrs Maradick's old home falling to pieces.

'You didn't tell me the name of the bride,' I said. 'Is she someone he met while he was in Europe?'

'Dear me, no! She is the very lady he was engaged to before he married Mrs Maradick, only she threw him over, so people said, because he wasn't rich enough. Then she married some lord or prince from over the water; but there was a divorce, and now she has turned again to her old lover. He is rich enough now, I guess, even for her!'

It was all perfectly true, I suppose; it sounded as plausible as a story out of a newspaper; and yet while she told me I felt, or dreamed that I felt, a sinister, an impalpable hush in the air. I was nervous, no doubt; I was shaken by the suddenness with which the housekeeper had sprung her news on me; but as I sat there I had quite vividly an impression that the old house was listening – that there was a real, if invisible, presence somewhere in the room or the garden. Yet, when an instant afterwards I glanced through the long window which opened down to the brick terrace, I saw only the faint sunshine over the deserted garden, with its maze of box, its marble fountain, and its patches of daffodils.

The housekeeper had gone – one of the servants, I think, came for her – and I was sitting at my desk when the words of Mrs Maradick on that last evening floated into my mind. The daffodils brought her back to me; for I thought, as I watched them growing, so still and golden in the sunshine, how she would have enjoyed them. Almost unconsciously I repeated the verse she had read to me:

'If thou hast two loaves of bread, sell one and buy daffodils' – and it was at this very instant, while the words were still on my lips, that I turned my eyes to the box maze, and saw the child skipping along the graveled path to the fountain. Quite distinctly, as clear as day, I saw her come, with what children call the dancing step, between the low box borders to the place where the daffodils bloomed by the fountain. From her straight brown hair to her frock of Scotch plaid and her little feet, which twinkled in white socks and black slippers over the turning rope, she was as real to me as the ground on which she trod or the laughing marble boys under the splashing water. Starting up from my chair, I made a single step to the terrace. If I could only reach her – only speak to her – I felt that I might at last solve the mystery. But with the first flutter of my dress on the terrace, the airy little form melted into the quiet dusk of the maze. Not a breath stirred the daffodils, not a shadow passed over the sparkling flow of the water; yet, weak and shaken in every nerve, I sat down on the brick step of the terrace and burst into tears. I must have known that something terrible would happen before they pulled down Mrs Maradick's home.

The doctor dined out that night. He was with the lady he was going to marry, the housekeeper told me; and it must have been almost midnight when I heard him come in and go upstairs to his room. I was downstairs because I had been unable to sleep, and the book I wanted to finish I had left that afternoon in the office. The book – I can't remember what it was – had seemed to me very exciting when I began it in the morning; but after the visit of the child I found the romantic novel as dull as a treatise on nursing. It was impossible for me to follow the lines, and I was on the point of giving up and going to bed, when Doctor Maradick opened the front door with his latch-key and went up the stair.

I was still there when the telephone on my desk rang, with what seemed to my overwrought nerves a startling abruptness, and the voice of the superintendent told me hurriedly that Doctor Maradick was needed at the hospital. I had become so accustomed to these emergency calls in the night that I felt reassured when I had rung up the doctor in his room and had heard the hearty sound of his response. He had not yet undressed, he said, and would come down immediately while I ordered back his car, which must just have reached the garage.

'I'll be with you in five minutes!' he called as cheerfully as if I had summoned him to his wedding.

I heard him cross the floor of his room, and before he could reach the head of the staircase, I opened the door and went out into the hall in order that I might turn on the light and have his hat and coat waiting. The electric button was at the end of the hall, and as I moved towards it, guided by the glimmer that fell from the landing above, I lifted my eyes to the staircase, which climbed dimly, with its slender mahogany balustrade, as far as the third story. Then it was, at the very moment when the doctor, humming gayly, began his quick descent of the steps, that I distinctly saw – I will swear to this on my death-bed – a child's skipping-rope lying loosely coiled, as if it had dropped from a careless little hand, in the bend of the staircase. With a spring I had reached the electric button, flooding the hall with light; just as I did so, while my arm was still outstretched behind me, I heard the humming voice change to a cry of surprise or terror, and the figure on the staircase tripped heavily and stumbled with groping hands into emptiness. The scream of warning died in my throat while I watched him pitch forward down the long flight of stairs to the floor at my feet. Even before I bent over him, before I wiped the blood from his brow and felt for his silent heart, I knew that he was dead.

Something – it may have been, as the world believes, a misstep in the dimness, or it may have been, as I am ready to bear witness, an invisible judgment – something had killed him at the very moment when he most wanted to live.

Marjory E. Lambe

THE RETURN

A NIGHT that was wild with wind and pitiless rain. Wind that tore at hair and clothing with gusty, bitter fingers; rain that lashed and drove and whimpered, like the sound of that croaking voice that had been stilled two years ago.

How he had whimpered, that old man! Surprised in the act of returning his ill-gotten gains to their stronghold, he who had always been so poor that he could not afford a living wage for his servants, nor an education for his son. Caught out, with his wealth around him to prove his lies!

The man who was tramping back towards the gloomy house in its nest of trees set his jaw in sullen, grim determination. For two years had that wealth lain there, useless and yet safe from prying eyes.

He alone, whose hand had struck him down, knew the secret of its hiding-place, and now that suspicion had died down and the law was quiet – aye, as quiet as that thing that lay in the churchyard yonder – he could come back and search for his rightful treasure in peace.

Rightful, did you say? Why, to be sure there was the old man's son, but his image was faint and shadowy in the mind of his father's murderer. Murder! How the word clung! The very trees seemed to whisper it as he passed. An ugly word, for an ugly thing.

It was not a nice thought, even now, to enter that shuttered house far away from the village, to force his way into the great gloomy room where that old man had whimpered before the look of horror in his eyes had turned to astonishment, and then – blind fear.

He drew his hat down over his eyes and plodded on, his hands buried deep in his pockets, and the sound of his heavy boots muffled in the soft mud until they were drowned altogether in the wind.

A dark bend in the road and the lights of the village shone out, blurred with rain. Recognition, he told himself, was impossible, and yet as he drew near the cheerful doorway of the 'White Horse' he hesitated.

Bodily fatigue and nervous strain combined in a craving for a draught of burning spirits – a draught that would cheer him and help to still that voice that cried at him in the darkness. Besides, he had thought a moment ago that he had seen an old white face peering at him from behind a tree-trunk in the hedge. Such fancies must be drowned and quickly, too.

After all, it was two years. There had never been more than two servants up at the house; himself and Benjamin Strong, the gardener. When he had fled the country the old man had been nearly as old as his master; it was ten chances to one that he was dead, too, by now. He had no one else to fear, therefore, except the son, and him he dismissed with a contemptuous shrug of his shoulders.

A shadow all his life, obsequious to the slightest whim of the old man, he would have left the neighbourhood long ago. He could not have kept up that great house on one hundred a year, which was all that his father had left him.

Once more he congratulated himself on the cunning that had induced him to move the body aside and hastily pack away the money into its hiding-place. Even if the house had been sold it would still be there. No one knew of it save himself. He was the only living soul who knew of its existence.

Exultation rose strong again in his breast, and he pushed open the door of the bar and entered.

Across the haze of tobacco smoke he seemed to hear his own voice asking for brandy, neat, and there was a ring in it that was unlike himself. He smiled as he tossed off the spirit, and asked for more.

He did not know that the girl looked at him strangely, he did not notice that the conversation in the room had ceased at his entrance, and that staring eyes were directed curiously towards him. But he did know that the girl took up his money and tossed it carelessly into an open drawer, and he knew that the tobacco smoke had wreathed itself into an old, avaricious face, bending low over it and looking up cunningly at him with a smile of triumph.

'Must have followed me in,' he muttered, and drew his hand over his eyes. It went then, vanished as suddenly as it had come, and he found that the girl was looking at him with frightened eyes.

'D'you want any change?' she asked, and then as he did not seem to understand, repeated in a louder voice: 'Any change?'

He tried to control his shaking voice, tried to speak distinctly.

'No,' he said. 'No. No change at all. He is just the same. Tell me,' he added, bending forward eagerly and laying a hot, dry hand on her arm, 'is he always like that? Does he still look at you and then at the money?'

She shook off his hand.

'Get along with you,' she said disgustedly. 'I thought you were ill. You are only drunk.' But her eyes were watching him closely and she was trying to see the expression of his face beneath the low brim of his hat.

He felt furiously indignant.

'Never been drunk in my life,' he assured her. 'Never. Always a steady character. Always.'

'Well, you are unsteady enough tonight,' she told him partly over her shoulder as she turned away, and a general laugh made him aware that he had attracted considerable attention, and that in spite of her seeming indifference she was regarding him curiously. Fear, returning swiftly, whispered of recognition, and with a muttered curse he thrust his shaking hands into his pockets and went out.

As the door swung to behind him a man stepped up to go in and the light fell full on his face. He was old, but he was still upright, and the face, though wrinkled, was full of health and vigour. The man in the shadows stepped back quickly into the darkness, and although the other did not glance in his direction, it was some moments before he could control his nerves sufficiently to go on. For the man who had passed him was Benjamin Strong.

Alone once more, he fumbled for his handkerchief and wiped away the sweat that had started to his face. Then he pulled himself together as far as his ragged nerves would permit and started on the last lap of his journey.

The house was not far now. Two turnings and a stretch of dark lane brought him to a gate, gleaming white in the darkness.

His fingers were some time unfastening it, although it was only latched, but it swung open at last with a grating against the gravel. As he made his way up the long, grass-grown avenue he told himself that the wind had risen. How it roared in the bare branches above his head, now rising to a scream as if it were an old voice screaming in that last cry for mercy, now dying away to a whisper –

The click of the gate behind him made him start. He had left it open. Had it shut of its own accord, or was it because someone had brushed it in passing through?

He breathed a sigh of relief when the house loomed up before him. It was evidently still empty, for the windows were shuttered and they had boarded up that little window at the side, but the boards were insecurely fastened, and a pocket-knife and hasty fingers quickly removed them.

A cracked voice muttering:

'That's the way in,' made him sweat with fear until he realised that it was himself.

It was better inside the house than in the gusty avenue, with the wind full of strange sounds. He had thought he had heard a footstep on the gravel a moment ago, a slow slouching footstep, like that of an old man –

Matches refused to light when struck by trembling fingers, but he knew his way so well that he could grope along by the wall as far as the stairs. Each board creaked as he mounted, and halfway up he stopped short, shaking, for a door had slammed somewhere in the distance. He waited for five gasping seconds, but no further sound reached him except the wind in the trees, and cursing himself for a frightened fool, he stumbled on.

But his limbs were trembling and his hands were clammy with sweat.

He reached the room at last, and had used up all his matches before he remembered his electric-torch.

The furniture remained the same as it had been that night. The chairs were pushed back, the tablecloth was dragged half off the table, and the very vase of flowers that he had knocked over in the struggle was smashed on the floor with the dry dead flowers scattered in all directions.

'Dead,' he muttered aloud, and grew weirdly, horribly afraid.

The spring by the fireplace was stiff with disuse, but it worked at last, and his fears momentarily vanished as he bent over the secret drawer. Eager fingers groped their way into the dim recesses, and at last, with a gasp of trembling joy, he drew out roll after roll of notes, bag after bag of coins.

'Hundreds of pounds!' he croaked. 'Hundreds! And all mine! Hundreds of —'

And then stopped quite suddenly, the words frozen on his lips.

Only the creaking of a board, that was all, but he knew as well as if he could see it, that that shuffling footstep had followed him from the avenue, through the window and up the stairs. He could hear it coming slowly down the corridor.

With a sobbing gasp he flashed his torch upon the slowly opening door, and as the white arc of light lit up the open space he saw that grinning wizened face looking in at him.

The white hair was streaked with blood, the skin was yellow across the skeleton face, but the bloodless lips were drawn back in a grin of pure triumph.

The old man had come back to guard his treasure, and suddenly his wretched victim knew that he had not come for the money. That was only the bait that had set the trap —

The shuffling footsteps came nearer, and with them the grinning face, and then it was that something snapped in his brain. A wild scream rang through the silent house, the torch dropped to the ground, and he pitched forward into a darkness that seemed to hold the mocking laughter of fiends.

'What shall we do with him, sir?'

The old man's son threw a contemptuous glance at the prostrate figure at his feet.

'You'd better take him away, Inspector. Hold the candle nearer. Isn't dead, is he?'

'No, sir. A fit, I should say.'

'Poor devil! He's been punished enough already. As for me, I don't care what you do with him. He showed me the way to the secret hiding-place, and that was all that I wanted.'

He turned to a white-faced girl who was standing behind him.

'And you deserve half the spoils, Bessie, for spotting him.'

She shivered slightly.

'I wasn't alone, sir. There wasn't a man in the bar that didn't spot him, too, and it only wanted Benjamin Strong to settle it.' She shivered again and glanced over her shoulder into the shadows. 'Wonder what he thought he saw, sir, when you pushed open the door?'

The old man's son laughed.

'Nerves, my dear,' he said, 'and a guilty conscience, that's all.'

But his laughter did not ring quite true and his eyes followed hers into the shadows beyond the door, for he fancied he had heard a low, wicked chuckle by the stairs. He stepped to the doorway and listened, and was it only a rat in the walls or did a shuffling footstep pass on down to the empty hall?

Returning quickly to the dimly-lit room, he was met by the Inspector.

'I made a mistake, sir,' he said. 'The man is dead.'

Margery Lawrence

THE HAUNTED SAUCEPAN

'YES,' said the long lean man in the corner, 'I have had one odd experience that I suppose certainly comes under the heading of "Spook" stories. Not that I ever *saw* the ghost – I never saw a real ghost in my life. But this was odd. Yes. Odd . . . tell you? Yes, of course, if you like, Saunderson! Ask that youngster by the drinks to pour me out another whisky-and-splash, if she will – thanks, Laurie! Now then. Here's the yarn, and don't interrupt. . . .

'I was hunting for a flat in London – say about three seasons ago – a furnished flat, as I didn't know how long I was going to stay in England, and it wasn't worth getting my furniture out of store. Rents were pretty high in the district I wanted – somewhere about St James's or thereabouts – and I didn't want to go out far, as it was essential that I kept in touch with my business interests. I had almost given up in despair and concluded that I should have to go either to a hotel or my Club, when an agent rang me up and said he had a flat for me, he thought. The owner, a woman, was abroad – he thought I might find it just the thing. The address was just what I wanted, the rent almost incredibly low – I jumped into a taxi and rushed round to see it, feeling sure there must be a catch somewhere, but it was a delightful flat, nicely furnished and as complete in every detail as you could wish. I was cautious and asked all sorts of questions, but as far as the agent knew it was a straightforward deal enough – the lady was staying abroad indefinitely, the previous tenants had gone. . . . Why did they leave? I wanted to know . . . but the agent played with his pencil and assured me he didn't know. Illness in the family made them decide to leave very suddenly, he believed. . . . Well, at any rate, a week's time saw me settled in, with my faithful man Strutt to do for me – you know Strutt, of course – one of the best fellows that ever lived? He plays an important part in the remarkable story I'm going to tell you.

'The first evening I spent there seemed too delightful for words after the discomfort and inconvenience I had been enduring in various hotels for the last six months, and I drew a sigh of enjoyment as I stretched out my legs before the fire and sipped the excellent coffee at my elbow. Strutt had found me a woman of sorts to do the cooking – marvellous fellow Strutt! – and certainly she could cook, though the glimpse I had caught of her through the kitchen door as I went into the dining-room proved her a dour and in truth most ill-favoured looking old lady, with a chenille net, a thing I had thought as dead as the Dodo, holding up her back hair. I rang for some more coffee, and as usual, Strutt was at my elbow almost as my finger left the bell-push.

'"More coffee, please Strutt – and, by the way, a very good dinner," I said carelessly. "Where did you find this cook – she seems an excellent one?" Strutt took up my empty cup as he replied in his usual even voice – is there anything quite so woodenly self-contained as the well-trained valet's voice, I wonder?

'"She came one day to fetch something – day or so before you came in, sir, and I was here getting a few things ready for you. We got talking, sir, and I found she was servant to the lady who owns the flat, and caretaker when she left; she seemed a sensible useful sort of body, sir, and I engaged her – after trying to get references from the lady, sir, and failing, as nobody seemed to know her address, I took the liberty of exercising my own judgment, sir, and took her for a month on trial. I hope you think I did right, sir?"

'"Oh, of course," I said hastily – as indeed Strutt's judgment is invariably better than my own! "I should say she's a find, if she can keep up this standard of cooking. All right – tell her I'm pleased. . . ."

'The door closed noiselessly and I sank into a brown study. The flat was very silent and the pleasant crackle of the flames sounded loud in the stillness, like little pistol-shots – the deep leather chair was comfortable, and beneath the red lampshade rested three books I particularly wanted to read. With a sigh of satisfaction I reached for one, and was in five minutes so deep in it that the entrance of Strutt with my second cup of coffee passed almost unnoticed, and I gulped it down heedlessly as I read. Buried civilisations have always been my hobby, though I've never had the money to go and explore in person – this book was a new and thrilling account of some recent diggings and discoveries, and I devoured the thing till I woke with a start to realise that it was after twelve and the fire out!

'With a laugh and a shiver I struggled out of my chair flipped on the full light and poured myself out a whisky – the syphon hissed as I pressed down the jet, and I cursed Strutt's forgetfulness (most unlike him it was, too!) as I saw it was empty. Perhaps there was another in the kitchen – I went along there to look, feeling rather peevish and very sleepy. The kitchen was flooded with moonlight and all the pots and pans and bottles and things struck little high lights of silver – it was quite a pretty effect; there were several things on the stove, and I remember now that one, a little saucepan, had its lid not quite on – not fitted on levelly, I mean – and it had the oddest look for a moment, just as if it had cocked up its lid to take a sly look at me! I found a fresh syphon on the dresser, had a drink and went to bed; my last thought as I curled luxuriously between the cool linen sheets was that the woman who had had this flat furnished and fitted it up so perfectly must have been a sybarite in her tastes, since I had yet to find the article in her flat that did not show the true lover of luxury. I wondered idly why she had left it, with all its contents, even to linen, plate, pots and pans . . . then sleep came, and I sank into unconsciousness, my query unanswered. I must have slept some two hours, I think, when I was awakened by a sudden attack of pain, of all extraordinary things! I awoke shaking and gasping, my hands alternately clutching my throat and stomach as the most awful griping agonies seized me, throwing me into convulsive writhings as the pain twisted me into knots and the sweat poured down my face, or fits of frantic coughing that I thought must surely split my lungs – I felt as though I had swallowed some ghastly acid that was burning my very vitals out ! . . . Feebly I reached for the bell, but before I touched it Strutt was in the room, awakened by my coughing, and bending anxiously over me.

'"My God, sir, what's the matter? You waked me coughing! Wait a second, sir, and I'll get you a drop of brandy. . . . "

'The spirit spilled against my chattering teeth, for I was shaking like a man with ague, and my staring eyes were glazed with pain – poor old Strutt's face was a study – he's always been very devoted to me. A few drops went down my throat, however, and after another dose of it I seemed to feel a shade better, and lay back against the pillows panting and shivering. My pyjamas were damp and streaked with perspiration, and now my perceptions were coming back to me and I began to wonder – why this attack, and what on earth had happened to cause it? Strutt bustled about my room getting out a fresh pair of pyjamas, his anxious eye flitting back to me every minute. No need to worry any further though, as I was rapidly returning to my normal healthy self – but this only made it stranger.

'Strutt approached the bed.

'"You feeling better now, sir? If you'll take my advice you'll change them damp things and let me rub you down before you go to sleep again."

'Feeling almost sound again, though still shaken from the memory of that ghastly ten minutes, I slipped out of bed and stood lost in speculation as Strutt rubbed me – certainly, back in bed in a few minutes in clean pyjamas, with a stiff brandy-and-soda inside me, I could not understand what on earth could have attacked me so terribly, yet passed away so entirely, leaving no trace – for I felt as well as before the attack.

'"Strutt," I said, "Heaven only knows what was the matter with me – it can't have been anything I've eaten, since you've probably had the same, and you're all right. But it was the most damnable attack – fever's nothing to it.

Besides, it *wasn't* fever; I've had too many bouts of that not to know it. Wonder if my heart's all right?"

'"I should have said so, sir, but it might be as well to see the doctor to-morrow. What sort of pain was it? You'll forgive me saying so, sir, but you looked simply ghastly. Never seen fever make you look so – never, sir!" Strutt's voice held conviction – moreover, the fellow had seen me through enough fever to know. I knitted my brows:

'"What did I have? Clear soup – a sole – piece of steak and vegetables. All well cooked – oh, and a savoury – mushrooms on toast. Mushrooms!"

'I looked at Strutt triumphantly – for a minute I thought I'd hit it.

'"Mushrooms – she must have got hold of some poisonous stuff, not real mushrooms. It's easily done – "

'"Beg your pardon, sir," said Strutt firmly, "but that can't be it. Being rather partial to mushrooms myself, sir, I took a few – and Mrs Barker she did, too . . . so that can't be the reason. There's nothing else you had, sir, barring your coffee, which I made myself – the second lot at least, as Mrs Barker had gone home when you rang."

'I lay back on my pillows silenced, but more puzzled than ever – however, I was too thankful to feel well again to worry very much over the cause of my strange attack.

'"Well, I can't worry any more over it, Strutt. Turn out the lights. I shall see the doctor in the morning."

'I did, and his report confirmed my own opinion and added not a little to my puzzlement – I was as sound as a bell in every respect; even the trace of occasional fever left by my long sojourn in the East seemed to have vanished. Old Macdonald punched me in the ribs as he said goodbye, and grinned.

'"Don't you come flying to me next time you get a pain under your pinny from a whisky or two too many, young fellow-me-lad – go for a good long tramp and blow it away. You're as strong as a young horse, and as for heart – don't you try to pull any of that stuff on me. You've got a heart that'll work like a drayhorse, and never turn a hair. . . ."

'I walked up St James's more puzzled than ever – what on earth had happened to me last night? In the light of my present feeling of supreme health and well-being my last night's agonies seemed more inexplicable than ever – obviously old Mac thought I had been more or less tight and exaggerated a nightmare into this. . . . It was very irritating – yet I still had the vivid memory of that terrible, choking, burning sensation, the torturing pains that had gripped my frame, tearing and wrenching me, it seemed, till my very bones groaned and quivered within me. Good Lord! – a dream? Still lost in thought about the whole curious affair I ran full tilt into an old chum of mine on the steps of the Club – George Trevanion, who seized me delightedly by the hand and poured forth questions. We dined together that night at the Club and spent a long time yarning over the fire afterwards – when we parted Trevanion had promised to dine with me the next night – I was, I admit, rather keen on showing him my new quarters. I had been so engrossed in talking shop – we're both engineers – and there had been so many things to say that I had forgotten to tell him, as I had meant, about my remarkable attack of pain, an omission that annoyed me a little, as having spent thirty years knocking about the world he might have been able to put his finger at once on the cause of it.

'There were some letters lying on the table in the dark little hall of my flat as I let myself in. I picked them up; nothing interesting, only some bills and an invitation or two. I dropped them again and turned to hang up my coat. The kitchen door opened into the hall, and when I entered it had been shut – now I saw when I turned that it had swung noiselessly open, and I could see into the moonlit kitchen, the usual little place one finds in these small flats. The gas stove was in line with the door, with various utensils upon it ready for use in the morning – I think there was a large kettle and two saucepans, a big one and a little enamel one. The open door made me jump for a second, but of course I said "draughts" and thought so – I paused a second to light a cigarette – and the match dropped from my fingers and sputtered out upon the carpet. I held the unlighted cigarette between my fingers as I stared. As I am a living man, this is what I saw – or thought I saw. The saucepan – the little one on the stove, nearest the door – seemed to lift its lid a shade – it seemed to tilt, ever so slightly, cautiously, and from beneath its tilted lid, it looked at me! Yes, I suppose it doesn't sound as horrible as I want it to, but I swear to you that was the most eerie thing I ever saw, or want to see. . . . For a second I stood cold and dumb, my mouth sticky with fright – somehow the utter banality of the thing made it more terrifying – then I swore at myself, strode into the kitchen and seized the saucepan, holding it to the light.

'It was, of course, a mere trick of light – I remember noticing the previous night how brilliantly the moonlight streamed into the kitchen – but good heavens, it had shaken me for a minute, positively! That attack last night must have upset my nerves more than I knew – Lord, what a fool! I put the saucepan back, laughing heartily, and going into the hall, picked up my letters again, still grinning at my own folly. I glanced back at the kitchen as I went along to my room – I could still see the stove and the silent row of pans upon it. The lid of the little saucepan was still askew – it still had the absurd air of watching me stealthily from beneath it! There almost seemed a menace in its very stillness. . . . I laughed again as I got into bed. It seemed so lunatic – fancy being scared of a saucepan . . . good Lord, a chunk of tin, an absurd piece of ironmongery – it just shows you what light and a few jangled nerves can do for one! . . .

'I slept splendidly, and awoke hungry as a hunter, and flung myself into work that day like a giant refreshed. Trevanion and I met at the Club about six-thirty for a cocktail, and had several cocktails – it was good to see the old man again; we'd been boon companions in all sorts of odd places, and I really didn't know how much I'd missed him till we met again. We walked back to the flat about seven fifteen and found a rattling good dinner awaiting us – I'd told Strutt to put Mrs Barker on her mettle, and, by Jove! she turned us out a feed fit for a king. Cream soup, oysters done with cheese – marvellous things they were – roast chicken and salad and a soufflé that melted in your mouth; we were too occupied appreciating flavours to talk much at first, but at last Trevanion sat back, regarding me with reverence, and drew a long breath of repletion.

'"Man, you must be a perfect Croesus! Where on earth did you strike the cash to pay for this place, this feeding, and your *cordon bleu* in the kitchen, I should like to know?"

'I grinned with triumph, sipping the last drops of my claret.

'"Why, sheer luck, dear boy – the rent of this flat is a mere flea-bite – the cook fell into my hands with the flat, and being a bit of an epicure I feel justified in spreading myself a trifle in the feeding line – especially when an old companion in crime like you turns up!"

'Trevanion's brow wrinkled.

'"A flat in St James's – for a flea-bite rental? Are you sure you're not being done somehow, old man? It seems to me almost impossible."

'I shrugged as I rose and we sought our arm-chairs by the smoke-room fire; the reason why was still as obscure to me as ever, and after a while we dismissed the subject and began to talk of other things. Strutt brought in coffee and liqueurs, and the hours passed imperceptibly as we chewed our pipes and yarned over old times, adventures old and new. At last Trevanion looked at the clock and laughed, putting down his pipe.

'"Good Lord, look at the time! Time I got along to my place, though I don't boast palatial quarters like these of yours, you lucky devil. Come and dine with me one night next week anyway, and I'll see if I can't raise a good drink or two for you, though I can't promise a dinner anywhere near your standard. . . . " He was standing by the door, his hand on the handle, and I was on the hearthrug knocking out the dottle of my pipe; suddenly we both fell silent, and his sentence broke off short as we stood listening. In the silence, down the passage came the sound of something boiling – on the cold stove, black and silent since Mrs Barker left two hours ago! We looked at each other, our mouths open with astonishment, then Trevanion laughed.

"'What an odd noise – just like a kettle or something boiling. Suppose your man's been making a drop of toddy for himself on the Q.T. and left the thing on. . . . " For some reason we stared at each other, hard, as he spoke. I know that I, for one, knew somehow that Strutt had not left the gas burning – the kitchen door was open, but from where we stood we could not see into it: the smoke-room door was round an angle. The moonlight streamed into the dark passage through the invisible open door, and with the moonlight came the distant sound of bubbling and boiling – like water in a kettle – or saucepan. . . . In the silence there seemed, however ridiculous it may sound, a sort of quiet menace in the sound – with a jerk I slewed round from the hearth and made towards the door.

"'Probably it's only a draught – wind bubbling through a crevice or something of the sort. Come on, let's see at all events."

'Personally, the last thing I really wanted to do was to go into that kitchen – that beastly kitchen, as mentally I had already begun to call it; here was the door open again – Strutt assured me he had shut it when Mrs Barker left, and always did – there was something in the atmosphere of the whole flat now that I didn't like at all. But my funk was as yet not even definitely acknowledged even to myself, and I strode down the passage with my chin set, and round the angle into the kitchen. The bubbling sounds, clear and distinct till the second I turned the corner, ceased on the instant, and dead silence succeeded. In the moonlit kitchen Trevanion and I stared at each other blankly. The stove held only one utensil, the little enamel saucepan I had noticed before, but the gas beneath it was unlit; its lid was close down. . . . Trevanion was rattling the window, examining the catch, a frown of bewilderment on his brow – I took up the saucepan, vaguely disturbed, and peered inside it; empty of course.

"'Well, upon my soul, this is rum!" said Trevanion, scratching his head. "There doesn't seem to be a chink anywhere that could let in a draught – air bubbling through a knot-hole *might* make a noise like that. . . . I suppose there isn't another gas-jet left alight anywhere that might make a sound like water boiling – is the geyser on?'

'The geyser was not on, nor was there any other gas-jet, the flat being lighted by electricity – at last we gave it up as a bad job, and gaped at each other, completely floored. Trevanion scratched his head again, then laughed and shrugged his shoulders as he reached for his hat.

"'Well – it's the most extraordinary thing I ever knew – still, there's probably some perfectly simple reason for it. 'Phone me when you find out, Connor, old man; it's left me guessing for the present, and I'd really like to know what it is. Never heard anything so clearly – nor so odd, confound it! Think you must have some spook that boils water for its ghostly toddy! . . . "

'Trevanion's cheery laugh died away down the street, and I slammed the door of the flat and stood for a minute, chin in hand, thinking. Damn it, something *had* been boiling, I'd take my oath – but what? As if in answer to my thought, a faint sound broke the stillness of the flat again – the bubbling of a boiling kettle – or saucepan? Why was it that somehow I always thought of a saucepan when that sound started? It was faint at first, but grew more distinct as I listened, every muscle taut with strain – now whatever the damned thing was, I *would* catch it!

'The kitchen door stood ajar, of course – I had shut it when we went to look at the geyser, but it was open again when we came out of the bathroom – undoubtedly the sound came from the kitchen . . . cautious, I took a step forward, though my back crept unaccountably as I did so, and craning forward, I peered round the door. The little saucepan stood where I had put it, on the stove, still cold and unlit – but it was boiling! The lid was rakishly aslant, and tilted a shade every second or so as the liquid, whatever it was, bubbled inside, and gusts of steam came out as I gaped, dumbfounded – somehow as I listened, the noise of the bubbling shaped itself into a devilish little song, almost as if the thing was singing to itself, secretly and abominably . . . chortling to itself in a disgusting sort of hidden way, if you know what I mean! I gave a half-gasp of sheer fright, and do you know, instantly the saucepan was . . . just an ordinary saucepan again, silent on the stove! I made myself go in, though I admit I was shaking with nerves – I took it up; cold and empty. . . . Well, cursing myself for a fool, I took a stiff drink and despite a horrible little shivery feeling that there was more in this than I liked, told myself sternly that I must have had one whisky too many and mistaken light and the noise of a stray mouse might have made, for the whole thing. I knew, of course, inside me, that it wasn't so, and I *had* seen that abominable saucepan boiling some infernal brew – but I wouldn't admit it, and scrambled into bed with, I confess, considerable speed, and not a few glances over my shoulder into the dark.

'However, I slept well again, and awoke laughing at myself not a little, but with sneaking thankfulness that Trevanion had also made a bit of an ass of himself over the mysterious noise! I lay for a few minutes blinking in the shafts of sunlight that filtered through my blinds, and reached for my watch – it was nine o'clock! Cursing Strutt for his laziness – I always had my bath at eight-thirty, confound him – I rang the bell. A shuffling step came along the passage, and the sullen lined face of Mrs Barker peeped in. I stared at her, then snapped:

'"What on earth's the matter with Strutt? It's nine o'clock!"

'The woman studied me in silence with her narrow, secret eyes for a few seconds – what an old hag she was, really, I thought impatiently! – then jerked her thumb over her shoulder.

'"E's took bad with summat – dunno what. Bin writhin' and cursin' like a good 'un . . ." Her lips wreathed themselves into a mirthless grin, and I eyed her with even less favour than before.

'As she spoke I heard a faint moaning coming from poor old Strutt's room – curtly ordering Mrs Barker back to her kitchen I scrambled out of bed and went down the passage – poor Strutt was lying fully dressed on the bed, his lips blue and dry with pain, his limbs twitching convulsively – he was quite beyond speech, but his eyes implored help. I tore off his collar and shouted to Mrs Barker for brandy – the poor fellow's looks really frightened me to death. Bit by bit we pulled him round – though it struck me at the time that the woman's help was given none too willingly; and at last Strutt sat up, shaky, but himself. I sat on the bed staring at him, more concerned than I liked to say.

'"What on earth happened, Strutt? It seemed much the same sort of attack I had the other night – you'd better go and see my doctor, I can't have you cracking up like this. When did it come on?"

'Strutt cleared his throat, his voice still husky and strained with pain.

'"I got up about seven, sir, as usual, or perhaps a little before – Mrs Barker was late, so I made myself some tea and boiled an egg. I hadn't eaten it so very long, sir, before I began to feel as if something was on fire inside me, sir – awful the pain was, I couldn't move nor cry out – not a word. I dunno what it was, sir, but I'll take my oath it's the same sort of thing you was taken with the other night."

'I frowned and meditated.

'"Well, you'd better see Macdonald. This is beyond me. . . ."

'Strutt was duly overhauled by the doctor and reported sound in wind and limb – this fresh puzzle made me feel almost as if there must be something in superstitions after all, and there must be a curse on my new flat. I was still lost in speculation about it when I met Trevanion in Bond Street, very spruce and dapper from lunching with the lady he happened to favour at the moment. He buttonholed me at once.

'"Hullo, Connor, spotted the ghost yet?" I shook my head.

'"Spotted it – I wish I could! Listen – there seems no end to the extraordinary things that are coming my way lately . . ." And I plunged into the story, beginning with my own attack of illness and winding up with what I had seen – or thought I had seen – in the kitchen after he had left, and Strutt's mysterious collapse this morning. Trevanion listened intently, not laughing as I half-expected . . . it seems a queer place to discuss a bogey-tale, the corner of Bond Street on a fine spring morning, but it struck neither of us at the time.

'"It's certainly odd," Trevanion said at last, "it's the oddest yarn I've heard for a long time. Frankly, if it wasn't you – and if I hadn't heard that noise myself last night – I'd of course say it was too much whisky and you were seeing things – But . . . look here, I'll come up to your place to-night, say about eleven-thirty, and we'll try an experiment – I've got an idea slowly working its way out! So long, old man."

'I was relieved he had not laughed, and guessed, from his serious attitude towards the whole incomprehensible thing, that he must have been more impressed than I had thought with the episode of the mysterious bubbling – what connection had that, if any, with the equally mysterious attacks of pain that had seized both Strutt and myself? The whole thing obtruded itself upon my work, which did not go particularly well in consequence, and I was still cogitating when the bell rang that night, and Strutt let in Trevanion, accompanied by a dog, to my great astonishment. We shook hands warmly.

'"Didn't know you'd got a dog," I said, "but while you were about it couldn't you have found a better specimen than this mouldy old semi-demi-collie?" Trevanion grinned at me mysteriously. When Strutt had gone out of the room he bent forward and whispered:

'"This is the experiment!"

I gaped, and Trevanion went on, as the old beast settled himself down in front of the blazing fire.

'"First and foremost, may I give this old beast a feed? – he's rather hungry, I'm afraid. It's the porter's dog from the Club. I borrowed him for to-night. Yes – as you say, he's a bit of a cheesehound, but not a bad old beast. What about that feed?"

'"Of course," I said, "I daresay there are some bones in the kitchen – I'll tell Strutt." Trevanion stopped my upraised hand on the way to the bell.

'"I don't want Strutt, thanks old man. I want to give this myself – warm up some scraps for him; you know the sort of thing." I stared rather, then shrugged my shoulders; I knew Trevanion too well to ask him too many questions at the start of a thing.

'"Oh, all right, my dear fellow, though I really don't see why this fuss about warm stuff – you sound as if the beast was a Derby winner!"

'"I'm not as cracked as I seem," asserted Trevanion, going into the kitchen now brightly lighted and as cheerful as could well be imagined, "you leave this to your Uncle Stalky – it's all part of the experiment!" I left him rummaging among pots and pans and betook myself to an armchair and my book on Egypt, till the entrance of my friend, the dog at his heels licking his lips after his feed, interrupted me. Throwing himself down in the opposite armchair, Trevanion reached for the whisky – I cocked an amused eyebrow at him.

'"Finished your incantations over the kitchen stove, Trev?" I said, using my old abbreviation of his name. Trevanion laughed as he filled his pipe.

"'You can pull my leg as much as you like, my dear chap, when we're through with this thing. It may be capable of an ordinary explanation – nine out of ten times it is – but there's always the faint possibility of the tenth time cropping up. D'you remember that case of the Box that Wouldn't keep Shut – when you and I were working on that road near Lahore? That was creepy if you like . . ." I nodded, silenced – for the moment I had forgotten that odd story, never fully explained. Trevanion went on:

"'Well, I believe, from what I felt here the other night, and from various other little things – more than ever if the little experiment I've just tried on Ben here succeeds – I believe that we've got here one of the few cases of genuine 'queerness.' Something really uncanny, I mean." I interrupted him, my back creeping uncomfortably.

"'What have you tried on the dog, then?" Trevanion looked at me oddly.

"'Fed him out of the saucepan – the saucepan that bubbled !" he said at last. My back crept again, though I did not quite get what he was driving at – I stared, puzzled.

"'But what – I don't quite see your drift, Trev. What should that show you?"

"'If I'm right we shall soon see," Trevanion returned, "but I don't want to tell you all my ideas entirely before we've got through the end of this sitting, as they might colour your impressions, and I want to leave your mind as open as possible to-night. . . . Now about twelve I propose that you and I and old Ben shut ourselves up in the kitchen – and see if anything happens. I believe if we're right, and there *is* something more to this than the things of everyday life, the dog's behaviour will show it. Beasts are much more susceptible to psychic influence than we are, especially dogs and cats. . . . At any rate, it's worth trying to see if he *does* seem to sense anything – if he does that will prove that you and I are not both slightly off our chumps" . . . A strangled gasp from Ben interrupted him, and like a flash we turned – the poor old dog was in convulsions of mortal agony, his eyes starting from his head, writhing and twisting, and snapping wildly at our hands as we tried to help him! I rushed for brandy and warm milk, and between us we got him round, and sat back staring at each other, our skins prickling faintly with a horrid little fright – at least mine was.

"'I'm dead right in my first guess, I think," Trevanion said soberly, stroking the head of the still panting and exhausted dog. "Poor old Ben then! I boiled some scraps in that infernal saucepan – it was hard on Ben, but I had to find out somehow whether my idea was right, and by Jove it is! Everything cooked in that thing half-poisons people – or gives them an attack like poisoning. . . ."

"'D'you think there's something in the paint?" I hazarded. Trevanion was not sure – it was only an ordinary enamel saucepan – he didn't think so. Ben lay panting on the rug before the fire, still rather a wreck, but regaining his strength every minute – I stooped down and patted him.

'"We shall have to give him another five minutes or so to recover," said Trevanion, "poor old brute – never mind, he'll be all right in a jiff. I don't mind telling you, though, that it will take us all our nerve to face that kitchen, and that infernal saucepan . . . that bubbling noise was quite the most unpleasant and disturbing thing I ever heard. The actual homeliness of it seeming to hide a sort of sinister meaning – and the purr of a boiling kettle is such a jolly thing as a rule. . . ." I nodded – I didn't want to think about it overmuch just then to tell the truth, so I resolutely hunted out cards and we played poker for half an hour or so, till Strutt came in with a fresh syphon, and with his usual correct "Anything more, sir? Good night, sir," went off to his own quarters.

'Trevanion, with a glance at the clock – it marked just twelve, or a few minutes before – got up and waked the old dog, who was sleeping by this time with his chin on his paws. It was twelve o'clock . . . in silence we turned the lights low and tiptoed along to the kitchen. The door was open, of course, but otherwise the whole place looked demure to a degree. We had brought cushions and rugs with us, and threw them into a corner, the furthest away from the stove, near the window, from where we could watch both door and stove – and saucepan – without being too close. I felt, as usual, a horrid little reluctance to enter the room, but Trevanion's large presence went a long way towards scotching that – besides, I meant to see what we might see, however I funked it. Settling ourselves down, I rummaged in my pocket for my pipe, and realised the dog was not with us. Trevanion craned out from his corner, calling softly – the old beast's eyes gleamed from the shadows in the hall beyond . . . he put a cautious nose across the threshold, and retreated at once, ears flat. Trevanion looked at me and nodded.

'"You see? There is a funny atmosphere here. Come on, Ben, old man – come on . . ." By dint of much coaxing the dog crept into the room, unwilling enough but obedient, and we made room for him beside us. But he would not lie down, and kept raising his head and sniffing the air, his eyes watchful, puzzled, and full of a vaguely stirring fear. The silence grew steadily as the minutes passed – even the occasional low-toned remarks we exchanged to start with died into the all enveloping silence, and we puffed our pipes solemnly, our eyes glued to Ben's shaggy head. The air seemed to grow steadily colder, too, as we sat there, despite the warmth of the spring night air that stole through the slightly opened window. As the silence deepened the cold seemed to intensify too – there seemed to come a cold, dumb menace into the atmosphere, that fastened upon us so gradually that we scarcely perceived its beginnings till we were surrounded, soaked in it. My hands were frozen, and my mind, too, seemed to have grown cold and numbed: Trevanion told me later he felt just the same. Ben's yellow hair was fluffed out into a ruff round his head, his wary eyes, old, but alert, wandering ceaselessly round and round the little kitchen. The moonlight, flooding the whole place with eerie white light, helped the general uncanny effect – the shadows lay sharp-edged, black, behind every piece of furniture – the grandfather clock seemed to hide a long lean thing that peered furtively at us with narrow horrible eyes . . . Trevanion moved his leg and coughed – our eyes met and I read the same thought in his mind – was the silence, helped by our vivid imagination, already over-excited by the episode of poor old Ben, going to work on our nerves till we made shapes and sounds out of mere shadows and the silence of the night? At this moment, the dog suddenly decided for us – with a faint wuff of uneasiness he sat up, his eyes on the open door; I could hear nothing, but obviously his ears, more finely attuned to degrees of sound, had caught something in the dark flat that vaguely distressed him. Ordinarily any dog would have promptly gone out to investigate, but Ben remained, stiff-poised, his head held forwards his paws braced against the floor – Trevanion nudged me to watch him, but I did not need it – then suddenly the dog flattened himself down between us, his head low, his eyes fixed on the door, shivering in every limb. At the same moment it seemed to me that I heard a faint movement in the darkness beyond the door – very faint, but definite. The sound, it seemed to me, of a door being shut with the most delicate care so as to avoid any possible creaking or snap of the latch. The exquisite caution of the sound made it peculiarly horrible – I felt my hair rise as I strained my ears, wondering if the sound could possibly be my imagination? . . . The pause of silence that followed was almost worse – it was like the pause made by someone, having shut the door, waiting outside to be certain they were not heard . . . I took a firm grip of myself, glanced at Trevanion – his hand was cold too, but we were both steady enough . . . we waited – as a matter of fact I doubt if we could either of us have moved then, we were held in the fascination of fear. Suddenly Ben gave a terrified whimper and burrowed wildly into the rugs – another sound broke the awesome stillness. A faint movement in the passage, at the far end – on tiptoe, pausing for greater stealth, *Something* stole towards the kitchen door! The cold draught seemed to grow even colder, it lifted our hair and stirred Ben's rough coat . . . my flesh crept softly and horribly on my bones as I gripped Trev's clammy hand and stared at the door, setting my teeth as the Thing in the passage trailed softly nearer and nearer. I say trailed because that so nearly describes the sound – a faint footstep accompanied by a soft rustle like a trailing skirt. At this moment I became aware of another phenomenon – there grew a heavy scent in the air, like patchouli, I think . . . at any rate a definite perfume that seemed to herald Whatever approached. Our throats dry with fright, we shrank close to each other, staring at the dog as he moaned and whimpered – and the steps drew near, and paused outside the kitchen door, as if Whoever walked that night stood still to peer at us through the crack of the door . . . and laughed at us through the chink! For sheer terror, that beat all I had ever known, yet still the spell held us both motionless, staring, as Ben, shaking, his eyes bulging, slowly raised himself as if to face something. Dead silence – neither Trevanion nor I could see a thing – but the dog's eyes, fixed about five feet from the floor, followed – Someone – who entered. The moonlight lay white and sheer unbroken across the kitchen floor, yet Someone entered – paused – and walked towards the stove. As our terrified eyes followed Ben's, fixed on the Invisible, there came the faint click of a cautious hand moving among the pots and pans on the stove – and suddenly, upon the silence broke a sinister little sound – the clink of a saucepan lid, carefully lifted. My eyes bolting, dumb, I gaped – as I dreaded, the lid of the little saucepan was just raised, and from beneath it, there seemed to steal a faint curl of steam, thin and blue and horrible; it seems an absurd thing, but this just finished me – the spell of sheer terror that had held us both broke, and with a yell of mortal fear I flung aside the rugs and bolted past that horrible stove like a maniac, Trevanion at my heels, blundering madly over poor old Ben as he ran. We gained the smoke-room, and slamming the door upon the Horror that ruled that uncanny kitchen, we sank into two chairs, sweating with fright. I was white and clammy, and Trevanion's hand shook against the glasses as he poured us out each a stiff tot of whisky . . . even now in the silence there stole upon the air that vile sound of bubbling; there was almost a note of meditation in it now, as if the soul behind that hateful little purring noise was pleased, and sat grinning to itself, planning new evil – a mocking, threatening little note. Oh, it was beyond words vile and awful, that sound – and to know, as now we did know, that Something – Someone – did actually, *sans* human light, gas or anything of that sort, set a-boiling in that horrible little saucepan some devil's brew of some sort, every night of the Lord I'd spent in that flat! My skin crept again as I thought of it, and I took a hasty gulp of whisky. Trevanion's voice broke the silence, still rather shaky.

'"Well! – I said you had a spook, Connor – and by Jove, you've got a beauty! I frankly admit I'm not going past the door of that kitchen again to-night – I'm claiming a shakedown on the floor if you can't sleep two in your bed!"

'His laugh was rather harsh, but it served its purpose, and I shook myself together. Putting down my glass, I patted Ben, his rough hair now beginning to lie down and the light of terror fading from his eyes.

'In the distance, but more faintly, still purred that infernal sound.

'"What is it, in the name of the Lord?" I ejaculated. Trevanion's normal senses were rapidly returning – he lit a cigarette.

'"I don't know, for certain, but we must interrogate your man Strutt. I think you'll find he knows more about this than you think – he passed the door of the kitchen when I was feeding Ben, and I saw him jump and look at the saucepan in a furtive sort of way – I pretended not to see him. Then he glanced at the shelf where it sometimes stands, and looked puzzled . . . I'm going to pump him. Obviously the whole thing centres round that infernal saucepan. . . . Anyway, we're both too knocked up to do any more to-night – let's turn in, and we'll thrash the whole thing out to-morrow."

'We slept like logs, Trevanion on the couch in my room, buried in rugs and pillows. I woke to broad daylight and Strutt at my shoulder with a cup of tea. I always had a weakness for early tea, feminine though it sounds. Trevanion was already awake. As my man turned to hand him his tea, Trevanion looked up at him.

'"Strutt," he said, "did you boil the water for the tea in the – saucepan?"

'There was a pause, and Strutt's eyes, first blank, then full of a passionate relief, stared back at Trevanion's intent blue ones.

'"You – know sir? Then, thank God, I'm not mad . . ." I turned sharply.

'"What, Strutt, you must have seen something, too!"

'"Seen something, sir! . . . Well, gentlemen, if you knew what a relief it is to know you know, and don't think me crazy nor drunk – well, I can't tell you what it is. The last two days have been fair hell – beg your pardon, sir, but it's true – and I didn't dare tell you, sir, for fear you'd think I was mad or I'd bin drinking! . . . Strutt's strained eyes, blue circled, told their own tale, and the passionate, almost tearful relief in his voice was nakedly real – I felt a very definite admiration for Strutt as I realised what terrors he must have fought down all alone during the past few days. Trevanion nodded, his eyes alert with interest.

'"Go on, Strutt – this is most interesting. Now tell me; when you made the coffee for Mr Connor the first night he was here, did you use this saucepan for boiling the water – or a kettle?"

'Strutt's eyes looked back unflinchingly at Trevanion's – I think we both knew his answer before he said it though.

'"The saucepan, sir. The kettle was leaking. The little enamel saucepan – the – the – one that *boils*, sir." Strutt's voice suddenly sank to a dreadful whisper, and although it was broad daylight, we involuntarily shuddered.

'"And the day you were taken ill?" My man nodded.

'"Yessir – I'd boiled an egg for my breakfast in it . . . I've . . . wanted to speak to you about all this before, sir, but it all seemed so crazy I didn't like . . . I was afraid if I told you all I seen and heard you'd think I'd taken to drink, sir . . ."

"'Lord, not now!" I said fervently. "After last night I'd believe anything of this infernal flat! Go on, Strutt, for goodness' sake. Tell us all you know about the thing – don't keep anything back."

"'Well, sir – the first night I come in here, the night you were taken ill, I left your room to see if everything was all right, and I heard something singing in the kitchen, like a kettle on the boil – bubbling and steaming like. I thought, well I must have left something on, or Mrs Barker, but I went in, and blest if everything wasn't quiet, and as cold and dark as Egypt! Not a sign . . . well, I was scared, but I thought I must have bin half asleep – but I got back to my room and left the door open, and in a few minutes the same noise come again. I tiptoed out then, sir, you may bet, to try and catch whatever made that noise – and round the corner I could see that little saucepan boiling away like fury . . . You don't think I'm drunk, sir?"

"'By George, we don't – I don't. Go on – what did you do?"

"'I went in, sir – don't mind saying it took a lot of doing – I'd a given a month's salary not to – but I didn't want to feel done, and I still thought I *must* be seeing things. . . . Well, sir, the minute I stepped round that door that blamed thing stopped dead – as true as I'm standing here. Wasn't even warm – well, I bolted back to my room, and that's a fact. Well, in the morning I thought I *must* have been mad or seeing things – but I didn't like the look of that saucepan till I got to feel it was behaving silly to act so, and I boiled that egg in it to show I didn't care. . . . Well, after I was took ill like you, sir, I said I wasn't going to meddle any more with the beastly thing, and I took and threw it into the dustbin – but last night it was back again – and begging your pardon, sirs, I wouldn't touch the . . . thing if I was you. There's something about it's not right – don't you touch it."

'Strutt's troubled voice ceased, and Trevanion's eyes met mine. He nodded.

"'You're right, Strutt. All you say goes to prove my theory. Obviously everything cooked in that thing produces acute symptoms of some sort of poisoning – arsenical, I should say, but we can find out the details later. Now what in the world is the story connected with this saucepan – I take it all the things here belonged to the woman who had this flat before?"

"'Yessir – so I understand. Mrs Barker was with her a long time, and took care of the place when she left – I heard yesterday what we didn't know when you put in for this flat, sir; that three lots of tenants had had it and left very sudden. I did hear that one or two of them fell ill all of a sudden – I'm certain this saucepan'll be at the bottom of their going, sir – anyway they none of them stayed more than a month or so."

"Mrs Barker – Mrs Barker –" mused Trevanion. "Now I wonder whether that old soul knows anything. . . ." As he spoke there seemed a faint shuffle outside the door, and bouncing out of bed, I flung it open; Mrs Barker herself was outside, her wrinkled, wicked old face alive with rage and fear, her knotted hands twisted in her apron. We all stared, then Trevanion seized her wrist as she tried to glide away.

"'No, you don't, old lady! What were you listening for, I should like to know?" She eyed him sullenly and venomously, but vouchsafed no reply; dragging her into the room, Trevanion shut the door determinedly.

"'Look here, there's something here I don't like, Connor. Do you suppose this is all a plant by this old hag, for reasons of her own?"

'I shook my head, still blank – evil old woman as she looked now, her face all twisted with hate, I did not see how in the world she could have been responsible for all the strange things we had, the three of us, witnessed the last few days.

"'You know – something!" Trevanion said sternly, "now you tell us the whole truth about this beastly business and it'll be all right for you . . . if not –"

"'I shan't tell you – besides, there ain't nothin' to tell," the old woman answered sullenly – Strutt suddenly interrupted her.

"'You're lying – beg your pardon, sir, but I seen her laugh when Mr Connor was took ill. Now, you wicked old sinner, you tell all you know about this, as you're told – or I'll make you eat something cooked in that saucepan . . ."

'It was horrible – the hag crumpled like a shot rabbit at the threat, and put up her trembling, gnarled hands – her deadly terror was dreadfully sincere. . . . I put up my hand.

"'All right, Strutt – let her go, Trev. She'll tell us."

'Her voice shaky and strained, sullen, but vanquished, the old woman began her story. Shall I ever forget that scene, the untidy room, Trevanion and me in pyjamas, drinking it in, while Strutt, immovably correct as ever, with his back to the door as she talked? The story was incomplete; much had to be taken for granted, but it was a sufficiently grim picture that she conjured up before us of her late mistress. Young, beautiful, hard as marble; an old husband standing between her and her own ends. . . . A lover – lovers – and riches to be gained by his death. One lover a doctor, a mysterious packet of powder seen to be given by him to the woman one day when the old woman was prying round – then the empty paper, found thrown away, with a few grains of white powder in the creases. Afterwards, gradually weakening health of the husband, only helped by the constant solicitude of his young wife, the apple of his eye . . . she was tireless in her goodness to him – how many times did she not rise in the middle of the night, to brew soup or tea or anything he fancied? At last he grew so that he would take nothing she had not prepared . . . his attacks of pain were terrible, folks said – seemed to twist him all to pieces – heart, the doctor said – the young doctor that was Madam's friend was attending him, and he and Madam used to laugh together on the stairs when he left the old man – then the death of the husband, and hasty burial. . . . The doctor was crazy about Madam, and one night Mrs Barker heard them planning to be married very soon – she told him she was making her will in his favour and laughingly insisted he should return the compliment. . . . He did, and Mrs Barker was called in to witness it; they were very merry together, and Madam insisted on making some of her special punch for him to drink to their happiness in. . . . Madam came laughing into the kitchen, and seemed to talk and laugh even to the saucepan as she boiled the water for the punch. She sent Mrs Barker away then – but the doctor never got his honeymoon. Next day he was found dead in the flat, and Madam was away with another man, a Spaniard she was running an affair with at the same time. . . . No – they said it was heart failure, but Mrs Barker – well, she thought a lot of things she didn't say. What was the use? and Madam left her instructions to take care of the place till it was let, and it was a good job; but she never fancied anything cooked in that saucepan somehow – put it up on a shelf till one day the new tenants used it and got sick and left. . . . Same thing happened again with the next people, and they used to say they saw things and heard the kettle or something boiling when there was nothing there. Yes, Madam used a funny scent – began with "p" but she couldn't say the word – all over the place it was some nights. . . . Couldn't say she'd ever actually seen anything – she took good care to go to bed early when she was living in the flat, and, anyway, it never come further than the kitchen. . . . Yes . . . (defiantly) she 'ad used the thing on purpose once or twice! She was a poor woman, and caretakin' was a good job when you got a post like this and no one to interfere; yes, she 'ad used it before to scare out tenants 'cos she wanted to stick to her job, and she didn't care. There were lots of other flats in London. No – She – It – never came unless that there saucepan was there on the stove as it used to be – yes, she'd missed it the day Strutt threw it into the dustbin, and looked about there till she had found and re-instated it. Of course she wanted us to go, like the rest – the agents were so sick of tenants leaving that they'd said if we went they shouldn't bother to let the place again. . . . Sorry – why should she be? Nobody never died of it that she heard of – on'y got attacks like the old man used to get. . . .

'The door closed on her dismissed figure, and Trevanion's stare met mine. With one accord we said:

'"My God, what a horrible yarn!"

'Gingerly we went into the kitchen and picked up the saucepan, smooth and harmless-looking instrument of a ruthless woman's crimes. Gingerly I handed it to Strutt.

'"For heaven's sake tie a stone to the vile thing, Strutt, and sink it in the Thames – or burn it – get rid of it somehow. We seem to have struck one of the most unpleasant stories I ever heard – however, once rid of this I don't think we shall be bothered any further, as obviously this horrible little thing is the 'germ' of the haunting . . ." which indeed was true, the ghostly bubbling and boiling never troubled the flat more, nor did the kitchen door persist in opening. The ghost was laid – but I often speculate on the fate probably in store for the unfortunate wretch now in love with the woman whose white hands once brewed death for her husband and lover in that uncanny saucepan.'

Mary Webb

MR TALLENT'S GHOST

THE first time I ever met Mr Tallent was in the late summer of 1906, in a small, lonely inn on the top of a mountain. For natives, rainy days in these places are not very different from other days, since work fills them all, wet or fine. But for the tourist, rainy days are boring. I had been bored for nearly a week, and was thinking of returning to London, when Mr Tallent came. And because I could not 'place' Mr Tallent, nor elucidate him to my satisfaction, he intrigued me. For a barrister should be able to sum up men in a few minutes.

I did not see Mr Tallent arrive, nor did I observe him entering the room. I looked up, and he was there, in the small firelit parlour with its Bible, wool mats and copper preserving pan. He was reading a manuscript, slightly moving his lips as he read. He was a gentle, moth-like man, very lean and about six foot three or more. He had neutral coloured hair and eyes, a nondescript suit, limp-looking hands and slightly turned-up toes. The most noticeable thing about him was an expression of passive and enduring obstinacy.

I wished him good evening, and asked if he had a paper, as he seemed to have come from civilization.

'No,' he said softly, 'no. Only a little manuscript of my own.'

Now, as a rule I am as wary of manuscripts as a hare is of greyhounds. Having once been a critic, I am always liable to receive parcels of these for advice. So I might have saved myself and a dozen or so of other people from what turned out to be a terrible, an appalling, incubus. But the day had been so dull, and having exhausted Old Moore and sampled the Imprecatory Psalms, I had nothing else to read. So I said, 'Your own?'

'Even so,' replied Mr Tallent modestly.

'May I have the privilege?' I queried, knowing he intended me to have it.

'How kind!' he exclaimed. 'A stranger, knowing nothing of my hopes and aims, yet willing to undertake so onerous a task.'

'Not at all!' I replied, with a nervous chuckle.

'I think,' he murmured, drawing near and, as it were, taking possession of me, looming above me with his great height, 'it might be best for me to read it to you. I am considered to have rather a fine reading voice.'

I said I should be delighted, reflecting that supper could not very well be later than nine. I knew I should not like the reading.

He stood before the cloth-draped mantelpiece.

'This,' he said, 'shall be my rostrum.' Then he read.

I wish I could describe to you that slow, expressionless, unstoppable voice. It was a voice for which at the time I could find no comparison. Now I know that it was like the voice of the loud speaker in a dull subject. At first one listened, taking in even the sense of the words. I took in all the first six chapters, which were unbelievably dull. I got all the scenery, characters, undramatic events clearly marshalled. I imagined that something would, in time, happen. I thought the characters were going to develop, do fearful things or great and holy deeds. But they did nothing. Nothing happened. The book was flat, formless, yet not vital enough to be inchoate. It was just a meandering expression of a negative personality, with a plethora of muted, borrowed, stale ideas. He always said what one expected him to say. One knew what all his people would do. One waited for the culminating platitude as for an expected twinge of toothache. I thought he would pause after a time, for even the most arrogant usually do that, apologizing and at the same time obviously waiting for one to say: 'Do go on, please.'

This was not necessary in his case. In fact, it was impossible. The slow, monotonous voice went on without a pause, with the terrible tirelessness of a gramophone. I longed for him to whisper or shout – anything to relieve the tedium. I tried to think of other things, but he read too distinctly for that. I could neither listen to him nor ignore him. I have never spent such an evening. As luck would have it the little maidservant did not achieve our meal till nearly ten o'clock. The hours dragged on.

At last I said: 'Could we have a pause, just for a few minutes?'

'Why?' he inquired.

'For . . . for discussion,' I weakly murmured.

'Not,' he replied, 'at the most exciting moment. Don't you realize that now, at last, I have worked up my plot to the most dramatic moment? All the characters are waiting, attent, for the culminating tragedy.'

He went on reading. I went on awaiting the culminating tragedy. But there was no tragedy. My head ached abominably. The voice flowed on, over my senses, the room, the world. I felt as if it would wash me away into eternity. I found myself thinking, quite solemnly:

'If she doesn't bring supper soon, I shall kill him.'

I thought it in the instinctive way in which one thinks it of an earwig or a midge. I took refuge in the consideration how to do it? This was absorbing. It enabled me to detach myself completely from the sense of what he read. I considered all the ways open to me. Strangling. The bread knife on the sideboard. Hanging. I gloated over them. I was beginning to be almost happy, when suddenly the reading stopped.

'She is bringing supper,' he said. 'Now we can have a little discussion. Afterwards I will finish the manuscript.' He did. And after that, he told me all about his will. He said he was leaving all his money for the posthumous publication of his manuscripts. He also said that he would like me to draw up this for him, and to be trustee of the manuscripts.

I said I was too busy. He replied that I could draw up the will to-morrow.

'I'm going to-morrow,' I interpolated passionately.

'You cannot go until the carrier goes in the afternoon,' he triumphed. 'Meanwhile, you can draw up the will. After that you need do no more. You can pay a critic to read the manuscripts. You can pay a publisher to publish them. And I in them shall be remembered.'

He added that if I still had doubts as to their literary worth, he would read me another.

I gave in. Would anyone else have done differently? I drew up the will, left an address where he could send his stuff, and left the inn.

'Thank God!' I breathed devoutly, as the turn of the lane hid him from view. He was standing on the doorstep, beginning to read what he called a pastoral to a big cattle-dealer who had called for a pint of bitter. I smiled to think how much more he would get than he had bargained for.

After that, I forgot Mr Tallent. I heard nothing more of him for some years. Occasionally I glanced down the lists of books to see if anybody else had relieved me of my task by publishing Mr Tallent. But nobody had.

It was about ten years later, when I was in hospital with a 'Blighty' wound, that I met Mr Tallent again. I was convalescent, sitting in the sun with some other chaps, when the door opened softly, and Mr Tallent stole in. He read to us for two hours. He remembered me, and had a good deal to say about coincidence. When he had gone, I said to the nurse: 'If you let that fellow in again while I'm here, I'll kill him.'

She laughed a good deal, but the other chaps all agreed with me, and as a matter of fact, he never did come again.

Not long after this I saw the notice of his death in the paper.

'Poor chap!' I thought, 'he's been reading too much. Somebody's patience has given out. Well, he won't ever be able to read to me again.'

Then I remembered the manuscripts, realizing that, if he had been as good as his word, my troubles had only just begun.

And it was so.

First came the usual kind of letter from a solicitor in the town where he had lived. Next I had a call from the said solicitor's clerk, who brought a large tin box.

'The relations,' he said, 'of the deceased are extremely angry. Nothing has been left to them. They say that the manuscripts are worthless, and that the living have rights.'

I asked how they knew that the manuscripts were worthless.

'It appears, sir, that Mr Tallent has, from time to time, read these aloud –'

I managed to conceal a grin.

'And they claim, sir, to share equally with the – er – manuscripts. They threaten to take proceedings, and have been getting legal opinions as to the advisability of demanding an investigation of the material you have.'

I looked at the box. There was an air of Joanna Southcott about it.

I asked if it were full.

'Quite, sir. Typed MSS. Very neatly done.'

He produced the key, a copy of the will, and a sealed letter.

I took the box home with me that evening. Fortified by dinner, a cigar and a glass of port, I considered it. There is an extraordinary air of fatality about a box. For bane or for blessing, it has a perpetual fascination for mankind. A wizard's coffer, a casket of jewels, the alabaster box of precious nard, a chest of bridal linen, a stone sarcophagus – what a strange mystery is about them all! So when I opened Mr Tallent's box, I felt like somebody letting loose a genie. And indeed I was. I had already perused the will and the letter, and discovered that the fortune was moderately large. The letter merely repeated what Mr Tallent had told me. I glanced at some of the manuscripts. Immediately the room seemed full of Mr Tallent's presence and his voice. I looked towards the now dusky corners of the room as if he might be looming there. As I ran through more of the papers, I realized that what Mr Tallent had chosen to read to me had been the best of them. I looked up Johnson's telephone number and asked him to come round. He is the kind of chap who never makes any money. He is a free-lance journalist with a conscience. I knew he would be glad of the job.

He came round at once. He eyed the manuscripts with rapture. For at heart he is a critic, and has the eternal hope of unearthing a masterpiece.

'You had better take a dozen at a time, and keep a record,' I said. 'Verdict at the end.'

'Will it depend on me whether they are published?'

'*Which* are published,' I said. 'Some will have to be. The will says so.'

'But if I found them all worthless, the poor beggars would get more of the cash? Damnable to be without cash.'

'I shall have to look into that. I am not sure if it is legally possible. What, for instance, is the standard?'

'I shall create the standard,' said Johnson rather haughtily. 'Of course, if I find a masterpiece –'

'If you find a masterpiece, my dear chap,' I said, 'I'll give you a hundred pounds.'

He asked if I had thought of a publisher. I said I had decided on Jukes, since no book however bad, could make his reputation worse than it was, and the money might save his credit.

'Is that quite fair to poor Tallent?' he asked. Mr Tallent had already got hold of him.

'If,' I said as a parting benediction, 'you wish you had never gone into it (as, when you have put your hand to the plough, you will), remember that at least they were never read aloud to you, and be thankful.'

Nothing occurred for a week. Then letters began to come from Mr Tallent's relations. They were a prolific family. They were all very poor, very angry and intensely uninterested in literature. They wrote from all kinds of viewpoints, in all kinds of styles. They were, however, all alike in two things – the complete absence of literary excellence and legal exactitude.

It took an increasing time daily to read and answer these. If I gave them any hope, I at once felt Mr Tallent's hovering presence, mute, anxious, hurt. If I gave no hope, I got a solicitor's letter by return of post. Nobody but myself seemed to feel the pathos of Mr Tallent's ambitions and dreams. I was notitifed that proceedings were going to be taken by firms all over England. Money was being recklessly spent to rob Mr Tallent of his immortality, but it appeared, later, that Mr Tallent could take care of himself.

When Johnson came for more of the contents of the box, he said that there was no sign of a masterpiece yet, and that they were as bad as they well could be.

'A pathetic chap, Tallent,' he said.

'Don't, for God's sake, my dear chap, let him get at you,' I implored him. 'Don't give way. He'll haunt you, as he's haunting me, with that abominable pathos of his. I think of him and his box continually just as one does of a life and death plea. If I sit by my own fireside, I can hear him reading. When I am just going to sleep, I dream that he is looming over me like an immense, wan moth. If I forget him for a little while, a letter comes from one of his unutterable relations and recalls me. Be wary of Tallent.'

Needless to tell you that he did not take my advice. By the time he had finished the box, he was as much under Tallent's thumb as I was. Bitterly disappointed that there was no masterpiece, he was still loyal to the writer, yet he was emotionally harrowed by the pitiful letters that the relations were now sending to all the papers.

'I dreamed,' he said to me one day (Johnson always says 'dreamed', because he is a critic and considers it the elegant form of expression), 'I dreamed that poor Tallent appeared to me in the watches of the night and told me exactly how each of his things came to him. He said they came like "Kubla Khan".'

I said it must have taken all night.

'It did,' he replied. 'And it has made me dislike a masterpiece.'

I asked him if he intended to be present at the general meeting.

'Meeting?'

'Yes. Things have got to such a pitch that we have had to call one. There will be about a hundred people. I shall have to entertain them to a meal afterwards. I can't very well charge it up to the account of the deceased.'

'Gosh! It'll cost a pretty penny.'

'It will. But perhaps we shall settle something. I shall be thankful.'

'You're not looking well, old chap,' he said. 'Worn, you seem.'

'I am,' I said. 'Tallent is ever with me. Will you come?'

'Rather. But I don't know what to say.'

'The truth, the whole truth –'

'But it's so awful to think of that poor soul spending his whole life on those damned . . . and then that they should never see the light of day.'

'Worse that they should. Much worse.'

'My dear chap, what a confounded position!'

'If I had foreseen *how* confounded,' I said, 'I'd have strangled the fellow on the top of that mountain. I have had to get two clerks to deal with the correspondence. I get no rest. All night I dream of Tallent. And now I hear that a consumptive relation of his has died of disappointment at not getting any of the money, and his wife has written me a wild letter threatening to accuse me of manslaughter. Of course that's all stuff, but it shows what a hysterical state everybody's in. I feel pretty well done for.'

'You'd feel worse if you'd read the boxful.'

I agreed.

We had a stormy meeting. It was obvious that the people did need the money. They were the sort of struggling, under-vitalized folk who always do need it. Children were waiting for a chance in life, old people were waiting to be saved from death a little longer, middle-aged people were waiting to set themselves up in business or buy snug little houses. And there was Tallent, out of it all, in a spiritual existence, not needing beef and bread any more, deliberately keeping it from them.

As I thought this, I distinctly saw Tallent pass the window of the room I had hired for the occasion. I stood up; I pointed; I cried out to them to follow him. The very man himself.

Johnson came to me.

'Steady, old man,' he said. 'You're overstrained.'

'But I did see him,' I said. 'The very man. The cause of all the mischief. If I could only get my hands on him!'

A medical man who had married one of Tallent's sisters said that these hallucinations were very common, and that I was evidently not a fit person to have charge of the money. This brought me a ray of hope, till that ass Johnson contradicted him, saying foolish things about my career. And a diversion was caused by a tremulous old lady calling out: 'The Church! The Church! Consult the Church! There's something in the Bible about it, only I can't call it to mind at the moment. Has anybody got a Bible?'

A clerical nephew produced a pocket New Testament, and it transpired that what she had meant was: 'Take ten talents'.

'If I could take one, madam,' I said, 'it would be enough.'

'It speaks of that too,' she replied triumphantly. 'Listen! "If any man have one talent . . ." Oh, there's everything in the Bible!'

'Let us,' remarked one of the thirteen solicitors, 'get to business. Whether it's in the Bible, or not, whether Mr Tallent went past the window or not, the legality or illegality of what we propose is not affected. Facts are facts. The deceased is dead. *You've* got the money. *We* want it.'

'I devoutly wish you'd got it,' I said, 'and that Tallent was haunting you instead of me.'

The meeting lasted four hours. The wildest ideas were put forward. One or two sporting cousins of the deceased suggested a decision by games – representatives of the would-be beneficiaries and representatives of the manuscript. They were unable to see that this could not affect the legal aspect. Johnson was asked for his opinion. He said that from a critic's point of view the MSS. were balderdash. Everybody looked kindly upon him. But just as he was sunning himself in this atmosphere, and trying to forget Tallent, an immense lady, like Boadicea, advanced upon him, towering over him in a hostile manner.

'I haven't read the books, and I'm not going to,' she said, 'but I take exception to that word balderdash, sir, and I consider it libellous. Let me tell you, I brought Mr Tallent into the world!' I looked at her with awesome wonder. She had brought that portent into the world! But how . . . whom had she persuaded? . . . I pulled myself up. And as I turned away from the contemplation of Boadicea, I saw Tallent pass the window again.

I rushed forward and tried to push up the sash. But the place was built for meetings, not for humanity, and it would not open. I seized the poker, intending to smash the glass. I suppose I must have looked rather mad, and as everybody else had been too intent on business to look out of the window, nobody believed that I had seen anything.

'You might just go round to the nearest chemist's and get some bromide,' said the doctor to Johnson. 'He's overwrought.'

Johnson, who was thankful to escape Boadicea, went with alacrity.

The meeting was, however, over at last. A resolution was passed that we should try to arrange things out of court. We were to take the opinions of six eminent lawyers – judges preferably. We were also to submit what Johnson thought the best story to a distinguished critic. According to what they said we were to divide the money up or leave things as they were.

I felt very much discouraged as I walked home. All these opinions would entail much work and expense. There seemed no end to it.

'Damn the man!' I muttered, as I turned the corner into the square in which I live. And there, just the width of the square away from me, was the man himself. I could almost have wept. What had I done that the gods should play with me thus?

I hurried forward, but he was walking fast, and in a moment he turned down a side-street. When I got to the corner, the street was empty. After this, hardly a day passed without my seeing Tallent. It made me horribly jumpy and nervous, and the fear of madness began to prey on my mind. Meanwhile, the business went on. It was finally decided that half the money should be divided among the relations. Now I thought there would be peace, and for a time there was – comparatively.

But it was only about a month from this date that I heard from one of the solicitors to say that a strange and disquieting thing had happened – two of the beneficiaries were haunted by Mr Tallent to such an extent that their reason was in danger. I wrote to ask what form the haunting took. He said they continually heard Mr Tallent reading aloud from his works. Wherever they were in the house, they still heard him. I wondered if he would begin reading to me soon. So far it had only been visions. If he began to read . . .

In a few months I heard that both the relations who were haunted had been taken to an asylum. While they were in the asylum they heard nothing. But, some time after, on being certified as cured and released, they heard the reading again, and had to go back. Gradually the same thing happened to others, but only to one or two at a time.

During the long winter, two years after his death, it began to happen to me.

I immediately went to a specialist, who said there was acute nervous prostration, and recommended a 'home'. But I refused. I would fight Tallent to the last. Six of the beneficiaries were now in 'homes', and every penny of the money they had had was used up.

I considered things. 'Bell, book and candle' seemed to be what was required. But how, when, where to find him? I consulted a spiritualist, a priest and a woman who has more intuitive perception than anyone I know. From their advice I made my plans. But it was Lesbia who saved me.

'Get a man who can run to go about with you,' she said. 'The moment

He appears, let your companion rush round by a side-street and cut him off.'

'But how will that –?'

'Never mind. I know what I think.'

She gave me a wise little smile.

I did what she advised, but it was not till my patience was nearly exhausted that I saw Tallent again. The reading went on, but only in the evenings when I was alone, and at night. I asked people in evening after evening. But when I got into bed, it began.

Johnson suggested that I should get married.

'What?' I said, 'offer a woman a ruined nervous system, a threatened home, and a possible end in an asylum?'

'There's one woman who would jump at it. I love my love with an L.'

'Don't be an ass,' I said. I felt in no mood for jokes. All I wanted was to get things cleared up.

About three years after Tallent's death, my companion and I, going out rather earlier than usual, saw him hastening down a long road which had no side-streets leading out of it. As luck would have it, an empty taxi passed us. I shouted. We got in. Just in front of Tallent's ghost we stopped, leapt out, and flung ourselves upon him.

'My God!' I cried. 'He's *solid!*'

He was perfectly solid, and not a little alarmed.

We put him into the taxi and took him to my house.

'Now, Tallent!' I said, 'you will answer for what you have done.'

He looked scared, but dreamy.

'Why aren't you dead?' was my next question.

He seemed hurt.

'I never died,' he replied softly.

'It was in the papers.'

'I put it in. I was in America. It was quite easy.'

'And that continual haunting of me, and the wicked driving of your unfortunate relations into asylums?' I was working myself into a rage. 'Do you know how many of them are there now?'

'Yes. I know. Very interesting.'

'Interesting?'

'It was in a great cause,' he said. 'Possibly you didn't grasp that I was a progressive psychoanalyst, and that I did not take those novels of mine seriously. In fact, they were just part of the experiment.'

'In heaven's name, *what* experiment?'

'The plural would be better, really,' he said, 'for there were many experiments.'

'But what for, you damned old blackguard?' I shouted.

'For my *magnum opus*,' he said modestly.

'And what is your abominable *magnum opus*, you wicked old man?'

'It will be famous all over the world,' he said complacently. 'All this has given me exceptional opportunities. It was so easy to get into my relations' houses and experiment with them. It was regrettable, though, that I could not follow them to the asylum.'

This evidently worried him far more than the trouble he had caused.

'So it was *you* reading, every time?'

'Every time.'

'And it was you who went past the window of that horrible room when we discussed your will?'

'Yes. A most gratifying spectacle!'

'And now, you old scoundrel, before I decide what to do with you,' I said, 'what is the *magnum opus*?'

'It is a treatise,' he said, with the pleased expression that made me so wild. 'A treatise that will eclipse all former work in that field, and its title is – "An Exhaustive Enquiry, with numerous Experiments, into the Power of Human Endurance".'

Enid Bagnold

THE AMOROUS GHOST

IT was five o'clock on a summer morning. The birds, who had woken at three, had long scattered about their duties. The white, plain house, blinkered and green-shuttered, stood four-square to its soaking lawns, and up and down on the grass, his snow-boots planting dark blots on the grey dew, walked the owner. His hair was uncombed, he wore his pyjamas and an overcoat, and at every turn at the end of the lawn he looked up at a certain window, that of his own and his wife's bedroom, where, as on every other window on the long front, the green shutters lay neatly back against the wall and the cream curtains hung down in heavy folds.

The owner of the house, strangely and uncomfortably on his lawns instead of in his bed, rubbed his chilly hands and continued his tramp. He had no watch on his wrist, but when the stable clock struck six he entered the house and passing through the still hall he went up to his bathroom. The water was luke-warm in the taps from the night before, and he took a bath. As he left the bathroom for his dressing-room he heard the stirring of the first housemaid in the living-rooms below, and at seven o'clock he rang for his butler to lay out his clothes.

As the same thing had happened the day before, the butler was half-prepared for the bell; yawning and incensed but ready dressed.

'Good morning,' said Mr Templeton rather suddenly. It was a greeting which he never gave, but he wished to try the quality of his voice. Finding it steady he went on, and gave an order for a melon from the greenhouse.

For breakfast he had very little appetite, and when he had finished the melon he unfolded the newspaper. The door of the dining-room opened, and the parlourmaid and housemaid came in and gave him their notice.

'A month from to-day, sir,' repeated the parlourmaid to bridge the silence that followed.

'It's nothing to do with me,' he said in a low voice. 'Your mistress is coming home to-night. You must tell her of these things.'

They left the room.

'What's the matter with those girls?' said Mr Templeton to the butler who came in.

'They haven't spoken to me, sir,' said the butler untruly; 'but I gather there has been an upset.'

'Because I chose to get up early on a summer morning?' asked Mr Templeton with an effort.

'Yes, sir. And there were other reasons.'

'Which were?'

'The housemaid,' said the butler with detachment, as though he were speaking of the movements of a fly, 'has found your bedroom, sir, strewn with clothes.'

'With my clothes?' said Mr Templeton.

'No, sir.'

Mr Templeton sat down. 'A nightgown?' he said weakly, as though appealing for human understanding.

'Yes, sir.'

'More than one?'

'Two, sir.'

'Good God!' said Mr Templeton, and walked to the window whistling shakily.

The butler cleared the table quietly and left the room.

'There's no question about it,' said Mr Templeton under his breath. 'She was undressing . . . behind the chair.'

After breakfast he walked down his two fields and through a wood with the idea of talking to Mr George Casson. But George had gone to London for the day, and Mr Templeton, faced with the polish on the front door, the polish on the parlourmaid, and the sober look of the *Morning Post* folded on the hall table, felt that it was just as well that he had not after all to confide his incredible story. He walked back again, steadied by the air and exercise.

'I'll telephone to Hettie,' he decided, 'and make sure that she is coming to-night.'

He rang up his wife, told her that he was well, that all was well, and heard with satisfaction that she was coming down that night after her dinner-party, catching the eleven-thirty, arriving at twelve-fifteen at the station.

'There is no train before at all,' she said. 'I sent round to the station to see, and owing to the strike they run none between seven-fifteen and eleven-thirty.'

'Then I'll send the car to the station and you'll be here at half-past twelve. I may be in bed, as I'm tired.'

'You're not ill?'

'No. I've had a bad night.'

It was not until the afternoon, after a good luncheon and a whisky-and-soda, that Mr Templeton went up to his bedroom to have a look at it.

The dream curtains hung lightly blowing in the window. By the fireplace stood a high, wing, grandfather chair upholstered in patterned rep. Opposite the chair and the fireplace was the double bed, in one side of which Mr Templeton had lain working at his papers the night before. He walked up to the chair, put his hands in his pockets, and stood looking down at it. Then he crossed to the chest of drawers and drew out a drawer. On the right-hand side were Hettie's vests and chemises, neatly pressed and folded. On the left was a pile, folded but not pressed, of Hettie's nightgowns. Mr Templeton noted the crumples and creases on the silk.

'Evidence, evidence,' he said, walking to the window, 'that something happened in this room after I left it this morning. The maids believe they found a strange woman's nightgowns crumpled on the floor. As a matter of fact they are Hettie's nightgowns. I suppose a doctor would say I'd done it myself in a trance.'

'Two nights ago?' he thought, looking again at the bed. It seemed a week. The night before last as he lay working, propped up on pillows and cushions and his papers spread over the bed, he had glanced up, absorbed, at two o'clock in the morning and traced the pattern on the grandfather chair as it stood facing the empty grate with its back towards him, just as he had left it, when he had got into bed. It was then that he had seen the two hands hanging idly over the back of the chair as though an unseen owner were kneeling in the seat. His eyes stared, and a cold fear wandered down his spine. He sat without moving and watched the hands.

Ten minutes passed, and the hands were withdrawn quickly as though the occupant of the chair had silently changed its position.

Still he watched, propped, stiffening, on his pillows, and as time went on he fought the impression down. 'Tired,' he said. 'One's read of it. The brain reflecting something.' His heart quietened, and cautiously he settled himself a little lower and tried to sleep. He did not dare straighten the litter of papers around him, but with the light on he lay there till the dawn lit the yellow paint on the wall. At five he got up, sleepless, his eyes still on the back of the grandfather chair, and without his dressing-gown or slippers he left the room. In the hall he found an overcoat and his warm snow-boots behind a chest, and unbolting the front door he tramped the lawn in the dew.

On the second night (*last* night) he had worked as before. So completely had he convinced himself after a day of fresh air that his previous night's experience had been the result of his own imagination, his eyesight and his mind hallucinated by his work, that he had not even remembered (as he had meant to do) to turn the grandfather chair with its seat towards him. Now, as he worked in bed, he glanced from time to time at its patterned and concealing back, and wished vaguely that he had thought to turn it round.

He had not worked more than two hours before he knew that there was something going on in the chair.

'Who's there?' he called. The slight movement he had heard ceased for a moment, then began again. For a second he thought he saw a hand shoot out at the side, and once he could have sworn he saw the tip of a mound of fair hair showing over the top. There was a sound of scuffling in the chair, and some object flew out and landed with a bump on the floor below the field of his vision. Five minutes went by, and after a fresh scuffle a hand shot up and laid a bundle, white and stiff, with what seemed a small arm hanging, on the back of the chair.

Mr Templeton had had two bad nights and a great many hours of emotion. When he grasped that the object was a pair of stays with a suspender swinging from them, something bumped unevenly in his heart, a million black motes like a cloud of flies swam in his eyeballs; he fainted.

He woke up, and the room was dark, the light off, and he felt a little sick. Turning in bed to find comfort for his body, he remembered that he had been in the middle of a crisis of fear. He looked about him in the dark, and saw again the dawn on the curtains. Then he heard a chink by the washstand, several feet nearer to his bed than the grandfather chair. He was not alone; the thing was still in the room.

By the faint light from the curtains he could just see that his visitor was by the washstand. There was a gentle clinking of china and a sound of water, and dimly he could see a woman standing.

'Undressing,' he said to himself, 'washing.'

His gorge rose at the thought that came to him. Was it possible that the woman was coming to bed?

It was that thought that had driven him with a wild rush from the room, and sent him marching for a second time up and down his grey and dewy lawns.

'And now,' thought Mr Templeton as he stood in the neat bedroom in the afternoon light and looked around him, 'Hettie's got to believe in the unfaithful or the supernatural.'

He crossed to the grandfather chair, and taking it in his two hands was about to push it on to the landing. But he paused. 'I'll leave it where it is to-night,' he thought, 'and go to bed as usual. For both our sakes I must find out something more about all this.'

Spending the rest of the afternoon out of doors, he played golf after tea, and eating a very light dinner he went to bed. His head ached badly from lack of sleep, but he was pleased to notice that his heart beat steadily. He took a couple of aspirin tablets to ease his head, and with a light novel settled himself down in bed to read and watch. Hettie would arrive at half-past twelve, and the butler was waiting up to let her in. Sandwiches, nicely covered from the air, were placed ready for her on a tray in the corner of the bedroom.

It was now eleven. He had an hour and a half to wait. 'She may come at any time,' he said (thinking of his visitor). He had turned the grandfather chair towards him, so that he could see the seat.

Quarter of an hour went by, and his head throbbed so violently that he put the book on his knees and altered the lights, turned out the brilliant reading lamp, and switched on the light which illumined the large face of the clock over the mantelpiece, so that he sat in shadow. Five minutes later he was asleep.

He lay with his face buried in the pillow, the pain still drumming in his head, aware of his headache even at the bottom of his sleep. Dimly he heard his wife arrive, and murmured a hope to himself that she would not wake him. A slight movement rustled around him as she entered the room and undressed, but his pain was so bad that he could not bring himself to give a sign of life, and soon, while he clung to his half sleep, he felt the bedclothes gently lifted and heard her slip in beside him.

Feeling chilly he drew his blanket closer round him. It was as though a draught was blowing about him in the bed, dispelling the mists of sleep and bringing him to himself. He felt a touch of remorse at his lack of welcome, and putting out his hand he sought his wife's beneath the sheet. Finding her wrist his fingers closed round it. She too was cold, strange, icy, and from her stillness and silence she appeared to be asleep.

'A cold drive from the station,' he thought, and held her wrist to warm it as he dozed again. 'She is positively chilling the bed,' he murmured to himself.

He was awakened by a roar beneath the window and the sweep of a light across the wall of the room. With amazement he heard the bolts shoot back across the front door. On the illuminated face of the clock over the fireplace he saw the hands standing at twenty-seven minutes past twelve. Then Mr Templeton, still gripping the wrist beside him, heard his wife's clear voice in the hall below.

The art of writing a successful ghost story in under 150 words is a notoriously difficult one – but here are two of the best examples to be found anywhere.

Marjorie Bowen

THE ACCIDENT

MURCHISON was amazed at the speed with which he escaped from the flaming car, across the common, for he could now see the red blaze on the lonely road in the distance: they were fools to row, he and Bargrave, and send the cursed vehicle over like that; he had not ceased running since he had felt the first shock of the released fire from the wreckage.

He wondered why they had quarrelled: the fright had seared his memory; but he certainly knew he loathed Bargrave; the landscape was oddly dim, like the dimness of an eclipse.

Murchison, still fleeing, suddenly saw Bargrave in front of him, also hurrying – an attenuated, grey wisp of a Bargrave, blown thin by the forlorn breeze.

Murchison yelled in triumph:

'So you were killed, you silly fool!'

'Do you think that you're alive?' jeered the ghost of Bargrave, then Murchison knew that he also had no body and that the red flames were not the blaze of the burning car but the light of their future destination.

woke up. He was in his bed at home. It had all been a bad dream.

Marjorie Bowen

A PERSISTENT WOMAN

TEMPLE, exhausted, resolved to leave his wife; their atrocious quarrels were killing him; he was still shaken by the furies of this morning's disagreement when he returned home with bitter reluctance; difficult to get free of Sarah, but it must be done; Temple was resolved.

She met him in the sombre lane that led to their house, and clung to his arm in silence; she was repentant, no doubt, but Temple would not relent; he was mute and tried to shake her off, but she clung with great tenacity.

When they reached their home he found it full of commotion; out of a phantasmagoria someone told him that his wife had been discovered in the pond – 'Suicide, poor thing!' and his brother whispered: 'You're free.'

But Temple grinned at the spiteful shape hugging his arm and knew he never could be free from Sarah.

Phyllis Bottome

THE WAITING-ROOM

ELAINE Marlowe sat on the Rohns Terrasse and looked down over Göttingen. She had the timeless feeling that comes after a long journey. Everything had arrived safely and was put away and recovered from, and as she sat there, on that delicious May morning, she felt deeply, tenderly settled. The still, tranquil sunshine rested on her hands, on the newborn green of the beech leaves, as softly and unsubstantially as if the leaves and her hands were both transparent – light resting upon light.

Beneath her lay the little russet town dipped deep in gardens. The tall massive tower of the Jacobiokirche seemed to be pulling its heavy church up with it into the vague blue air. The German tower lacked the flying grace of an English spire or the slender stateliness of an Italian campanile, but it had a beauty and a vivid strength all its own.

The twin towers of the Johanniskirche had never settled which of their quaint and obstinately unlike spires should really have been allowed to soar. They rose up above the solid grave old Rathaus in a perpetual silent strife, stone against stone. Elaine knew what the little squat high-roofed houses beneath them were like; all carved and painted, pillow-shaped wooden rollers over the doorways, steep bulging roofs, as if time like a wind was playing beneath them, drawing them in here, and furling them out there, above their timbered beams.

The windows looked out from overhanging eaves like deep-set eyes from under frowning brows.

The narrow streets were still cobbled and full of youths with slashed faces, brave from recent duels, flying by on bicycles, their incredible saucer-shaped caps looking as if they must be gummed or growing out of their round-shaped heads. There had been changes, of course, since she was here. These gentle, stiff, simple, and good-humoured people, clean and honest like their Anglo-Saxon cousins, had flamed into monsters of iniquity for the rest of the world, and the rest of the world had seemed to them a herd of vindictive and wanton oppressors. There was a certain clumsiness about them, then as now, the clumsiness of the rigid mind, of the over-disciplined, unplastic will. Dick had once said to her: 'It's the fatality of the good mixed with the stupid. We all share it. We are good to ourselves, we are stupid to others, and out of our stupidity comes violence, suspicion, hate, cruelty, and panic. Wicked people get stopped, but a clumsy person does such unexpected things – you can't stop them; and when their intentions are good, too, they naturally won't stop themselves.'

This morning Elaine did not feel the war as she usually felt it – even now, after all these years, as a fresh weight of pity and horror. It seemed too remote from the lovely covering of the spring. She thought of the little town with love. An almost singing happiness filled her whole heart. She could not move her hand on the fluttering white tablecloth without joy.

She had been alone for a long time without feeling in the least lonely; for the *Terrasse* was full of bird songs, and the occasional visits of bees and butterflies were personal matters. They carried with them on their wings part of her happiness.

Suddenly she heard voices, and saw advancing along the *Terrasse* three very long and massive forms. A man with an immense red neck followed meekly by two large women, with very small hats above broad, smiling faces and strange clothes which seemed to have passed through centuries of fashion without taking from them so much as one coherent thought. Elaine was not as a rule very fond of large, loud people, but she had a peculiar sensation as her eyes rested upon this advancing group. She felt an overwhelming desire to protect them, as if they were secretly afraid of something that she knew they needn't be afraid of, and she was touched by them – by their secret pathos – almost to tears. It was all the difference between seeing a note of music printed on a page and hearing it sound suddenly from some beautifully toned instrument. They were dreadfully real to her. They bore down upon Elaine, loud, beaming, with a quite curious physical solidity wedging their vast circumferences into the delicate light. She was thankful that there were empty tables on each side of her, because in spite of her sympathy she had a conflicting sense of being anxious to get out of their way. It was a curious guilty feeling as if she knew something that they had forgotten or had forgotten something which they knew.

They advanced yet nearer, their cheerful moving sounds enveloping her. They approached the table at which she sat as if she was not there. Elaine made a wavering gesture with her hands towards one of the empty tables. They didn't look at all angry or brutal, but they ignored her defensive gesture. They came straight up to her table and the most massive of the ladies sat down in Elaine's chair. It was then that Elaine realised that she was dead. She didn't have even to withdraw herself from the lady. She simply wasn't there. A thought had been there and the thought was gone.

Elaine felt as if she was plunging into a cold sea. A wash of unknown consciousness swept over her. It was startling to find that what she had supposed were her hand and her dress, the very lovely lines of the wisteria-coloured dress she had just bought in Paris, only existed when she herself suggested existence to them. What more might come to her – what more might leave her – unprotected by any walls of sense from the strange secrets of the universe?

When had she died? She remembered nothing about it. Ever since Dick's death she had been subject to recurrent attacks of breathlessness, for which the doctors had found various reasons and no remedies. They had been very distressing, but the last had been the least severe. She had thought it was going to be very bad, when it had quite suddenly stopped.

But if she was dead, why was she at Göttingen? It was the last place she had ever allowed herself to think of. She had disciplined her clamorous mind so severely that the very name Göttingen had gone out of her consciousness. Those dreadful memories, which had fought day and night like wild beasts over her prostrate heart, had been driven away or lost. She never saw Göttingen even in her dreams. But now when memory deepened into reality, when she was left alone and unprotected face to face with it, she felt no pain. Nothing, not even the lonely coldness of the unknown, shook her deep central security.

She looked at the scene of her life's disaster without a pang. It had been such a silly little thing – plunging into the warm, untroubled sea of their happiness like the swift, unseen fin of a murderous shark! They were utterly wrapped up in each other; and with the years this condition of their love had deepened and grown safe about them. Their perfect marriage was the secret exasperation of those less fortunate than themselves, and the torch of hope to the inexperienced and the romantic. They never really quarrelled. Their hottest discussions had a mild unreality about them; they knew that no difference of opinion could shake the continuity of their love. Behind all possible differences they were always – just Elaine and Dick. And Elaine was the whole world to Dick and Dick the whole world to Elaine. Nothing but an accident could happen to them.

If she could possibly help it – after the time when she thought of nothing else – Elaine never allowed herself to remember the cause of their quarrel. But she let herself remember it now with a smile of tenderness for such foolishness. They had quarrelled as to which of their mothers they should visit first on their return to England. Both of them were attached to their mothers and to each other's mother.

There had never been an instant's difficulty about these fortunate relationships. Dick's mother thought Elaine as perfect for Dick as any young woman, not his mother, could be. Elaine's mother thought Dick the pick of all possible husbands for her unique Elaine.

But though these relationships were ideal and needed very little keeping up, the affection of these desirable mothers-in-law for each other was distinctly less ideal. Elaine's mother often thought that it was really extraordinary that such a delightful son-in-law as Dick should have such a grasping, exacting mother, and Dick's mother felt it little less than a miracle that so satisfactory a daughter-in-law as Elaine could have been produced by a jealous, scheming woman like Elaine's mother. Both of them loved having their children to stay with them and neither of them liked their children staying with the other mother.

Elaine's mother was delicate; special consideration was due to her on this account. Dick's mother lived nearer the Channel Ports and was slightly the more unreasonable of the two old ladies. What Elaine feared, but unfortunately had not said, was that if they visited Dick's mother first, her mother would allow the fine gold of Dick's image to become dimmed. It was for Dick's reputation Elaine was secretly fighting. Dick felt the same about Elaine and his mother and it was for Elaine's white record that he fought.

Neither of them suspected that in the other this exquisite care for the Beloved's characters was the root of a preposterous claim. Both credited the other with incredible and thick-witted selfishness, heightened by unreasoning obstinacy. So they had sat and quarrelled in the warm May sunshine – how many years ago! – passionately dear to each other, wildly hurt, and hurting back as wildly! There was no reason for it at all. Neither of them cared in the least which mother they visited first. Neither of them stopped to find out whether this hated thing they were fighting in a mask was after all nothing but the beloved face which they would die to save. They said terrible things to each other. Finally Dick, who was most sensitive to the power of words, and secretly knew his mother to be the more unreasonable of the two, got up and said, 'I can't stand any more of this! I shall go for a walk alone. We can settle our plans when I return!' and Elaine had said icily, 'Do, if you wish!' instead of 'Darling, let's do whatever you like!' which had lain so close to the other speech that she hardly knew which she had said, till afterwards.

They were sitting in the Theaterplatz under a copper beech; against its bronzed dull red a clever waiter had set pots of scarlet geraniums. The sun played through the dark metallic lustre of the beech leaves, and flamed on the broad fiery petals of the geraniums. Memory went on unflinchingly now, and quite without that cold terror Elaine had always felt as she approached any of the avenues of thought down which she might catch a glimpse of the Arch-Fear.

Dick stepped onto the road without looking, without perhaps caring, and a great car swooped out of the white distance, caught him, and killed him before her eyes. There had been no time for a word, or a smile, no time for anything but the interminable fussy ministrations of the Göttingen authorities. They had all been kind. She was able, borne up by the wings of disaster, to remember what Dick would have liked, to give them as little trouble as possible, and as much recognition of their kindness.

The shipwreck came afterwards. And now she didn't mind thinking even about that! Curious! How long the journey must have been, and she was dead, and this was Göttingen! Why was she here? Was it because she was a criminal and had killed him and so must always haunt the scene of her crime? But wasn't it the murdered, more often than the murderer, who was to be found there? Ah! if it only could be! If only for a fraction of what she supposed must be Eternity, she could see him face to face! This had been her perpetual human longing, only to know that he existed, only to know where he was! But she nourished no illusions. Dick had not returned to her. She had found him neither among the Living nor among the Dead, if there were any other dead. She felt lonely now – conscious that she had lost not only Dick but everybody else – even the human beings she saw weren't so human to her as when she was human to them.

She knew now why her heart had gone out to the Germans who came to her table, and why she was sorry for them. What she had wanted to tell them was that Death was not dreadful. What she wanted to express to them was that she was much more like them than she had ever known, she was almost part of them, only when one was alive one did not understand that all living things were the same; and that to hurt each other was to hurt oneself.

Dick had always told her thoughts were things and she realised now how true his particular theory had been. Her thoughts – which she felt hadn't yet begun to grow or change to meet the new condition she was in – were still clothed with familiar appearances. She had her human form when she thought about it, not when she didn't. She smelt, saw, heard, felt, not with the organs of sense, but out of one intangible sense which gave her everything, a unity that space no longer controlled nor was time concerned in it.

She said to herself: 'I will walk to the Theaterplatz,' but she was conscious that she didn't walk there. She was there, just as if she chose to think about it, she was in the Rohns Terrasse, and at the same time. It was not confusing because automatically what you did not think of ceased to exist – you saw only what you selected to see.

Once one was in one place at one time, now one was always – everywhere; and it was less strange than that once one could only go from one room to another. She saw the copper beech, and close to the bright geraniums, with their old sun-warmed scent, were the rows of little white tables. She thought of herself as she had been eight years ago and she no longer wore the wisteria dress, but a lovely pale grey-green garment Dick had chosen for her, with a flame-coloured crêpe de chine hat. She thought methodically of the very shoes and stockings, the emerald ring on her ungloved hand. She wondered if she was smiling the same smile, the last one she had not had to smile on purpose. She thought she would find the table where they had had iced coffee – and the quarrel. Perhaps God had sent her here simply to lay the ghost of that quarrel forever, and to lay ghosts you had to go through everything that made the ghost rise.

She found the table. It was the lunch hour and none of the tables were empty. Some one was sitting at hers. But in a moment she remembered it didn't really matter. She saw Them, but quite obviously from the Rohns Terrasse episode – They didn't see her. If she spoke to Them, it was like the murmur of summer bees, and if she touched Them, they thought it only the wind against their cheeks.

She could without disturbing her fellow guest sit down, and, blotting him out of her line of vision, relive her memories until she had brought them all safely into the strange peace. But when she reached the table he had seen her. He rose and their eyes met. She supposed it was their eyes. For she saw Dick, saw him again as if it was just now – only just now, that they were swept apart by Death – by that silly little thing – now passed away forever.

She said what had lain in her heart and almost on her lips ever since. 'Ah Dick where *were* you all the time?' And he said, 'My darling, I never left here, I just waited.'

Catherine Wells

THE GHOST

SHE was a girl of fourteen, and she sat propped up with pillows in an old four-poster bed, coughing a little with the feverish cold that kept her there. She was tired of reading by lamplight, and she lay and listened to the few sounds that she could hear, and looked into the fire. From downstairs, down the wide, rather dark, oak-panelled corridor hung with brown ochre pictures of tremendous naval engagements exploding fierily in their centres, down the broad stone stairs that ended in a heavy, creaking, nail-studded door, there blew in to her remoteness sometimes a gust of dance music. Cousins and cousins and cousins were down there, and Uncle Timothy, as host, leading the fun. Several of them had danced into her room during the day, and said that her illness was a 'perfect shame,' told her that the skating in the park was 'too heavenly,' and danced out again. Uncle Timothy had been as kind as kind could be. But – Downstairs all the full cup of happiness the lonely child had looked forward to so eagerly for a month, was running away like liquid gold.

She watched the flames of the big wood fire in the open grate flicker and fall. She had sometimes to clench her hands to prevent herself from crying. She had discovered – so early was she beginning to collect her little stock of feminine lore – that if you swallowed hard and rapidly as the tears gathered, that you could prevent your eyes brimming over. She wished some one would come. There was a bell within her reach, but she could think of no plausible excuse for ringing it. She wished there was more light in the room. The big fire lit it up cheerfully when the logs flared high; but when they only glowed, the dark shadows crept down from the ceiling and gathered in the corners against the panelling. She turned from the scrutiny of the room to the bright circle of light under the lamp on the table beside her, and the companionable suggestiveness of the currant jelly and spoon, grapes and lemonade and little pile of books and kindly fuss that shone warmly and comfortingly there. Perhaps it would not be long before Mrs Bunting, her uncle's housekeeper, would come in again and sit down and talk to her.

Mrs Bunting, very probably, was more occupied than usual that evening. There were several extra guests, another house-party had motored over for the evening, and they had brought with them a romantic figure, a celebrity, no less a personage than the actor Percival East. The girl had indeed broken down from her fortitude that afternoon when Uncle Timothy had told her of this visitor. Uncle Timothy was surprised; it was only another schoolgirl who would have understood fully what it meant to be denied by a mere cold the chance of meeting face to face that chivalrous hero of drama; another girl who had glowed at his daring, wept at his noble renunciations, been made happy, albeit enviously and vicariously, by his final embrace with the lady of his love.

'There, there, dear child,' Uncle Timothy had said, patting her shoulder and greatly distressed. 'Never mind, never mind. If you can't get up I'll bring him in to see you here. I promise I will. . . . But the *pull* these chaps have over you little women,' he went on, half to himself. . . .

The panelling creaked. Of course, it always did in these old houses. She was of that order of apprehensive, slightly nervous people who do not believe in ghosts, but all the same hope devoutly they may never see one. Surely it was a long time since any one had visited her; it would be hours, she supposed, before the girl who had the room next her own, into which a communicating door comfortingly led, came up to bed. If she rang it took a minute or two before any one reached her from the remote servants' quarters. There ought soon, she thought, to be a housemaid about the corridor outside, tidying up the bedrooms, putting coal on the fires, and making suchlike companionable noises. That would be pleasant. How bored one got in bed anyhow, and how dreadful it was, how unbearably dreadful it was that she should be stuck in bed now, missing everything, missing every bit of the glorious glowing time that was slipping away down there. At that she had to begin swallowing her tears again.

With a sudden burst of sound, a storm of clapping and laughter, the heavy door at the foot of the big stairs swung open and closed. Footsteps came upstairs, and she heard men's voices approaching. Uncle Timothy. He knocked at the door ajar. 'Come in,' she cried gladly. With him was a quiet-faced greyish-haired man of middle age. Then uncle had sent for the doctor after all!

'Here is another of your young worshippers, Mr East,' said Uncle Timothy.

Mr East! She realised in a flash that she had expected him in purple brocade, powdered hair, and ruffles of fine lace. Her uncle smiled at her disconcerted face.

'She doesn't seem to recognise you, Mr East,' said Uncle Timothy.

'Of course I do,' she declared bravely, and sat up, flushed with excitement and her feverishness, bright-eyed and with ruffled hair. Indeed she began to see the stage hero she remembered and the kindly-faced man before her flow together like a composite portrait. There was the little nod of the head, there was the chin, yes! and the eyes, now she came to look at them. 'Why were they all clapping you?' she asked.

'Because I had just promised to frighten them out of their wits,' replied Mr East.

'Oh, how?'

'Mr East,' said Uncle Timothy, 'is going to dress up as our long-lost ghost, and give us a really shuddering time of it downstairs.'

'*Are* you?' cried the girl with all the fierce desire that only a girl can utter in her voice. 'Oh, why am I ill like this, Uncle Timothy? I'm not ill really. Can't you see I'm better? I've been in bed all day. I'm perfectly well. Can't I come down, Uncle *dear* – can't I?'

In her excitement she was half out of bed. 'There, there, child,' soothed Uncle Timothy, hastily smoothing the bedclothes and trying to tuck her in.

'But *can't* I?'

'Of course, if you want to be thoroughly frightened, frightened out of your wits, mind you,' began Percival East.

'I do, I *do*,' she cried, bouncing up and down in her bed.

'I'll come and show myself when I'm dressed up, before I go down.'

'Oh please, please,' she cried back radiantly. A private performance all to herself! 'Will you be perfectly *awful*?' she laughed exultantly.

'As ever I can,' smiled Mr East, and turned to follow Uncle Timothy out of the room. 'You know,' he said, holding the door and looking back at her with mock seriousness, 'I shall look rather horrid, I expect. Are you sure you won't mind?'

'*Mind* – when it's you?' laughed the girl.

He went out of the room, shutting the door.

'Rum-ti-tum, ti-tum, ti-ty,' she hummed gaily, and wriggled down into her bedclothes again, straightened the sheet over her chest, and prepared to wait.

She lay quietly for some time, with a smile on her face, thinking of Percival East and fitting his grave, kindly face back into its various dramatic settings. She was quite satisfied with him. She began to go over in her mind in detail the last play in which she had seen him act. How splendid he had looked when he fought the duel! She couldn't imagine him gruesome, she thought. What would he do with himself?

Whatever he did, she wasn't going to be frightened. He shouldn't be able to boast he had frightened *her*. Uncle Timothy would be there too, she supposed. Would he?

Footsteps went past her door outside, along the corridor, and died away. The big door at the end of the stairs opened and clanged shut.

Uncle Timothy had gone down.

She waited on.

A log, burnt through the middle to a ruddy thread, fell suddenly in two tumbling pieces on the hearth. She started at the sound. How quiet everything was. How much longer would he be, she wondered. The fire wanted making up, the pieces of wood collecting together. Should she ring? But he might come in just when the servant was mending the fire, and that would spoil his entry. The fire could wait. . . .

The room was very still, and, with the fallen fire, darker. She heard no more any sound at all from downstairs. That was because her door was shut. All day it had been open, but now the last slender link that held her to downstairs was broken.

The lamp flame gave a sudden fitful leap. Why? Was it going out? Was it? – no.

She hoped he wouldn't jump out at her, but of course he wouldn't. Anyhow, whatever he did she wouldn't be frightened – really frightened. Forewarned is forearmed.

Was that a sound? She started up, her eyes on the door. Nothing.

But surely, the door had minutely moved, it did not sit back quite so close into its frame! Perhaps it was – She was sure it had moved. Yes, it had moved – opened an inch, and slowly, as she watched, she saw a thread of light grow between the edge of the door and its frame, grow almost imperceptibly wider, and stop.

He could never come through that? It must have yawned open of its own accord. Her heart began to beat rather quickly. She could see only the upper part of the door, the foot of her bed hid the lower third. . . .

Her attention tightened. Suddenly, as suddenly as a pistol shot, she saw that there was a little figure like a dwarf near the wall, between the door and the fireplace. It was a little cloaked figure, no higher than the table. How *did* he do it? It was moving slowly, very slowly, towards the fire, as if it was quite unconscious of her; it was wrapped about in a cloak that trailed, with a slouched hat on its head bent down to its shoulders. She gripped the clothes with her hands, it was so queer, so unexpected; she gave a little gasping laugh to break the tension of the silence – to show she appreciated him.

The dwarf stopped dead at the sound, and turned its face round to her.

Oh! but she was frightened! it was a dead white face, a long pointed face hunched between its shoulders, there was no colour in the eyes that stared at her! How did he do it, how *did* he do it? It was too good. She laughed again nervously, and with a clutch of terror that she could not control she saw the creature move out of the shadow and come towards her. She braced herself with all her might, she mustn't be frightened by a bit of acting – he was coming nearer, it was horrible, horrible – right up to her bed. . . .

She flung her head beneath her bedclothes. Whether she screamed or not she never knew. . . .

Some one was rapping at her door, speaking cheerily. She took her head out of the clothes with a revulsion of shame at her fright. The horrible little creature was gone! Mr East was speaking at her door. What was it he was saying? *What?*

'*I'm ready now,*' he said. '*Shall I come in, and begin?*'

Eleanor Scott

'WILL YE NO' COME BACK AGAIN?'

THE friends of Annis Breck (who were not many, and were all female) generally spoke with respect of her Sound Good Sense, her Practical Ability and her Capabilities. Her foes (who were more, but still not many) said that she was hard, commercial and unimaginative. Every one else said that you could never really *know* Miss Breck, she was so – and left it at that. Her idea of opening a hostel for working girls in Burley was, everyone agreed, just like her, though they said so for different reasons. She had done so much, one way and another, for girls. Women and their rights (or, more often, wrongs) had always been her strong point; and of course, added the foes, she always had a keen eye to the main chance. If Annis Breck took up a thing, you might be pretty sure there was money in it. She'd make this hostel a very paying thing, see if she didn't. But when they heard that she had taken Queen's Garth, they wondered if she would. They then said that these 'business women' . . . ! and again left it at that.

For, they pointed out, Queen's Garth had stood empty for years. It had been unfortunate in its owners. The last of the original family, old Miss Campbell, was the only survivor of a clan that had lived in the house ever since it was built in the seventeenth century. They had apparently specialised in strong-minded females, who had very occasionally condescended to marry, but had always ruled with a rod of iron, having a deep-rooted suspicion of men and a determination to keep them well under. How they had ever married at all was a marvel; no doubt it had been entirely for practical, and never for romantic, reasons. The family had now died out, it was true, but (said the foes, nastily) it seemed that the tradition of the firm female and the rod of iron was to endure. They pitied the girls, they said.

Then came the friends. Annis was wonderful, they knew that, but had she really *considered*? Did she realise all it *meant*? The house had stood empty so long. The furniture, they knew, had been lovely – Sheraton and Chippendale and all sorts of gems – but it must be simply dropping to pieces now. The house was charming, of course, and dirt cheap, and the rooms beautifully large, but, my *dear! Think* of the work, with all those stairs and twisting passages, and no conveniences to speak of. Besides, there was some story –

oh, no one *believed it*, of course, but you know what maids *are*. They'd turn every echo and waving curtain into a ghost. And water, always such a problem in these picturesque old places . . . Still, Annis probably knew best. So practical, dear Annis!

Annis herself felt not the smallest doubt as to her venture. She never did, which, no doubt, was why so many of them succeeded. She took Queen's Garth as soon as she saw it, stairs and ghost and water and all. She did not underrate these disadvantages, but she simply accepted them because she knew as soon as she saw the old red house that she 'belonged.' Almost unconsciously she felt that; she closed her bargain on the spot.

She meant to open the hostel on New Year's Day. Alterations must be made, of course, and equally of course they would not be made in time unless she personally saw that they were. You could never trust men to keep their word. So she moved, early in December, into Queen's Garth, to keep an eye on the men, make curtains, and so on, and arrange everything properly. Organisation, she said, was the key to success. Anything could be done by good organisation.

She said this to Lucy Ferrars, an old friend of W.S.P.U. days, who had called to ask Annis to speak at a meeting. Lucy was always getting up meetings and asking Annis to speak at them, and Annis was always irritated sooner or later by Lucy's absolute lack of the power to organise. Her meetings were never successful. So she repeated her formula about the necessity of organisation, *àpropos* of the hostel, but hoping that Lucy would take it to heart. Apparently she didn't – Annis thought it was that she wouldn't.

'How *marv'*lous you are,' was all that she said in the bleating voice that irritated Annis so badly. 'Marv'lous. And what *perfect* furniture, Annis. So quaint.'

Miss Breck shuddered.

'I s'pose you've got it all in here,' pursued Lucy.

Annis gave up the hope of impressing her with the necessity of organisation, and allowed the talk to turn to furniture.

'Oh, no,' she replied, bored but tolerant. 'The house is practically all furnished, and it's all eighteenth century stuff.'

'My *dear*! It must have cost you a *fortune!*' gasped Lucy.

'Not a bit of it. No one wanted it. You see, the furniture goes with the house. Some clause in the old lady's will – seems it was the rule in the family. It makes it awfully – personal,' she added, half to herself, passing her fingers lightly over the back of an elegant Chippendale chair. 'It's very lucky for me,' she went on, smiling dryly, 'that people are so idiotically superstitious. I should never have got the house otherwise . . .'

She broke off, turning her head sharply.

'What is it?' breathed Lucy, her prominent eyes goggling, her mouth gaping.

'Nothing,' said Annis, relaxing her attitude. 'I thought I saw someone – a reflection in my glasses, no doubt. For the moment I thought one of the men had come back. . . . You'll stay and have some tea, won't you, Lucy? Bachelor's Hall, of course, but I make myself very comfortable.'

'Are you all alone?' asked Lucy, still round-eyed.

'Oh, yes. No sense in having maids for one person – especially as I hear they're going to be hard to keep! But I can cook, you know. You will stay, won't you?'

'Oh, no, thank you very much,' said Lucy hastily. 'I – it's getting late – it's dark so very early now. I have such a lot to do – this meeting, you know – I *think* I must go, dear, thank you so much. . . .'

She babbled all the way to the door, and annoyed Annis very much by stopping on the threshold, half in and half out, to press her to come and sleep with her until the house should be ready and there were 'girls and maids and people' for company. She gave no reason for this suggestion – Lucy, Annis reflected with amusement, didn't know the meaning of the word 'reason' – but was very persistent and incoherent. Annis got rid of her with difficulty.

It was nearly dark when she turned back into the house. She made it a rule to go the rounds of all the rooms each night, to make sure that there were no open windows or smouldering cigarette ends ('You know what men are!') – and now, thanks to Lucy's maunderings, she would have to do this by the inadequate light of an electric torch, since candles carried in the hand were hardly safe. She thought, as she tripped over forgotten and unnecessary steps and felt her way along the winding passages, that the house was more inconvenient than she had thought. Odd that, with all its twists and turns, it should somehow seem familiar. One would soon get used to its irregularities. And the girls wouldn't mind. Girls, she reflected bitterly, never mind anything really badly. Girls were what men had made them – giddy, fickle, heartless. They had found that faith and loyalty and depth of feeling didn't pay – thanks to men.

'*Men!*' she muttered aloud, slamming a door. 'Men! All alike! Just use women and throw them away – forget they exist. No wonder girls . . .'

She stopped short. A tiny sound, like the faint echo of a sob, caught her ear.

She stood, listening intently. No – not a sound. Or – yes, there it was again – a sound of muffled, pitiful, hopeless crying.

For a moment she stood there, straining every sense. Then suddenly relief swept over her.

'It's a child,' she thought. 'Some child who's brought one of the men his tea, and got left behind. . . . It was just here somewhere.'

She walked briskly down the passage, making encouraging sounds, opening every door, examining every room, flashing the beam of her torch into every corner. The house was empty and still.

'Very odd,' thought Annis, annoyed. 'It must have been some trick of the wind.'

And she finished her rounds and went back to her cosy little sitting-room, with its Georgian furniture and Victorian silhouettes, to study catalogues and reports. She spent a peaceful and busy evening, and slept extra well in consequence.

The morning was sunny and mild, and Annis seized the opportunity to go over the garden, which she had not yet investigated, with a view to turning it to the best advantage for 'her girls.' The lawns should be cut and rolled and turned into courts for tennis and badminton; the gravelled courtyard outside the old stables would be excellent for netball; she might fix up fives in the stables themselves. And she would leave bits of real garden simply for rest. She would keep the old flower-borders, with their fragrant hedges of rosemary and lavender and lad's love. Rosemary, that's for remembrance. And lad's love – there was some song about it –

What is lad's love and the love of a lad?
Lad's love is green and grey;
And the love of a lad is merry and sad –
Here yesterday – gone to-day.
Heigh-ho, hey!
Here yesterday – gone to-day!

Yes, there was something melancholy, as well as sweet, about lad's love. Perhaps that should go. . . .

But the old rose-garden, with its formal beds and stone seats and sundial, must certainly remain. She liked the sundial. It would have a motto, she was sure – 'Time flieth, hope dieth' – why did the words come into her head? She had not seen them anywhere that she remembered.

She strolled across. Yes, she was right. The words were almost obliterated, worn and overgrown with moss, but they were there. She leant over the slab, tracing them with an idle finger.

'Time flieth, hope . . .'

Annis suddenly stiffened. She remained, her hands resting lightly on the old stone slab, her eyes bent on the motto; but she, too, might have been carved in stone. For she felt, as certainly as she had ever felt anything, that someone stood behind her, reading the words over her shoulder – someone sneering, hating, despising her. . . . She could hear her pulses beating in her throat – she could not breathe. . . .

And then, as suddenly, these symptoms passed. She was alone in the winter sunshine, and a robin sang sweet and shrill in the bare rose-trees. She drew a deep breath, looked slowly round her, and walked thoughtfully into the house.

It was some time before she threw off the impression of those few seconds; but when she did she was very much ashamed of herself, and in consequence, very angry.

'Idiot!' she said crossly to herself. 'Been overdoing it, I suppose, like all the other fools. . . . I'll go to bed early to-night.'

It was Saturday, and the workmen went early, so Annis was able to make her rounds in the bleak light of a winter afternoon. She looked very carefully through each room, and then locked it. She wasn't going to have the trouble she'd had last night over that imaginary child. She'd make sure, this time, that every room was empty before she locked it – the big bedrooms with the old four-poster beds, the little slip of a room with the spinet, the pale old drawing-room that still smelt faintly of pot-pourri – she examined and locked them all.

What a lot of rooms there were! – and each with some trace of occupation. Why, in this one there was an old-fashioned work-table with needlework still in it, the needle rusted into the stuff! How could people ever have done that endless, jigsaw patchwork, she wondered as she took it up. But how pretty some of the stuffs had been! Those scraps of blue silk with tiny bright posies – charming. She touched the silk lovingly. Then she stood, her fingers stiffening, listening intently.

The spinet. Quite unmistakably she heard the faltering, tinkling notes of unpractised fingers – scales, broken by false notes, or ending abruptly. In the pauses there came little sobbing sounds. . . . Annis stood motionless in the gathering dusk, her cold fingers clutching the old, old patchwork, listening to the faint, jingling notes of the spinet in the locked room next door. . . .

The sound changed. There was a jangle, as if the performer had dropped weary hands from the keys; and then, very slowly and uncertainly, there came an air, picked out with one faltering hand – the old, plaintive, haunting tune, 'Will ye no' come back again?'

It, too, broke off half finished, and again there came the sound of hopeless, muffled weeping. . . .

Or was it rain? Rain was pattering softly on the windows. There was no other sound except the beating of her own heart. . . .

Annis thrust the old patchwork back into the table. She ran, stumbling, to the door, locked it behind her, fled back to her own little sanctum, and locked herself in. She stood leaning against the door, breathing hard and unevenly, her hand still on the latch.

What was that – that pale figure facing her, with wide, staring dark eyes in a white face. . . . Only herself, reflected in the panel mirror opposite the door.

For a moment it had looked different. . . . But it was only herself, Annis Breck, white-faced, with staring, frightened eyes. . . .

She crossed to the hearth and sat down. She was trembling violently. She sat looking with some surprise at her own shaking hands. The rain beat softly on the windows, melancholy and persistent. The grey, rain-swept garden sighed in the evening wind.

Annis rose, rather unsteadily, and went across to put up the shutters. The garden was so sad, grey in the rain. The sundial glimmered in the dusk. Was that –? No, only a mist-wreath curving about the dial – it has dissolved already. But oh, how dreary, how melancholy! She put up the old white shutters hurriedly, and at an incredibly early hour sought the comfort and security of her bed.

Annis awoke with a start. What was it that had awakened her? Surely she had heard something. Was it a voice? A name, echoing in her ears? Or was it the spinet – 'Will ye no' come back again?' 'Time flieth, hope dieth.' Yes – and a girl – a girl dressed in a frock of blue silk, patterned with tiny gay posies – a girl at the spinet – a girl by the sundial, tracing the sad old motto, while slow tears dropped on the stone slab – a girl called Annis. . . .

The girl had her own face. She understood it now. And his name – ah, how had she ever forgotten it? – his name had been Richard. . . .

E. M. Delafield

❧

SOPHY MASON COMES BACK

'HAVE you ever, actually, seen a ghost?'

It wasn't, as it is so often, a flippant enquiry. One was serious, on that particular subject, with Fenwick. He was keen on psychical research, although it was understood that he took a line of his own, and neither accepted, nor promulgated, arbitrary interpretations of any kind.

He answered cautiously:

'I've seen what the French call a *revenant*, undoubtedly.'

'Was it frightening?' asked one of the women, timidly.

Fenwick shook his head.

'I wasn't frightened,' he admitted. 'Not by the ghost or spirit – whichever you like to call it. Still less have I been so by so-called "haunted rooms" with mysterious noises and unexplained openings of doors, and so on. But once, in the house where I saw the *revenant* – I was frightened.'

'Do you mean – wasn't it the ghost that frightened you, then?'

'No,' said Fenwick, and his serious, clever face wore a look of gravity and horror.

We asked if he would tell us about it.

'I'll try, but I may have to tell the story backwards. You see, when I came into it, everything was over – far away in the forgotten past, not just on the other side of the war, but right back in the late eighties. You know – horse-drawn carriages, and oil-lamps, and the women wearing bonnets, and long, tight skirts, all bunched up at the back. . . . In a French provincial town, naturally, things were as much behind the times then, as they are now. (This happened in France by the way – did I tell you?) It isn't necessary to give you the name of the town. It was somewhere in the *midi*, where the Latins are – very Latin indeed.

'Well, there was a house – call it Les Moineaux. One of those tall, narrow French houses, white, with blue shutters, and a straight avenue of trees leading to the front steps, and a formal arrangement of standard rose-bushes on either side of the blue front-door.

'It was quite a little house, you understand – not a *château*. It had once belonged to a very small community of contemplative monks – they'd made the garden and the avenue, I believe. When the monks became so few in number that they were absorbed into another Order, the house stayed empty for a bit. Then it was bought by a wine-merchant, as a gift for his wife, who used it as a country villa for herself and her children every summer. This family lived at – well, in a town about twenty kilometres away. They could either drive out to Les Moineaux, or come by the *diligence*, that stopped in the village about half a mile away from the house. Most of the year, the house remained empty, and no one seems to have thought that a caretaker was necessary. Either the peasants round there were very honest, or there was nothing worth taking in the house. Probably the thrifty madame of the wine-merchant brought down whatever they required for their summer visits, and took it all away again when they left. There were big cupboards in the house, too – built into the wall – and she could have locked anything away in those, and taken the key.

'The family consisted of monsieur and madame, three or four children, and an English girl, whom they all called "mees," who was supposed to look after the children, and make herself generally useful.

'Her name was Sophy Mason; she was about twenty when she came to them, and is said to have been very pretty.

'One imagines that she was kept fully occupied. Madame would certainly have seen to it that she earned her small salary, and her keep; and, as is customary in the French middle-class, each member of the household was prepared to do any job that needed doing, without reference to "my work" or "your work." Sophy Mason, however, was principally engaged with the children. Quite often, in the spring and early summer, she was sent down with them to Les Moineaux for a few days' country air, while monsieur and madame remained with the business. They must have been go-ahead people, by the way, far in advance of their time, for "the mees" seems to have been allowed to keep the children out of doors, quite in accordance with the English traditions, and entirely contrary to the usual French fashion of that date and that class.

'The peasants, working in the fields, used to see the English girl, with the children, running races up and down the avenue, or going out into the woods to pick wild strawberries. Sophy Mason could speak French quite well, but she was naturally expected to talk English with the children, and, except for a word or two with the people at the farm, from which milk and butter and eggs were supplied to Les Moineaux, there was in point of fact no one for her to talk to, when monsieur and madame were not there.

'Until Alcide Lamotte came on the scene.

'All I can tell you about him is that he was the son of a farmer – a big, red-headed fellow, of an unusual type, and certainly possessing brains, and a compelling personality.

When he and Sophy Mason met first, he was in the middle of his compulsory three years' military service, and home at the farm *en permission*.

'One can imagine it – this English girl, who'd been in France over a year without, probably, exchanging a word with anyone but her employers, their children, and perhaps an occasional old *curé* coming in for a game of cards in the evening – left to her own devices in the more or less isolated villa – and late spring, or early summer, in the vine country. What happened was, of course, inevitable. No one knows when or how their first meetings took place, but passions move quickly in that country. By the time monsieur and madame did appear, to inaugurate their usual summer *vie de campagne*, the neighbouring peasantry were perfectly aware that *le roux*, as they called him, was Sophy Mason's lover.

'Whether they betrayed her to her employers or not, one doesn't know. Personally, I imagine they didn't. In that country, and to that race, neither love nor passion appears as a crime, even when marital infidelity is involved, and in this case it was merely a question, for the girl, of deceiving her mistress, and Lamotte – also a free agent – was one of themselves. Almost certainly, madame found out for herself what was going on.

'There must have been a crisis – *une scène de première classe*. Perhaps madame kept watch – was peeping through the crack of a door just left ajar, when "the mees" stole in – noiselessly, as she hoped – from a moonlight tryst in the woods where the wild strawberries had grown a few weeks earlier.

'"What! Depraved, deceitful creature, to whom I have entrusted my innocent children! . . ."

'The French are nothing if not dramatic.

'I suspect that madame enjoyed herself, making the most of the scene, whilst poor Sophy Mason, ashamed and guilty, was frightened out of her wits. Perhaps she saw herself sent back to the Bloomsbury boarding-house of the aunt who was her only living relation, disgraced, and with no hope of ever getting another situation.

'As a matter of fact, madame forgave her. Sophy Mason was useful, the children liked her, she was very cheap – and perhaps, at the bottom of her heart, madame was not very seriously shocked at Sophy's lapse from virtue.

'At all events, after extracting a promise that she would never meet Alcide again, except for one farewell interview, madame told Sophy that she might stay.

'The farewell interview, I believe, took place in madame's presence – she'd stipulated for that. Something – one can only guess that it may have been some pathetic, scarcely disguised hint from the girl – indicated to madame's acute perceptions that if Alcide had proposed marriage Sophy would have been ready, and more than ready, to have him. But Alcide, of course, did nothing of the kind. He accepted his dismissal with a sulky acquiescence that he would certainly not have shown if Sophy Mason – more astute and less passionate – had not so readily yielded to him every privilege that he chose to demand.

'There was an unpleasant and humiliating moral to be drawn from his attitude, and it may safely be presumed that madame did not hesitate to draw it, probably in forcible language. Sophy Mason, poor child, was left to her tears and her disgrace.

'But those pangs of shame and disappointment were to give place to a much more real cause for distress.

'In the autumn, Sophy Mason discovered that she was going to have a baby.

'It is, given her youth and probable upbringing, quite likely that the possibility of such a thing had never presented itself to her. But that madame had apparently not foreseen such a contingency is much more difficult to explain.

'It may, of course, be that she attributed more sophistication to the girl than poor Sophy Mason actually possessed, and that she asked a leading question or two that Sophy answered without really understanding.

'One thing is certain: that Sophy Mason did not dare to tell her employer of her condition. She had recourse, instead, to a far more hopeless alternative.

'She appealed to her lover.

'At first, by letter. She must have written several times, if one draws the obvious inference from the only reply of his that was seen by anyone but the recipient. It is an illiterate, ugly scrawl, evidently written in haste, telling her not to write again, and concluding with a perfunctory endearment. It was probably those few, meaningless last words that gave the unfortunate Sophy courage for her final imprudence. It seems fairly certain that she was, actually, imaginatively in love with Alcide, whereas with him, of course, the attraction had been purely sensual, and had not outlasted physical gratification. In fact, I have no doubt, personally, that the usual reaction had set in, and that the mere thought of her was probably as repellent to him as it had once been alluring. Sophy, however, could not, or would not, believe that everything was over, and that she was to be left to confront disgrace and disaster alone. Under the pretext of meeting some imaginary English friends, she obtained leave of absence from madame, and went down to Les Moineaux on a day in late October.

'Either she had made an assignation beforehand with Alcide, or, as seems a good deal more probable, she had learnt that he was home again, on the termination of his military service, and counted on taking him by surprise. She must have made up her mind that if only she could see him again, and plead with him, he would, in the phrase of the time, "make an honest woman of her."

'The interview between them took place. What actually occurred can only be a matter of conjecture.

'That it took place at Les Moineaux is a proved fact, and I – who have seen the house – can visualise the setting of it. They would have gone into the living-room, where only the bare minimum of furniture had been left, but from the ceiling of which dangled, magnificently, a huge candelabra of pale pink glass, swinging from gilt chains. The gaudy beauty, and tinkling light music of the candelabra have always seemed to me to add that touch of incongruity that sharpens horror to the unbearable pitch. Beneath its huddled glitter, Sophy Mason must have wept, and trembled, and pleaded, in an increasing terror and despair.

'Lamotte was a southerner, a coarse, brutal fellow, with the strong animal passions of his years, and of his race. Whether what followed then was a premeditated crime, or a sudden impulse born of violent rage and exasperation, will never be known. With apparently no other weapon than his own powerful hands, Alcide Lamotte, probably by strangulation, murdered Sophy Mason.

'When the girl failed to return home, her employer, apparently, neglected to make any serious enquiry into her fate. Madame, who had perhaps suspected her condition, affected to believe that the girl had run away to England, in spite of the fact that her few belongings had been left behind.

'Possibly they were afraid of a scandalous discovery, but more probably, with the thriftiness of their class, they dreaded being put to expense that would, they well knew, never be made good by Sophy's only relation, in distant England.

'The aunt, in point of fact, behaved quite as callously as the French couple, and with even less excuse. Sophy Mason was the illegitimate child of her dead sister, and when, eventually, she learnt of the girl's disappearance, she is said to have taken up the attitude of asserting: "Like mother, like daughter," and declaring that Sophy had certainly gone off with a lover, like her mother before her.

'Conveniently for madame, if she wanted to convince herself and other people of the truth of that theory, Alcide Lamotte suddenly made off, towards the end of the same month, and was reported to have gone to America. Of course, said madame, they had gone together. Sophy had been traced as far as Les Moineaux without the slightest difficulty, and where she had spent the intervening weeks, between that visit and her alleged departure to America with her lover, no one seems to have enquired.

'The only clue to the mystery was that last letter, written by Lamotte, that Sophy had left behind her, and that was found and read by her employers, and in the fact that when, in the summer following her disappearance, the wine merchant and his family went as usual to Les Moineaux, they found unmistakable evidence that the house had been entered by a back door, of which the lock had been picked.

'Nothing else seemed to have been tampered with, or disturbed in any way, and the whole affair was allowed to drop in a fashion that, in this country and at this date, appeared almost incredible.'

Fenwick paused for a while, before resuming.

'My own connection with the story, came more than forty years later. All that I have told you, was conjectured, or found out many years after it happened. I warned you that I might have to tell the story backwards.

'The wine-merchant of Sophy Mason's story was the connecting link. During the war, I came to know his son – a middle-aged man, once the youngest of the children in the avenue of Les Moineaux.

'I need not trouble you with any account of how we had come to know one another well – it was no stranger than the story of many other relationships established during the war-years.

'We met from time to time, long after the Armistice had taken place, and in the summer of 1925, when I was in France, Amédé, my friend, invited me to pay him a visit, in the *midi*. He had quite recently married a girl many years younger than himself, and in accordance with French provincial custom, was living with her in the house of his parents – or rather, of his father, for the mother had been dead for some time.

'The wine-merchant himself was over seventy – a hale and hearty old man, well looked after by an unmarried daughter, and still in perfect possession of all his faculties.

'Whilst I was with them, an observation on my part as to the facility with which all the family spoke English, occasioned an allusion to Sophy Mason – the English "mees" of forty-five years earlier.

'The old man, I remember, referred to her mysterious disappearance, but without giving any great importance to the story, and attaching to it, as a mere matter of course, the old explanation of the flight to America with Lamotte.

'In that light one would doubtless have accepted, and then forgotten it, but for two things. One of these was something that was told me by Amédé, and the other the coincidence – if you like to call it so – that forms the whole point of the story. Amédé's revelation, that was purposely not made in the presence of his father, was as follows:

'About fifteen years previously, shortly before the death of his mother, she had made over to him Les Moineaux, the little country villa that had belonged to her.

'Amédé was fond of the place, although he had no intention of ever living there, and long after the other brothers and sisters had scattered, when their mother was dead, and their father no longer cared to move from home, he continued to visit it periodically.

'It was, therefore, to Amédé that some peasants one day came, with an account of a gruesome discovery made in the wood near the house – that very wood where Sophy Mason used to take the children of her employers to pick wild strawberries.

'In a deep ditch, under the leaf-mould of more than a quarter of a century, had been uncovered, by the merest chance, the skeleton of a woman. Curiously enough – or perhaps not so curiously, taking into account the mentality of the uneducated – the older generation of villagers viewed the discovery with more horror than surprise, and displayed little hesitation in identifying the protagonists of the tragedy. The story of Sophy Mason's disappearance had survived the years, and Amédé's enquiries brought to light a singular piece of evidence.

'A woman was found who remembered, many years before, a revelation made by a servant-girl on her deathbed. This girl – a disreputable creature – had declared that on a certain October afternoon she had been in the wood, with her lover, and that, from their place of concealment, they had seen something terrible – a gigantic youth, with red hair, half-carrying and half-dragging the body of a woman, whom he had subsequently flung into the ditch, and covered with earth and stones from the hedge.

'Neither the girl, nor the man with her – who was, incidentally, married to another woman – had dared reveal their horrible discovery, fearing lest their own guilty connection should thereby come to light. This girl, in point of fact, died shortly afterwards, and her story, told on her deathbed, had actually been disbelieved at the time by her hearers, because the narrator was known to have the worst possible reputation and to be a notorious liar.

'The woman to whom it was told swore that she had never actually repeated the story, but that rumours of it had long been rife and that the wood, in consequence, had been shunned for years.

'The name of Alcide Lamotte, curiously enough, seems not to have been directly mentioned. The Lamotte family were the chief land-owners in the place, and were accounted rich and powerful, and *le roux* himself had never been heard of since his disappearance to America.

'My friend Amédé, hearing the strange echo of the past, doubted greatly what course to adopt. It is easy to say that an Englishman, in his place, would have doubted not at all. The Englishman has a natural respect for the law that is certainly lacking in the Latin. Remember, too, that it had all happened so long ago – that the only known witness of the crime was a woman of ill-repute, long since dead – that poor Sophy Mason – if it was indeed she who had been done to death – had no one to demand a tardy investigation into her fate – and finally, that by the law of France, a man cannot be brought to trial for a crime that is only discovered after the lapse of a certain number of years. Amédé, contenting himself with giving the minimum of the information in his possession – all of which, it must be taken into account, depended upon hearsay – to the authorities, saw to the burial of the unidentified remains.

'There the story would have ended, so far as such things can ever be said to end, but for the coincidence of which I spoke.

'Fifteen years later, whilst I was on my visit to Amédé's old father, and just after Amédé had told me of this strange and hidden postscript to the mystery of Sophy Mason, after an absence of close on forty-one years, Alcide Lamotte returned to the neighbourhood.

'And here, at last, is where such first-hand knowledge as I possess, begins. It is here that I, so to speak, come into the story.

'For I met Alcide Lamotte.

'He had come back – but, of course, he was not the wild, half-civilised lout – *le roux* – of a lifetime ago. He was, actually a naturalised American, and a rich and successful man.

'There was no one left to recognise him, and, indeed, he now even called himself by a different name, and was Al Mott, from Pittsburg.

'You understand – I am not telling you a detective story, and trying to make a mystery. It *was* Alcide Lamotte, but when he came to the old wine-merchant's house, Amédé and his father didn't know it. That is to say, the old man certainly didn't – and Mr Mott called, the first time, with a business introduction, in regard to a sale of land. Amédé, when he found that, in spite of his Americanised appearance, the visitor was not only a Frenchman, but also conversant with the immediate neighbourhood, connected him with the district of Les Moineaux, but only in that vague, unemphatic fashion that just fails to put two and two together until, or unless, something happens that produces a sudden, blinding flash of illumination.

'There was certainly nothing about Al Mott, from Pittsburg, to recall the half-legendary figure of *le roux*.

'He was a big corpulent man, perfectly bald, with a hard, heavy face, and great pouches below his eyes.

'His manners were not polished, but noisy and genial.

'Neither Amédé nor his father took a fancy to him, but they were *hommes d'affaires*, there was a transaction to be concluded, and one evening he was asked to supper, and came.

'It was an evening in late October.

'The old man, of course, was there, and Amédé and his young, newly married wife. The aunt – the one that lived with them – had gone away for a few days.

'The evening, from the beginning, did not go very well. Madame Amédé, the bride, was an inexperienced hostess, and the guest was not of a type to put her at her ease.

'Amédé, who was madly in love with his wife, kept on watching her.

'For my part, I felt an extraordinary uneasiness. You all know, I believe, what is usually meant by the word "psychic" applied to an individual, and you know, too, that it has often been applied to me. I can only tell you that, in the course of that evening, I knew, beyond any possibility of doubt, certain things not conveyed to me through the normal channels of the senses. I knew that the other guest, the man sitting opposite to me, had, somehow, some intimate connection with tragedy and violence, and I knew, too, that he was evil. At the same time I was aware, more and more as the evening went on, that something which I can only describe as a wave, or vibration, of misery, was in the atmosphere and steadily increasing in intensity.

'Afterwards, Madame Amédé told me that she had felt the same thing.

'She and her husband, it is worth remembering, were in the keyed-up, highly wrought state of people still in the midst of an overwhelming emotional experience. That is equal to saying that they were far more susceptible than usual to atmospheric influence.

'The old wine-merchant, Amédé's father, was the only person, beside Mott himself, unaware of tension.

'He made a casual allusion to the countryside, and then to Les Moineaux – but not referring to it directly by name.

'Mott replied, and the conversation went on.

'But in that instant, without any conscious process of reasoning or induction, the connection was made in my mind.

'I knew him for Alcide Lamotte, and I saw that Amédé did too. My eyes, and those of Amédé met, for one terrible second, the knowledge flashing from one to the other.

'Both of us, I know, became utterly silent from that moment. Alcide, of course, went on talking. He was very talkative, and under the influence of wine, was becoming loud and boastful. He began to tell the old man, who was alone in paying attention to him, about his early struggles in America, and then his increasing successes there.

'He spoke in French, of course, the characteristic, twanging drawl of the *midi*, and with, actually, a queer kind of American intonation, noticeable every now and then. I can remember very vividly the effect of relentlessness that his loud tones, going on and on, made in the small room.

'He was still talking when – the thing happened.

'You can, of course, call it what you like. An apparition – a collective hallucination – or the result produced by certain psychological conditions that are perhaps not to be found once in a hundred years – but that were present that night.

'The feeling of unease that had been with me all the evening was intensified, and then – it suddenly left me altogether, as though some expected calamity had taken place, and had proved more endurable than the suspense of awaiting it. In its place, I experienced only a feeling of profound sadness and compassion.

'I *knew*, with complete certainty, that some emanation of extreme unhappiness was surrounding us. Then Madame Amédé, who sat next to me, spoke, just above her breath:

'"*What is it?*"

'There were two sounds in the room. . . . One was the excited, confident voice of Alcide, now in the midst of his triumphant story, the other was a succession of sobs and stifled, despairing wails.

'The second sound came from the corner, exactly facing the place where Lamotte was sitting.

'There was a door there, and it opened slowly. Framed in the doorway, I saw her – a young girl, in the dress of the late eighties, with a scared, pitiful face, sobbing and wringing her hands.

'That was my *revenant* – Sophy Mason come back.

'I told you, when I began the story, that the – the apparition had not frightened me. That was true.

'Perhaps it was because I knew the story of the poor betrayed girl, perhaps because I have, as you know, been interested for years in psychic manifestations of all kinds. To me, it seemed apparent, even at that moment, that the emotional vibrations of the past, sent out by an anguished spirit all those years ago, had become perceptible to us because we were momentarily attuned to receive them.

'In my own case, the attunement was so complete that, for an instant or two, I could actually catch a glimpse of the very form from which those emotional disturbances had proceeded.

'Amédé and his wife – both of them, as I said before, in an unusually receptive condition – heard what I did. Amédé, however, saw nothing – only an indistinct blur, as he afterwards described it. His wife saw the outlines of a girl's figure. . . .

'It all happened you understand, within a few minutes. First, that sound of bitter crying, and then the apparition, and my own realisation that the Amédés were terror-struck. The old man, Amédé's father, had turned abruptly in his chair with a curious, strained look upon his face – uneasy, rather than frightened. He told us afterwards that he had seen and heard nothing, but had been suddenly conscious of tension in the room, and that then the expression on his son's face had frightened him. But he admitted, too, that sweat had broken out upon his forehead, although it was not hot in the room.'

'But Alcide Lamotte?'

'Alcide Lamotte,' said the narrator slowly, 'went on talking loudly – without pause, without a tremor. He perceived nothing until Madame Amédé, with a groan, fell back on her chair in a dead faint. That of course, broke up the evening abruptly. . . .

'You remember, what I told you at the beginning? It wasn't the poor little *revenant* that frightened me – but I *was* afraid, that evening. I was afraid, with the worst terror that I have ever known, of that man who had lived a crowded lifetime away from the passionate, evil episode of his youth – who had changed his very identity, and had left the past so far behind him that no echo from it could reach him. Whatever the link had been once, between him and Sophy Mason – and who can doubt that, with her, it had survived death itself – to him, it now all meant nothing – had perished beneath the weight of the years.

'It was indeed that which frightened me – not the gentle, anguished spirit of Sophy Mason – but the eyes that saw nothing, the ears that heard nothing, the loud, confident voice that, whilst those of us who had never known her were yet tremblingly aware of her, talked on – of success, and of money, and of life in Pittsburg.'

Hester Gorst

THE DOLL'S HOUSE

WHAT makes it so much more terrible is that there was no reason why it should happen. It was as if the earth had opened suddenly and showed a chasm down which we must fall. There should be something to warn us when life has prepared one of its chasms. We are so pitifully helpless against it. *I* was so happy. Fate had given me all I wanted. Friendship, enough money to give my various hobbies free play, and good health. Could a man want more?

My work was congenial, if not invigorating. I made models for the British Museum, and occasionally lectured on mummies there. The fact of my pottering about the Museum so much gave me my taste for antiques. I adored old china, old glass, and had quite a nice little collection of Ming and Ling. But what I was keenest on was old furniture, and in this I did not follow the usual bent. I limited myself to the miniature chests and mirrors that were the advertisement pieces before our catalogues were invented. I loved tiny things and, whereas there is many a doubtful antique in the grown-up furniture, one rarely finds it worth a dealer's while to copy these liliputian relics. My specimens were nearly always in good condition, too. All this may sound very childish, but we are all childish in some way or another. So I frequented auction sales and searched among musty old shops to find what I wanted. And then one day I found the horrible thing.

It stood in the dark corner of an auction room – a perfect model of a house. Not the regulation doll's house whose whole front opens at once, but a house only accessible through windows and doors. It was an architect's model in wood made in Georgian style, and painted to resemble red brick. One could imagine it being sent to some gentleman with a letter appending to say: 'Here is a house I can build you. It will cost such and such an amount.' It stood about two feet from the ground – a house of three storeys. The porch had two minute wooden pillars which must have been stone in the real thing. The tiny windows, facing every side, had real sashes to push up and down, and through them one could see dark rooms, mysterious and empty, with doors standing ajar. I turned to my catalogue for information. 'Lot 153,' I read, 'a well-preserved and exceptionally perfect model of a house in late eighteenth century.' So it was not an advertisement piece, but a genuine copy of a

Georgian mansion. I felt a thrill of excitement. How exquisite it would look among my other treasures. Eagerly I sought out my special dealer. He looked contempt when I told him the amount I was prepared to go to. 'Why you will get it for half that, sir. There ain't much demand for that sort of stuff not nowadays. It takes up too much room, and it's not the sort of thing a kid could make use of, seeing it's all shut-up.' It was as he had said. Lot 153 was secured at a ridiculously low figure, and was delivered at my flat next day.

I neglected a model of a particular species of toad I was making for the Museum in order to unpack and install my precious acquisition. Jack Harland came in while I was littering the place with paper.

'Hello!' he said. 'What have you got here?'

I proudly exhibited it. 'A genuine Georgian manor. There are not many private collections that can boast of that. Even the South Kensington hasn't got a whole one.'

Jack was peering through the little windows. 'Very choice,' he remarked. 'I wish I could get into the damned thing. I can see the stairs, and there is a jolly big fire-place in the hall. Whoever did it took acres of trouble. It's funny there's no way of getting inside.'

'No way in the world, except through the door,' I said, laughing. 'You should eat a bit of mushroom like Alice in Wonderland and get the right size.'

'I wonder why they had it made?' my friend went on. He was more romantic than I was. 'It seems odd to have a model of a house when they could have had a sketch. Perhaps it's got some dark history, a haunted room or something.'

'Then they would have had to make a model ghost to fit,' said I. 'I'll listen-in to-night for some bone rattling.'

Jack and I went to college together – in fact, we had known each other all our lives. He lectured on history at various schools, and read obscure works on alchemy in his spare time.

This search for knowledge brought him to the British Museum, and he would sometimes follow me round with the crowd on the mummy lecture days, driving me nearly mad by asking idiotic questions. He had heaps of friends, and yet he never seemed to forget he had known me longer than anyone. For all his good looks and cleverness, which gave him far more opportunities than I had, he always said he enjoyed being with me best. He was the dearest pal a man ever had. To-night we were dining together. I parted from Jack about two o'clock, saying I must get back to my modelling. In fact the particular species of toad was rather on my mind, and I felt I must finish it. Jack suggested returning with me, but I knew it would mean no work if he did. The reptile had to be sent to the moulders in the morning.

'Well, don't forget to watch out for the ghost in the new house,' he said. And I left him.

I worked till about three o'clock and then went to bed. I was dead beat, for the toad, being more or less extinct, had to be reconstructed from diagrams, which is exhausting work. However, directly I got to sleep I began to dream. A most extraordinary dream. I had shrunk in an astonishing degree, and was standing inside the door of the miniature house, looking towards the large dark hall which Jack and I had seen through the windows. Up to now the dream was natural enough, but then it changed. I was not the mild young man of my waking hours. Rather I had become somebody intensely alive, someone with a special and a very horrible purpose. I did not know who I was or what the purpose was, but I know I went creeping up the deserted staircase very swiftly and quietly so as not to let someone in an upper room hear me. The dusty banisters were icy cold. I must be some old Georgian rake, I thought, coming home very drunk and very late. In a moment I shall be making excuses to my wife. But why should the house be empty of furniture and carpets? However softly I trod, the bare boards would creak a little. I gained the first floor and crept through a dark, empty bedroom. Then I became aware that always a little ahead was the noise as if someone else was creeping, creeping away from me. As I shut one door another one would open. If I had been my ordinary self I would have been blue with funk, but now I only wanted to find that someone who was hidden. My whole being was centred upon this search. The part of my mind which still remained myself dared not ask what was to be done with the quarry when it was found. I knew I was becoming merged in this other one, and that his sinister intent would soon be wholly mine.

When I woke it was broad daylight, and my charwoman was knocking at the door. All day the atmosphere generated by that dream remained with me. I felt nervy and strung up. Jack had an engagement for dinner, but he said he would drop in later in the evening. When I told him about my experience he looked worried.

'If I were you I should scrap the thing. There must be something nasty about it.'

'But it's such a find,' I remonstrated. 'I've never seen anything like it before.'

'I daresay,' he said. 'But you never know what's happened in these cases. I mean to say, what sort of influences are about.'

Jack studied alchemy and was much more a believer in the supernatural than I was.

'Why should anyone want to make a thing like that?' he went on. 'You can't get into it – It's no use for a kid to play with.'

'Well, what do you think it was for?' I asked.

'How can I tell? but it may be a sort of memento. Some blighter who had done somebody in, wanting to have something to remember it by. So he had a model of the house made. Pervert, you know. Gave him great pleasure to kill whoever it was.'

'But why should I dream about it?'

'How can I tell? Probably his beastly influence going on. I'd scrap the thing if I were you.'

But I could not find it in my heart to do that. It looked so marvellous among my collection of miniatures of bureaux and dainty mirrors and tiny chairs. Whoever it was who designed it was an artist.

That night I was in the house again. This time, however, I was evidently one with the searcher. Was growing in cunning and quickness of step. I knew what I was trying to do would have taken only one night to fulfil, yet night after night in the following week I searched without attaining my desire. My hate of the terrified thing which I pursued grew in strength. I was irritated by its continually thwarting me. No shred of pity balked my ardour. Once I nearly had it in my grasp. It was a slight form, easily handled and easy to kill, but in the darkness it again evaded me. I could hear its terrified gasping on the stairs above.

'What's the good of going on like this?' said Jack. 'I should put the whole thing on the fire.'

'I wish I could tell what happens at night,' I said to him. 'Whether I get out of bed, or whether anything happens in the darned building. With all this excitement going on inside, it seems impossible for it to be as placid as it looks now.'

Jack rubbed his chin. 'I don't see the use of knowing.'

I was surprised that my friend, who was keen on occult subjects as a rule, should sheer off this case, which should have been full of interest for him.

'Well,' I said, 'let's try one night. You sleep here and find out if I do get up. Whatever happens I promise to bung the whole thing in the fire in the morning, although it seems a criminal thing to do.'

'Alright, we'll do that if it will cure you. It will be a funny thing if we both have the same dream and go chivvying each other round.'

'I don't see how that can happen. The person who I am hunting is a woman. There couldn't be two of us looking for her.'

Jack looked at me in a disgusted way. 'I think the whole thing is vile. And you talk about it quite coolly. I hope that swine, whoever he was, swung for it.'

'But he hasn't done anything yet,' I argued. 'He may never have done anything. She probably escaped and lived to a good old age. It's his sensations of hate have registered themselves in the house, but there doesn't need to have been any tragedy.'

I fixed up a bed for Jack in my sitting-room , and we dined fairly early so as to be in bed in good time. Jack arrived with a heavy stick so as to smash the house if it kicked up a row.

'Or I'll shove it through the windows if I see you creeping about, and stop your little games.'

We were both rather excited because I had just got a book published on the anatomy of prehistoric beasts, which had been given quite a good review. Jack had got engaged to be married. This last event was a big blow to me, but Jack was so evidently in the Seventh Heaven, I tried to be happy with him.

'Diana hates anything creepy,' he confided. 'That's mostly been the reason why I snubbed you up about the house. I was interested, but Diana didn't like it. She said it was frightfully dangerous to get in contact with malevolent intelligences, they can have influences over your mind.'

'I'm sure your fiancée would weep if she knew the doom which waits for the exquisite thing in the morning.' I stroked the Georgian house tenderly. 'How can you be so heartless as to keep me to my promise?' The only way of persuading Jack to stay the night had been to say I would burn the model next day.

'You won't have any peace till you do. I believe it's possessed by a devil.'

I looked at my treasure as it stood among my collection, with the tenderness of a mother towards a naughty child. The afternoon sun shone in through the quaint windows, lighting up the dark hall and staircase. I inserted my finger under the sash and lifted one of them.

'That will give it an airing for to-night.'

'Don't be a fool,' said my pal.

In spite of the arrangement to go to bed early, we sat up talking till late. There was bitterness to me in the thought that soon I should not have Jack all to myself any more. I was very glad for his sake, but I knew there would be a great void in my life when I could not see him so much. Love makes us very humble, but I wondered whether he would ever find anyone willing to give everything up for him, or to share the last penny as I was.

We went to bed at last. Jack said he would sleep in the sitting-room. I had offered him my bed.

'It's better not to disturb the usual routine,' he said, laughing. 'I don't know what you expect to happen, but you had better stay put in your old place.' After that he rolled himself up on the sofa and went to sleep. 'I'm sure to wake if you come in here.'

I could not sleep for a long time. No fear of the dream kept me awake, for I looked upon it now only as a curious but quite innocuous phenomenon. It was as if my ego objected to being ousted by that seeker, whoever he was, and strove to keep him out as long as possible. I lay awake thinking of Jack and his engagement. I tried to school myself to the thought that very soon he would not be able to pop in and out of the flat any old time, and I could almost hate Diana and him for making me suffer. I knew I would miss him terribly. Then, when I thought of his happy face and all the eager plans he had been making, I felt a cad for putting my future loneliness before his joy. I began to wonder what that stranger that haunted my house must have felt. Was his return some expression of his subconscious self which had come to the surface with his death? Can jealousy, love, hatred, be hidden from their possessor, yet leave their atmosphere in some place where they have lived? That thing which we call the subconscious self which hoards up impressions and sensations without our knowing could surely control our actions. The seeker in my house had murder in his heart, but he may not have committed murder. Or had a murder been committed, and was it the resistance of my ego that retarded its re-enactment? I knew suddenly that I was deadly tired of these nocturnal rambles. That I wanted to sleep naturally and dream of normal things. I wondered whether the action of destroying the house would accomplish this. If it did, where would that influence that haunted it go? Up the chimney, I supposed. A strong desire to get up and burn the thing there and then possessed me. It would be interesting to see whether my dream changed. I wanted it to be changed. Cautiously I tiptoed to the sitting-room door. If Jack was awake I would tell him my plan, ask him to help me. The fire was out and the room was in complete darkness. 'Jack,' I whispered. He was asleep. We had arranged his bed so that it barred the way to the table where the little house stood. Jack was a light sleeper and would wake if he felt me fumbling across his bed. What would be the good of waking him for nothing? I would wait till to-morrow to burn the thing and have one more dream in it to-night. I returned to bed and was soon asleep.

The hall was dark and sinister. Once more I was creeping through it. Slinking silently up the stairs. Half-way up the first flight a thing happened which was different from the other dreams. The moon shone through a window in the landing. As luck would have it I was in shadow, but I saw clearly a crouching figure leaning over the top of the banisters. I knew it was waiting for me, quaking at the fall of my step. Ready to fly. Ever through its long martyrdom it had waited, watching for me at the top of the stairs, and I had never known it was there. I wondered whether there was perhaps another staircase in the house that I could negotiate. Why not creep up behind this trembling thing and so end the pursuit? Still deep in the shadow I retraced my steps downstairs and trod softly across the dark hall. Under the stairs was a door which I had never been through. It was open. No need to make any noise. Now, very quietly, I felt along the wall. I was in a passage a few feet long. My foot struck against something. It was the first step of a staircase. Very cautiously I stole up it. My hands groped for each step above me. They were steeper stairs than the flight in the hall, stairs used by the servants, no doubt. Then another door at the top. I pushed it open. It was covered with baize, so that the servants on their way up or downstairs should not disturb their employers. The moonlight flooded the passage behind the door. It must have been a dreadful thing to see that door open so silently in the empty house. The figure still crouched at the top of the stairs. I leapt forward swiftly and struck at its head with a sure aim. There came a long wailing cry. A white face which I seemed to know very well stared up at me. Then the face was gone, and I saw a twisted heap upon the ground. I woke.

I was standing in the sitting-room. My back turned to the table where the house stood. I was conscious that I had been standing there some time, and had been beating at something with what I held in my hand. I looked at my hand and saw it clasped Jack's stick. I was holding it by the point and the heavy handle hung-downwards – broken. Jack was lying on the floor in his pyjamas. His eyes were shut and there was a trickle of blood coming from his mouth. 'Jack,' I whispered sickly. But there was no answer. He was dead.

Edith Olivier

THE NIGHT NURSE'S STORY

NURSE Webber had tea alone in the Nurses' Sitting-room. The maid who
let her in had told her that every nurse on the staff was out, and she guessed
that it wouldn't be long before they had another call. 'But they don't stop
long,' she had added cheerily. 'The patients keeps on dying, and the nurses
keeps on coming in. It's nice to have plenty of change though, isn't it?' Nurse
Webber agreed that it was, but when the maid had left her, she felt strange,
sitting there alone after the friendly crowd in the Hospital. She suddenly felt
that 'private nursing' would be a cold and inhuman exchange for the stirring
atmosphere of the great wards. She ate her bread and butter, and she
wondered how soon Matron would have finished the 'interview' which was
occupying her, and whether there would be time before she appeared, to
make a piece of toast on her knife by the fire. She thought not, and she was
thankful that she had so decided when the door opened almost immediately,
and Matron entered to find the new nurse 'making herself at home' very
demurely at the tea-table, instead of kneeling on the hearthrug scorching both
her own face and a piece of bread.

Matron greeted Nurse Webber in her quick kind manner. She gave the
impression that her friendly welcome was the prelude to some important
piece of work which must be done at once. Nurse Webber felt that she had
been plainly told that no time was ever wasted in the West Square Nursing
Home. This did not perturb her. She had not forgotten her Hospital training.

'I am afraid I shall have to send you out to-night, Nurse,' Matron said
brightly. 'I have no one else coming in till to-morrow night, and we have an
urgent case. An old lady has had a fall and injured herself internally. Can you
be ready by six? I must order a car to take you out, as there's no station
anywhere near the place.'

'I shan't take more than half an hour to unpack and repack,' replied Nurse
Webber; 'and then I shall be ready to start as soon as you wish, Matron.'

'I'll show you your room,' said Matron, 'and leave you to get on with it.'
And she wasted no more words, but left the new Nurse alone in the room with
her trunk and her suitcase.

At six o'clock Nurse Webber was leaving the Home by the door through which she had entered it for the first time little more than an hour earlier. Matron came to see her off.

'Do you know Eustace Grange?' she asked the chauffeur.

'More or less,' replied the man. 'It's an out-of-the-way place, and I'm not sure of the road after Chisholme. But I can ask.'

'If there's anyone out to ask on a night like this,' said Matron.

'Well, we'll get there somehow. I've never been done yet, and I don't think I'm likely to be this time.'

The dark wet November night had evidently had no effect on the spirits of the stout little chauffeur; and he gaily drove Nurse Webber away to her first private case.

They were certainly going to an 'out-of-the-way' place, for they quickly left the main road and began climbing about the Moor, taking farm roads which zigzagged over steep hills, and turning ever into narrower lanes where no signposts marked the way. And Matron had been right. They met no one to ask.

Nurse Webber felt nervous. The journey was taking longer than she expected. If the chauffeur, as he had said, did not know the way, by what instinct did he continue to turn and twist about this unknown piece of country?

She tapped on the glass.

'Do you think we are going right, driver?'

'I think so, Sister. It's somewhere out here, I know. We had to turn left in Chisholme, and keep on turning left; and that's what we've been doing ever since.'

'Let us stop and ask at the next house.'

'Right you are, Sister, though there aren't many about, are there? I don't seem to think we shall find one till we get to the one we want. But I'll certainly ask if I get a chance.'

And a chance came at the next corner.

A man was standing there, evidently on the look-out for a car, for as they approached he stepped into the road and signalled for them to stop.

'Is that the Nurse?' he called.

'That's right,' said the chauffeur.

'I knew you'd never find the house, and I've been out here for more than an hour waiting for you.'

'I'm glad you came,' said Nurse Webber, in her sedate voice. 'I was beginning to think we must have got off the road.'

'I wonder you didn't,' said their guide, as he got up beside the driver.

'How is the patient?' asked Nurse Webber, trying to assume what she thought must be the manner of an experienced private nurse.

'I fear my poor dear old aunt will hardly get through the night. In fact I don't know what we may find when we get in. I've been out nearly an hour and a half, and it's touch and go all the time.'

They drove for another quarter of an hour, going downhill all the way. The road was damp and slimy, and the car skidded about most unpleasantly. Nurse Webber was immensely relieved when they came up against the bulk of a house, looming close upon them out of the darkness, which it made still darker. The car stopped with a last skid.

'Waynfleet is my name,' said the man, as he opened the door for the nurse to get out.

The name seemed in some way familiar, but she could not remember where she had heard it.

'And my patient is Miss Parker, isn't she?'

'Near enough. My poor aunt is not likely to answer to that or to any other name till the books are opened on the Day of Judgment,' said Mr Waynfleet.

Nurse Webber's half-conscious dislike of him became definite. He spoke cynically, as if he were alluding to an absurd fairy story.

She said nothing, but went past him into the house.

The hall was elaborately and expensively furnished. Taste alone had been economized in its decoration. The pile of the carpets was incredibly thick. It muffled all sound. Nurse Webber made her way through a crowd of gilt tables, Buol cabinets, velvet-covered armchairs, and marble pedestals on which stood statues of stout women carved by German artists. Every available space was filled by a crowd of *objets d'art*. The drawers of the big bureau were open, and a half-filled trunk stood beside it, while another, locked and corded, stood near the door.

No servant came to meet them.

'I should like to go to my room to change my things,' said Nurse Webber; 'and then I can go at once to the patient.'

'I'll send a housemaid to you,' said Mr Waynfleet; but without waiting to do so, he himself took the nurse upstairs and showed her her room.

'My aunt is next door,' he said, 'but they will come and show you round.'

Nurse quickly changed into uniform, but the maid was at the door even before she was ready.

'I will show you where everything is,' she said; and with the manner of one who wishes to curtail conversation, she swiftly led the way out of the room. She showed Nurse Webber the kitchen, the bathroom, the lavatory, the housemaid's cupboard, and a small dressing-room in which a fire was burning.

'You'll have to heat up everything you want in here,' she said. 'We haven't any gas, so there's not a ring. Most nurses grumble about it.'

'Have you had other nurses?' asked Nurse Webber. 'I thought Miss Parker had only just had her accident.'

'She's chronic,' replied the other, in a tone of some irony. 'One accident leads to another.'

Nurse Webber disliked her too.

'May I go to my patient's room?' she asked.

'Surely. I'll put your supper in the dressing-room. What do you want for the night?'

Nurse Webber shortly ran through the list of her requirements – teapot and kettle, bread and butter, and a couple of eggs; she was shown the store of invalid foods; and she learnt where extra china was kept. It was a new experience to be alone in a strange house to shift for herself through the dark hours, and she felt rather helpless as she went at last into the sick-room.

Miss Parker seemed to be asleep. It was difficult to guess her age, for though the hand which lay upon the counterpane was not the hand of a young woman, yet her skin was singularly smooth, and there was no sign of grey in her thick black hair. Nurse Webber thought that the immovable face had that look of calm youth which she had seen on the faces of the dead, and yet Miss Parker did not in other ways look as if she were near death. Her face bore no signs of suffering or weakness.

The housemaid led the nurse across the room, and the two women stood side by side looking down upon Miss Parker's motionless figure. The invalid lay quite still, and seemed unconscious of their scrutiny.

Then the housemaid spoke, and her voice sounded curiously clear and thin. She bent over the apparently sleeping woman, saying, 'Nurse is here, madam.'

Miss Parker, who was lying on her back, turned her face to one side with surprising vigour. The gesture was pettish. It suggested dismissal, but she said nothing.

'Good evening, Miss Parker,' said Nurse. 'I hope you are feeling a little better.'

'I don't want any of Mr Waynfleet's nurses,' said Miss Parker. 'You can tell him so.'

'I hope you will let me try to make you a little more comfortable,' said Nurse Webber, wishing that her patient would open her eyes.

'Between you, you will, in the end, I don't doubt. But not yet. Not yet. I have still some fight left in me. I'm not so old and stupid as he says.'

Nurse looked interrogatively towards the housemaid, to find the woman had silently left the room. The space where she had stood seemed now to possess an emptiness which was positive, not negative, as though she had left behind her the invisible mould of the form which had vanished.

Nurse could get no further response from the figure in the bed, and she now busied herself with preparations for the night. On a table by the window were some bottles of medicines and some charts. She found that Miss Parker's temperature varied very little, and that it had been taken at six o'clock that evening. By whom, she wondered. It had then been a few points above normal. Apparently the patient was washed at nine o'clock each night, and then had a cup of ovaltine. Nurse Webber prepared the little meal, and she went to the bed. The invalid still ignored her, and the house was as silent as the grave. Nurse Webber felt very lonely.

Miss Parker made no protest while her face was sponged, but it was impossible to rouse her sufficiently to induce her to swallow any of the ovaltine; and Nurse Webber's first entry on the chart was the record of a failure to give the patient her usual meal.

As she turned from the chart, she saw that she had inadvertently dated the entry 'November 6, 1932', instead of '1933'. She wondered at finding she had made such a slip so late in the year, and then she observed that all the previous records showed the same error. Her predecessor had opened the page with the wrong date, and had so continued throughout. The persistence of such a mistake struck Nurse Webber as significant. There had then been no one in the house sufficiently interested to observe it.

In fact she began to feel that there was no one in the house at all. At any rate, all of its occupants must have gone early to bed, for though it was not yet ten o'clock, the only light which still burned seemed to be her own. When she carried the rejected cup of ovaltine to the sink, the light she turned on in the passage threw a faint sickly beam down the long narrow darkness, and as she watched its course she realized that if everyone had indeed gone to bed they had told her nothing of the geography of the house. What was behind the various closed doors? Where could she find anyone if her patient did indeed die in the night? Mr Waynfleet seemed to have thought this might happen, though she herself saw no signs of immediate collapse.

Nurse Webber went down the corridor, tapping one by one on each of the doors. There was no reply. The people in this house slept early and soundly.

She decided that there was nothing to do but to settle down too for the night, so she drew her chair close beside a shaded lamp which stood on a table some way from the bed, and she pulled out the patchwork quilt she was making. Obviously there was nothing to be done for the patient, and the long, lonely night stretched before her in a vista of uninterrupted needlework.

Now and again she crossed the room to look at Miss Parker, and to take her pulse. There was never any change, and the patient continued to appear quite unaware of her presence.

As she returned from one of these journeys, her eye chanced to fall upon the label on one of the medicine bottles. It was addressed to 'Miss Power'. Nurse Webber looked at it again. Surely 'Parker' had been the name told her by Matron, and she knew it was the name she herself had used to Mr Waynfleet. She tried to recall his reply, and she seemed to remember that he had not quite accepted the name of Parker. What did it mean? It frightened her to think that she actually was not certain who was the patient she was watching in that horrible silent house.

And then she remembered the Letter of Recommendation she had brought from the Home, and which so far she had had no opportunity of presenting. It was still in her case. She fetched it from her room, and read it under the lamp. It was clearly addressed to:

'Miss Parker, Eustace Grange, Chisholme.'

Miss Parker. Miss Power. There could be no further question. The unresponsive figure lying in that bed was not the patient she had been sent to nurse, and, if not, the house to which Mr Waynfleet had led her could not be Eustace Grange? Where then was she now?

Waynfleet? Waynfleet? Yes, the name was certainly familiar. She began to feel as if she had always known it, and yet she could not say what associations it brought. Something sinister. Perhaps it was a detective story.

Feverishly she picked up her patchwork, and tried to concentrate on it.

When she next looked up, she saw a figure standing by the bed, gazing intently down upon the face of the sick woman. Mr Waynfleet had come so silently into the room that she had heard no sound, and he had crossed it without crossing her line of vision. She certainly had not heard him open the door, but now as she glanced toward it she saw that he had not only opened it, but had shut it behind him. He ignored her presence, and after a moment he bent down to listen to his aunt's breathing. Nurse Webber watched him curiously. His back was towards her, and she could not see what it was that he was doing with something he held in his hand. The complete silence of his movements was uncanny. She felt as if she were watching a scene from outside a closed window.

And then, all of a sudden, she realized that he had quickly, and very deftly, thrown over his aunt's face a large white handkerchief, which he now drew tightly over it. There was a gurgling sound, and the fumes of chloroform filled the room. Nurse Webber sprang to her feet, and leapt across the room. She seized Mr Waynfleet's arm, and wrestled with him with all her force. She found herself thrown on to the bed, with the old woman under her, the smell of chloroform overpowering her too. But now her hands were on the handkerchief, and she tried with all her might to tear it from her patient's face. She would not see her murdered before her eyes. She fought wildly, and then Mr Waynfleet's hand closed round her throat. It seemed as cold as ice. She tried to bite it, but it eluded her, though it still gripped her throat like cold steel, and still the fumes of chloroform swayed about her like tipsy waves.

They vanquished her at last.

She opened her eyes, feeling broken and sick. The room was in utter darkness. Mr Waynfleet had evidently turned out the light as he went away, and he must have been gone for some time, for the fire, which had previously been burning brightly, had now burnt out. She tried to remember where she was, and what had been happening. As her memory returned, she realized that she must be in the room with a murdered woman. But had Miss Power actually been murdered? It might yet be possible to save her life. Nurse Webber crawled to the door and turned on the switch. There was no result. The light must be off at the main. Then her blood ran cold. She was petrified with terror. Still she knew she must do what she could. She was a nurse, and there lay her patient. Even in this darkness, she must get that handkerchief off. She began to feel her way round the room, groping for the bed. Her hand traversed a blank wall. Where was the bed? Where indeed was any of the furniture? Everything was gone. The bed, her chair, the table on which she had left her needlework, the sofa, the . . . The room was empty . . . empty. . . . All she could be sure of was that she herself had woken in darkness with a murdered woman somewhere nearby. And the murderer? How near was he? How soon would those cold hands grab her again? She was afraid to scream, for no one but Mr Waynfleet would hear her, and her cries would tell him that he had not killed her as yet.

Then she began to think that she could not still be in the room in which she had lost consciousness. Of course he hadn't removed the furniture, but had carried her out, and had thrown her into an empty room. Could she escape? She wondered if she dared try to get out of this silent room, to find herself face to face with the unknown terrors of the house outside. She stood very still, listening. A clock was ticking beside her. She recognized the sound. It had exasperated her earlier in the night as she had sat at work. But where could that clock be now for the table on which it had stood had gone like everything else? It was that insistent little sound which decided her. She must get away at all costs, for surely it meant that Mr Waynfleet himself was nearby, with the clock ticking in his hand. Till now she had moved slowly and cautiously, feeling carefully for indications of her whereabouts, but now she almost ran round the room, groping for the door. She expected to find it locked, but it wasn't. Instead, it opened so easily that she almost fell backwards as it came towards her. Quickly she shut it behind her, and was in the corridor. Here it seemed rather less dark, for the outline of the staircase window glimmered before her as a guide. It showed her where the stairs must be. She paused, listening. Again she heard the clock still ticking a few feet away. It had come out of the room too. Frantic, she ran to the staircase, seized the banister, and hurled herself somehow down the stairs. As she passed the window, a cold draught caught her face, and even in the darkness she was able to see that one of the panes was broken. How could this have happened, for certainly there had been no window broken when she arrived? As she fled down the stairs, her mouth was suddenly full of dusty cobwebs. They clung to her face, sticky, and exuding a musty smell. She ran through them and reached the house-door. It was locked. She felt for the bolts and found them at once, but they were not drawn. It was not they which kept her prisoner. The door was locked on the outside. Then once more she heard the clock ticking at her side. This time she screamed, hurling herself wildly against the door. There was no response, and her shrieks went echoing up the stairs and added to her panic. Then she clung to the handle of the door and waited.

Hours seemed to pass, and now there was indeed in the air, a faint promise of dawn. It was hardly twilight as yet, but it was possible to make out that the hall too was completely empty. The door and the staircase stood where they had stood last night, but everything else had vanished. All that rich ornate furniture was gone. As she wildly peered into the lessening darkness, Nurse Webber began to think that she must have come down by some other staircase, to find in the back part of the house, a hall exactly like the one by which she had entered.

Her straining eyes came to the staircase window, and she remembered that fresh stream of cold air which had entered by it. It could not be far from the ground.

'I'll break every pane rather than stay here another moment,' she said to herself, and she staggered upstairs and felt for the bolt. She found it. It moved, and she flung the window open as far as it would go. Wisps of night mist blew into the house as she leapt on to the sill, and let herself down by her hands. It was quite a short drop, and she was free.

She stood up and listened. The clock had ceased to tick. She had left it behind her in the house.

She turned and tried to run, but it was heavy going, for the earth was damp and sodden, and dead wet weeds clung to her legs and bedraggled her skirt. The garden was full of last year's neglected growths. Several times she tripped and all but fell, but she found the gate at last, and got into the lane outside. Then she ran with all the speed she could summon from her quaking limbs.

A man was whistling, and she heard steps coming to meet her. There was an early morning sound of pots and pans.

Nurse Webber was face to face with the dairyman on his way to milk the cows. She threw herself upon him.

'Help me. Take me away,' she gasped. 'Where am I? Oh, get me away from that awful house.'

She stood there in her nurse's uniform, her cap awry, and her teeth chattering.

'Why, Sister, what's happened?' said the man. 'Where have you come from? How did you get here at this hour of day?'

'I had a case. I went there last night. That house at the end of the lane. Oh, it was awful. I can't go back there. Tell me how I can get away.'

'At the end of the lane? What house?'

'The stone house behind the laurel hedge.'

'What, Laurel Lodge? You can't mean that. That house is empty. Has been empty since this time last year when Mr Waynfleet murdered his poor old aunt and her nurse. But he swung for it . . .'

Then the dairyman saw that Nurse Webber had fainted in a heap at his feet.

Winifred Holtby

THE VOICE OF GOD

ONCE upon a time an inventor made an instrument by which he could listen in to the past.

Being a shy man, he kept himself to himself and told nobody of his invention; but he found his new instrument more entertaining than his wireless set, and would sit for hours when his day's work was over listening in to Queen Victoria scolding Prince Albert on a wet Sunday at Balmoral, or to Mr Gladstone saying whatever he did say in 1868.

One evening it happened that a young reporter, hurrying home from the offices of the *Daily Standard*, was knocked off his motor-cycle just outside the inventor's window. Though shy, the inventor was a kind man, and without waiting to switch off his instrument, he ran down, invited the young man in, bound his cut hands and offered him a brandy and soda.

'And how do you feel now?' he asked.

The reporter listened to the instrument, which was just then recording an interview between King Charles II and a lady friend, and he said, 'Thank you very much. I feel all right, but I think I must have had a bang on the head. I keep on hearing things.'

'What sort of things?' asked the inventor.

'Well, the sort of things you don't generally hear over the wireless,' said the reporter, and he blushed.

'But that isn't exactly the wireless,' said the inventor, and he explained exactly what it was.

'But that's impossible!' cried the reporter. 'It's more than impossible. It's a scoop.' And he ran straight off and telephoned to his newspaper.

The news editor was a cautious man, but he did not want to miss anything, so he sent down a senior reporter who arrived in time to hear Mrs Disraeli telling Mr Disraeli what she really thought about Queen Victoria. Then he rang up the editor, who sent down the dramatic critic, the chief sporting correspondent, three photographers, and the editor of the financial page. The inventor let them listen in to Nelson bombarding the neutral fleets at Copenhagen, but they said that this was not really British, and could not be genuine. So the inventor then tuned in to the last directors' meeting of the

Daily Standard, and they heard the proprietor telling the editor just what he thought about the advertising figures; and after that they were convinced. They acquired the exclusive news rights on the instrument.

The invention as news was an immense success.

The proprietor of the *Daily Standard* himself wrote a column explaining that the instrument was a striking example of British enterprise, revealing to the world the whole story of our empire's greatness. The Federation of British Industries issued a statement that it would be good for trade and help to restore confidence in our empire market. The scientists said that it would enlarge the field of human knowledge, and the editor of the *Daily Standard* ordered a symposium, on 'If I could listen in to the past, which scene would I choose, and why?' commissioning contributions from a movie star, a tennis champion, an Atlantic flyer, an ex-Secretary of State for India, and a Dean.

The Dean sat down to write his contribution explaining that of all past scenes he would prefer to hear that in which John Knox denounced Mary Queen of Scots. But when he came to say why he preferred this, he found no good reason except the true one, which was that he disliked all women and thought well of their detractors; but this he felt, was not good journalism.

So he sat biting his pen and contemplating a row of his own published works on Plotinus, Origen, the British Empire and other sacred subjects; and as he looked at them, he had a great idea.

It was a really great idea. The longer he thought of it the more he was impressed, as a priest by its solemnity, as a patriot by its power, and as a journalist by its superb news value.

He tore up his tribute to John Knox and scribbled along a sheet of foolscap half a dozen headlines: 'When Christ returns to London'; 'The Scientist's Miracle'; 'The Voice of God.'

Then he began to write his greatest article.

Three mornings later, the readers of the *Daily Standard* left their breakfast bacon while they repeated to each other, 'Can it be true? Surely it can't be true.'

For the Dean had written that the invention was an instrument chosen by God Himself to enable man to hear the Voice of Christ. For two thousand years the world had tried to reconstruct from the inspired fragments of the Gospels the full record of His tremendous doctrine. The time had come to confess that Man had failed. Much was incomprehensible; much uncertain. Scholars had argued, armies fought and martyrs died because of Man's imperfect understanding. But now science, the handmaid, not the enemy, of religion, had wrought the miracle, and men might listen again, not only to the true Sermon on the Mount, not only to the evidence of the Resurrection, but to all those lessons which had never been recorded, to the full story of that

Perfect Life. Everything would at last be known beyond all doubt. To the housewife in Clapham, to the savage in an African forest, to the Chinese mandarin and the professional footballer, the Voice of God Himself at last would speak.

The first time, wrote the Dean, that the Voice of God was heard on earth, the world was unprepared for it. Society was ignorant, the listeners few, the words went unrecorded. The Jews, a servile and uncultured people, proved quite unworthy of their splendid privilege, and responded only by the Crucifixion. But when God spoke a second time, the world would be awaiting him. He would speak, not to a group of Jewish fishermen, but to a Great Imperial People. The whole resources of science and learning would lie at His disposal. Now would be no indifference, no misunderstanding. Suddenly, as in the twinkling of an eye, society would be changed. Worldliness and materialism, selfishness and sloth would flee away for ever and we should be summoned to a new crusade for righteousness and true religion.

The effect of the Dean's article was instantaneous. Letters poured in to the inventor. Questions were asked in the House of Commons. Special services were held in every church and chapel. A Baptist minister, stripping off his clothes, girded himself in sackcloth and ran down Piccadilly crying, 'The Kingdom of Heaven is at hand. Repent ye in the name of the Lord.' He tried also to live on locusts and wild honey, but locusts he could not obtain, though Messrs. Fortnum & Mason offered to procure some if given reasonable notice. The Vatican held aloof, but a rich manufacturer of wireless instruments offered to finance the construction of a new, larger instrument capable of listening in to Palestine two thousand years ago, and wrote off the cost as Advertisement Expenses.

The offer was accepted, the instrument made, the public informed, and a date fixed for the first hearing.

But then the trouble began.

The *Daily Standard*, having acquired exclusive news rights on the instrument, demanded that nothing should be published save through its columns or under its auspices. The Archbishop of Canterbury considered that the invention should be placed in a consecrated building, Westminster Abbey or St Paul's Cathedral. The Nonconformists all protested that the established Church had no monopoly of the Word of God, and the Rationalist Press declared that, this being a matter for scientific evidence, the sooner it was secularised the better. *The Times* brought out a special supplement on 'Church, Empire, and the Voice of God,' but took no line that could offend the Government.

At length a compromise was reached.

The instrument remained where it had been constructed, in the inventor's house, but the Archbishop was permitted to bless the freehold property, which had just been acquired by the *Daily Standard*. The instrument was connected by wireless with loud speakers placed in every public hall and church and chapel in the kingdom. The King and Queen consented to attend a First Reception Service at Westminister Abbey, and the *Daily Standard* organised a vast meeting in Wembley Stadium at which its readers could hear the first words spoken by the Voice.

The day arrived; the crowds collected; the massed bands of Guards in the arena played the Hallelujah Chorus. Led by a world-famed contralto, the audience joined in the community singing of 'Abide with Me.' The massed bands played a great fanfare on their trumpets. The people rose and stood in breathless silence, broken only by sobs of emotion and scattered sighs as strong men fainted from the strain.

Then, out of the silence, amplified on the hundreds of loud speakers, the Voice spoke.

The people listened.

At first they listened with awe, then with bewilderment, then with increasing agitation.

For the Voice spoke in a completely unknown language. They could not understand a word of it.

The editor of the *Daily Standard*, listening in at his private office, flung off his earphones in a rage. 'Something's gone wrong. The instrument's out of order. Ring through to the inventor at once and tell him that if he lets us down, I'll have him hounded out of England. It's a farce. It's a flop. With the King listening too, it's an insult to His Majesty. Why, a hitch here will send our circulation down by thirty-five per cent.'

But the inventor declared that nothing was wrong with his instrument. The voices that they heard were indeed voices, speaking in Galilee two thousand years ago, and speaking, as might be expected, in Aramaic dialect. 'Did you expect,' asked the inventor with surprise, 'that they would speak in English?'

As that was, indeed, just what the editor had expected, there really was nothing to say. Being a man of initiative, however, he had a microphone connected with the loud speakers at the stadium, and informed the waiting public that they had heard at last the authentic Voice of God. This fact alone should be sufficient to transform the whole course of their lives; but in order to make the Voice not only heard but comprehensible, English translations would be published henceforward serially in the *Daily Standard*, until the great sacred record was complete.

Having done that, the editor sent immediately to all the known scholars of oriental languages, offering immense salaries to those who could translate archaic Aramaic. Contrary to his expectation, the response was not immediate. In spite of its circulation of three million, very few scholars read the *Daily Standard*, and when approached personally, one declared that he was correcting examination papers for the Final Honours School of Oriental Languages at Oxford and did not wish to be disturbed. Another was excavating remains in Mesopotamia, a third was due to sail for a summer school in San Francisco, a fourth stated that he had never read the *Daily Standard*, never wished to read the *Daily Standard*, and refused to co-operate in any enterprise organised by the *Daily Standard*, even if it were the Second Coming itself. The Catholic theologians were forbidden to handle the matter unless the instrument was transferred to the control of His Holiness at Rome. A learned Unitarian quarrelled with an Anglo-Catholic about the translation of the first sentence that he heard, and the inventor himself, worn out by wrangling and discussion, succumbed to influenza and died after three days' distressing illness.

His death was followed by extraordinary demonstrations. The *Daily Standard*, relying upon the work of quite inferior scholars, published each morning a translated extract which it declared to be an authentic interpretation of the Voice. The scholars, bound to secrecy, shut up in their office, listened day and night to sounds recorded by the instrument. But as in Palestine two thousand years before, the Voice did not immediately reveal itself to listeners as the Voice of God, so now in Fleet Street it was difficult to distinguish the speaker of the words received. Sometimes the sentences recorded seemed quite trivial, sometimes incomprehensible, and sometimes it was quite impossible to translate their unfamiliar dialect. Yet each day the scholars had to be ready with their copy in order that the *Daily Standard* might not disappoint its readers. On one occasion, after the publication of a profoundly eloquent address on righteousness, the scholars discovered that it had been spoken by a Pharisee who was later condemned by the Voice for his hypocrisy. The scholars immediately informed the editor, asking him to publish an acknowledgement of error, but he replied by his usual formula, 'The *Daily Standard* never makes mistakes,' and told them to get on with their own business.

For the sales of the *Daily Standard* were now quite unprecedented. No scoop in the whole history of journalism equalled this. From every country in the world came orders from millions of excited readers, longing for the new revelation which should change their lives.

It is true that not every one was happy. The *Evening Express*, the *Daily Standard*'s rival, published allegations that the scholars were tampering with the instrument. Students of oriental languages disagreed about the translations and filled the correspondence columns with amendments. Spain and Italy, as the leading Catholic countries, complained that England, being heretical, had no right to the instrument. The Soviet Government, bitterly distressed, declared that all the misery of Tsarist Russia, the lice, poverty, ignorance of infant hygiene, primitive sanitation and illiterate peasantry, had been due to this perverse and degrading interest in God, and that the attempt to revive it must be checked at once. The American House of Representatives, as a precautionary measure, rushed through a new tariff law, a bigger navy programme and an amendment to the constitution. The International Federation of Trades Unions summoned a special conference at Amsterdam to discuss the bearing upon trade-union regulations of the command that those who have been bidden to walk one mile should walk two, and the Stock Exchange suffered an unheard-of slump under the threat of the command to sell all that one had and give it to the poor. The National Savings Association made a plea for suppression of those passages relating to 'take no thought for the morrow,' and the World League for Sexual Reform temporarily suspended its activities. The Zionists petitioned the League of Nations for special police protection, and the British Israelites, after a meeting in the Albert Hall, led a demonstration against the Jews, Freemasons, Theosophists and revolutionaries that ended in a free fight outside the offices of the *Daily Standard*.

The editor of the *Daily Standard* responded heroically. He summoned his readers to a new crusade for the Protection of the Holy Voice, adopting the slogan, 'Keep it Pure and Keep it British.' The Churches, restive and uncertain, failed to check the rising excitement of the people. A bishop was assassinated. An Oxford professor, who dared to question the authenticity of one published message, ate powdered glass in his boiled celery, and died in dreadful pain, while an attempt was made by armed and desperate robbers to kidnap the instrument from the inventor's house.

Finally, martial law was proclaimed in London. Day after day fresh bloodshed was reported. The Council of the League of Nations held three special sessions, and two British Cabinet Ministers died of apoplexy.

None watched these events with greater concern and foreboding than the Dean. He felt himself responsible. Had he been content to praise the admirable Knox, had his journalistic acumen not overcome his original impulse, bloodshed and misery, violence and scandal would have been avoided. Men would still have ignored the Gospels, or each would have continued to interpret them according to his own immediate interest. Economic advantage would have counter-balanced ethical law, and all would have been as well as ever.

The Dean repented his vainglorious action.

He witnessed the increase of mob violence. He read of the order to the New Crusaders to shoot at sight any one seen to tamper with the instrument. He made up his mind what he must do.

One night he went by himself to the inventor's house. As the most distinguished ecclesiastical journalist on the *Daily Standard* he was at once admitted, the guards believing that he had come to write up a new descriptive article on 'The Instrument in Action.' He went into the room where the invention stood, and knelt before its complex mechanism.

'O God,' he prayed, 'Your Voice has spoken to us through the centuries, and always those who had ears to hear have heard, as You once warned us. We heard according each to our capacity. Two thousand years ago we were unprepared for Your high doctrine; to-day, O Lord, we are no more prepared. It is too much for us. Whenever You speak we fall into strange madness. In Your Name we have slain, tortured, burned and persecuted; we have waged wars; we have thrust men into prison. We have heard You call us to whatever work our own desire indicated. When left alone we can, through patience, learn a little kindliness, a little wisdom. The Churches have, through years of long endeavour, adapted Your teaching to the needs of men, remembering their difficulties and limitations. But when You speak, Your council of perfection destroys our humble work of compromise. It is too high for us. We cannot stand it. Depart from us, for we are sinful men, O Lord.'

Then, raising the hatchet which he had brought with him for this purpose, he smashed the instrument, crushing its fragile valves and tearing its slender wires till it was quite destroyed.

Hearing the noise, the guards rushed in and found him hurling the screws and nuts around the room. They fired, and he fell with a dozen bullets in his body.

The destruction of the instrument was final, for since the death of the inventor nobody knew how to make another. The excitement aroused by the possibility of obtaining full records of the Voice died down; indeed, many began to doubt whether it had been ever heard.

The sales of the *Daily Standard* suffered a temporary decline, but this was received by the editor with the philosophic resignation of the really great. 'Ah, well,' he said, 'if the Dean hadn't gone gaga I should have to have put a stop to it all myself some time, for though a stunt like that is excellent for circulation, the uncertainty and excitement is bad for trade and puts a check on advertising. After all, taking it by and large, advertisements matter more than circulation. What about starting a new crusade for really womanly women and pleasing the big drapers? I think that, on the whole, it should pay better.'

Cynthia Asquith

THE FOLLOWER

MRS Meade had been in the nursing home with heart trouble for three weeks, and her doctor, to whom she had confided the terror that obsessed her, had at last persuaded her to see the famous psycho-analyst, Dr Stone. She awaited his visit in great trepidation. It would not be easy to tell him of her fantastic experiences – 'hallucinations' her own doctor insisted on calling them.

A quarter of an hour before the time when she expected Dr Stone, there was a knock on the door.

'I'm a little early, Mrs Meade,' said a smooth voice from behind the screen, 'and I must ask you to forgive my fancy dress ball appearance. I was very careless with a spirit lamp and am obliged to wear this mask for some time.'

As he approached her bedside, Mrs Meade saw that her visitor's face was entirely concealed by a black mask with two small holes and a slit for his eyes and mouth.

'Now, Mrs Meade,' he said, seating himself in a chair close to the bed. 'I want you to tell me all about this mysterious trouble that is thought to be affecting your physical health. Please be perfectly frank with me. When did this – shall I say obsession? – begin, and what precisely is it?'

'Very well,' said Mrs Meade. 'I will try to tell you the whole story. It began years ago – when I first went to live in Regent's Park. One afternoon I was most disagreeably struck by the appearance of a man who was loafing about outside the Baker Street Tube Station. I can't tell you how strong and horrible an impression he made on me. I can only say that there was something utterly hateful about his face, with its bold, malignant eyes – lashless eyes that searched me like unshaded lights. He seemed to leer at me with a "so there you are!" sort of look, and the queer thing was that, though I had never to my knowledge seen him and – as I say – his appearance came to me as a shock, yet it was not a shock of complete surprise. In the violent distaste I felt for him there was a faint element of – shall I say sub-sub-conscious recognition? – as though he reminded me of something I had once dreamt or imagined. I don't know! I vaguely noticed that he had on a black slouch hat and no tie but a sort of greenish muffler round his neck. Otherwise his clothes were ordinary. Like the description of Mr Hyde, he gave an impression of deformity without any nameable malformation. His face was horrible – moistly pale like . . . like a toadstool! It's no good! I *can't* describe him! I can only repeat that the aversion he inspired in me was extraordinarily violent. I was conscious of his stare as I hurried past him and went down the steps, and it was a great relief to disappear into the lift and be whirled away in the Tube. Though I had plenty to do that day I could not quite dismiss him from my mind, and when I returned by Tube late in the evening it was a horrid shock to find him lurking at the top of the steps just as though he were waiting for me. This time there was no doubt that he definitely leered at me, and I thought he faintly shook his head. I hurried past him. Soon I had that horrid sense of being followed and glanced over my shoulder. Sure enough, there he was – just a few paces behind! and, as I turned, he slightly raised his hat. I almost ran home, and I cannot say what a relief it was to hear my front door slam behind me. Well, I saw him the next day and the next, and practically every day. The distaste with which I recognized him became a definite shudder, and each time his cynical glance seemed to grow bolder. Several times he followed me towards my house, but never right up to the door. I made tentative inquiries at the little shops round the Tube Station, but no one seemed to have noticed him. The dread of meeting him became an absolute obsession. Soon I gave up going in the Tube and would make long detours in order to avoid that upper part of Baker Street.'

'You minded him as much as all that, did you?' asked the doctor.

'Yes.'

'Go on, don't let me interrupt you.'

'For some time,' continued Mrs Meade, 'I did not see him and then there was a hideous incident. Returning from a walk in the park one day I saw quite a large crowd just outside the gate. A little girl had been run over. An ambulance man was carrying her lifeless form, and a policeman and some women were attending to the demented mother. Amongst all those shocked and pitying faces, suddenly I saw one vile, mocking face, its familiar features horribly distorted in a gloating grin. With positive glee he pointed at the dead child and then he turned *and leered at me.*

'After this horrible encounter you may be sure I shunned Upper Baker Street, but one day, just as I was starting to walk through the park, the heaviest rain I have ever seen came on, so I rushed towards the taxis at the top of the street and jumped into the first on the rank. A small boy opened the door for me, and, to avoid getting my hat wet, I gave him the address to give the driver. To my surprise we started off at a terrific pace. I looked up and saw a rather crouched back and a greenish muffler. The speed at which we were going was insane, and I banged on the window. The driver turned. Imagine my nightmare horror when I recognized that dreaded face, grinning at me through the glass. Heaven knows why we did not crash at once. Instead of watching the road, the creature on the box kept turning round to grin and gloat at me. We went faster and faster – whirling through the traffic. I was so sick with horror that, in spite of the appalling speed, I would at all costs have jumped out, but – struggle as I might – I could not turn the handle. I think I screamed and screamed and screamed. I was simply flung about the taxi. At last there was an appalling shock. . . .

'I can just remember the tinkle of breaking glass and the awful pain in my head – and then no more.

'When I came to, I was in a hospital where for hours I had been unconscious from concussion. I began to ask questions but could only learn that I had been picked up from the debris of a taxi which had crashed into some railings, and that it was a miracle I had not been killed. As for the driver, he had unaccountably disappeared before the police arrived and no one claimed to have seen him. The taxi bore no number and could not be identified. The police were completely baffled.

'After this I insisted on leaving the neighbourhood, and made my husband take a house in Chelsea.

'Nearly a year passed and I began to hope that I should never see him again; but I became ill, and after endless consultations a very serious operation was decided on. Everything was arranged and the evening before the date fixed I drove to the nursing home with the sinking sensation natural to the occasion. I rang the bell and the door was promptly opened by a short man. I almost screamed. In spite of the incongruous livery, *it was him*! There he stood – sickly pale as ever, and with that awful, evil, *intimate* smile.

'In a wild panic I sprang from the door and back into the taxi which was waiting with my luggage. Directly I got home I cancelled the operation. In spite of all the Harley Street opinions, I recovered. The operation was proved unnecessary.'

Mrs Meade paused in her narrative. The listener spoke.

'Then this being – whatever he is – on this occasion may be said to have done you a good turn?' he asked.

'Yes,' answered Mrs Meade, 'perhaps, but it didn't make me dread him any the less. Oh, the ghastly dreams I had! – that I had been given the anaesthetic and was thought to be unconscious, but I *wasn't*, and I saw the surgeon approach and, as he bent over me, his face was THE FACE!'

'Did you ever see him again, Mrs Meade?'

'I'm sorry,' answered the patient hastily, 'but the next time I saw him, I cannot tell you about. It is still too unbearable. There are things one cannot speak about. It was then I understood why he had pointed at that dead child and leered at me out of his vile little eyes. That was a long time ago, but the dread is always with me. You see, I still have one child left – I am always looking for what I fear. I can never leave my house without expecting to see him. What if one day I should meet him *in my house*?'

'I do not think you will ever do that, Mrs Meade.'

'I suppose you think the whole thing is an illusion, Doctor Stone? And in any case I don't suppose I have been able to give any impression of what – it – he – the creature is like,' sighed Mrs Meade.

The listener rose from his chair and leant over the invalid.

'Is – his – face – like this?' he asked, and, as he spoke, he whipped off his mask.

No one who heard it will ever forget Mrs Meade's scream.

Two nurses rushed into her room, followed by Doctor Stone, who, punctual to his appointment, had that moment arrived.

The dead woman lay on the bed.

There was no one else in the room.

F. M. Mayor

MISS DE MANNERING OF ASHAM

Oct. 9.

My dear Evelyn,

As you say you really are interested in this experience of mine, I am doing what you asked, and writing you an account of it. You can accept it as a token of friendship for, to tell you the truth, I had been trying to forget it, whatever it was. I hope in the end to bring myself to the belief that I never had it, but at present my remembrance is more vivid than I care for.

Yours affectionately

MARGARET LATIMER

You remember my friend, Kate Ware? She had been ill, and she asked me to stay in lodgings with her at an East Coast resort. 'It is simply Brixton-by-the-Sea, with a dash of Kensington,' Kate wrote, 'but I ought to go, because my aunt lives there, and likes to see me. So come, if you can bear it.'

'I think we might take a day off,' said Kate one morning, after we had been there a week. 'Too much front makes me think there really is no England but this. Let's have some sandwiches, and bicycle out as far away as we can.'

We came to a wayside inn, so quiet, so undisturbed, so cheerful in its quietness, that we felt at last we had found the soothing and rest we were in need of. Yes, I suppose our nerves were a little unstrung; at any rate, being high school mistresses, we knew what nerves were. But hitherto I have felt capable of controlling mine, only, as Hamlet says, I have bad dreams. And Kate is rather strange by nature; I do not think her nerves make her any stranger.

'Now,' said Kate, when we had finished our meal – she always settles everything – 'I propose we borrow the pony here, and have a drive. I don't like desecrating these solitary lanes, which have existed for generations and generations before bicycles, with anything more modern than Tommy.'

Kate generally wants to have a map, and know exactly where she is going, but to-day we agreed to take the first turn to the left, and see where it led to. It was a sleepy afternoon, and Tommy trotted so gently that we were all three dozing, before we had gone a mile or two. Then we came to what had been magnificent wrought iron gates with stone pillars on either side. The pillars were now ruined, and the wall beyond was falling down. Kate said, 'Let's go in.' I said it was private, but we did go in.

We came into an avenue of laurels, resembling the sepulchral shrubberies with which our fathers and our fathers' fathers loved to surround their residences, only those were generally more serpentine. It must have been there many years, and had had time to grow so high as to block out almost all the sky. It was very narrow, and the dankness, the closeness, the black ground that never gets dry, which have always oppressed me in such places, seemed almost intolerable here. I thought we should never get out to the small piece of white light we saw at the end of it. At the same time I dreaded what I expected to find there; one of those great, lugubrious, black mausoleums of a mansion, which so often are the complement of the shrubbery. But this avenue seemed to have been planted at haphazard, for it led only to another gate, and that opened on a neglected park. We saw before us an expanse of unfertile-looking grass, and then the horizon was completely hidden by ridges of very heavy greenish-black trees. There were other trees scattered about; they looked very old, and some had been struck by lightning. I felt sorry for their wounds; it seemed as if no one cared whether they lived or died.

There was a small church standing at the left-hand corner of the park, so small that it must have been a chapel for the private worship of the owners of the park; but we thought they could not have valued their church, for there was actually no path to it, nothing but grass, long, rank and damp.

I do not know when it was that I became so certain that I abhorred parks, but I remember it came over me very strongly all of a sudden. I was extremely anxious that Kate should not know what I felt. However, I said to her that grandeur was oppressive, and that after all I preferred small gardens.

'Yes,' said Kate, 'one might feel too much enclosed, if one lived in a park, as if one could never get out, and as if other things. . . .'

Here Kate stopped. I asked her to go on, and she said that was all she had to say. I don't know if you want to hear these minute details, but nearly everything I have to tell you is merely a succession of minute details. I remember looking up at the sky, because I wanted to keep my eyes away from the distant trees. I did not like to see them – it seems a very poor reason for a woman of thirty-eight – because they were so black. When I was six years old, I was afraid of black, and also, though I loved the country, I used to feel a sense of fear and isolation, if the sun was not shining, and I was alone in a large field; but then a child's mind is open to every terror, or rather it creates a terror out of everything. I thought I had as much forgotten that condition as if I had never known it. I should have supposed the weight of my many grown-up years would have defended me, but I assure you that I felt all at once that I was – what after all we are – as much at the mercy of the universe as an insect.

I remember when I looked up at the sky I observed that it had changed. As we were coming it had had the ordinary pale no-colour aspect, which it bears for quite half the days in the year. Some people grumble at it, but it is very English, and if you do not like it, or more than like it, relish it, you cannot really relish England. The sky had now that strange appearance to which days in the north are liable; I do not think they know anything about it in Italy or the south of France. It is a fancy of mine that the sudden strangeness and wildness one finds in our literature is due to these days; it is something to compensate us for them.

If I said the day was dying, you would think of beautiful sunsets, and certainly the day could not be dying, for it was only three o'clock in the afternoon, but it looked ill; and the grey of the atmosphere was not that silvery grey, which I think the sweetest of all the skies in the year, but an unwholesome grey, which made the trees look blacker still. I should have felt it a relief if only it had begun to rain, then there would have been a noise; it was so utterly silent.

Just as I was wondering where I should turn my eyes next, Tommy came to a sudden stop, and nearly jerked us out of the cart. 'Clever,' said Kate, 'you're letting Tommy stumble.'

But it was simply that Tommy would not go on. He was such a mild little pony too, anxious, as Kate said, to do everything one asked, before one asked him.

'Tommy's frightened,' said Kate. 'He's all trembling and sweating.'

Kate got out, and tried to soothe him, but for some time it was very little good.

'It's another snub for the men of science,' said Kate. 'Tommy sees an angel in the way. Animals are very odd you know. Haven't you noticed dogs scurrying past ghosts in the twilight? I am so glad we haven't got their faculties.'

Then Tommy all at once surprised us by going on as quietly as before.

We drove a little further, and we came to the hall. It was built 150 years before the mausoleum period, but it could not well have been drearier, though it must formerly have been a noble Jacobean mansion. It was not that it looked out of repair; a house can be very cheerful, in fact rather more cheerful, if it is shabby. And here there was a terrace with greenhouse plants in stucco vases placed at intervals, and also a clean-shaven lawn, so that man must have been there recently; nevertheless it seemed as if it had been abandoned for years.

I cannot tell you how relieved I was when a respectable young man in shirt sleeves made his appearance. It is Kate generally who talks to strangers, but the moment he was in sight I felt I must cling to him, as a protection. I felt Tommy and Kate no protection.

I apologized for trespassing in private grounds.

'No trespassing at all, miss, I'm sure.' He went on to say he wished it happened oftener, Colonel Winterton, the owner, being hardly ever there, only liking to keep the place up with servants, and 'if there wasn't a number of us to make it lively, one room being shut up and all,' he really did not know —

It did not seem right to encourage him on the subject of a shut-up room; we changed the conversation, and asked him about the church.

He said it was a very ancient church, and there was tombs and that, people came a wonderful way to see. Not that he cared much about them himself.

Kate, who is fond of sight-seeing, declared she would visit the church.

I would not go, though I should like to have seen the tombs. I said I must hold the pony. The young man said he was a groom, and would hold the pony for us. Then I said I was tired: Kate said she would go alone. She started.

'Don't go down there, miss,' said the groom, 'the grass is so wet. Round by the right it's better.'

His way looked the same as hers to me, but Kate followed his advice.

I talked to the groom while Kate was away, and I was glad to hear that he liked the pictures in reason, and that his father was a saddler, living in the High Street of some small town. This was cheerful and distracting to my thoughts, and I had managed to become so much interested that it was the young man who said, 'There's the lady coming back.'

'Well,' I said, 'what was the church like?'

'It was locked,' Kate answered, 'however, it was nice outside.'

'But Kate,' I said, 'how pale you are!'

'Of course I am,' said Kate. 'I always am.'

The young man hastened to ask if he should get Kate a glass of water.

'Oh dear no, thank you,' said Kate. 'But I think we might be going now. Is there any other road out? I don't want to drive exactly the same way back.'

There was, and we set off. As soon as we had said good-bye to the young man, Kate began: 'About Grace Martin; what do you think of her chances for the Certificate?' and we talked about the Certificate until we got back to the inn. As to that oppressed feeling, I could hardly imagine now what it was. It had passed, and the world seemed its usual dear, safe self, irritating and comfortable. It was clearing up, and the trees and hedges looked as they generally look at the end of August. They were dusty and a little shabby, showing here and there a red leaf, occasional bits of toadflax, and all those little yellow flowers whose names one forgets, but to which one turns tenderly in recollection, when seeing the beauty of foreign lands. My thoughts broke away from our conversation now and then to wonder what I could possibly have been afraid of.

They gave us tea at Tommy's home, and the innkeeper's wife was glad to have some conversation.

'Yes, the poor old Hall, it seems a pity the Colonel coming down so seldom. He only bought it seven years ago, and he seems tired of it already, and then only bringing gentlemen. Gentlemen spend more, but I always think there's more life with ladies. It's changed hands so often. Yes, there's a shut-up room. They say it was something about a housemaid many years ago and a baby, if you'll excuse my mentioning it, but I'm sure I couldn't say. If you listen to all the tales in a village like this, in a little place you know, one says one thing and one another. I come from Norwich myself.'

'The church looks rather dismal,' said Kate. 'The churchyard is so overgrown.'

'Yes, poor Mr Fuller, he's a nice gentleman, though he is so high. First when he come there was great goings on, services and antics. He says to me, "Tell me, Mrs Gage, is that why the people don't come?" "Oh," I says, "well, of course, I've been about, and seen life, so whether it's high or low, I just take no notice." I said that to put him off, poor gentleman, because it wasn't that. They won't come at all hardly after dark, particularly November; December it's better again; and for his communion service, what he sets his heart on so, we have such a small party, sometimes hardly more than two or three, and then he gets so downhearted. He seems to have lost all his spirit now.'

'But why is it better in December?'

'I'm sure I couldn't tell you, miss, but they always say those things is worse in November. I always heard my grandfather say that.'

I had rather expected that what I had forgotten in the day would come back at night, and about two, when I was reading *Framley Parsonage* with all possible resolution, I heard a knock at the door, and Kate came in.

'I saw your light,' said she. 'I can't sleep either. I think you felt uncomfortable in the park too, didn't you? Your face betrays you rather easily, you know. Going to the church, at least not going first of all, but as I got near the church, and the churchyard – ugh! However, I am *not* going to be conquered by a thought, and I mean to go there to-morrow. Still, I think, if you don't very much mind, I should like to sleep in here.'

I asked her to get into my bed.

'Thank you, I will,' said she. 'It's very good of you, Margaret, for I'm sure you loathe sharing somebody's bed as much as I do, but things being as they are —'

The next morning Kate was studying the guidebook at breakfast.

'Here we are,' said she. '"Asham Hall is a fine Jacobean mansion. The church, which is situated in the park, was originally the private chapel of the de Mannerings. Many members of the family are buried there, and their tombs are well worth a visit. The inscriptions in Norman French are of particular interest. The keys can be obtained from the sexton." Nothing about the shut-up room; I suppose we could hardly hope for it. We must see the tombs, don't you think so?'

Kate was one who very rarely showed her feelings, and I knew better than to refer to last night.

We bicycled to the Hall. It was a very sweet, bright windy morning, such a morning as would have pleased Wordsworth, I think, and may have brought forth many a poem from him.

'Now,' said Kate, 'when we get into the park, we'll walk our bicycles over the grass to the church.'

I began: then exactly the same feeling came over me as before, only this time there could be nothing in calm, beautiful nature to have produced it. The trees, though dark, did not look at all sinister, but stately and benignant, as they often do in late August, and early September. Whatever it was, it was within me. I felt I could not go to the church.

'You go on alone,' I said.

'You'd better come,' said Kate. 'I know just what you feel, but it will be worse here by yourself.'

'I think perhaps I won't,' I said.

'Very well,' said Kate. 'Bicycle on and meet me at the other gate.'

I said I was a coward, and Kate said she did not think it mattered being a coward. I meant to start at once, but I found something wrong with the bicycle. It took quite half an hour to repair, but as I was repairing it all my oppression passed, and I felt light and at ease. By the time I was ready, Kate had visited the tombs, and was coming out of the church door. I looked at her going down the path, and saw there was another woman in the churchyard. She was walking rather slowly. She came up behind Kate, then passed quite close to Kate on her left side. I was too far off to see her face. I felt thankful Kate had someone with her. I mounted; when I looked again the woman was gone.

I met Kate outside the church. She always had odd eyes; now they had a glittering look, half scared and half excited, which made me very uncomfortable. I asked her if she had spoken to the woman about the church.

'What woman? Where?' said Kate.

'The one in the churchyard just now.'

'I didn't see anyone.'

'You must have. She passed quite close to you.'

'Did she?' said Kate. 'She passed on my left side then?'

'Yes, she did. How did you know?'

'Oh, I don't know. We give the keys in here, and let's bicycle home fast, it's turned so cold.'

I always think Kate rather manlike, and she was manlike in her extreme moodiness. If anything of any sort went wrong, she clothed herself in a mood, and became impenetrable. Such a mood came on her now.

'I don't know why I never will tell things at the time,' said Kate next day. It was raining, and we were sitting over a nice little fire after tea. 'It's a sign of great feebleness of mind, I think. However, if you like to hear about Asham Church, you shall. I saw the tombs, and they are all that they should be. I hope the de Mannerings were worthy of them. But the church; perhaps being a clergyman's daughter made me take it so much to heart, but there was a filthy old carpet rolled up on the altar, all the draperies are full of holes, the paint is coming off, part of the chancel rail is broken, and it seems an abode of insects. I did not know there were such forsaken churches in England. That rather spoilt the tombs for me, also an uncomfortable idea that I did not want to look behind me; I don't know what I thought I was going to see. However, I gave every tomb its due. Then, when I was in the churchyard, I had the same feeling as last time; I could not get it out of my head that something I did not like was going to happen the next minute. Then I had that sensation, which books call the blood running chill; that really means, I think, a catch in one's heart as if one cannot breathe; and at the same time I had such an acute consciousness of someone standing at my left side that I almost felt I was being pushed, no one being there at all, you understand. That lasted a second, I should think, but after that I felt as if I were an intruder in the churchyard, and had better go.'

One afternoon a week later, the great-aunt of the smart townlike landlady at our lodgings came to clear away tea. First of all she was deferential and overwhelmed, but I have never known anyone have such a way with old ladies and gentlemen of the agricultural classes as Kate. In a few moments Mrs Croucher was sitting on the sofa with Kate beside her.

'Asham Hall,' said she. 'Why, my dear mother was sewing maid there, when she was a girl. Oh dear me, yes, the times she's told me about it all. Oh, it's a beautiful place, and them lovely laurels in the avenue, where Miss de Mannering was so fond of walking. It was the old gentleman, Mr de Mannering, he planted them; they was to have gone right up to the Hall, so they say. There was to be wonderful improvements, he was to have pulled down the old Hall and built something better, and then he hadn't the money. Yes, even then it was going down, for Mr William, that was the only son, that lived abroad, he was so wild. Yes, my mother was there in the family's time, not with them things which hev a-took it since.'

'You don't think much of Colonel Winterton, then?'

'Oh, I daresay he's a kind sort of gentleman, they say he's very free at

Christmas with coals and that, but them new people they comes and goes, it stands to reason they can't be like the family. In the village we calls them jumped-up bit-of-a-things, but I'm sure I've nothing to say against Colonel Winterton.'

'Are there any of the family still here?'

'Oh no, mum. They've all gone. Some says there's a Mr de Mannering still in America, but he's never been near the place.'

'It's very sad when the old families go,' said Kate sympathetically.

'Oh, it is, mum. Poor old Mr de Mannering; but the place wasn't sold till after his death. My mother, she did feel it.'

'Was there a room shut up in your mother's time, Mrs Croucher?'

'Not when she first went there, mum.'

'It was a housemaid, wasn't it?'

'Not a housemaid,' with a look of important mystery. 'That's what they say, and it's better it *should* be said; I shouldn't tell it to everybody, but I don't mind telling a lady like you; it wasn't a housemaid at all.'

'Not a housemaid?'

'No; my mother's often told me. Miss de Mannering, she was a very high lady, well, she was a lady that *was* a lady, if you catch my meaning, and she must have been six or seven and forty, when she was took with her last illness. And the night before she died, my mother she was sitting sewing in Mrs Packe's room (she was the lady's maid, my mother was sewing maid, you know) and she heard Doctor Mason say, "Don't take any notice of what Miss de Mannering says, Mrs Packe. People get very odd fancies, when they're ill," he says. And she says, "No, sir, I won't," and she comes straight to my mother, and she says, "If you could hear the way she's a-going on. 'Oh, my baby,' she says, 'if I could have seen him smile. Oh, if he had lived just one day, one hour, even one moment.' I says to her, says Mrs Packe to my mother, 'Your baby, ma'am, whatever are you talking about?' It was such a peculiar thing for her to say," says Mrs Packe. "Don't you think so, Bessie?" Bessie was my mother. "I'm sure I don't know," says my mother; she never liked Mrs Packe. "Miss de Mannering didn't take no notice," Mrs Packe went on, "then she says, 'If only I'd buried him in the churchyard.' So I says to her, 'But where did you bury him then, ma'am?' and fancy! she turns round, and looks at me, and she says, 'I burnt him.'" Well, that's the truth, that's what my mother told me, and she always said, my mother did, Mrs Packe had no call to repeat such a thing.'

'I think your mother was quite right,' said Kate. 'Burnt! Poor Miss de Mannering must have been delirious. It is such a frightful. . . .'

'No, my mother didn't like carrying tales about the family,' said Mrs Croucher, engaged on quite a different line of thought. And whether it was that she had heard the story so often, or whether it was that they are still more inured to horrors in the country – I have observed far stranger things happen in the country than in the town – Mrs Croucher did not seem to have any idea that she was relating what was terrible. On the contrary, I think she found it homely, recalling a happy part of her childhood.

'Then,' went on Mrs Croucher, 'Mrs Packe, she says to my mother, "You come and hear her," she says, and my mother says, "I don't like to, whatever would she say?" "Oh," says Mrs Packe, "she don't take any notice of anything, you come and peep in at the door." "So I went," my mother says, "and I just peeped in, but I couldn't see anything, only just Miss de Mannering lying in bed, for there was no candle, only the firelight. Only I heard Miss de Mannering give a terrible sigh, and say very faint, but you could hear her quite plain, 'Oh, if only I'd buried him in the churchyard.' I wouldn't stay any longer," says my mother, "and Miss de Mannering died at seven in the evening next day." Whenever my mother spoke of it to me, she always said, "I only regretted going into her room once, and that was all my life. It was taking a liberty, which never should have been took."'

'But,' said Kate, framing the question with difficulty, 'did anybody —? Had anybody had a suspicion that Miss de Mannering —?'

'No, mum. Miss de Mannering was always very reserved, she was not a lady that was at all free in her ways like some ladies; not like you are, if you'll excuse me, mum. Not that I mean she would have said anything to anyone of course, and she had no relations, no sisters, and they never had no company at the Hall, and the old gentleman, he'd married very late in life, so he was what you might call aged, and the servants was terrible afraid of him, his temper was so bad; even Miss de Mannering had a wonderful dread of him, they said.

'There was a deal of talk among the servants after what Mrs Packe said, and there was a housemaid, she'd been in the family a long time, and she remembered one winter years before, I daresay eighteen or twenty years before, Miss de Mannering was ailing, and she sent away her maid, and then she didn't sleep in her own room, but in a room in another part of the house not near anyone, that's the room they shut up, mum. And they remembered once she was ill for months and months, and her nurse that lived at Selby, when she was very old, she got a-talking as sometimes old people will, she died years after Miss de Mannering, and she let out what she would have done better to keep to herself.

'It wasn't long after Miss de Mannering's death they began to say you could see her come out of that there room, walk down the stairs, out at the front door, down through the park, along the avenue, and back again to the house, and then across the park to the churchyard. And of course they say she's trying to find a place for her baby. Then there's some as says Mr Northfield, what lived at Asham before Colonel Winterton came, he saw her. They say that's why he sold it. Mr Fuller they say he's spoke to her; they say that's why he's turned so quiet.

'Then there's some say, Miss Jarvis – she kept The Blue Boar in the village, when I was a girl – she used to say, that Miss Emily Robinson, the daughter of Sir Thomas Robinson, who bought the place from Mr Seaton, who bought it after Mr de Mannering's death – he wasn't much of a "Sir" to my mind, just kept a draper's shop in London, the saying was – she was took very sudden with the heart disease, and was found dead, flat on her face in the avenue. Of course the tale was, she met Miss de Mannering and she laid a hand on her. The footman that was attending Miss Robinson – she was regular pomped up with pride *she* was, and always would have a footman after her – he says he *see* a woman quite plain come up behind her, and then she fell. He told Mr Jarvis. Poor Mrs Dicey – they was at the Hall before the Northfields – she went off sudden too at the end, but she was always sickly, and I don't hold with all those tales myself.

'But people will believe anything. Why, not long ago, well, perhaps twenty years ago, in Northfield's time, there was a footman got one of the housemaids into trouble, and of course there's new people about in the village since the family went, and they say the room was shut up along of *her*. It's really ridickerlous.'

'Did you ever see her, Mrs Croucher?'

'Not to say see her, mum, but more than once as I've been walking in the park, I've *heard* her quite plain behind me. That was in November. November is the month, as you very well know, mum,' – I could see Kate was gratified that it was supposed she should know – 'and you could hear the leaves a-rustling as she walked. There's no need to be frightened, if you don't take no notice, and just walk straight on. They won't never harm you; they only gives you a chill.'

'Did your mother ever see her?'

'If she did, she never would say so. My mother wouldn't have any tales against Miss de Mannering. She said she never had any complaints to make. There was a young man treated my mother badly, and one day she was crying, and Miss de Mannering heard her, and she comes into the sewing-room, and she says, "What is it?" and my mother told her, and Miss de Mannering spoke very feeling, and said, "It's very sad, Bessie, but life is very sad." In general Miss de Mannering never spoke to anybody.

'My mother bought a picture of Miss de Mannering, if you young ladies would like to see it. Everything was in great confusion when Mr de Mannering died. Nothing had been touched for years, and there were all Miss de Mannering's dresses and her private things. No one had looked through them since her death. So what my mother could afford to buy she did, and she left them to me, and charged me to see they should never fall into hands that would not take care of them. There's a lot of writing I know, but I'm not much of a scholar myself, though my dear mother was, and I can't tell you what it's all about, not that my mother had read Miss de Mannering's papers, for she said that would never have been her place.'

Mrs Croucher went to her bedroom and brought us the papers and the portrait. It was a water-colour drawing dated Bath, 1805. The artist had done his best for Miss de Mannering with the blue sash to match the bit of blue sky, and the coral necklace to match her coral lips. The likeness presented to us was that of a young woman, dark, pale, thin, elegant, lady-like, long-nosed and plain. One gathers from pictures that such a type was not uncommon at that period. I should have been afraid of Miss de Mannering from her mouth and the turn of the head, they were so proud and aristocratic, but I loved her sad, timid eyes, which seemed appealing for kindness and protection.

Mrs Croucher was anxious to give Kate the portrait, 'for none of 'em don't care for my old things.' Kate refused. 'But after you are gone,' she said, for she knows that all such as Mrs Croucher are ready to discuss their deaths openly, 'if your niece will send her to me, I should like to have Miss de Mannering; I shall prize her very much.'

Then Mrs Croucher withdrew, 'for I shall be tiring you two young ladies with my talk.' It is rather touching how poor people, however old and feeble, think that everything will tire 'a lady,' however young and robust.

We turned to Miss de Mannering's papers. It was strange to look at something, written over a century ago, so long put by and never read. I had a terrible sensation of intruding, but Kate said she thought, if we were going to be as fastidious as all that, life would never get on at all. So I have copied out the narrative for you. I am sure, if Mrs Croucher knew you, she would feel you worthy to share the signal honour she conferred on us.

MISS DE MANNERING'S NARRATIVE

It is now twenty-two years since, yet the events of the year 1805 are engraved upon my memory with greater accuracy than those of any other in my life. It is to escape their pressing so heavily upon my brain that I commit them to paper, confiding to the pages of a book what may never be related to a human friend.

Had my lot been one more in accordance with that of other young women of my position, I might have been preserved from the calamity which befell me. But we are in the hands of a merciful Creator, who appoints to each his course. I sinned of my own free will, nor do I seek to mitigate my sin. My mother, Lady Jane de Mannering, daughter of the Earl of Poveril, died when I was five years old. She entrusted me to the care of a faithful governess and nurse, and owing to their affectionate solicitude in childhood and girlhood I hardly missed a mother's care. Of my father I saw but little. He was violent and moody. My brother, fourteen years older than I, was already causing him the greatest anxiety by his dissipation. Some words of my father's, and a chance remark, lightly spoken in my hearing, made an ineffaceable impression on me. In the unusual solitude of my existence I had ample, too ample, leisure to brood over recollections which had best be forgotten. Cheerful thoughts, natural to my age, should have left them no room in my heart. When I was thirteen years old, my father said to me one day, 'I don't want you skulking here, you're too much of a Poveril. Everyone knows that a Poveril once, for all their pride, stooped to marry a French waiting-maid. That's why every man Jack of them is black and sallow, as you are.' I fled from the room in terror.

Another day Miss Fanshawe was talking with the governess of a young lady who had come to spend the afternoon with me. They were walking behind us, and I heard their conversation.

'Is not Miss Maynard beautiful?' said Miss Adams. 'I believe that golden hair and brilliant eye will make a sensation even in London. What a pity Miss de Mannering is so black! Fair beauties are all the rage they say, and her eyes are too small.'

'Beauty is a very desirable possession for a young woman,' said Miss Fanshawe, 'but one which is perhaps too highly valued. Anyone may have beauty; a milkmaid may have beauty; but there is an air of rank and breeding which outlasts beauty, and is, I believe, more prized by a man of fastidious taste. Such an air is possessed by Miss de Mannering in a remarkable degree.'

My kind, beloved Fan! but at fifteen how much rather would I have shared the gift possessed by milkmaids! From henceforth I was certain I should not please.

Miss Fanshawe, who never failed to give me the encouragement and confidence I lacked, died when I was seventeen and had reached the age which, above all others in a woman's life, requires the comfort and protection of a female friend. My father, more and more engrossed with money difficulties, made no arrangement for my introduction to the world. He had no relations, but my mother's sisters had several times invited me to visit them. My father however, who was on bad terms with the family, would not permit me to go. The most rigid economy was necessary. He would allow no guests to be invited, and therefore no invitations to be accepted. The Hall was situated in a very solitary part of the country, and it was rare indeed for any visitor to find his way thither. My brother was forbidden the house. Months, nay years passed, and I saw no one.

Suddenly my father said to me one day, 'You are twenty-five, so that cursed lawyer of the Poverils tells me; twenty-five, and not yet married. I have no money to leave you after my death. Write and tell your aunt at Bath that you will visit her, and she must find you a husband.'

Secluded from society as I had been, the prospect of leaving the Hall and being plunged into the world of fashion filled me with the utmost apprehension. 'I entreat you, sir, to excuse me,' I cried. 'Let me stay here. I ask nothing from you, but I cannot go to Bath.'

I fell on my knees before him, but he would take no denial, and a few weeks after I found myself at Bath.

My aunt, Lady Theresa Lindsay, a widow, was one of the gayest in that gay city, and especially this season, for she was introducing her daughter Miss Leonora.

My father had given me ten pounds to buy myself clothes for my visit, but, entirely inexperienced as I was, I acquitted myself ill.

'My dear creature,' said my cousin in a coaxing manner that could not wound. 'Poor Nancy in the scullery would blush to see herself like you. You must hide yourself completely from the world for the next few days like the monks of La Trappe, and put yourself in Mamma's hands and mine. After that time I doubt not Miss Sophia de Mannering will rival the fashionable toast Lady Charlotte Harper.'

My dear Leonora did all in her power to set me off to the best advantage, to praise and encourage me, and my formidable aunt was kind for my mother's sake. But my terror at the crowd of gentlemen, that filled my aunt's drawing-room, was not easily allayed.

'I tremble at their approach,' I said to Leonora.

'Tremble at their approach?' said Leonora. 'But it is their part to tremble at ours, my little cousin, to tremble with hopes that we shall be kind, or with fears that we shall not. I say my little cousin, because I am a giantess,' she was very tall and exquisitely beautiful, 'and also I am very old and experienced, and you are to look up to me in everything.'

I wished to have remained retired at the assemblies, but Leonora always sought me out, and presented her partners to me. But my awkwardness and embarrassment soon wearied them, and after such attentions as courtesy required they left me for more congenial company. Certainly I could not blame them; it was what I had anticipated. Yet the mortification wounded me and I said to my cousin, 'It is of no use, Leonora. I can never, never hope to please.'

'Those who fish diligently,' she replied, 'shall not go unrewarded. A gentleman said to me this evening, "Your cousin attracts me; she has so much countenance." Captain Phillimore is accounted a connoisseur in our sex. That is a large fish, and I congratulate you with all my heart.'

Captain Phillimore came constantly to my aunt's house. Once he entered into conversation with me. Afterwards he sought me out; at first I could not believe it possible, but again he sought me out, and yet again.

'Captain Phillimore is a connexion not to be despised by the ancient house of de Mannering,' said my aunt. 'There are tales of his extravagance it is true, and other matters; but the family is wealthy, and of what man of fashion are not such tales related? Marriage will steady him.'

Weeks passed by. It was now April. My aunt was to leave Bath in a few days, and I was to return home; the season was drawing to its close. My aunt was giving a farewell reception to her friends. Captain Phillimore drew me into an anteroom adjoining one of the drawing-rooms. He told me that he loved me, that he had loved me from the moment he first saw me. He kissed me. Never, never can I forget the bliss of that moment. 'There are,' he said, 'important reasons why our engagement must at present be known only to ourselves. As soon as it is possible I will apprise my father, and hasten to Asham to obtain Mr de Mannering's consent. Till then not a word to your aunt. It will be safest not even to correspond.' He told me that he had been summoned suddenly to join his regiment in Ireland and must leave Bath the following day. 'I must therefore see you once more before I go. The night is as warm as summer. Have you the resolution to meet me in an hour's time in the garden? We must enjoy a few minutes' solitude away from the teasing crowd.'

I, who was usually timid, had now no fears. I easily escaped unnoticed. The whole household was occupied with the reception. At the end of a long terrace there was an arbour. Here we met. He urged me to give myself entirely to him, using the wicked sophistries which had been circulated by the infidel philosophers of France; that marriage is a superstitious form with no value for the more enlightened of mankind. But alas, there was no need of sophistries. Whatever he had proposed, had he bidden me throw myself over a precipice, I should have obeyed. I loved him as no weak mortal should be loved. When his bright blue eye gazed into mine, and his hand caressed me, I sank before him as a worshipper before a shrine. With my eyes fully open I yielded to him.

I returned to the house. My absence had not been observed. My cousin came to my room, and said with her arch smile, 'I ask no question, I am too proud to beg for confidences. But I know what I know. Kiss me, and receive my blessing.'

I retired to rest, and could not sleep all night for feverish exaltation. It was not till the next day that I recognized my guilt. I hardly dared look my aunt and cousin in the face, but my demeanour passed unnoticed; for during the morning a Russian nobleman attached to the Imperial court, who had been paying Leonora great attentions, solicited her hand and was accepted. In the ensuing agitation I was forgotten, and my proposal that I should return to Asham a day or two earlier was welcomed. My aunt was anxious to go to London without delay to begin preparations for the wedding.

She made me a cordial farewell, engaging me to accompany her to Bath next year. 'But, Mamma,' said Leonora, 'I think Captain Phillimore will have something to say to that. All I stipulate is that Captain and Mrs Phillimore shall be my first visitors at St Petersburgh.'

Their kindness went through me like a knife, and I returned to Asham with a heavy heart.

'Where is your husband?' was my father's greeting.

'I have none, sir,' said I.

'The more fool you,' he answered, and asked no further particulars of my visit.

Time passed on. Every day I hoped for the appearance of Captain Phillimore. In vain; he came not. Certainty was succeeded by hope, hope by doubt, doubt by dread. I would not, I could not despair. Ere long it was evident that I was to become a mother. The horror of this discovery, with my total ignorance of Captain Phillimore's whereabouts, caused me the most miserable perturbation. I walked continually with the fever of madness along the laurel avenue and in the Park. I went to the Church, hoping that there I might find consolation, but the memorials of former de Mannerings reminded me too painfully that I alone of all the women of the family had brought dishonour on our name.

I longed to pour out my misery to some human ear, even though I exposed my disgrace. There was but one in my solitude whom I could trust; my old nurse, who lived at Selby three miles off. I walked thither one summer evening, and with many tears I told her all. She mingled her tears with mine. I was her nursling, she did not shrink from me. All in her power she would do for me. She knew a discreet woman in Ipswich, whither she might arrange for me to go as my time approached, who would later take charge of the infant. She suggested all that could be done to allay suspicion in the household and village.

At first my aunt and cousin wrote constantly, and even after Leonora's marriage I continued to hear from Russia. My letters were short and cold. When I knew that I was to be a mother, I could not bear to have further communication with them. My aunt wrote to me kindly and reproachfully. I did not answer, and gradually all correspondence ceased. Yet their affectionate letters were all I had to cheer the misery of those ensuing months. I shall never forget them. Although it was now summer, the weather was almost continuously gloomy and tempestuous. There were many thunder storms, which wrought havoc among our elm trees in the Park. The rushing of the wind at night through the heavy branches and the falling of the rain against my window gave me an indescribable feeling of apprehension, so that I hid my head under the bedclothes that I might hear nothing. Yet more terrible to me were the long days of August, when the leaden sky oppressed my spirit, and it seemed as if I and the world alike were dead. I struggled against the domination of such fancies, fancies perhaps not uncommon in my condition, and in general soothed by the tenderness of an indulgent husband. I could imagine such tenderness. Night and day Captain Phillimore was in my thoughts. No female pride came to my aid; I loved him more passionately than ever.

On the 20th November some ladies visited us at the Hall. We had a common bond in two cousins of theirs I had met frequently in Bath. They talked of our mutual acquaintance. At length Captain Phillimore's name was mentioned. Shall I ever forget those words? 'Have you heard the tale of Captain Phillimore, the all-conquering Captain Phillimore? Major Richardson, who was an intimate of his at Bath, told my brother that he said to him at the beginning of the season, "What do you bet me that in one season I shall successfully assault the virtue of the three most innocent and immaculate maids, old or young, in Bath? Easy virtue has no charms for me, I prefer the difficult, but my passion is for the impregnable," and Major Richardson assures my brother that Captain Phillimore won his bet. Mr de Mannering, we are telling very shocking scandals; three ladies of strict virtue fallen in one season at Bath. What is the world coming to?'

My father had appeared to pay little heed to their chatter, but he now burst forth, 'If any woman lets her virtue be assaulted by a rake, she's a rake herself. Should such a fate befall a daughter of mine, I should first horsewhip her, and then turn her from my doors.'

During this conversation I felt a stab at the heart, so that I could neither speak nor breathe. How it was my companions noticed nothing I cannot say. I dared not move, I dared not leave my seat to get a glass of water to relieve me. Yet I believe I remained outwardly at ease, and as soon as speech returned, I forced myself to say with tolerable composure, 'Major Richardson was paying great attention to Miss Burdett. Does your brother say anything of that affair?'

Shortly afterwards the ladies took their leave.

I retired to my room. I had moved to one in the most solitary part of the house, far from either my father or the servants. I tried in vain to calm myself, but each moment my fever became more uncontrollable. I dispatched a messenger to my nurse, begging her to come to me without delay. I longed to sob my sorrows out to her with her kind arms round me. The destruction of all my hopes was as nothing to the shattering of my idol. My love was dead, but though I might despise him, I could not, could not hate him.

Later in the day I was taken ill, and in the night my baby was born. My room was so isolated that I need have little fear of discovery. An unnatural strength seemed to be given me, so that I was able to do what was necessary for my little one. He opened his eyes; the look on his innocent face exactly recalled my mother. My joy who shall describe? I was comforted with the fancy that in my hour of trial my mother was with me. I lay with my sweet babe in my arms, and kissed him a hundred times. The little tender cries were the most melodious music to my ears. But short-lived was my joy; my precious treasure was granted me but three brief hours. It was long ere I could bring myself to believe he had ceased to breathe. What could I do with the lovely waxen body? The horror that my privacy would be invaded, that some intruder should find my baby, and desecrate the sweet lifeless frame by questions and reproaches, was unendurable. I would have carried him to the churchyard, and dug the little grave with my own hands. But the first snow of the winter had been falling for some hours; it would be useless to venture forth.

The fire was still burning; I piled wood and coal upon it. I wrapped him in a cashmere handkerchief of my mother's; I repeated what I could remember of the funeral service, comforting and tranquillizing myself with its promises. I could not watch the flames destroy him. I fled to the other end of the room, and hid my face on the floor. Afterwards I remember a confused feeling that I myself was burning and must escape the flames. I knew no more, till I opened my eyes and found myself lying on my bed, with my nurse near me, and our attached old Brooks, the village apothecary, sitting by my side.

'How do you feel yourself, Miss de Mannering?' said he.

'Have I been ill?'

'Very ill for many weeks,' said he, 'but I think we shall do very well now.'

My nurse told me that, as soon as my message had reached her, she had set out to walk to Asham, but the snow had impeded her progress, and she was forced to stop the night at an inn not far from Selby. She was up before dawn, and reached the Hall, as the servants were unbarring the shutters. She hastened to my room, and found me lying on the floor, overcome by a dangerous attack of fever. She tended me all the many weeks of my illness, and would allow none to come near me but the doctor, for throughout my delirium I spoke constantly of my child.

The doctor visited me daily. At first I was so weak that I hardly noticed him, but my strength increased, and with strength came remembrance. He said to me one morning, 'You have been brought from the brink of the grave, Miss de Mannering. I did not think it possible that we should have saved you.'

In the anguish of my spirit I could not refrain from crying out, 'Would God that I had died.'

'Nay,' said he, 'since your life has been spared, should you reject the gift from the hands of the Almighty?'

'Ah,' I said in bitterness. 'You do not know —'

'Yes, madam,' said he, looking earnestly upon me, 'I know all.'

I turned from him trembling.

'Do not fear,' he said. 'The knowledge will never be revealed.'

I remained with my face against the wall.

'My dear Madam,' he said with the utmost kindness. 'Do not turn from an old man, who has attended you since babyhood and your mother also. My father and my father before me doctored the de Mannerings, and I wish to do all in my power to serve you. A physician may sometimes give his humble aid to the soul as well as to the body. Let me recall to your suffering soul that all of us sinners are promised mercy through our Redeemer. I entreat you not to lose heart. Now for my proper domain, the body. You must not spend your period of convalescence in this inclement native county of ours. You must seek sun and warmth, and change of scene to cheer your mind.'

His benevolence touched me, and my tears fell fast. Amid tears I answered him, 'Alas, I am without friends; I have nowhere to go.'

'Do not let that discourage us,' he said with a smile, 'we shall devise a plan. Let me sit by my own fireside with my own glass of whisky, and I shall certainly devise a plan.'

By his generous exertions I went on a visit to his sister at Worthing. She watched over me with a mother's care, and I returned to Asham with my health restored. Peace came to my soul; I learnt to forgive him. The years passed in outward tranquillity, but in each succeeding November, or whenever the winds were high or the sky leaden, I would suffer, as I had suffered in the months preceding the birth of my child. My mind was filled with baseless fears, above all that I should not meet my baby in Heaven, because his body did not lie in consecrated ground. Nor were the assurances of my Reason and my Faith able to conjure the delusion: yet I had –

Here the writing stopped.

'Wait, though,' said Kate, 'there's a letter.' She read the following:

3 Hen and Chicken Court,
Clerkenwell.
March 7, 1810.

Madam,

I have been told that my days are numbered. Standing as I do on the confines of eternity, I venture to address you. Long have I desired to implore your forgiveness, but have not presumed so far. I entreat you not to spurn my letter. God knows you have cause to hate the name of him who betrayed you. Yes, Madam, my vows were false, but even at the time I faltered, as I encountered your trusting and affectionate gaze, and often during my subsequent career of debauchery has that vision appeared before me. Had I embraced the opportunity offered me by Destiny to link my happiness with one as innocent and confiding as yourself, I might have been spared the wretchedness which has been my portion.

I am Madam, your obedient servant,

Frederic Phillimore.

I could not speak for a minute; I was so engrossed with thinking what Miss de Mannering must have felt when she got that letter.

Kate said, 'I wonder what she wrote back to him. How often it has been folded and refolded, read and re-read, and do you see where words have got all smudged? I believe those are her tears, tears for that skunk!'

But I felt I could imagine better than Kate all that letter, with its stilted old-fashioned style, which makes it hard for us to believe the writer was in earnest, would have meant to Miss de Mannering.

'To-morrow is our last afternoon,' said Kate. 'What do you think,' coaxingly, 'of making a farewell visit to Asham?'

But though Miss de Mannering is a gentle ghost, I do not like ghosts; besides, now I know her secret, I *could* not intrude upon her. So we did not go to Asham again. Now we are back at school, and that is the end of my story.

Stella Gibbons

ROARING TOWER

MY father bent his head to kiss me, but I turned my face away and his lips brushed the edge of my veil instead. Over his shoulder I met my mother's grieved eyes, and my own filled with tears.

I lowered my veil, with trembling fingers, murmured some words which I have now forgotten, and stepped into the compartment, my father holding open the door for me. On the seat in the corner lay a bunch of white roses, a copy of a ladies' journal, and a basket packed with my refreshment for the journey.

My heart was like stone. The roses, picked from the garden of our house in Islington, softened it not a whit. I moved them aside carefully and sank into my corner seat. I said not a word; and my father and mother stood in silence too; how I wished they would go away!

'You will write to-morrow, my child, and tell us what your journey was like and how your Aunt Julia is?' said my mother.

'Yes, Mamma.' My lips felt stiff and cold.

'Remember, Clara, we shall expect you to take full advantage of the Cornish air, and to return to us in a very different frame of mind and quite restored to health.' My father's voice was a warning.

'Yes, Papa.'

I folded my black-gloved hands on my lap, and stared out of the window, avoiding my mother's eyes.

The passions which invade a heart at nineteen, like a beautiful menacing army, seem faded and small enough if one looks back on them after a lapse of fifty years, as I am doing now, but on the late summer morning I describe, as I waited with my parents under the dome of the railway station, no heart could have been fiercer, and yet colder, than mine. One voice, which I should never hear again, sounded in my ears, and one face, which I had promised to forget, filled my eyes.

'All else' (as that German philosopher wrote) 'was folly.'

Well, my parents had parted us; and my heart was broken; and there was no more to be said. I wished the train would start, so that I could be alone.

The journey was uneventful. My Aunt Julia was not wealthy enough to afford a carriage, and when, on the evening of the same day, I got out of the train at the Cornish town of N — I found that I must take a fly to the village two miles hence where she lived, which was near the sea.

I found an ancient carriage, driven by a surly-looking old man in a great cape, and the porter, with this old fellow's help, hoisted my trunk into the driver's seat, gave me a gallant arm into the carriage with a wink at the cabby, and we were off.

We left the town behind; and at last, in twilight, we came to the end of the last lane, and faced a little sandy bay in which broke the waves of the open sea. On the other side of the bay stood the village where my aunt lived.

The horse slackened his pace almost to a walk and the wheels slid in the fine sand as we crossed the bay; the soft sound of the falling waves and the lights shining in the village windows were balm to me.

Suddenly I saw something which – even then – startled and impressed me so much that I leaned forward and plucked at the driver's cape.

'What is that – what are those ruins there, on the left?' I asked, pointing.

He did not turn his head in the direction in which I pointed and I had some difficulty in hearing his surly, indistinct reply, which came after a pause:

'That be the Roaring Tower,' he said at last, curling his whip round his horse's ribs.

I looked, with a livelier interest than I had looked at any object for months past, at the indistinct outline of the ruined circular tower, which faced the breaking waves, and which was almost covered by a fine bush of wild roses. It was no more than a circular rim of stone, higher at some points than at others, but the circle was unbroken. It stood by itself, in the lowest curve of the low cliff encircling the bay.

I remember that I sat upright in the swaying carriage, as we drew nearer to the village, and eagerly studied the tower until a curve in the cliff hid it from sight; and even when it had disappeared, I saw it plainly in my mind's eye, like the dazzling memory of a light after it has gone out.

My Aunt Julia's greeting was kindly but reserved, as befitted a welcome to a troublesome and headstrong niece who had been so imprudent as to bestow her affections on an unsuitable wooer. I was given to understand that my month's stay with her was not to be a time of idle repining – 'mooning,' I remember she called my listless air. I was to help her with hemming sheets, with her fowls, and with her garden.

But after I had made my bed in the mornings, tidied my room, and helped Bessie to feed the fowls my time was my own until midday dinner; and this was the time I liked best of all – as much, that is, as I liked any 'time' in those unhappy days.

I clambered from rock to rock, waded through pools in a bitter dream, and saw with unseeing, unhappy eyes the conservatories and hothouses of the sea, green fronds and purple and red, swaying below me in innocent beauty.

But I only grieved the more to see them. Was I not alone in the midst of beauty, and would be so for ever? And my heart grew harder, my tongue less apt to exclaim or praise, and my thoughts turned every day more and more inward upon myself.

The Roaring Tower, which, you may be sure, was the first place I visited on the first day of my stay, became my favourite haunt. Its rose-bush was in fullest flower, and no matter at what time of the day I visited it, the first sound I heard as I flung myself down on the parching grass, breathless with my climb up the cliffside, was the sustained, slumberous drone of the wild bees, ravaging the open chalices of the roses.

I have written 'the first sound I heard.'

But there was another sound.

I learned, before I had been staying with Aunt Julia a week, whence the Tower got its strange name.

It was the noon of a burning and cloudless day. I was returning languidly along the cliff-edge from a walk to a village which lay inland, swinging my hat in my hand, my eyes half closed against the waving glitter of the grass and the smiting glitter of the sea.

I was not thinking of anything in particular, not even of my sorrow; my mind lay like a black marsh under the sun – flowerless, stagnant. If there was a thought hovering at the back of my head (I can write it now with a smile) it was a hopeful surmise that there might be fresh fish for dinner. But had I been taxed with this I should have denied it with anger. I hugged my grief; it was all I had. Nothing could heal it; it was a deathless wound.

Alas! the bitterest lesson I have since learned is how gently and remorselessly Time steals even our dearest wounds from us.

As I drew near the Tower I glanced, as usual, in its direction. A little group of village people stood about it, the women clustering together at some distance, the men scattered round it in a broken circle, like a doubtful advance guard.

As I drew near I heard an indescribable sound which seemed to come from no particular spot but from the whole surrounding air, which I thought at first (for lack of better knowledge) to be the drone of bees in swarm.

It was a soft, hollow, furious roaring, such a sound as a giant distant waterfall might make; the sound I have heard that great hunter, my Uncle Max, describe when he told us how his heart would shake in his body to hear, in the dead of night, the solemn far-off voices of lions at their wooing and hunting in the starlit desert.

The sound rose and fell in waves, exactly as the roaring of an animal rises and falls.

As I advanced over the grass, intending to ask one of the women what was amiss, I saw my own inward uneasiness reflected in the sly, downward glances of the village people.

'What is it? What's the matter?' I asked sharply of a woman near me. 'What is that strange noise?'

She hesitated, glancing appealingly at the man by her side, but he avoided her eyes. I repeated my question imperiously.

'It's only the Roaring Tower,' she said at last, reluctantly. 'When the rose-bush is all out, and on sweltering hot days, miss, the Tower roars, like you can hear.'

'But what is it? What makes that awful sound?'

Again there was silence. The other villagers were looking curiously at me; a few of them drew slowly near to our little group, but no one attempted to answer me.

At length, from the back of the group, a man's doubtful voice volunteered:

'They say it's the water under the Tower, miss. There's a great cave under the Tower, so they say, and when the tide gets into it it makes that noise.'

There were one or two half-hearted assents to this.

But I was not satisfied; the explanation was plausible and yet unconvincing. But the uneasy manner of the villagers and their inquisitive eyes repelled me, and I hastened to leave the spot.

I had been with Aunt Julia a week when one morning I went out into the kitchen to give Bessie some linen which she had promised to wash for me.

She was not there, but at a corner of the kitchen table sat a little fair-haired girl, busy with paper and pencils, which she used from a painted box at her elbow. This was Jennie, Bessie's niece, whom my aunt allowed to play in the kitchen as she was a good, quiet child.

'Good morning, Miss Clara,' she whispered, looking shyly at me.

'Where is your aunt, Jennie?' I asked, impatiently; I wanted to be off to the seashore. 'She must wash these ruffles for me to-day, I shall need them for church to-morrow.'

'She's gone to market, Miss Clara, and won't be back for an hour or more.'

'Then it's very forgetful and careless of her. They will never be dry and pressed in time for to-morrow. Give them to her as soon as she comes in, Jennie, and say I must have them by this evening.'

But just as I was flouncing out of the kitchen, my annoyance increased by Jennie's solemn, timid stare, I stopped suddenly and picked up her pencil-box from the table.

'Why – there's the Roaring Tower!' I said, half to myself in a new voice, full of the pleasure I felt at the sight of the picture painted on the lid of the box. 'Where did you get this, Jennie? Who painted it? And what's this queer creature with the snout, close to the Tower?'

'Davy gave me that,' drawled Jennie. 'Daft Davy, they call him. He's not right in the head. He painted the box for me with that queer beast. And Davy said he's seen it.'

I stared at her, and back at the box, wondering where the weak-minded old man could have found his model for the gross, long-snouted monster with four brown paws which he had painted squatting close to the Tower.

'You mustn't tell lies, Jennie. It's wicked,' I said, primly.

'But Davy *has* seen it, Miss Clara,' Jennie persisted. 'Long ago, when he was a little boy. That's the noise we hears, coming out of the Tower, when the rose-bush is all out. That's why it's called the Roaring Tower. It's that poor bear-thing, shut up in there, and he can't get away, Davy says.'

I continued to stare at her. She did not seem at all frightened; one little hand was posed over her drawing, as though she was about to go on with her game.

'Well —' I said at last, drawing a deep breath, 'you are a very wicked little girl to repeat Davy's lies, Jennie. You ought to be ashamed of yourself.' But my voice did not sound so severe as I should have liked.

'Yes, Miss Clara. I'm sorry,' whispered Jennie, anxiously, and then I went towards the door. But at the door I paused, and called back to her, curiously:

'Weren't you frightened, Jennie, when Davy told you about it?'

'Oh, no, Miss Clara,' she replied, sedately. 'He don't hurt people, that bear-thing don't. Everyone's afeard of him round here, and no one's sorry for him a bit, but he don't hurt people. He only wants to get away home, Davy says.'

Well, after such a talk between us, where should my steps go but towards the Tower, that afternoon, when my aunt was taking her nap in the garden?

I crossed the sands, and climbed the gentle slope towards it. There it was, half-mantled with its rose-bush, its very stones steeped in quivering heat and silence. Bees droned in the flowers and butterflies reeled above the higher branches.

I crossed the grass and mounted the fallen stone which I always used as a step whenever I wanted to look down on to the circle of grass inside the Tower.

In the early morning the rose-bush and the wall cast a lop-sided shadow half-way across the grass, and at sunset the shadow reappeared on the other side, but now, at high noon, when I looked down on the grass, it was shadowless, clear and deep as emeralds.

I leaned my elbows on the broken stone rim and stared downwards. My thoughts were vague. Certainly, I was not afraid, and this now seems strange to me, for Daft Davy's drawing depicted a beast that was enough to put queer thoughts into the mind of a better-balanced girl than I was.

But all I felt, idling there in the heat and drowsy silence, was a kind of mischievous curiosity, and a return of the inexplicable pity I had experienced when I heard the Tower at its roaring.

As I lingered, more asleep than awake, an infinitely soft tremor began to jar in the air, scarce distinguishable from the far-off rumour of the sea, and it grew in volume, rising above the sound of the waves and the bees until it dominated them entirely, and I realised that the Tower was roaring, and that I stood, like a swimmer on a sea-girt spit of sand, in the full tide of its sound.

Then, indeed, my heart began to beat a little faster. I glanced quickly over my shoulder, and took my elbows from the wall, and prepared for flight.

But I did not go – I stayed, and no one was more surprised than myself. For pity had come back into my heart; that astonishing, irrational pity for a mere sound which I had felt before.

I hesitated on my stone pedestal, gripping the wall with one hand, and peering down into the silent pit of green. There was nothing there, of course. The grass burned coolly in the sunlight, the bees hung among the roses. And the soft, piteous sound roared about me in waves, abandoned, despairing.

Frightened and moved as I was, I did a strange thing. I hung over that empty pit, calling softly: 'Can you hear me? Poor soul! Poor tormented creature! Can I help you? I would if I could.'

The foolish words, banal and human, faltered back from the airy but impassable wall of beauty presented by rose-bush and glimmering grass. I called again, over the ominous hollow:

'Listen! I am here. I would pray for you, if prayers would help you. You poor, lost thing, you! You have a friend left on earth, if you care to have her. I will do what I can. . . .'

My eyes streamed with the first unselfish tears I had shed for months. Scarce knowing what I did, I put my hands firmly on the wall, and vaulted the low drop into the hollow. Heaven alone knows what purpose I thought that would serve!

I landed with a jarring shock, staggered forward, and fell on my hands and knees in the grass. I was conscious that all I could see of the familiar world I had left was a rough circle of bluest sky, against which the rose-bush moved in the wind.

All about me, stunning the ears with soft reiteration, rose and fell the voice of Roaring Tower.

'Well!' I said aloud, shakily, scrambling to my feet, and standing with my back almost touching the wall as though I were at bay. 'Here I am, in the middle of things, with a vengeance. I must go through with it now.'

But the words were unnecessarily bold. Nothing happened, not even the catastrophe expected. These feelings, relieved by my shower of tears, slowly grew calmer. The roaring seemed to be dying down in long exhausted peals of sound, or else my ears were growing used to it.

'Of course. The tide is going out,' I murmured, walking slowly round the circle of grass, brushing the wall with the tips of my fingers. 'How silly of me.'

I blushed for my tears and pity of a few moments ago.

My prison was not really a prison. I knew I could get out the moment I wanted to by scrambling up the six feet or so of rough wall, which provided more footholds than I needed. But I liked to linger there, shut away from the world in the sunshine and silence. I sat down on the grass, under the overhanging mass of the rosebush, and leaned back against the wall with a tired sigh.

How deep the quiet was! For now the roaring had ceased. Not a bee droned, not a butterfly stirred. The air of summer, cooled in this pit of silence, smelled sweet.

It would be easy for me to write at this point, 'I must have fallen asleep.'

But I know, as I know that my body must soon die, that I did not sleep, even for a few seconds. I was awake, wide awake. And I saw what I saw.

A shadow rose from the emerald grass.

It was brown, and large, larger by many times than I was, and at first it seemed like a thickening of the air immediately above the grass, and I blinked my eyes once or twice, thinking they were still dim from my recent tears. But the shadow persisted. It grew darker and thicker, and began to take shape. It was squat, obese, crouching, with a small head sunk between its shoulders, a long snout, and four paws drawn up ratlike against its furred sides.

I bent forward, blinking my eyes again; I even rubbed them with my fists, but the shadow did not move. And as I watched it, the faint sound jarred again on the still air, rose to a rumour of noise, fell to a whisper, and rose again.

The Tower was roaring, and the sound came from the throat of the monster before me, with its head flung back. The creature – vision, spectre, whatever it may have been – turned its head from side to side as it roared, as though in extremity of anguish; I caught the glint of its oblique eyes as the head swayed.

Did the monster look at me? Strange question, with more than a hint of ludicrousness! How can one speak, in sober earnest, of looks exchanged between a dweller in this world and a visitor from some world at which I cannot even guess? But it seems to me, remembering, that the beast recognized my presence there, for soon it made a blundering, circular movement and turned its head towards me, still roaring piteously, as though entreating my help.

So we faced each other, I and the Voice of Roaring Tower, and as I looked, every feeling driven from my heart suddenly flooded back in a huge wave of pity.

I held out my hands, I spoke to the monstrosity before me as though it could understand: 'Is there anything I can do?' I whispered. 'Shall I fetch a clergyman?'

But even as the foolish words left my dry lips the brown shadow changed.

I cannot describe what followed. I am only a human being; the pen of one of Milton's archangels would be needed for that.

The shadow streamed upwards, melting as it streamed. It seemed to be drawn straight into the zenith, sucked by some invisible strength.

I had, for a terrifying flash of time, a glimpse of huge wings, feathered with copper plumes from tip to tip, of a face crowned with hair like springing rays of gold, a wild face, smiling down on me in ecstasy, of a sexless body, veined again with gold as a leaf is veined. A blinding shock passed through my frame, which may have been (may the creature's God forgive me if I blaspheme) an embrace of gratitude.

Then it had gone. It had gone as though I had never seen it.

There was nothing left. The Roaring Tower was empty as a sun-dried bone; I could feel that, as I sat with my eyes now closed. Virtue had gone out of the very roses; they were mysterious only with the mystery of all growing things.

Presently I roused myself, and after several attempts climbed out of the Roaring Tower.

Weak as a kitten, I sauntered home by the sea's margin. The crisping foam ran to my feet; I could trace its snow under my tired, lowered lids. The slow, strong sea wind, blowing along the evening clouds, smoothed my cheeks. I thought of nothing. My mind was calm as the sands stretched before me.

I was not unhappy any more. I looked at the great sky, the sand, the darkening sea, the flower-fringed cliffs, and thought, with tired pleasure, how rich I was in having many, many years before me in which to love their beauty.

For now they belonged to me, as all beauty did. This was the gift of that terrible spirit I had pitied in the Tower. My pity, I believed, had released it, and in return it had swept personal sorrow out of my heart, and made me free of all beauty.

I felt strangely impersonal, as (with our human limitations) we imagine a grain of sand or a clover-flower must feel. Light-footed, unthinking, calm, I idled homewards with the homing light.

That was fifty years ago.

During the rest of the time I stayed there, I asked cautious questions of my aunt, Daft Davy, and in the village, but never a shred of a legend could I find that might explain (if explanation were possible) what had happened in Roaring Tower. Davy was terrified, and refused to answer me; and my aunt stared at me as though I had gone mad.

But the gift of Roaring Tower has never left me throughout my long life filled to the brim with sorrow and happiness. Part of me is untouchable; part of me can always escape into the watching, surrounding beauty of the natural world, and be free.

Is it to be wondered at, now I am too old a woman to make concessions to those who believe that this world is the only world we shall ever inhabit, that I am not afraid to die?

Unhaunted, voiceless, a mere ruin of stones, the Roaring Tower may stand to this day. But I have never returned there to see.

D. K. Broster

JUGGERNAUT

I

'I REALLY do think, Aunt Flora, that we shall be comfortable here! This Mrs Wonnacott seems very obliging, and the rooms aren't at all stuffy, and not too *aspidistrian*, as that clever young man we met at the Vicarage last week called it. And there's a splendid view of the sea-front – much better, really, because we are on the first floor; so that will make up, won't it, for your having to go up and down the stairs? – Now, you are not resting your leg, as Dr Philipson said you were to, in between! Wait a moment; here's a most convenient little chair, better than that beaded footstool – how delightful to see a beaded footstool again – it reminds me of dear Grandmamma. . . . Is that quite comfortable? I expect Mrs Wonnacott will be in any moment now with the teapot, as everything else seems to be on the table. Cucumber sandwiches, too – how very nice!'

The active tongue which would shortly sample those sandwiches was not new to either of its principal functions. Speech had flowed copiously from it – nearly always cheerful and good-natured speech – for some five and thirty years. Primrose Halkett, its proprietress, was a spare, dark, alert, girlish woman, who shared the kindly temperament, though not the comfortable habit of body, of her Aunt Flora, the elder Miss Halkett, with whom she lived in the country. Miss Flora Halkett herself, the victim of a rather badly sprained ankle, had come to Middleport for a short change of air after her enforced seclusion at Grove Cottage, and since her medical attendant had recommended her to use her leg, in moderation, the cautious ascent and descent of one flight of stairs, together with a certain amount of walking, had not beeen forbidden her.

The limb in question, of a size capable of supporting her solid frame, extended on the chair provided by her niece. Miss Flora Halkett looked appraisingly round the comfortable ornament-bedecked sitting-room of 'Bêche-de-Mer' – for Mrs Wonnacott's husband, after reading a novel about some Pacific island, had bestowed this singular appellation upon his dwelling under the impression that it was the French for 'seabeach.' In her late fifties, of the type of British spinster who not long ago would have worn a decent mushroom hat with strings – somewhat longer ago a bonnet with intensively cultivated pansies packed under the brim – Miss Halkett had surmounted her large, square, florid face and greying fair hair with a black béret, more striking than becoming. For though (despite the béret) she looked, and actually was, one of those exceedingly worthy and untiring women who form the standby of a country parish, Aunt Flora might with some accuracy be said to Lead Two Lives, and under different names too. If need arose she would take her niece's place at the organ in church, she reigned almost supreme in the Women's Institute, but she was also a writer, and not a writer of stories for the parish magazine – though in moral tone her books were unimpeachable.

The Gift (as her friends alluded to it) had come upon Miss Flora Halkett suddenly and late, for it was only between six and seven years ago that the Muse had dropped a stray plume from her wing upon Miss Flora's writing-table, near the G. F. S. account book. The pen thus put into so unlikely a hand must have been feathered with crimson, since this good, kindly lady with a sense of humour wrote thrillers of the most improbable type – and sold them too – but not as 'Miss Halkett.' For when she first launched her inexperienced literary craft and discovered the turbulence of the waters which it seemed appointed for her to navigate, she had promptly taken to herself the cloak of a masculine pseudonym, fearing that if the Vicar or some member of the Mothers' Union came upon her real name displayed upon the cover of *The Murder Swamp*, he or she might be scandalized. But to her almost shocked gratification she subsequently discovered that the Vicar had read 'Theobald Gardiner's' thriller with avidity, though unaware of its real attribution, and he later accepted a substantial donation towards the new blowing apparatus for the organ out of the yield of the swamp in question. In the same way the advance royalties of *Tiger or Dagger*, just completed during Mr Gardiner's recent seclusion, were assigned to the financing of this holiday for herself and the faithful Primrose.

Tea now appearing, in a large Britannia-metal teapot enriched with repoussé roses, Miss Halkett removed herself from her chair to the table, with a view to doing fuller justice to the meal. And indeed the chronicling of deeds of terror had never affected her appetite, nor did the 'Things' which in her stories walked behind her heroes on lonely moors, or waited, gorilla-like, to strangle her heroines in underground passages, ever sit beside *her* bed or deprive her of a single night's rest.

After tea, aunt and niece sat at the open window and looked forth upon the Mecca of their pilgrimage, the ocean, bounded on the hither side by the relentless concrete of the 'front,' at the glass-sided shelters full of forms reading, knitting, or merely torpid, and at the remarkable architecture of the new pier pavilion, which recalled at one moment Byzantium, at another Mandalay. Primrose sniffed the salt air appreciatively, her tongue going merrily the while, and Miss Halkett smoked her after-tea cigarette (one of the daily four, which were never exceeded) and asserted that she felt she would soon be able to walk as far as the West Cliff, of whose unspoilt beauty she had heard so much.

'But not for some time yet, Aunt Flora!' expostulated Primrose, ready to check the ardour which not long ago had conveyed Miss Halkett's bulk half-way up the rough track of Ben Nevis. 'You *must* go slow for a bit – start with walking to the end of the promenade and coming back in a bath-chair. There *are* bath-chairs here; I see a little row of them farther along.'

'It will have to be a solid bath-chair, then,' replied Miss Flora, chuckling, as she crushed out the end of her cigarette. 'Primrose, have you counted the number of china ornaments on this mantelpiece? There are twenty-three, including the miniature litter of pigs. I must make a note of it, for I think I might stage my next book in a seaside town like Middleport.'

'Because stories of your kind never happen there!' interpreted Primrose admiringly. 'Oh, Aunt Flora, how original of you!'

'I'm not sure,' admitted Theobald Gardiner, with commendable candour, 'that my particular brand of story could happen anywhere!'

The fine evening of the Miss Halketts' arrival was succeeded by a morning of lashing rain. A leaden sea tumbled in untidy hostility among the long centipede legs of the pier, and slapped vigorously against its inveterate enemy, the wall of the sea-front. Occasionally a burst of spray would come sousing over the pavement of the promenade, and it was Primrose's somewhat childish amusement to sit at the rain-washed window and watch for victims among the very few stalwarts who tramped up and down despite the weather. At the table Theobald Gardiner wrestled, Laocoon-like, with the galley-proofs of a former masterpiece, *The Death Stairs*, of which she had recently sold the second serial rights to a small provincial newspaper. This step she was now near to regretting, for the compositor of the *Bulsworth Gazette and Springshire Advertiser* was endowed with an uncanny faculty for converting her intended tragedy into comedy, a metamorphosis which was not actually very difficult of accomplishment.

'Primrose!' suddenly screamed the outraged authoress, 'this really is the limit! Not content with having made my rich banker a *baker*, the scoundrel has turned "the dreadful bond which linked them" into "*the dreadful bone which licked them*"!'

But Primrose's gaze did not move from the sea-front. 'How tiresome!' she concurred absently. 'Of course it should be "the bone which they licked," shouldn't it?'

'You are obviously not attending, dear! There is no question of bone-licking by anyone – no question of a *bone* at all! It should be *bond* – b, o, n, d. – Good gracious, here's another misprint at the bottom of this slip - "a man of noble *berth*" – as if it were a matter of a state-cabin! – What is interesting you so much, Primrose, that you have no attention to spare for the incredible villainies of this printer?'

Primrose jumped round. 'I'm *so* sorry, Aunt Flora! How dreadful of me! And your proofs are sliding all over the place.' She knelt down and began to collect some galleys – endued as usual with a slithery life of their own – from the floor. 'I was only looking at a bath-chair going to and fro along the front, and wondering what sort of invalid was brave enough to be out in such weather.'

'Rather foolish, whoever it is. Have you the next galley there? – it should begin: "*Feverishly he clutched*. . . ." That's it. Was it a man or a woman in the bath-chair?'

'I could not see, Aunt Flora, because, of course, the hood was up – or down, whichever you like to call it. – Aunt Flora, the printer of this paper ought really to be dismissed! I've just seen something in a slip you haven't done yet – something I'm sure you never wrote: "Taking her hand he conducted her, silly sheep, towards the" . . . *Oh!*' Primrose's voice broke off on a note of horror.

'"*Silly Sheep*,"' exclaimed Theobald Gardiner, roused to fresh fury. 'Heavens above, it should be "*still asleep*"! It is where the mysterious Sylvester, having sent Miranda into a hypnotic trance – you remember? – at the séance, takes her into the cabinet which he has arranged to have removed while she is inside, and so to abduct her. Don't tell me this criminal fool has muffed the cabinet too; he *can't* have made anything else out of that word! – What are you so red about?'

'Well,' answered her niece, with a real Victorian blush, 'he hasn't actually altered the word, but for some reason he has put it into italics, so that it looks French . . . and you know what it means in French, Aunt Flora!'

Miss Halkett did not find walking for any length of time as easy as she had anticipated, and though at first she fought against the idea of taking a bath-chair when tired, she soon came not to dislike this method of transport, save that she wished, for the sake of the bath-chairman, that she weighed rather less. 'Otherwise, Primrose,' she observed after her first experience, 'there is a kind of Cleopatrish sensation about it, except that I am sure Cleopatra's slaves were younger and more upstanding.'

The bath-chairmen of Middleport were certainly neither young nor vigorous, nor did they unduly exert themselves, with the exception of one old man, and he almost the frailest-looking of them all, who seemed always to be either on his way to fetch a fare, or on his way back after depositing one, so that never did the Miss Halketts actually see any occupant of his vehicle, particularly as, whatever the weather, the hood was invariably forward.

'Perhaps that is what is meant by "plying for hire,"' observed Primrose one day as they were returning on foot to 'Bêche-de-Mer,' and had just espied this particular old man dragging his machine along the front. 'He is certainly more energetic than the other old creatures, and I am almost sure it was him I —'

'*He*, Primrose!' corrected the authoress.

'He (of course) that I saw that day in the storm. And have you noticed, Aunt Flora, that though we never actually see anybody in his bath-chair, he always pulls it – he's pulling it now – as if there were a weight inside? I mean, you can nearly always tell from the way a bath-chairman walks —'

'Yes, yes, of course one can. But, though I personally should never try to hire him, because he doesn't look strong enough, I had not noticed that fact about your old man.' Indeed, Miss Flora's powers of observation had latterly been in abeyance, owing to the cloud spread upon her faculties by the sins of the compositor of the *Springshire Advertiser*.

Two or three days later, however, her attention was drawn, if indirectly, to the 'plying' bath-chairman. She and Primrose had walked nearly to the extreme end of the sea-front, when a heavy shower of rain drove them into a shelter, already nearly full. When the rain had stopped, it left the surface of the promenade so wet that Primrose was afraid of her aunt slipping, while the approach of lunch-time did not admit of their waiting for it to dry. The stand being too far away, Primrose volunteered to catch some cruising bath-chair, and, after hovering about for a little outside the shelter, she returned to announce that she could see one coming along, which appeared to be empty; and was off again.

But when she had posted herself in the route of the slowly advancing vehicle, and it became clear to her that it really was empty, it became clear also that the man pulling it was 'her' old chairman, whom Miss Flora would have qualms about engaging.

'But it's quite a short way to Mrs Wonnacott's,' thought Primrose, and started forward. 'Stop, chairman, stop! There's a lady in that shelter wanting you!'

The old man did not appear to hear, but went on past her with his head bowed forward, slowly tugging, for all the world like an automaton pulling a heavy weight. Yet the bath-chair was quite empty, though shrouded up against the rain. Primrose put herself directly in front of the chairman, and he was obliged to stop.

'There's a lady here wants you to take her quite a short way – and in the direction you are going!'

Without raising his eyes the elderly chairman replied, in a voice little more than a whisper: 'Sorry, ma'am, but this chair is engaged.'

'But if you are on your way to fetch a fare,' insisted Primrose, 'surely you could take this lady in that direction, and drop her? She is lame, and I am afraid she may slip on the wet pavement.'

The bath-chairman raised his eyes. They were of a clear pale blue, an innocent blue, almost like a child's, though no one could have mistaken them for the untroubled eyes of youth.

'Lame? Did you say she was *lame*, ma'am? With a stick?' he questioned, in a tone which for a second suggested yielding to her demand. Then he shook his head, in the old straw hat which contrasted with his decent and little-worn black suit. 'No, ma'am, I'm sorry, but Mrs Birling wouldn't like the chair being used.'

Primrose drew back. 'I didn't know, of course, that it was a private chair,' she said. 'I'm sorry.'

'There is no call to apologise, ma'am,' said the elderly chairman, with courtesy and even dignity, and starting the bath-chair again with a slight effort, went slowly on his way.

'It's no good,' announced Primrose, arriving back, slightly dashed, at the shelter. 'There's no one in his chair, but he won't take you; he said some lady or other wouldn't like it.'

No sooner had she uttered the words than a female of that unmistakable type which abounds in seaside shelters, wearing a long magenta knitted coat, looked up from her book and said: 'It's a waste of time, if you don't mind my telling you, ever to try to get old Cotton to take you in that bath-chair of his. He's been queer, you know, ever since Mrs Birling's death.'

'Mrs Birling – that's the name!' exclaimed Primrose. 'But is she *dead*? He said just now that the chair was hers – or at least he implied it!'

'That's just how he's queer,' explained her informant, who had evidently the advantage of being either a resident or a frequent visitor at Middleport. Everyone else in the shelter woke to attention, with the exception of an old gentleman in the corner doing the *Daily Telegraph* crossword. 'Mrs Birling always used to employ Cotton – had him for years. A bad-tempered old thing she was, but rich – and mean. However, when she died about a couple of years ago she did leave him a legacy in her will – quite a nice little sum, I believe – and since then he has dragged that empty chair of his about in all weathers, and won't let anyone get in. . . . Under the circumstances,' she added to herself, 'I'm not sure that I should care to.' But this remark was caught by neither of the Miss Halketts, particularly as Miss Flora began instantly upon the objection that, as he was a licensed bath-chairman, he surely was obliged to take up persons wishing to hire him.

'Oh,' said the lady in magenta, resuming her book, 'no one bothers about that here. You see, he was always such a respectable old man that people are sorry for him, and he doesn't take up room on the stand. You may have noticed that he is never there.'

It was only after the Miss Halketts had left the shelter that the old gentleman of the crossword looked up and asked: 'Why didn't you tell those women straight away that what keeps most people from worrying Cotton for a lift is that they know what happened in that bath-chair?'

The open mouths of the non-resident listeners emitted one simultaneous '*What* happened?'

II

'Dinner's ready, Dad,' announced Mrs Sims, appearing in the door-way of the shed. 'Now, you can leave dusting your old chair, surely, till afterwards, or you won't get your rabbit-pie hot, and you like rabbit-pie, don't you?'

The shed stood in the yard behind the little tobacco and sweet shop whose proprietor, Mabel Cotton, had married 'from service.' It was nearly two years ago that her father, after the death of her mother, had come to live with them – he and his bath-chair and his 'bat in the belfry' about it. But since Mabel and Will Sims had arrived at the resolve not openly to combat 'Dad's crazy notions,' life had become easier in the little house over the shop. No more would Mabel burst out, 'Don't be so absurd, Dad – it ain't right to go on so! You weren't that fond of the old lady when she was alive – old terror, I thought she was!' only to provoke a flash of brittle, evanescent anger in the old man, and to drive him to stay out the longer on the sea-front with his inseparable companion. For her husband had counselled her to leave the subject as much as possible alone; not to encourage the poor old chap, but not to thwart him. And the plan had seemed to work; at any rate, there wasn't the worry involved in continual protests.

'You know,' Mabel Sims had said one evening some months after this decision had been taken – 'you know, Will, if Mrs Birling hadn't left Dad that fifty pounds I don't believe there'd have been any of this trouble. The – the other affair alone wouldn't have made him carry on like this. It's his gratitude – silly kind of gratitude I call it, hauling that old chair about in all weathers, with that crape bow and all! It's getting worse, too.'

They were covering up the shop for the night. 'If you ask me,' said her husband, as he locked the till, 'I don't think he does it out of anything so – so human as gratitude.'

'Goodness, don't you? What is it, then? Just pig-headedness?'

'I don't rightly know,' replied Will Sims. 'But it's my belief, from things

I've sometimes heard him muttering to himself in that shed, that he hates the thought of Mrs Birling.'

Duster in hand, his wife stared at him. 'Well, I never! Come to think of it, though, she must have given him a fair shock. I don't wonder, in a way, that he has a special kind of feeling for that wretched chair of his. I've often thought about that day up at the West Cliff. Poor old Dad! Well, anyhow, I'll go on sticking to your advice, Will, and not try to stop him doing what he likes.'

That conversation had taken place the previous winter. Since then some gradual grinding process had been at work on poor old Dad. Every day he seemed a little more whittled away; the neat black clothes which he had worn since the death of his wife hung more loosely upon him, the flesh of his mild, thin face had gained in transparency – and the octopus-like tentacles of his obsession enwrapped him ever more straitly. And yet neither his daughter nor her husband could quite penetrate to the core of his delusion, and indeed it seemed as if old Cotton himself was too confused in mind to do so either. What exactly did he think he was doing pulling the old chair about – did he imagine that Mrs Birling sat in it still?

Mabel Sims had often asked herself that question. It was not far from her thoughts now as she looked at her father across the table, where he sat gazing abstractedly at the half-eaten contents of his plate. They were alone together, for it was early-closing day, and Will Sims had gone over to the carnival at Shenstone, Middleport's neighbour and rival.

'Dad, never mind if you can't finish your pie. There's a nice little milk-pudding in the oven. I'll get it out now.'

The old man, however, pushed back his chair. 'I don't want no more to eat, thank you, Mabel. The pie was very good. I'll go back and finish my polishing – must do some extra polishing after the rain.' He looked at her sideways as she lifted the pie from the table, and went on gravely: 'Something awkward happened this morning – something She wouldn't have liked.'

His daughter did not need to ask who She was. She and It – round those two pronouns her father's conversation (what there was of it) tended increasingly to revolve.

'What was it, Dad? You mean the rain was awkward?' Mabel asked, in the kindly, but only half-attentive, voice of one speaking to a child, and she turned away with the pie.

'No, not the rain itself . . . though I suppose it wouldn't have happened but for the rain. A lady stopped me on the front and wanted to hire it.'

'Well, that does happen sometimes, don't it, Dad?' commented Mrs Sims brightly, as she went to the oven. 'I suppose you just told her it wasn't for hire, like you always do.'

Her father was fidgeting with a spoon on the table. 'She didn't want it for herself,' he replied. 'It was for another lady, what wasn't there, who was lame, she said.'

'Well?' asked Mabel Sims, opening the oven door.

'Don't you see, Mabel, what it seems like?' asked the old man in an agitated voice. 'Don't you see what it might be? Like as if She was wanting It again!'

'Dad, I never heard such absolute nonsense!' said his daughter sharply, abandoning the withdrawal of the milk-pudding and her usual neutral attitude at the same time. She was roused by the fear of a new complication in the 'belfry.' 'There's heaps of ladies with game legs about – in fact, I never saw such a place as Middleport for dot-and-go-one old women. Some days there don't seem one as can plant her feet straight! Besides,' she added triumphantly, 'you said just now that Mrs Birling wouldn't have liked this lady asking for the chair, so it couldn't have been her that was wanting it! Go along now, and finish your old polishing, and then come in for a rest and I'll make you a nice cup of tea.'

'I shan't have time for a rest; I shall have to go out again this afternoon,' replied her father, with a little sigh. 'But thank you, Mabel, all the same; maybe I'll come in for a cup first.' He went slowly out of the room, and his daughter pushed the oven door to with her knee rather more violently than became her vow of non-interference.

'Drat that blessed bath-chair!' she said under her breath.

Outside in the little yard Will Sims's nasturtiums, trained against the tarred wall of the shed, were glowing in the sun. Very slowly old Cotton unlocked the door of that edifice, which was always fastened when It was inside and unattended. Will had once kept a watering-pot and a few tools there too, but now only his bicycle was adjudged worthy to share the repose of his father-in-law's bath-chair. With a hesitation almost amounting to reluctance the old man entered, picked up his polishing materials from a little shelf, and resumed his labours; and though they were practically unnecessary, it was a good quarter of an hour before he desisted from them and stood back to survey the result.

The vehicle was one of the old solid type designed to shield its occupant from the weather as thoroughly as the extinct hansom cab, but it had undergone modifications which had deprived it of the hinged flaps which used to meet over the legs of the passenger and of the kind of window which could be closed at need. A waterproof apron had superseded the former, while the window had gone entirely – both greatly to the lightening of the chair's weight. For the rest, this converted antique was so well kept that it belied its probable age.

After a moment or two's contemplation old Cotton proceeded to address it, rubbing his hands together, his body bowed forward and a pale smile upon his lips.

'The West Cliff, ma'am? Yes, of course, of course, if you fancy it! I'll just beat up the new cushion a bit.'

He bent the hinges of the hood, stiff with disuse, and folded that protection back against the pushing handle behind. It could then be seen that a large crape bow had been pinned across the back of the inside of the chair. Below this reposed, in gaudy incongruity, a cheap new cushion, orange, purple, and black, while a striped rug of silk waste lay primly folded on the seat.

'You're quite sure as you want to go up there again, ma'am, in spite of . . . You haven't been up there since, you know . . . You really would like to go . . . ?' he mumbled, bending over these adjuncts.

His monologue, however, came to a close as, appearing to remember something, he hastily unfastened the waterproof apron over the lower part of the chair, and groping about under it, brought up a book in the durable but unattractive uniform of the Free Library. It was labelled *Diseases of the Heart*. Opening it at a page already indicated by a strip of paper, old Cotton read a few lines several times over; then, shaking his head, he thrust the book down again into its hiding-place.

His lower lip was trembling, and he began to mutter again, but this time to himself. 'I believe it *was* Her this morning! Then She will be angry. . . . Oh dear, oh dear, it's so difficult to know what She really wants!' Yet there was a smile, a fixed, mechanical smile, on his face as he plumped up the ugly cushion, and spread the rug out as if over some person's knees. It vanished, however, as if it had been turned off, as he put the hood forward again, and it was with a heavy sigh that he took his old black-ribboned straw hat off a peg and dragged the bath-chair out into the sunshine.

III

The afternoon was indeed so tempting that Miss Flora and her niece hired a car and went for a country drive. Coming back, they halted on top of the famous West Cliff before descending to the level portions of Middleport. It was a remarkable phenomenon that this headland, with its bracing air, fine sweep of view, and gorse-clad spaces, had neither been appropriated by the local golf club nor ruined by pavilions and houses, a phenomenon only to be explained by the fact that it had been bequeathed to the town on condition that it was always kept in its natural state. It was therefore undisfigured – except, of course, by the usual revolting jetsam, periodically removed, of orange-peel, torn wrappers, and sandwich-paper, by which British democracy commemorates its visits to any place of beauty or interest. There were a few seats, a gravel path or two, nothing more; even the main road cut straight across the landward side of the promontory.

The Miss Halketts were so much pleased to find the West Cliff practically deserted (the result, they surmised, of the attractions of Shenstone carnival) that they decided to dismiss their car, and after enjoying the breezy solitude to walk down to the spot where they could take the tram back to Middleport. Slowly and peaceably the two ladies proceeded therefore over the grass towards the verge, and when they reached the point sat upon a seat and enjoyed the view over a pale and silken sea. Far out on the horizon the smoke of invisible steamers created phantom coasts of cloud; nearer at hand, headlands, which aunt and niece tried vainly to identify stretched beyond each other into the haze; and at their feet the turf, studded with pink thrift, fell away in a gentle slope to the true edge of the cliff, whence the rock plunged sheer to an inaccessible beach below.

When at last they started back towards the road it could not be denied that the distance thereto seemed to have increased, and while they rested upon a seat a little farther back Primrose gently rated her aunt, and now bewailed the unusual solitude which rested upon the West Cliff.

Not until they rose to continue their way were they aware that Heaven had sent Miss Flora a means of conveyance. Round a large gorse bush at some short distance there came suddenly into sight a bath-chair, drawn – as usual – by an old man.

'What luck!' exclaimed Miss Flora, waving her stick to attract his attention.

'But, Aunt,' interposed Primrose, doubtfully, 'I'm afraid it's that old Cotton, who won't take anyone!'

To her surprise the bath-chairman put on a spurt, and bringing his vehicle to rest a few yards away, came shambling towards them, his hands fluttering over each other. 'I thought I should find you up here, ma'am,' he said, addressing Miss Flora. There was a faint tinge of the fawning in his manner. 'The chair's all ready, nice new cushion and all.'

'You don't mind, then –' began Miss Primrose.

Yet perhaps the old man did mind. His gaze had riveted itself upon Miss Flora's béret, and for a moment he looked like a lost and puzzled dog. 'I don't know, after all, 'he said hesitatingly. 'I think perhaps I'd better not.' But he still stood there.

'Oh come, I'm lame, you know – though only temporarily. You'll take me down as far as the tram, I'm sure!' And, smiling her jolly smile, Miss Halkett advanced towards the bath-chair. 'But I must have the hood back, or I can't get in.'

Quite suddenly, for no reason that was at all apparent, the old man was once more all eagerness to comply. 'Yes, yes, I'll take you down, ma'am; I'll take you down. I was thinking of going myself. It's the only thing left to do, I've decided . . . so if you really wish it . . . that is, if She wishes it . . .' He was already putting back the hood; now he unfastened the apron and stood with the striped rug over his arm.

'Aunt Flora,' whispered Primrose, catching her arm, 'don't go in his chair! Don't let him take you; he's so very queer! And look, there's a crape bow on it!'

'Do you imagine he's going to abduct me!' whispered back Miss Flora, chuckling. 'Only light people are in danger of abduction. Dear me, that's rather witty!' She was so pleased with her unintentional *bon mot* that she took no notice of the funereal adornment beyond saying under her breath, 'Very morbid, poor fellow!' and forthwith clambered in, the chair creaking a little beneath her weight.

'But what's this hard object down by my feet?' she inquired, as old Cotton assiduously spread the rug over her knees.

Stopping, he brought up the obstacle. 'Beg your pardon, ma'am, for leaving it there. It's the book what's made it quite certain and sure that I shall have to go down. I didn't quite believe it before about those drops in the capsicule thing –'

'What on earth is the man talking about?' quoth Miss Flora, but not as if she expected an answer.

Old Cotton stuffed the book with some difficulty into a pocket. 'Are you quite comfortable, ma'am?' he inquired. 'Got your stick and all? I see you haven't brought your air-cushion to-day. Now we'll go down, then.' He went forward to the handle, and the bath-chair, getting into motion, began to move off in the direction of the sea.

'No, not that way, Mr Cotton!' said Primrose loudly, catching hold of the pushing-handle at the back. 'We want to go down to the tram, not back to the edge of the cliff. Stop, stop! Aunt Flora, get out at once!'

Miss Flora, indeed, was already shouting in unison with her niece: 'Not this way! Turn round, man!' As old Cotton, however, appeared not to hear, but proceeded steadily and with a certain purposeful haste seawards, she began to follow Primrose's advice. Wrapped in the rug as she was, and further incommoded by the waterproof apron, this was not easy, though Primrose did her best to check the advance of the bath-chair by throwing her weight on to the rear handle. The scene ended, after a moment or two of confusion and something of panic, by the conveyance overturning and Miss Halkett rolling out on the ground.

Old Cotton, ashy white and shaking, helped the distracted Primrose to disentangle and raise the prostrate and indignant authoress, whose ankle, most fortunately, had sustained no additional damage.

'Oh, ma'am, I can't think how it happened!' he exclaimed in the accents of one smitten to the heart. 'How dreadful, how dreadful! Was it the wheel gave way? Such a thing hasn't never happened with me before . . . Oh, ma'am, indeed I hope you are not hurt!'

'Why on earth didn't you stop when I told you to?' demanded Miss Flora breathlessly, her béret at an uncommonly jaunty angle, as she was assisted to her feet. 'If you had done that it certainly wouldn't have happened!'

'But I thought you wanted to go down, ma'am!' replied the old man, looking worried again.

'So I did – down to the tram. I said so!' retorted the exasperated and shaken lady.

A mildly shocked expression came over old Cotton's face. 'The tram! Mrs Birling never went in a tram!' he said reproachfully.

'But I am not Mrs Birling, my good man! – No, Primrose, I am really all right. Don't fuss so!'

The old man passed his hand over his forehead. 'That's just what muddles me so,' he muttered. 'It's true that you couldn't well be Mrs Birling —"

'No, because she is dead, isn't she?' interposed Miss Flora, much more gently.

'She *died* right enough, yes, ma'am,' assented old Cotton in a slightly correcting tone. 'I ought to know that, if anyone does, because it was in this chair that she passed away. Still, I don't know as she's *dead*!'

'Passed away in this chair!' exclaimed both the ladies, their eyes going to the vehicle where it still lay sprawled upon its side on the grass.

'Yes, ma'am. Died of a heart disease with a name I never can get right – something like "engine."'

'Angina pectoris, I suppose,' murmured Miss Flora.

'Yes, ma'am, that was it. But they said that if she'd had the stuff to smell she wouldn't have died – not that day, anyhow.'

'Ah, nitrite of amyl. Yes, I've heard of it.'

'Yes, ma'am I expect that's what it was. Drops of some kind in a glass capsicule. No, she wouldn't have died.'

The old man, stooping, began to tug at the chair in an endeavour to get it upright again. Primrose, moved by pity, did the same, and together, not without difficulty, they heaved it on to its wheels and replaced its scattered contents.

'And this Mrs Birling,' said Primrose, cutting short old Cotton's humble thanks – 'this Mrs Birling died in your chair, and you could do nothing? How dreadful! No wonder you —' She pulled herself up.

'Yes, it was, ma'am,' assented the old man, looking from one lady to the other. 'Yes, I've often thought it was very dreadful. But, you see, I did want the money so bad; my poor wife was dying then, and there was some treatment as would have made it easier for her that she couldn't get at the Infirmary, and I knew Mrs Birling was leaving me something in her will. Many a time before that day I had thought to myself, knowing she had that bad heart, that if only the bad heart would carry her off soon, perhaps my poor Amy wouldn't have to suffer so.'

Both ladies recoiled.

'You are surely not – surely not trying to tell us that you murdered Mrs Birling!' cried Miss Flora, horrified, she who wrote so glibly of terror and slaughter and had never wittingly come within a hundred miles of any criminal.

The suggestion seemed to shock the old man in the black suit much less than its maker. 'Oh, *no*, ma'am!' he protested mildly. 'Because I didn't really believe about the drops. But this book I got from the Free Library says it's true. *Yes, it's true!*' he added suddenly in quite a different tone, a tone of anguish, and, pulling out his handkerchief, he wiped his forehead.

The scent of the gorse came warm upon the breeze. Primrose, fear in her eyes, was biting her long string of beads; Miss Halkett leant heavily upon her stick, also staring at the speaker, but neither of them moved or spoke. It was the inoffensive old man who broke the silence, looking not at his hearers, but out at the lazy sea beyond the cliff edge.

'Yes, it's two years now I've had to drag this chair about. Sometimes she's sitting in it, sometimes she doesn't come, but it's always heavy – getting heavier, too. Miss Sharpe – that was her companion – always carried those capsicules with the drops about with her in case Mrs Birling had another attack. She'd only had but two, and long enough ago; there really didn't seem much cha–danger of another. But that day Miss Sharpe had a bad sick headache; she couldn't come walking by the side of the chair; she stayed at home, but just to be on the safe side she gave the glass capsicule to me, and told me how I was to break it under the old lady's nose if she was took bad, which wasn't very likely to happen. She gave me a clean handkerchief on purpose for it. Mrs Birling was all for going up to the West Cliff that day, knowing there'd be nobody much about, because it was the carnival at Shenstone – like it is to-day – and she made me go, though it was cruel hot. She never had no mercy; she used to say: "There's fifty pounds down for you in my will, Cotton – you can go and ask my lawyer if there isn't – so you've no call to grumble whatever I ask you to do. . . ." Amy was very bad that day, so it come to me again, if only I could get that fifty pounds for her before it was too late. But I knew it was no good asking the old lady for it before the time; she would never part with a penny if she could help it. So it seemed such a chance, like, for poor Amy that when we got up here, and nobody about . . .

same as to-day. . . .' Still staring out to sea, he rolled his handkerchief round and round like a ball in his hands and repeated quietly, consideringly, 'It seemed such a chance.'

'What seemed – such a chance?' asked Miss Halkett in a whisper. Her face could not be called florid now.

'That she had one of them attacks up here. . . . Bad it was . . . I hadn't never seen one before. I broke the capsicule into the handkerchief, like Miss Sharpe had told me; I can smell the stuff now. . . . Then I thought of my Amy, and I – I shoved the handkerchief right down into my pocket, and put the hood of the chair over her quick, so as not to see, nor no one else if they *should* come by . . . and went and stood over there by the edge for a bit.' One hand left the other and went out to point. 'Yes, it was just over there . . . I told the doctor afterwards the stuff hadn't had no effect, but he said I done what I could for the old lady, because there was the glass crushed up on the handkerchief for him to see. It was Miss Sharpe as was blamed. . . . But Amy died before I got the money. . . . And I know that it's over there Mrs Birling wants me to go; even the chair sometimes seemed to be pushing a bit of late. Anyhow, I shall be glad not to have to pull it about no more; and I'm glad I've told somebody. But I'm sorry I frightened you, ladies, just now. . . . Good evening, and thank you for listening to me.'

His hearers were so frozen that they made no protest as old Cotton caught up the handle of the chair and started off at a brisk pace for the edge of the cliff. Then they woke to his purpose. Primrose again clutched the handle at the back, Miss Flora grabbed at the side of the chair, both by some fatality concentrating their resistance on the vehicle instead of on the old man who pulled it. And for a moment he, tired and spindly as he was, dragged them also forward for a few yards, until they reached the place where the turf, flushed with sea-pinks, began to slope to the ultimate verge, by which time their combined weight was too much for him. Old Cotton dropped the handle, turned on them one brief look of triumph, and holding on his hat, ran quietly down the incline.

No human eyes saw him go over, for they were tightly shut. But half a dozen gulls, screaming louder than Flora and Primrose Halkett, flapped indignantly up from their nests on the ledges below. An instant or two later came a fresh uprush of clamour and white wings, as the bath-chair, released by the two women only just in time for their own safety, ran with a kind of clumsy eagerness down the slope, then, toppling sideways followed its bond-slave over the cliff.

Elizabeth Bowen

THE HAPPY AUTUMN FIELDS

THE family walking party, though it comprised so many, did not deploy or straggle over the stubble but kept in a procession of threes and twos. Papa, who carried his Alpine stick, led, flanked by Constance and little Arthur. Robert and Cousin Theodore, locked in studious talk, had Emily attached but not quite abreast. Next came Digby and Lucius, taking, to left and right, imaginary aim at rooks. Henrietta and Sarah brought up the rear.

It was Sarah who saw the others ahead on the blond stubble, who knew them, knew what they were to each other, knew their names and knew her own. It was she who felt the stubble under her feet, and who heard it give beneath the tread of the others a continuous different more distant soft stiff scrunch. The field and all these outlying fields in view knew as Sarah knew that they were Papa's. The harvest had been good and was now in: he was satisfied – for this afternoon he had made the instinctive choice of his most womanly daughter, most nearly infant son. Arthur, whose hand Papa was holding, took an anxious hop, a skip and a jump to every stride of the great man's. As for Constance – Sarah could often see the flash of her hat-feather as she turned her head, the curve of her close bodice as she turned her torso. Constance gave Papa her attention but not her thoughts, for she had already been sought in marriage.

The landowners' daughters, from Constance down, walked with their beetle-green, mole or maroon skirts gathered up and carried clear of the ground, but for Henrietta, who was still ankle-free. They walked inside a continuous stuffy sound, but left silence behind them. Behind them, rooks that had risen and circled, sun striking blue from their blue-black wings, planed one by one to the earth and settled to peck again. Papa and the boys were dark-clad as the rooks but with no sheen, but for their white collars.

It was Sarah who located the thoughts of Constance, knew what a twisting prisoner was Arthur's hand, felt to the depths of Emily's pique at Cousin Theodore's inattention, rejoiced with Digby and Lucius at the imaginary fall of so many rooks. She fell back, however, as from a rocky range, from the converse of Robert and Cousin Theodore. Most she knew that she swam with love at the nearness of Henrietta's young and alert face and eyes which shone with the sky and queried the afternoon.

She recognized the colour of valediction, tasted sweet sadness, while from the cottage inside the screen of trees wood-smoke rose melting pungent and blue. This was the eve of the brothers' return to school. It was like a Sunday; Papa had kept the late afternoon free; all (all but one) encircling Robert, Digby and Lucius, they walked the estate the brothers would not see again for so long. Robert, it could be felt, was not unwilling to return to his books; next year he would go to college like Theodore; besides, to all this they saw he was not the heir. But in Digby and Lucius aiming and popping hid a bodily grief, the repugnance of victims, though these two were further from being heirs than Robert.

Sarah said to Henrietta: 'To think they will not be here to-morrow!'

'*Is* that what you are thinking about?' Henrietta asked, with her subtle taste for the truth.

'More, I was thinking that you and I will be back again by one another at table. . . .'

'You know we are always sad when the boys are going, but we are never sad when the boys have gone.' The sweet reciprocal guilty smile that started on Henrietta's lips finished on those of Sarah. 'Also,' the young sister said, 'we know this is only something happening again. It happened last year, and it will happen next. But oh how should I feel, and how should you feel, if it were something that had not happened before?'

'For instance, when Constance goes to be married?'

'Oh, I don't mean *Constance*!' said Henrietta.

'So long,' said Sarah, considering, 'as, whatever it is, it happens to both of us?' She must never have to wake in the early morning except to the birdlike stirrings of Henrietta, or have her cheek brushed in the dark by the frill of another pillow in whose hollow did not repose Henrietta's cheek. Rather than they should cease to lie in the same bed she prayed they might lie in the same grave. 'You and I will stay as we are,' she said, 'then nothing can touch one without touching the other.'

'So you say; so I hear you say!' exclaimed Henrietta, who then, lips apart, sent Sarah her most tormenting look. 'But I cannot forget that you chose to be born without me; that you would not wait —' But here she broke off, laughed outright and said: 'Oh, *see*!'

Ahead of them there had been a dislocation. Emily took advantage of having gained the ridge to kneel down to tie her bootlace so abruptly tht Digby all but fell over her, with an exclamation. Cousin Theodore had been civil enough to pause beside Emily, but Robert, lost to all but what he was saying, strode on, head down, only just not colliding into Papa and Constance, who had turned to look back. Papa, astounded, let go of Arthur's hand, whereupon Arthur fell flat on the stubble.

'Dear me,' said the affronted Constance to Robert.

Papa said: 'What is the matter there? May I ask, Robert, where you are going, sir? Digby, remember that is your sister Emily.'

'Cousin Emily is in trouble,' said Cousin Theodore.

Poor Emily, telescoped in her skirts and by now scarlet under her hatbrim, said in a muffled voice: 'It is just my bootlace, Papa.'

'Your bootlace, Emily?'

'I was just tying it.'

'Then you had better tie it. – Am I to think,' said Papa, looking round them all, 'that you must all go down like a pack of ninepins because Emily has occasion to stoop?'

At this Henrietta uttered a little whoop, flung her arms round Sarah, buried her face in her sister and fairly suffered with laughter. She could contain this no longer; she shook all over. Papa, who found Henrietta so hopelessly out of order that he took no notice of her except at table, took no notice, simply giving the signal for the others to collect themselves and move on. Cousin Theodore, helping Emily to her feet, could be seen to see how her heightened colour became her, but she dispensed with his hand chillily, looked elsewhere, touched the brooch at her throat and said: 'Thank you, I have not sustained an accident.' Digby apologized to Emily, Robert to Papa and Constance. Constance righted Arthur, flicking his breeches over with her handkerchief. All fell into their different steps and resumed their way.

Sarah, with no idea how to console laughter, coaxed, 'Come, come, come,' into Henrietta's ear. Between the girls and the others the distance widened; it began to seem that they would be left alone.

'And why not?' said Henrietta, lifting her head in answer to Sarah's thought.

They looked around them with the same eyes. The shorn uplands seemed to float on the distance, which extended dazzling to tiny blue glassy hills. There was no end to the afternoon, whose light went on ripening now they had scythed the corn. Light filled the silence which, now Papa and the others were out of hearing, was complete. Only screens of trees intersected and knolls made islands in the vast fields. The mansion and the home farm had sunk for ever below them in the expanse of woods, so that hardly a ripple showed where the girls dwelled.

The shadow of the same rook circling passed over Sarah then over Henrietta, who in their turn cast one shadow across the stubble. 'But, Henrietta, we cannot stay here for ever.'

Henrietta immediately turned her eyes to the only lonely plume of smoke, from the cottage. 'Then let us go and visit the poor old man. He is dying and the others are happy. One day we shall pass and see no more smoke; then soon his roof will fall in, and we shall always be sorry we did not go to-day.'

'But he no longer remembers us any longer.'

'All the same, he will feel us there in the door.'

'But can we forget this is Robert's and Digby's and Lucius's good-bye walk? It would be heartless of both of us to neglect them.'

'Then how heartless Fitzgeorge is!' smiled Henrietta.

'Fitzgeorge is himself, the eldest and in the Army. Fitzgeorge I'm afraid is not an excuse for us.'

A resigned sigh, or perhaps the pretence of one, heaved up Henrietta's still narrow bosom. To delay matters for just a moment more she shaded her eyes with one hand, to search the distance like a sailor looking for a sail. She gazed with hope and zeal in every direction but that in which she and Sarah were bound to go. Then – 'Oh, but Sarah, here *they* are, coming – they are!' she cried. She brought out her handkerchief and began to fly it, drawing it to and fro through the windless air.

In the glass of the distance, two horsemen came into view, cantering on a grass track between the fields. When the track dropped into a hollow they dropped with it, but by now the drumming of hoofs was heard. The reverberation filled the land, the silence and Sarah's being; not watching for the riders to reappear she instead fixed her eyes on her sister's handkerchief which, let hang limp while its owner intently waited, showed a bitten corner as well as a damson stain. Again it became a flag, in furious motion – 'Wave too, Sarah, wave too! Make your bracelet flash!'

'They must have seen us if they will ever see us,' said Sarah, standing still as a stone.

Henrietta's waving at once ceased. Facing her sister she crunched up her handkerchief, as though to stop it acting a lie. 'I can see you are shy,' she said in a dead voice. 'So shy you won't even wave to *Fitzgeorge*?'

Her way of not speaking the *other* name had a hundred meanings; she drove them all in by the way she did not look at Sarah's face. The impulsive breath she had caught stole silently out again, while her eyes – till now at their brightest, their most speaking – dulled with uncomprehending solitary alarm. The ordeal of awaiting Eugene's approach thus became for Sarah, from moment to moment, torture.

Fitzgeorge, Papa's heir, and his friend Eugene, the young neighbouring squire, struck off the track and rode up at a trot with their hats doffed. Sun striking low turned Fitzgeorge's flesh to coral and made Eugene blink his dark eyes. The young men reined in; the girls looked up at the horses. 'And my father, Constance, the others?' Fitzgeorge demanded, as though the stubble had swallowed them.

'Ahead, on the way to the quarry, the other side of the hill.'

'We heard you were all walking together,' Fitzgeorge said, seeming dissatisfied.

'We are following.'

'What, alone?' said Eugene, speaking for the first time.

'Forlorn!' glittered Henrietta, raising two mocking hands.

Fitzgeorge considered, said 'Good' severely, and signified to Eugene that they would ride on. But too late: Eugene had dismounted. Fitzgeorge saw, shrugged and flicked his horse to a trot; but Eugene led his slowly between the sisters. Or rather, Sarah walked on his left hand, the horse on his right and Henrietta the other side of the horse. Henrietta, acting like somebody quite alone, looked up at the sky, idly holding one of the empty stirrups. Sarah, however, looked at the ground, with Eugene inclined as though to speak but not speaking. Enfolded, dizzied, blinded as though inside a wave, she could feel his features carved in brightness above her. Alongside the slender stepping of his horse, Eugene matched his naturally long free step to hers. His elbow was through the reins; with his fingers he brushed back the lock that his bending to her had sent falling over his forehead. She recorded the sublime act and knew what smile shaped his lips. So each without looking trembled before an image, while slow colour burned up the curves of her cheeks. The consummation would be when their eyes met.

At the other side of the horse, Henrietta began to sing. At once her pain, like a scientific ray, passed through the horse and Eugene to penetrate Sarah's heart.

We surmount the skyline: the family come into our view, we into theirs. They are halted, waiting, on the decline to the quarry. The handsome statufied group in strong yellow sunshine, aligned by Papa and crowned by Fitzgeorge, turn their judging eyes on the laggards, waiting to close their ranks round Henrietta and Sarah and Eugene. One more moment and it will be too late; no further communication will be possible. Stop oh stop Henrietta's heartbreaking singing! Embrace her close again! Speak the only possible word! Say – oh, say what? Oh, the word is lost!

'Henrietta . . .'

A shock of striking pain in the knuckles of the outflung hand – Sarah's? The eyes, opening, saw that the hand had struck, not been struck: there was a corner of a table. Dust, whitish and gritty, lay on the top of the table and on the telephone. Dull but piercing white light filled the room and what was left of the ceiling; her first thought was that it must have snowed. If so, it was winter now.

Through the calico stretched and tacked over the window came the sound of a piano: someone was playing Tchaikowsky badly in a room without windows or doors. From somewhere else in the hollowness came a cascade of hammering. Close up, a voice: 'Oh, *awake*, Mary?' It came from the other side of the open door, which jutted out between herself and the speaker – he on the threshold, she lying on the uncovered mattress of a bed. The speaker added: 'I had been going away.'

Summoning words from somewhere she said: 'Why? I didn't know you were here.'

'Evidently – Say, who is "Henrietta"?'

Despairing tears filled her eyes. She drew back her hurt hand, began to suck at the knuckle and whimpered, 'I've hurt myself'.

A man she knew to be 'Travis', but failed to focus, came round the door saying: 'Really I don't wonder.' Sitting down on the edge of the mattress he drew her hand away from her lips and held it: the act, in itself gentle, was accompanied by an almost hostile stare of concern. 'Do listen, Mary,' he said. 'While you've slept I've been all over the house again, and I'm less than ever satisfied that it's safe. In your normal sense you'd never attempt to stay here. There've been alerts, and more than alerts, all day; one more bang anywhere near, which may happen at any moment, could bring the rest of this down. You keep telling me that you have things to see to – but do you know what chaos the rooms are in? Till they've gone ahead with more clearing, where can you hope to start? And if there *were* anything you could do, you couldn't do it. Your own nerves know that, if you don't: it was almost frightening, when I looked in just now, to see the way you were sleeping – you've shut up shop.'

She lay staring over his shoulder at the calico window. He went on: 'You don't like it here. Your self doesn't like it. Your will keeps driving your self, but it can't be driven the whole way – it makes its own get-out: sleep. Well, I want you to sleep as much as you (really) do. But *not* here. So I've taken a room for you in a hotel; I'm going now for a taxi; you can practically make the move without waking up.'

'No, I can't get into a taxi without waking.'

'Do you realize you're the last soul left in the terrace?'

'Then who is that playing the piano?'

'Oh, one of the furniture-movers in Number Six. I didn't count the jaquerie; of course *they're* in possession – unsupervised, teeming, having a high old time. While I looked in on you in here ten minutes ago they were smashing out that conservatory at the other end. Glass being done in in cold blood – it was brutalizing. You never batted an eyelid; in fact, I thought you smiled.' He listened. 'Yes, the piano – they are highbrow all right. You know there's a workman downstairs lying on your blue sofa looking for pictures in one of your French books?'

'No,' she said, 'I've no idea who is there.'

'Obviously. With the lock blown off your front door anyone who likes can get in and out.'

'Including you.'

'Yes. I've had a word with a chap about getting that lock back before to-night. As for you, you don't know what is happening.'

'I did,' she said, locking her fingers before her eyes.

The unreality of this room and of Travis's presence preyed on her as figments of dreams that one knows to be dreams can do. This environment's being in semi-ruin struck her less than its being some sort of device or trap; and she rejoiced, if anything, in its decrepitude. As for Travis, he had his own part in the conspiracy to keep her from the beloved two. She felt he began to feel he was now unmeaning. She was struggling not to condemn him, scorn him for his ignorance of Henrietta, Eugene, her loss. His possessive angry fondness was part, of course, of the story of him and Mary, which like a book once read she remembered clearly but with indifference. Frantic at being delayed here, while the moment awaited her in the cornfield, she all but afforded a smile at the grotesquerie of being saddled with Mary's body and lover. Rearing up her head from the bare pillow, she looked, as far as the crossed feet, along the form inside which she found herself trapped: the irrelevant body of Mary, weighted down to the bed, wore a short black modern dress, flaked with plaster. The toes of the black suède shoes by their sickly whiteness showed Mary must have climbed over fallen ceilings; dirt engraved the fate-lines in Mary's palms.

This inspired her to say: 'But I've made a start; I've been pulling out things of value or things I want.'

For answer Travis turned to look down, expressively, at some object out of her sight, on the floor close by the bed. 'I see,' he said, 'a musty old leather box gaping open with God knows what – junk, illegible letters, diaries, yellow photographs, chiefly plaster and dust. Of all things, Mary! – after a missing will?'

'Everything one unburies seems the same age.'

'Then what are these, where do they come from – family stuff?'

'No idea,' she yawned into Mary's hand. 'They may not even be mine. Having a house like this that had empty rooms must have made me store more than I knew, for years. I came on these, so I wondered. Look if you like.'

He bent and began to go through the box – it seemed to her, not unsuspiciously. While he blew grit off packets and fumbled with tapes she lay staring at the exposed laths of the ceiling, calculating. She then said: 'Sorry if I've been cranky, about the hotel and all. Go away just for two hours, then come back with a taxi, and I'll go quiet. Will that do?'

'Fine – except why not now?'

'Travis . . .'

'Sorry. It shall be as you say . . . You've got some good morbid stuff in this box, Mary – so far as I can see at a glance. The photographs seem more your sort of thing. Comic but lyrical. All of one set of people – a beard, a gun and a pot hat, a schoolboy with a moustache, a phaeton drawn up in front of mansion, a group on steps, a *carte de visite* of two young ladies hand-in-hand in front of a painted field —'

'*Give that to me!*'

She instinctively tried, and failed, to unbutton the bosom of Mary's dress: it offered no hospitality to the photograph. So she could only fling herself over on the mattress, away from Travis, covering the two faces with her body. Racked by that oblique look of Henrietta's she recorded, too, a sort of personal shock at having seen Sarah for the first time.

Travis's hand came over her, and she shuddered. Wounded, he said: 'Mary . . .'

'Can't you leave *me* alone?'

She did not move or look till he had gone out saying: 'Then, in two hours.' She did not therefore see him pick up the dangerous box, which he took away under his arm, out of her reach.

They were back. Now the sun was setting behind the trees, but its rays passed dazzling between the branches into the beautiful warm red room. The tips of the ferns in the jardiniere curled gold, and Sarah, standing by the jardiniere, pinched at a leaf of scented geranium. The carpet had a great centre wreath of pomegranates, on which no tables or chairs stood, and its whole circle was between herself and the others.

No fire was lit yet, but where they were grouped was a hearth. Henrietta sat on a low stool, resting her elbow above her head on the arm of Mamma's chair, looking away intently as though into a fire, idle. Mamma embroidered, her needle slowed down by her thoughts; the length of tatting with roses she had already done overflowed stiffly over her supple skirts. Stretched on the rug at Mamma's feet, Arthur looked through an album of Swiss views, not liking them but vowed to be very quiet. Sarah, from where she stood, saw fuming cataracts and null eternal snows as poor Arthur kept turning over the pages, which had tissue paper between.

Against the white marble mantelpiece stood Eugene. The dark red shadows gathering in the drawing-room as the trees drowned more and more of the sun would reach him last, perhaps never: it seemed to Sarah that a lamp was lighted behind his face. He was the only gentleman with the ladies: Fitzgeorge had gone to the stables, Papa to give an order; Cousin Theodore was consulting a dictionary; in the gunroom Robert, Lucius and Digby went through the sad rites, putting away their guns. All this was known to go on but none of it could be heard.

This particular hour of subtle light – not to be fixed by the clock, for it was early in winter and late in summer and in spring and autumn now, about Arthur's bedtime – had always, for Sarah, been Henrietta's. To be with her indoors or out, upstairs or down, was to share the same crepitation. Her spirit ran on past yours with a laughing shiver into an element of its own. Leaves and branches and mirrors in empty rooms became animate. The sisters rustled and scampered and concealed themselves where nobody else was in play that was full of fear, fear that was full of play. Till, by dint of making each other's hearts beat violently, Henrietta so wholly and Sarah so nearly lost all human reason that Mamma had been known to look at them searchingly as she sat instated for evening among the calm amber lamps.

But now Henrietta had locked the hour inside her breast. By spending it seated beside Mamma, in young imitation of Constance the Society daughter, she disclaimed for ever anything else. It had always been she who with one fierce act destroyed any toy that might be outgrown. She sat with straight back, poising her cheek remotely against her finger. Only by never looking at Sarah did she admit their eternal loss.

Eugene, not long returned from a foreign tour, spoke of travel, addressing himself to Mamma, who thought but did not speak of her wedding journey. But every now and then she had to ask Henrietta to pass the scissors or tray of carded wools, and Eugene seized every such moment to look at Sarah. Into eyes always brilliant with melancholy he dared begin to allow no other expression. But this in itself declared the conspiracy of still undeclared love. For her part she looked at him as though he, transfigured by the strange light, were indeed a picture, a picture who could not see her. The wallpaper now flamed scarlet behind his shoulder. Mamma, Henrietta, even unknowing Arthur were in no hurry to raise their heads.

Henrietta said: 'If I were a man I should take my bride to Italy.'

'There are mules in Switzerland,' said Arthur.

'Sarah,' said Mamma, who turned in her chair mildly, 'where are you, my love; do you never mean to sit down?'

'To Naples,' said Henrietta.

'Are you not thinking of Venice?' said Eugene.

'No,' returned Henrietta, 'why should I be? I should like to climb the volcano. But then I am not a man, and am still less likely ever to be a bride.'

'Arthur . . .' Mamma said.

'Mamma?'

'Look at the clock.'

Arthur sighed politely, got up and replaced the album on the circular table, balanced upon the rest. He offered his hand to Eugene, his cheek to Henrietta and to Mamma; then he started towards Sarah, who came to meet him. 'Tell me, Arthur,' she said, embracing him, 'what did you do to-day?'

Arthur only stared with his button blue eyes. 'You were there too: we went for a walk in the cornfield, with Fitzgeorge on his horse, and I fell down.' He pulled out of her arms and said: 'I must go back to my beetle.' He had difficulty, as always, in turning the handle of the mahogany door. Mamma waited till he had left the room, then said: 'Arthur is quite a man now; he no longer comes running to me when he has hurt himself. Why, I did not even know he had fallen down. Before we know, he will be going away to school too.' She sighed and lifted her eyes to Eugene. 'To-morrow is to be a sad day.'

Eugene with a gesture signified his own sorrow. The sentiments of Mamma could have been uttered only here in the drawing-room, which for all its size and formality was lyrical and almost exotic. There was a look like velvet in darker parts of the air; sombre window draperies let out gushes of lace; the music on the pianoforte bore tender titles, and the harp though unplayed gleamed in a corner, beyond sofas, whatnots, arm-chairs, occasional tables that all stood on tottering little feet. At any moment a tinkle might have been struck from the lustres' drops of the brighter day, a vibration from the musical instruments, or a quiver from the fringes and ferns. But the towering vases upon the consoles, the albums piled on the tables, the shells and figurines on the flights of brackets, all had, like the alabaster Leaning Tower of Pisa, an equilibrium of their own. Nothing would fall or change. And everything in the drawing-room was muted, weighted, pivoted by Mamma. When she added: 'We shall not feel quite the same,' it was to be understood that she would not have spoken thus from her place at the opposite end of Papa's table.

'Sarah,' said Henrietta curiously, 'what made you ask Arthur what he had been doing? Surely you have not forgotten to-day?'

The sisters were seldom known to address or question one another in public; it was taken that they knew each other's minds. Mamma, though untroubled, looked from one to the other. Henrietta continued: 'No day, least of all to-day, is like any other – surely that must be true?' she said to Eugene. 'You will never forget my waving my handkerchief?'

Before Eugene had composed an answer, she turned to Sarah: 'Or *you*, them riding across the fields?'

Eugene also slowly turned his eyes on Sarah, as though awaiting with something like dread her answer to the question he had not asked. She drew a light little gold chair into the middle of the wreath of the carpet, where no one ever sat, and sat down. She said: 'But since then I think I have been asleep.'

'Charles the First walked and talked half an hour after his head was cut off,' said Henrietta mockingly. Sarah in anguish pressed the palms of her hands together upon a shred of geranium leaf.

'How else,' she said, 'could I have had such a bad dream?'

'That must be the explanation!' said Henrietta.

'A trifle fanciful,' said Mamma.

However rash it might be to speak at all, Sarah wished she knew how to speak more clearly. The obscurity and loneliness of her trouble was not to be borne. How could she put into words the feeling of dislocation, the formless dread that had been with her since she found herself in the drawing-room? The source of both had been what she must call her dream. How could she tell the others with what vehemence she tried to attach her being to each second, not because each was singular in itself, each a drop condensed from the mist of love in the room, but because she apprehended that the seconds were numbered? Her hope was that the others at least half knew. Were Henrietta and Eugene able to understand how completely, how nearly for ever, she had been swept from them, would they not without fail each grasp one of her hands? – She went so far as to throw her hands out, as though alarmed by a wasp. The shred of geranium fell to the carpet.

Mamma, tracing this behaviour of Sarah's to only one cause, could not but think reproachfully of Eugene. Delightful as his conversation had been, he would have done better had he paid this call with the object of interviewing Papa. Turning to Henrietta she asked her to ring for the lamps, as the sun had set.

Eugene, no longer where he had stood, was able to make no gesture towards the bell-rope. His dark head was under the tide of dusk; for, down on one knee on the edge of the wreath, he was feeling over the carpet for what had fallen from Sarah's hand. In the inevitable silence rooks on the return from the fields could be heard streaming over the house; their sound filled the sky and even the room, and it appeared so useless to ring the bell that Henrietta stayed quivering by Mamma's chair. Eugene rose, brought out his fine white handkerchief and, while they watched, enfolded carefully in it what he had just found, then returning the handkerchief to his breast pocket. This was done so deep in the reverie that accompanies any final act that Mamma instinctively murmured to Henrietta: 'But you will be my child when Arthur has gone.'

The door opened for Constance to appear on the threshold. Behind her queenly figure globes approached, swimming in their own light: these were the lamps for which Henrietta had not rung, but these first were put on the hall tables. 'Why, Mamma,' exclaimed Constance, 'I cannot see who is with you!'

'Eugene is with us,' said Henrietta, 'but on the point of asking if he may send for his horse.'

'Indeed?' said Constance to Eugene. 'Fitzgeorge has been asking for you, but I cannot tell where he is now.'

The figures of Emily, Lucius and Cousin Theodore criss-crossed the lamplight there in the hall, to mass behind Constance's in the drawing-room door. Emily, over her sister's shoulder, said: 'Mamma, Lucius wishes to ask you whether for once he may take his guitar to school.' – 'One objection, however,' said Cousin Theodore, 'is that Lucius's trunk is already locked and strapped.' 'Since Robert is taking his box of inks,' said Lucius, 'I do not see why I should not take my guitar.' – 'But Robert,' said Constance, 'will soon be going to college.'

Lucius squeezed past the others into the drawing-room in order to look anxiously at Mamma, who said: 'You have thought of this late; we must go and see.' The others parted to let Mamma, followed by Lucius, out. Then Constance, Emily and Cousin Theodore deployed and sat down in different parts of the drawing-room, to await the lamps.

'I am glad the rooks have done passing over,' said Emily, 'they make me nervous.' – 'Why?' yawned Constance haughtily, 'what do you think could happen?' Robert and Digby silently came in.

Eugene said to Sarah: 'I shall be back to-morrow.'

'But, oh –' she began. She turned to cry: 'Henrietta!'

'Why, what is the matter?' said Henrietta, unseen at the back of the gold chair. 'What could be sooner than to-morrow?'

'But something terrible may be going to happen.'

'There cannot fail to be to-morrow,' said Eugene gravely.

'I will see that there is to-morrow,' said Henrietta.

'You will never let me out of your sight?'

Eugene, addressing himself to Henrietta, said: 'Yes, promise her what she asks.'

Henrietta cried: 'She *is* never out of my sight. Who are you to ask me that, you Eugene? Whatever tries to come between me and Sarah becomes nothing. Yes, come to-morrow, come sooner, come – when you like, but no one will ever be quite alone with Sarah. You do not even know what you are trying to do. It is *you* who are making something terrible happen – Sarah, tell him that that is true! Sarah —'

The others, in the dark in the chairs and sofas, could be felt to turn their judging eyes upon Sarah, who, as once before, could not speak –

– The house rocked: simultaneously the calico window split and more ceiling fell, though not on the bed. The enormous dull sound of the explosion died, leaving a minor trickle of dissolution still to be heard in parts of the house. Until the choking stinging plaster dust had had time to settle, she lay with lips pressed close, nostrils not breathing and eyes shut. Remembering the box, Mary wondered if it had been again buried. No, she found, looking over the edge of the bed: that had been unable to happen because the box was missing. Travis, who must have taken it, would when he came back no doubt explain why. She looked at her watch, which had stopped, which was not surprising; she did not remember winding it for the last two days, but then she could not remember much. Through the torn window appeared the timelessness of an impermeably clouded late summer afternoon.

There being nothing left, she wished he would come to take her to the hotel. The one way back to the fields was barred by Mary's surviving the fall of ceiling. Sarah was right in doubting that there would be to-morrow: Eugene, Henrietta were lost in time to the woman weeping there on the bed, no longer reckoning who she was.

At last she heard the taxi, then Travis hurrying up the littered stairs. 'Mary, you're all right, Mary – *another*?' Such a helpless white face came round the door that she could only hold out her arms and say: 'Yes, but where have *you* been?'

'You said two hours. But I wish —'

'I have missed you.'

'Have you? Do you know you are crying?'

'Yes. How are we to live without natures? We only know inconvenience now, not sorrow. Everything pulverizes so easily because it is rot-dry; one can only wonder that it makes so much noise. The source, the sap must have dried up, or the pulse must have stopped, before you and I were conceived. So much flowed through people; so little flows through us. All we can do is imitate love or sorrow. – Why did you take away my box?'

He only said: 'It is in my office.'

She continued: 'What has happened is cruel: I am left with a fragment torn out of a day, a day I don't even know where or when; and now how am I to help laying that like a pattern against the poor stuff of everything else? – Alternatively, I am a person drained by a dream. I cannot forget the climate of those hours. Or life at that pitch, eventful – not happy, no, but strung like a harp. I have had a sister called Henrietta.'

'And I have been looking inside your box. What else can you expect? – I have had to write off this day, from the work point of view, thanks to you. So could I sit and do nothing for the last two hours? I just glanced through this and that – still, I know the family.'

'You said it was morbid stuff.'

'Did I? I still say it gives off something.'

She said: 'And then there was Eugene.'

'Probably. I don't think I came on much of his except some notes he must have made for Fitzgeorge from some book on scientific farming. Well, there it is: I have sorted everything out and put it back again, all but a lock of hair that tumbled out of a letter I could not trace. So I've got the hair in my pocket.'

'What colour is it?'

'Ash-brown. Of course, it is a bit – desiccated. Do you want it?'

'No,' she said with a shudder. 'Really, Travis, what revenges you take!'

'I didn't look at it that way,' he said puzzled.

'Is the taxi waiting?' Mary got off the bed and, picking her way across the room, began to look about for things she ought to take with her, now and then stopping to brush her dress. She took the mirror out of her bag to see how dirty her face was. 'Travis –' she said suddenly.

'Mary?'

'Only, I –'

'That's all right. Don't let us imitate anything just at present.'

In the taxi, looking out of the window, she said: 'I suppose, then, that I am descended from Sarah?'

'No,' he said, 'that would be impossible. There must be some reason why you should have those papers, but that is not the one. From all negative evidence Sarah, like Henrietta, remained unmarried. I found no mention of either, after a certain date, in the letters of Constance, Robert or Emily, which makes it seem likely both died young. Fitzgeorge refers, in a letter to Robert written in his old age, to some friend of their youth who was thrown from his horse and killed, riding back after a visit to their home. The young man, whose name doesn't appear, was alone; and the evening, which was in autumn, was fine though late. Fitzgeorge wonders, and says he will always wonder, what made the horse shy in those empty fields.'

Pamela Hansford Johnson

THE EMPTY SCHOOLROOM

MY mother and father were in India and I had no aunts, uncles or cousins with whom I could spend my holidays; so I stayed behind in the drab and echoing school to amuse myself as best I could, my only companions the housekeeper, the maid, and Mademoiselle Fournier, who also had nowhere else to go.

Our school was just outside the village of Bellancay, which is in the north of France, four or five kilometres from Rouen. It was a tall, narrow house set upon the top of a hill, bare save for the great sweep of beech trees sheltering the long carriage drive. As I look back some twenty-seven years to my life there, it seems to me that the sun never shone, that the grass was always dun-coloured beneath a dun-coloured sky, and that the vast spaces of the lawns were broken perpetually by the scurry of dry brown leaves licked along by a small, bitter wind. This inaccurate impression remains with me because, I suppose, I was never happy at Bellancay. There were twenty or thirty other girls there – French, German or Swiss; I was the only English girl among them. Madame de Vallon, the headmistress, did not love my nation. She could not forget that she had been born in 1815, the year of defeat. With Mademoiselle Maury, the young assistant teacher, I was a little more at ease, for she, even if she did not care for me, had too volatile a nature not to smile and laugh sometimes, even for the benefit of those who were not her favourites.

Mademoiselle Fournier was a dependent cousin of our headmistress. She was in her late fifties, a little woman dry as a winter twig, her face very tight, small and wary under a wig of coarse yellow hair. To pay for her board and lodging she taught deportment; in her youth she had been at the Court of the Tzar, and it was said that at sixteen years of age she was betrothed to a Russian nobleman. There was some sort of mystery here, about which all the girls were curious. Louise de Chausson said her mother had told her the story – how the nobleman, on the eve of his wedding, had shot himself through the head, having received word that certain speculations in which he had for many years been involved had come to light, and that his arrest was imminent. . . . 'And from that day,' Louise whispered, her prominent eyes gleaming in the candlelight, 'she began to wither and wither and wither away, till her beauty was gone. . . .' Yes, I can see Louise now, kneeling upon her bed at the end of the vast dormitory, her thick plait hanging down over her nightgown, the little cross with the turquoise glittering at her beautiful and grainy throat. The others believed the story implicitly, except the piece about Mademoiselle Fournier's lost beauty. That they could not stomach. No, she was ugly as a monkey and had always been so.

For myself, I disbelieved in the nobleman; believed in the beauty. I have always had a curious faculty for stripping age from a face, recognizing the structure of the bone and the original texture of the skin beneath the disguisings of blotch, red vein and loosened flesh. When I looked at Mademoiselle Fournier I saw that the pinched and veinous nose had once been delicate and fine; that the sunken eyes had once been almond-shaped and blue; that the small, loose mouth had once pouted charmingly and opened upon romantic words. Why did I not believe in the nobleman? For no better reason than a distrust of Louise's information on any conceivable point. She was a terrible teller of falsehoods.

I was seventeen years old when I spent my last vacation at Bellancay, and knowing that my parents were to return to Europe in the following spring I watched the departure of the other girls with a heart not quite so heavy as was usual upon these occasions. In six months' time I, too, would be welcomed and loved, have adventures to relate and hopes upon which to feed.

I waved to them from a dormer window as they rattled away in fiacre and barouche down the drive between the beech trees, sired and damed, uncled and aunted, their boxes stacked high and their voices high as the treetops. They had never before seemed to me a particularly attractive group of girls – that is, not in the mass. There was, of course, Helene de Courcey, with her great olive eyes; Madeleine Millet, whose pale-red hair hung to her knees; but in the cluster they had no particular charm. That day, however, as, in new bonnets flowered and feathered and gauzed, they passed from sight down the narrowing file of beeches, I thought them all beautiful as princesses, and as princesses fortunate. Perhaps the nip in the air of a grey June made their cheeks rose-red, their eyes bright as the eyes of desirable young ladies in ballrooms.

The last carriage disappeared, the last sound died away. I turned from the window and went down the echoing stairs, flight after flight to the *salle-à-manger*, where my luncheon awaited me.

I ate alone. Mademoiselle Fournier took her meals in her own room upon the second floor, reading as she ate, crumbs falling from her lip onto the page. Tonight she and I, in the pattern of all holiday nights, would sit together for a while in the drawing room before retiring.

'You don't make much of a meal, I must say,' Marie, the maid, rebuked me, as she cleared the plates. 'You can't afford to grow thinner, Mademoiselle, or you'll snap in two.' She brought me some cherries, which I would not eat then but preferred to take out with me in the garden. 'I'll wrap them up for you. No! you can't put them in your handkerchief like that; you'll stain it.'

She chattered to me for a while, in her good nature trying to ease my loneliness. Marie, at least, had relations in the village with whom she sometimes spent her evenings. 'What are you going to do with yourself, eh? Read your eyes out as usual?'

'I shall walk this afternoon, unless I find it too chilly.'

'You'll find it raining,' said Marie, cocking a calculating eye toward the windows, 'in an hour. No, less, in half an hour.'

She busied herself wrapping up my cherries, which she handed to me in a neat parcel with a firm fingerloop of string. 'If it's wet you can play the piano.'

'You've forgotten,' I said, 'we have none now, or shan't have till they send the new one.'

Madame de Vallon had recently sold the old instrument, ugly and tinny, and with the money from the sale plus some money raised by parents' subscriptions had bought a grand pianoforte from Monsieur Oury, the mayor, whose eldest daughter, the musical one, had lately died.

'You can play on Mademoiselle Fournier's,' said Marie. 'She won't mind. You go and ask her.'

'What, is there another piano in the school?' I was amazed. I had been at Bellancay for seven years and had fancied no corner of the building unknown to me.

'Ah-ha,' said Marie triumphantly, 'there are still things you don't know, eh? You don't have to do the housework, or you'd be wiser.'

'But where is it?'

'In the empty schoolroom.'

I laughed at her. 'But they're all empty now! Whatever do you mean?'

'The one at the top,' she said impatiently, 'the one up the little flight of four stairs.'

'But that's the lumber room!'

'There's lumber in it. But it was a schoolroom once. It was when my aunt worked here. The piano's up there still, though *she* never plays it now.' Marie jerked her head skyward to indicate Mademoiselle Fournier upstairs.

I was fascinated by this information. We girls had never entered the lumber room because no attraction had been attached to it: to us it was simply a small grimy door in the attic, locked, we imagined, as we had never seen anyone go in or out. All we knew was that old books, valises, crates of unwanted china were sometimes stacked up there out of the way.

There! I have failed to make my point quite clear. I must try again. *There was no mystery whatsoever attaching to this room*, which is the reason why no girl had ever tried the handle. Schoolgirls are curious and roaming creatures; how better can they be kept from a certain path than by the positive assurance that it is a cul-de-sac?

Dismissing Marie, I determined to go and seek permission from Mademoiselle Fournier to play upon her pianoforte. Since the departure of the old one, I had missed my music lessons and above all my practicing; most of the girls were delighted to be saved a labour which to me, though I was an indifferent performer, had never been anything but a pleasure.

Mademoiselle had finished her meal and was just coming out upon the landing as I ran up the stairs to find her. I made my request.

She looked at me. 'Who told you about the instrument?'

'Marie.'

She was silent. Her brows moved up and down, moving the wig as they did so. It was a familiar trick with her when she was puzzled or annoyed. At last she said, without expression, 'No, you may not go up there,' and pushing me, hurried on downstairs.

At the turn of the staircase, however, she stopped and looked up. Her whole face was working with some unrecognizable emotion and her cheeks were burning red. 'Is there *no* place one can keep to oneself?' she cried at me furiously and, ducking her head, ran on.

When we sat that evening in the drawing room, in our chairs turned to the fireless grate, she made no reference to the little scene of that afternoon. I thought she was, perhaps, sorry for having spoken so sharply, for she asked me a few personal questions of a kindly nature and just before bedtime brought out a tin box full of sugared almonds, which she shared with me.

She rose a little before I did, leaving me to retire when I chose. I stayed for perhaps half an hour in that vast, pale room with its moth-coloured draperies and its two tarnished chandeliers hanging a great way below the ceiling. Then I took up my candle and went to bed.

Now I must insist that I was a docile girl, a little sullen, perhaps, out of an unrealized resentment against my parents for (as I thought) deserting me; but obedient. I never had a bad-conduct report from any of our teachers. It is important that this fact should be realized, so the reader shall know that what I did was not of my own free will.

I could not sleep. I lay open-eyed until my candle burned halfway down and the moon shifted round into the windowpane, weaving the golden light with its own blue-silver. I had no thought of any importance. Small pictures from the day's humdrum events flashed across my brain. I saw the neatly looped parcel of cherries, the currant stain at the hem of Marie's apron, the stark-blue bird on the bonnet of Louise de Chausson, who had left Bellancay to marry an elderly and not very rich nobleman of Provence. I saw the leaves scurrying over the grey lawns, saw a woodpecker rapping at the trunk of the tree behind the house. What I did not see was the face of Mademoiselle Fournier upturned from the stairway. She never entered my thoughts at all.

And so it is very strange that just before dawn I rose up, put on my dressing gown and sought about the room until I found a pair of gloves my father had had made for me in India, fawn-coloured, curiously stitched in gold and dark-green thread. These I took up, left the room and made my way silently up through the quiet house till I came to the door of the lumber room – or, as Marie had called it, the empty schoolroom. I paused with my hand upon the latch and listened. There was no sound except the impalpable breathing of the night, compound perhaps of the breathings of all who sleep, or perhaps of the movement of the moon through the gathered clouds.

I raised the latch gently and stepped within the room, closing the door softly behind me.

The chamber ran halfway across the length of the house at the rear of it, and was lighted by a ceiling window through which the moon rays poured lavishly down. It was still a schoolroom, despite the lumber stacked at the far end, the upright piano standing just behind the door. Facing me was a dais, on which stood a table and a chair. Before the dais were row upon row of desks, with benches behind. Everything was very dusty. With my finger I wrote DUST upon the teacher's table, then scuffed the word out again.

I went to the pianoforte. Behind the lattice-work was a ruching of torn red silk; the candle stumps in the sconces were red also. On the rack stood a piece of music, a Chopin nocturne simplified for beginners.

Gingerly I raised the lid and a mottled spider ran across the keys, dropped on hasty thread to the floor and ran away. The underside of the lid was completely netted by his silk; broken strands waved in the disturbed air and over the discoloured keys. As a rule I am afraid of spiders. That night I was not afraid. I laid my gloves on the keyboard, then closed the piano lid upon them.

I was ready to go downstairs. I took one glance about the room and for a moment thought I saw a shadowy form sitting upon one of the back benches, a form that seemed to weep. Then the impression passed away, and there was only the moonlight painting the room with its majesty. I went out, latched the door and crept back to my bed where, in the first colouring of dawn, I fell asleep.

Next day it was fine. I walked to the river in the morning, and in the afternoon worked at my petit-point upon the terrace. At teatime an invitation came to me. The mayor, M. Oury, wrote to Mademoiselle Fournier saying he believed there was a young lady left behind at school for the holidays, and that if she would care to dine at his house upon the following evening it would be a great pleasure to him and to his young daughters. 'We are not a gay house these days,' he wrote, 'but if the young lady cares for books and flowers there are a great number of both in my library and conservatory.'

'Shall I go?' I asked her.

'But of course! It is really a great honour for you. Do you know who the mayor's mother was before her marriage? She was a Uzes. Yes. And when she married M. Oury's father, a very handsome man, her family cut her off with nothing at all and never spoke to her again. But they were very happy. You must wear your best gown and your white hat. Take the gown to Marie and she will iron it for you.'

The day upon which I was to visit M. Oury was sunless and chilly. Plainly the blue dress that Marie had so beautifully spotted and pressed would not do at all. I had, however, a gown of fawn-coloured merino, plain but stylish, with which my brown straw hat would look very well.

Mademoiselle Fournier left the house at four o'clock to take tea with the village priest. She looked me over before she went, pinched my dress, tweaked it, pulled out the folds, and told me to sit quite still until the mayor's carriage came for me at half past six. 'Sit like a mouse, mind, or you will spoil the effect. Remember, M. Oury is not nobody.' She said suddenly, 'Where are your gloves?'

I had forgotten them.

'Forgetting the very things that make a lady look a lady! Go and fetch them at once. Marie!'

The maid came in.

'Marie, see Mademoiselle's gloves are nice, and brush her down once more just as you see the carriage enter the drive. I mustn't wait now. Well, Maud, I wish you a pleasant evening. Don't forget you must be a credit to us.'

When she had gone Marie asked for my gloves. 'You'd better wear your brown ones with that hat, Mademoiselle.'

'Oh!' I exclaimed, 'I can't! I lost one on the expedition last week.'

'Your black, then?'

'They won't do. They'd look dreadful with this gown and hat. I know! I have a beautiful Indian pair that will match my dress exactly! I'll go and look for them.'

I searched. The reader must believe that I hunted all over my room for them anxiously, one eye upon the clock, though it was not yet twenty minutes past four. Chagrined, really upset at the thought of having my toilette ruined, I sat down upon the edge of the bed and began to cry a little. Tears came very easily to me in those lost and desolate days.

From high up in the house I heard a few notes of the piano, the melody of a Chopin nocturne played fumblingly in the treble, and I thought at once, 'Of course! The gloves are up there, where I hid them.'

The body warns us of evil before the senses are half awakened. I knew no fear as I ran lightly up toward the empty schoolroom, yet as I reached the door I felt a wave of heat engulf me, and knew a sick, nauseous stirring within my body. The notes, audible only to my ear (not to Marie's, for even at that moment I could hear her calling out some inquiry or gossip to the housekeeper), ceased. I lifted the latch and looked in.

The room appeared to be deserted, yet I could see the presence within it and knew its distress. I peeped behind the door.

At the piano sat a terribly ugly, thin young girl in a dunce's cap. She was half turned toward me and I saw her piglike profile, the protruding teeth, the spurt of sandy eyelash. She wore a holland dress in the fashion of twenty years ago, and lean yellow streamers of hair fell down over her back from beneath the paper cone. Her hands, still resting on the fouled keyboard, were meshed about with the spider's web; beneath them lay my Indian gloves.

I made a movement toward the girl. She swivelled sharply and looked me full in the face. Her eyes were all white, red-rimmed, but tearless.

To get my gloves I must risk touching her. We looked at each other, she and I, and her head shrank, low between her hunching shoulders. Somehow I must speak to her friendlily, disarm her while I gained my objective.

'Was it you playing?' I asked.

No answer. I closed my eyes. Stretching out my hands as in a game of blindman's buff, I sought for the keyboard.

'I have never heard you before,' I said.

I touched something: I did not know whether it was a glove or her dead hand.

'Have you been learning long?' I said. I opened my eyes. She was gone. I took my gloves, dusted off the webs and ran, ran so fast down the well of the house that on the last flight I stumbled and fell breathless into Marie's arms.

'Oh, I have had a fright! I have had a fright!'

She led me into the drawing room, made me lie down, brought me a glass of wine.

'What is it, Mademoiselle? Shall I fetch the housekeeper? What has happened?'

But the first sip of wine had made me wary. 'I thought I saw someone hiding in my bedroom, a man. Perhaps a thief.'

At this the house was roused. Marie, the housekeeper and the gardener, who had not yet finished his work, searched every room (the lumber room, too, I think) but found nothing. I was scolded, petted, dosed, and Marie insisted, when the housekeeper was out of the way, on putting a soupçon of rouge on my cheeks because, she said, I could not upset M. le Maire by looking like a dead body – he, poor man, having so recently had death in his house!

I recovered myself sufficiently to climb into the carriage, when it came, to comport myself decently on the drive, and to greet the mayor and his two daughters with dignity. Dinner, however, was a nightmare. My mind was so full of the horror I had seen that I could not eat – indeed I could barely force my trembling hand to carry the fork to my lips.

The mayor's daughters were only children, eleven and thirteen years old. At eight o'clock he bade them say good night to me and prepare for bed. When they had left us I told him I thought I had stayed long enough: but with a very grave look he placed his hand upon my arm and pressed me gently back into my chair.

'My dear young lady,' he said, 'I know your history, I know you are lonely and unhappy in France without your parents. Also I know that you have suffered some violent shock. Will you tell me about it and let me help you?'

The relief of his words, of his wise and kindly gaze, was too much for me. For the first time in seven years I felt fathered and in haven. I broke down and cried tempestuously, and he did not touch me or speak to me till I was a little more calm. Then he rang for the servant and told her to bring some lime-flower tea. When I had drunk and eaten some of the sweet cake that he urged upon me I told him about the empty schoolroom and of the horror which sat there at the webbed piano.

When I had done he was silent for a little while. Then he took both my hands in his.

'Mademoiselle,' he said, 'I am not going to blame you for the sin of curiosity; I think there was some strange compulsion upon you to act as you did. Therefore I mean to shed a little light upon this sad schoolroom by telling you the story of Mademoiselle Fournier.'

I started.

'No,' he continued restrainingly, 'you must listen quietly; and what I tell you you must never repeat to a soul save your own mother until both Mademoiselle Fournier and Madame de Vallon, her cousin, have passed away.'

I have kept this promise. They have been dead some fourteen years.

M.Oury settled back in his chair. A tiny but comforting fire was lit in the grate, and the light of it was like a ring of guardian angels about us.

'Mademoiselle Fournier,' he began, 'was a very beautiful and proud young woman. Although she had no dowry she was yet considered something of a *partie*, and in her nineteenth year she became affianced to a young Russian nobleman who at that time was living with his family upon an estate near Arles. His mother was not too pleased with the match, but she was a good woman, and she treated Charlotte – that is, Mademoiselle Fournier – with kindness. Just before the marriage Charlotte's father, who had been created a marquis by Bonaparte and now, by tolerance, held a minor government post under Louis Philippe, was found to have embezzled many thousands of francs.'

'Her father!' I could not help but exclaim.

M. Oury smiled wryly. 'Legend has the lover the villain, eh? No; it was Aristide Fournier, a weak man, unable to stomach any recession in his fortunes. Monsieur Fournier shot himself as the gendarmes were on their way to take him. Charlotte, her marriage prospects destroyed, came near to lunacy. When she recovered from her long illness her beauty had gone. The mother of her ex-fiancé, in pity, suggested that a friend of hers, a lady at the Court of the Tzar, should employ Charlotte as governess to her children, and in Russia Charlotte spent nine years. She returned to France to assist her cousin with the school at Bellancay that Madame de Vallon had recently established.'

'Why did she return?' I said, less because I wished to know the answer than because I wished to break out of the veil of the past he was drawing about us both, and to feel myself a reality once more, Maud Arlett, aged seventeen years and nine months, brown hair and grey eyes, five foot seven and a half inches tall.

I did not succeed. The veil tightened, grew more opaque. 'Nobody knows. There were rumours. It seems not improbable that she was dismissed by her employer . . . why, I don't know. It is an obscure period in Charlotte's history.'

He paused to pour more tea for me.

'It was thought at first that Charlotte would be of great assistance to Madame de Vallon, teach all subjects and act as Madame's secretary. It transpired, however, that Charlotte was nervous to the point of sickness, and that she would grow less and less capable of teaching young girls. Soon she had no duties in the school except to give lessons in music and deportment.

'The music room was in the attic, which was then used as a schoolroom also. The pianoforte was Charlotte's own, one of the few things saved from the wreck of her home.'

M. Oury rose and walked out of the ring of firelight. He stood gazing out of the window, now beaded by a thin rain, and his voice grew out of the dusk as the music of waves grows out of the sea. 'I shall tell you the rest briefly, Mademoiselle. It distresses me to tell it to you at all, but I think I can help you in no other way.

'A young girl came to the school, a child; perhaps twelve or thirteen years of age. Her mother and father were in the East, and she was left alone, even during the vacations –'

'Like myself!' I cried.

'Yes, like yourself; and I have an idea that that is why she chose you for her . . . confidante.'

I shuddered.

He seemed to guess at my movement for, turning from the window, he returned to the firelight and to me.

'In one way, however, she was as unlike you as can possibly be imagined, Mademoiselle.' He smiled with a faint, sad gallantry. 'She was exceedingly ugly.

'From the first, Charlotte took a dislike to her, and it grew to a mania. The child, Therese Dasquier, was never very intelligent; in Charlotte's grip she became almost imbecile. Charlotte was always devising new punishments, new humiliations. Therese became the mock and pity of the school.'

'But Madame de Vallon; couldn't she have stopped it?' I interrupted indignantly.

'My dear,' M. Oury replied sadly, 'like many women of intellect – she is, as you know, a fine teacher – she is blind to most human distress. She is, herself, a kind woman: she believes others are equally kind, cannot believe there could be . . . suffering . . . torment . . . going on beneath her very nose. Has she ever realized *your* loneliness, Mademoiselle, given you any motherly word . . .? I thought not. But I am digressing, and that I must not do. We have talked too much already.

'One night Therese Dasquier arose quietly, crept from the dormitory and walked barefooted a mile and a half in the rain across the fields, to the river, where she drowned herself.'

'Oh, God,' I murmured, my heart cold and heavy as a stone.

'God, I think,' said Monsieur Oury, 'cannot have been attentive at that time . . .' His face changed. He added hastily, 'And God forgive me for judging Him. We cannot know – we cannot guess . . .' he continued rapidly, in a dry, rather high voice oddly unlike his own. 'There was scandal, great scandal. Therese's parents returned to France and everyone expected them to force the truth to light. They turned out to be frivolous and selfish people, who could scarcely make even a parade of grief for a child they had never desired and whose death they could not regret. Therese was buried and forgotten. Slowly, very slowly, the story also was forgotten. After all, nobody *knew* the truth, they could only make conjecture.'

'Then how did *you* know?' I cried out.

'Because Madame de Vallon came to me in bitter distress with the tale of the rumours and besought me to clear Charlotte's name. You see, she simply could not believe a word against her. And at the same time the aunt of

Marie, the maid, came to me swearing she could prove the truth of the accusations . . . Three days afterward she was killed in the fire which destroyed the old quarter of Bellancay.'

I looked my inquiry into his face.

'I knew which of the women spoke the truth,' he replied, answering me, 'because in Madame de Vallon's face I saw concern for her own blood. In the other woman's I saw concern for a child who to her was nothing.'

'But still, you *guessed* . . .' I protested.

He turned upon me his long and grave regard. 'You,' he said, 'you do not know the truth? Even you?'

I do not know how I endured the following weeks in that lonely school. I remember how long I lay shivering in my bed, staring into the flame of the candle because I felt that in the brightest part of it alone was refuge, how the sweat jumped out from my brow at the least sound in the stillness of midnight, and how, toward morning, I would fall into some morose and terrible dream of dark stairways and locked doors.

Yet, as day by day, night by night, went by with no untoward happening, my spirit knew some degree of easing and I began once more to find comfort in prayer – that is, I dared once again to cover my face while I repeated 'Our Father,' and to rise from my knees without fear of what might be standing patiently at my shoulder.

The holidays drew to an end. 'Tomorrow,' said Mademoiselle Fournier, folding her needlework in preparation for bed, 'your companions will be back with you once more. You'll like that, eh?'

Ever since my request and her refusal, she had been perfectly normal in her manner – I mean, she had been normally sour, polite, withdrawn.

'I shall like it,' I sighed, 'only too well.'

She smiled remotely. 'I am not a lively companion for you, Maud, I fear. Still, I am as I am. I am too old to change myself.'

She went on upstairs, myself following, our candles smoking in the draft and our shadows prancing upon the wall.

I said my prayers and read for a little while. I was unusually calm, feeling safety so nearly within my reach that I need be in no hurry to stretch out my hand and grasp it tight. The bed seemed softer than usual, the sheets sweet-smelling, delicately warm and light. I fell into a dreamless sleep.

I awoke suddenly to find the moon full on my face. I sat up, dazzled by her light, a strange feeling of energy tingling in my body. 'What is it,' I whispered, 'that I must do?'

The moon shone broadly on the great surfaces of gleaming wood, on the bureau, the tallboy, the wardrobe, flashed upon the mirror, sparkled on the spiralling bedposts. I slipped out of bed and in my nightgown went out into the passage.

It was very bright and still. Below me, the stairs fell steeply to the tessellated entrance hall. To my right the passage narrowed to the door behind which Mademoiselle Fournier slept, her wig upon a candlestick, her book and her spectacles lying on the rug at her side – so Marie had described her to me. Before me the stairs rose to the turn of the landing, from which a further flight led to the second floor, the third floor and the attics. The wall above the stair rail was white with the moon.

I felt the terror creeping up beneath my calm, though only as one might feel the shadow of pain while in the grip of a drug. I was waiting now as I had been instructed to wait, and I knew for what. I stared upward, my gaze fastened upon the turn of the stairs.

Then, upon the moonlit wall, there appeared the shadow of a cone. She stood just out of sight, her foolscapped head nodding forward, listening even as I was listening.

I held my breath. My forehead was ice-cold.

She came into view then, stepping carefully, one hand upholding a corner of her skirt, the other feeling its way along the wall. As she reached me I closed my eyes. I felt her pass by, knew she had gone along the passage to the room of Mademoiselle Fournier. I heard a door quietly opened and shut.

In those last moments of waiting my fear left me, though I could move neither hand nor foot. My ears were sharp for the least sound.

It came: a low and awful cry, tearing through the quiet of the house and blackening the moonlight itself. The door opened again.

She came hastening out, and in the shadow of the cap she smiled. She ran on tiptoe past me, up the stairs.

The last sound? I thought it had been the death cry of Mademoiselle Fournier; but there was yet another.

As Marie and the housekeeper came racing down, white-faced, from their rooms (they must have passed her as she stood in the shade) I heard very distinctly the piping voice of a young girl.

'*Tiens, Mademoiselle, je vous remercie beaucoup!*'

We went together, Marie, the housekeeper and I, into the room of Charlotte Fournier, and only I did not cry out when we looked upon the face.

'You see,' said Monsieur Oury, on the day I left Bellancay for ever to join my parents in Paris, 'she did make you her *confidante*. She gave to you the privilege of telling her story and publishing her revenge. Are you afraid of her now, knowing that there was no harm in her for *you*, knowing that she has gone for ever, to trouble no house again?'

'I am not afraid,' I said, and I believed it was true; but even now I cannot endure to awaken suddenly on moonlit nights, and I fling my arms about my husband and beg him to rouse up and speak with me until the dawn.

Elizabeth Jane Howard

THREE MILES UP

THERE was absolutely nothing like it.

An unoriginal conclusion, and one that he had drawn a hundred times during the last fortnight. Clifford would make some subtle and intelligent comparison, but he, John, could only continue to repeat that it was quite unlike anything else. It had been Clifford's idea, which, considering Clifford, was surprising. When you looked at him, you would not suppose him capable of it. However, John reflected, he had been ill, some sort of breakdown these clever people went in for, and that might account for his uncharacteristic idea of hiring a boat and travelling on canals. On the whole, John had to admit, it was a good idea. He had never been on a canal in his life, although he had been in almost every kind of boat, and thought he knew a good deal about them; so much indeed, that he had embarked on the venture in a light-hearted, almost a patronizing manner. But it was not nearly as simple as he had imagined. Clifford, of course, knew nothing about boats; but he had admitted that almost everything had gone wrong with a kind of devilish versatility which had almost frightened him. However, that was all over, and John, who had learned painfully all about the boat and her engine, felt that the former at least had run her gamut of disaster. They had run out of food, out of petrol, and out of water; had dropped their windlass into the deepest lock, and, more humiliating, their boathook into a side-pond. The head had come off the hammer. They had been disturbed for one whole night by a curious rustling in the cabin, like a rat in a paper bag, when there was no paper, and, so far as they knew, no rat. The battery had failed and had had to be re-charged. Clifford had put his elbow through an already cracked window in the cabin. A large piece of rope had wound itself round the propeller with a malignant intensity which required three men and half a morning to unravel. And so on, until now there was really nothing left to go wrong, unless one of them drowned, and surely it was impossible to drown in a canal.

'I suppose one might easily drown in a lock?' he asked aloud.

'We must be careful not to fall into one,' Clifford replied.

'What?' John steered with fierce concentration, and never heard anything people said to him for the first time, almost on principle.

'I said we must be careful not to fall *into* a lock.'

'Oh. Well there aren't any more now until after the Junction. Anyway, we haven't yet, so there's really no reason why we should start now. I only wanted to know whether we'd drown if we did.'

'Sharon might.'

'What?'

'Sharon might.'

'Better warn her then. She seems agile enough.' His concentrated frown returned, and he settled down again to the wheel. John didn't mind where they went, or what happened, so long as he handled the boat, and all things considered, he handled her remarkably well. Clifford planned and John steered: and until two days ago they had both quarrelled and argued over a smoking and unusually temperamental primus. Which reminded Clifford of Sharon. Her advent and the weather were really their two unadulterated strokes of good fortune. There had been no rain, and Sharon had, as it were, dropped from the blue on to the boat, where she speedily restored domestic order, stimulated evening conversation, and touched the whole venture with her attractive being: the requisite number of miles each day were achieved, the boat behaved herself, and admirable meals were steadily and regularly prepared. She had, in fact, identified herself with the journey, without making the slightest effort to control it: a talent which many women were supposed in theory to possess, when, in fact, Clifford reflected gloomily, most of them were bored with the whole thing, or tried to dominate it.

Her advent was a remarkable, almost a miraculous piece of luck. He had, after a particularly ill-fed day, and their failure to dine at a small hotel, desperately telephoned all the women he knew who seemed in the least suitable (and they were surprisingly few), with no success. They had spent a miserable evening, John determined to argue about everything, and he, Clifford, refusing to speak; until, both in a fine state of emotional tension, they had turned in for the night. While John snored, Clifford had lain distraught, his resentment and despair circling round John and then touching his own smallest and most random thoughts; until his mind found no refuge and he was left, divided from it, hostile and afraid, watching it in terror racing on in the dark like some malignant machine utterly out of his control.

The next day things had proved no better between them, and they had continued throughout the morning in a silence which was only occasionally and elaborately broken. They had tied up for lunch beside a wood, which hung heavy and magnificent over the canal. There was a small clearing beside which John then proposed to moor, but Clifford failed to achieve the considerable leap necessary to stop the boat; and they had drifted helplessly past it. John flung him a line, but it was not until the boat was secured, and they were safely in the cabin, that the storm had broken. John, in attempting to light the primus, spilt a quantity of paraffin on Clifford's bunk. Instantly all his despair of the previous evening had contracted. He hated John so much that he could have murdered him. They both lost their tempers, and for the ensuing hour and a half had conducted a blazing quarrel, which, even at the time, secretly horrified them both in its intensity.

It had finally ended with John striding out of the cabin, there being no more to say. He had returned almost at once, however.

'I say, Clifford. Come and look at this.'

'At what?'

'Outside, on the bank.'

For some unknown reason Clifford did get up and did look. Lying face downwards quite still on the ground, with her arms clasping the trunk of a large tree, was a girl.

'How long has she been there?'

'She's asleep.'

'She can't have been asleep all the time. She must have heard some of what we said.'

'Anyway, who is she? What is she doing here?'

Clifford looked at her again. She was wearing a dark twill shirt and dark trousers, and her hair hung over her face, so that it was almost invisible. 'I don't know. I suppose she's alive?'

John jumped cautiously ashore. 'Yes, she's alive all right. Funny way to lie.'

'Well, it's none of our business anyway. Anyone can lie on a bank if they want to.'

'Yes, but she must have come in the middle of our row, and it does seem queer to stay, and then go to sleep.'

'Extraordinary,' said Clifford wearily. Nothing was really extraordinary, he felt, nothing. 'Are we moving on?'

'Let's eat first. I'll do it.'

'Oh, I'll do it.'

The girl stirred, unclasped her arms, and sat up. They had all stared at each other for a moment, the girl slowly pushing the hair from her forehead. Then she had said: 'If you will give me a meal, I'll cook it.'

Afterwards they had left her to wash up, and walked about the wood, while Clifford suggested to John that they ask the girl to join them. 'I'm sure she'd come,' he said. 'She didn't seem at all clear about what she was doing.'

'We can't just pick somebody up out of a wood,' said John, scandalized.

'Where do you suggest we pick them up? If we don't have someone, this holiday will be a failure.'

'We don't know anything about her.'

'I can't see that that matters very much. She seems to cook well. We can at least ask her.'

'All right. Ask her then. She won't come.'

When they returned to the boat, she had finished the washing up, and was sitting on the floor of the cockpit, with her arms stretched behind her head. Clifford asked her; and she accepted as though she had known them a long time and they were simply inviting her to tea.

'Well, but look here,' said John, thoroughly taken aback. 'What about your things?'

'My things?' she looked inquiringly and a little defensively from one to the other.

'Clothes and so on. Or haven't you got any? Are you a gipsy or something? Where do you come from?'

'I am not a gipsy,' she began patiently; when Clifford, thoroughly embarrassed and ashamed, interrupted her.

'Really, it's none of our business who you are, and there is absolutely no need for us to ask you anything. I'm very glad you will come with us, although I feel we should warn you that we are new to this life, and anything might happen.'

'No need to warn me,' she said and smiled gratefully at him.

After that, they both felt bound to ask her nothing; John because he was afraid of being made to look foolish by Clifford, and Clifford because he had stopped John.

'Good Lord, we shall never get rid of her; and she'll fuss about condensation,' John had muttered aggressively as he started the engine. But she was very young, and did not fuss about anything. She had told them her name, and settled down, immediately and easily: gentle, assured and unselfconscious to a degree remarkable in one so young. They were never sure how much she had overheard them, for she gave no sign of having heard anything. A friendly but uncommunicative creature.

The map on the engine box started to flap, and immediately John asked, 'Where are we?'

'I haven't been watching, I'm afraid. Wait a minute.'

'We just passed under a railway bridge,' John said helpfully.

'Right. Yes. About four miles from the Junction, I think. What is the time?'

'Five-thirty.'

'Which way are we going when we get to the Junction?'

'We haven't time for the big loop. I must be back in London by the 15th.'

'The alternative is to go up as far as the basin, and then simply turn round and come back, and who wants to do that?'

'Well, we'll know the route then. It'll be much easier coming back.'

Clifford did not reply. He was not attracted by the route being easier, and he wanted to complete his original plan.

'Let us wait till we get there.' Sharon appeared with tea and marmalade sandwiches.

'All right, let's wait.' Clifford was relieved.

'It will be almost dark by six-thirty. I think we ought to have a plan,' John said. 'Thank you, Sharon.'

'Have tea first.' She curled herself on to the floor with her back to the cabin doors and a mug in her hands.

They were passing rows of little houses with gardens that backed on to the canal. They were long narrow strips, streaked with cinder paths, and crowded with vegetables and chicken huts, fruit trees and perambulators; sometimes ending with fat white ducks, and sometimes in a tiny patch of grass with a bench on it.

'Would you rather keep ducks or sit on a bench?' asked Clifford.

'Keep ducks,' said John promptly. 'More useful. Sharon wouldn't mind which she did. Would you, Sharon?' He liked saying her name, Clifford noticed. 'You could be happy anywhere, couldn't you?' He seemed to be presenting her with the widest possible choice.

'I might *be* anywhere,' she answered after a moment's thought.

'Well you happen to be on a canal, and very nice for us.'

'In a wood, and then on a canal,' she replied contentedly, bending her smooth dark head over her mug.

'Going to be fine tomorrow,' said John. He was always a little embarrassed at any mention of how they found her and his subsequent rudeness.

'Yes. I like it when the whole sky is so red and burning and it begins to be cold.'

'*Are* you cold?' said John, wanting to worry about it: but she tucked her dark shirt into her trousers and answered composedly:

'Oh no. I am never cold.'

They drank their tea in a comfortable silence. Clifford started to read his map, and then said they were almost on to another sheet. 'New country,' he said with satisfaction. 'I've never been here before.'

'You make it sound like an exploration; doesn't he, Sharon?' said John.

'Is that a bad thing?' She collected the mugs. 'I am going to put these away. You will call me if I am wanted for anything.' And she went into the cabin again.

There was a second's pause, a minute tribute to her departure; and, lighting cigarettes, they settled down to stare at the long silent stretch of water ahead.

John thought about Sharon. He thought rather desperately that really they still knew nothing about her, and that when they went back to London, they would, in all probability, never see her again. Perhaps Clifford would fall in love with her, and she would naturally reciprocate, because she was so young and Clifford was reputed to be so fascinating and intelligent, and because women were always foolish and loved the wrong man. He thought all these things with equal intensity, glanced cautiously at Clifford, and supposed he was thinking about her; then wondered what she would be like in London, clad in anything else but her dark trousers and shirt. The engine coughed; and he turned to it in relief.

Clifford was making frantic calculations of time and distance; stretching their time, and diminishing the distance, and groaning that with the utmost optimism they could not be made to fit. He was interrupted by John swearing at the engine, and then for no particular reason he remembered Sharon, and reflected with pleasure how easily she left the mind when she was not present, how she neither obsessed nor possessed one in her absence, but was charming to see.

The sun had almost set when they reached the Junction, and John slowed down to neutral while they made up their minds. To the left was the straight cut which involved the longer journey originally planned; and curving away to the right was the short arm which John advocated. The canal was fringed with rushes, and there was one small cottage with no light in it. Clifford went into the cabin to tell Sharon where they were, and then, as they drifted slowly in the middle of the Junction, John suddenly shouted: 'Clifford! What's the third turning?'

'There are only two.' Clifford reappeared. 'Sharon is busy with dinner.'

'No, look. Surely that is another cut.'

Clifford stared ahead. 'Can't see it.'

'Just to the right of the cottage. Look. It's not so dark as all that.'

Then Clifford saw it very plainly. It seemed to wind away from the cottage on a fairly steep curve, and the rushes shrouding it from anything but the closest view were taller than the rest.

'Have another look at the map. I'll reverse for a bit.'

'Found it. It's just another turn. Probably been abandoned,' said Clifford eventually.

The boat had swung round; and now they could see the continuance of the curve dully gleaming ahead, and banked by reeds.

'Well, what shall we do?'

'Getting dark. Let's go up a little way, and moor. Nice quiet mooring.'

'With some nice quiet mudbanks,' said John grimly. 'Nobody uses that.'

'How do you know?'

'Well, look at it. All those rushes, and it's sure to be thick with weed.'

'Don't go up it then. But we shall go aground if we drift about like this.'

'I don't mind going up it,' said John doggedly. 'What about Sharon?'

'What about her?'

'Tell her about it.'

'We've found a third turning,' Clifford called above the noise of the primus through the cabin door.

'One you had not expected?'

'Yes. It looks very wild. We were thinking of going up it.'

'Didn't you say you wanted to explore?' she smiled at him.

'You are quite ready to try it? I warn you we shall probably run hard aground. Look out for bumps with the primus.'

'I am quite ready, and I am quite sure we shan't run aground,' she answered with charming confidence in their skill.

They moved slowly forward in the dusk. Why they did not run aground, Clifford could not imagine: John really was damned good at it. The canal wound and wound, and the reeds grew not only thick on each bank, but in clumps across the canal. The light drained out of the sky into the water and slowly drowned there; the trees and the banks became heavy and black.

Clifford began to clear things away from the heavy dew which had begun to rise. After two journeys he remained in the cabin, while John crawled on, alone. Once, on a bend, John thought he saw a range of hills ahead with lights on them, but when he was round the curve, and had time to look again he could see no hills: only a dark indeterminate waste of country stretched ahead.

He was beginning to consider the necessity of mooring, when they came to a bridge; and shortly after, he saw a dark mass which he took to be houses. When the boat had crawled for another fifty yards or so, he stopped the engine, and drifted in absolute silence to the bank. The houses, about half a dozen of them, were much nearer than he had at first imagined, but there were no lights to be seen. Distance is always deceptive in the dark, he thought, and jumped ashore with a bow line. When, a few minutes later, he took a sounding with the boathook, the water proved unexpectedly deep; and he concluded that they had by incredible good fortune moored at the village wharf. He made everything fast, and joined the others in the cabin with mixed feelings of pride and resentment; that he should have achieved so much under such difficult conditions, and that they (by 'they' he meant Clifford), should have contributed so little towards the achievement. He found Clifford reading Bradshaw's *Guide to the Canals and Navigable Rivers* in one corner, and Sharon, with her hair pushed back behind her ears, bending over the primus with a knife. Her ears are pale, exactly the colour of her face, he thought; wanted to touch them; then felt horribly ashamed, and hated Clifford.

'Let's have a look at Bradshaw,' he said, as though he had not noticed Clifford reading it.

But Clifford handed him the book in the most friendly manner, remarking that he couldn't see where they were. 'In fact you have surpassed yourself with your brilliant navigation. We seem to be miles from anywhere.'

'What about your famous ordnance?'

'It's not on any sheet I have. The new one I thought we should use only covers the loop we planned. There is precisely three quarters of a mile of this canal shown on the present sheet and then we run off the map. I suppose there must once have been trade here, but I cannot imagine what, or where.'

'I expect things change,' said Sharon. 'Here is the meal.'

'How can you see to cook?' asked John eyeing his plate ravenously.

'There is a candle.'

'Yes, but we've selfishly appropriated that.'

'Should I need more light?' she asked, and looked troubled.

'There's no should about it. I just don't know how you do it, that's all. Chips exactly the right colour, and you never drop anything. It's marvellous.'

She smiled a little uncertainly at him and lit another candle. 'Luck, probably,' she said, and set it on the table.

They ate their meal, and John told them about the mooring. 'Some sort of village. I think we're moored at the wharf. I couldn't find any rings without the torch, so I've used the anchor.' This small shaft was intended for Clifford, who had dropped the spare torch-battery in the washing-up bowl, and forgotten to buy another. But it was only a small shaft, and immediately afterwards John felt much better. His aggression slowly left him, and he felt nothing but peaceful and well-fed affection for the other two.

'Extraordinary cut off this is,' he remarked over coffee.

'It is very pleasant in here. Warm, and extremely full of us.'

'Yes. I know. A quiet village, though, you must admit.'

'I shall believe in your village when I see it.'

'Then you would believe it?'

'No he wouldn't, Sharon. Not if he didn't want to, and couldn't find it on the map. That map!'

The conversation turned again to their remoteness, and to how cut off one liked to be and at what point it ceased to be desirable; to boats, telephones, and, finally, canals: which, Clifford maintained, possessed the perfect proportions of urbanity and solitude.

Hours later, when they had turned in for the night, Clifford reviewed the conversation, together with others they had had, and remembered with surprise how little Sharon had actually said. She listened to everything and occasionally, when they appealed to her, made some small composed remark which was oddly at variance with their passionate interest. 'She has an elusive quality of freshness about her,' he thought, 'which is neither naive nor stupid nor dull, and she invokes no responsibility. She does not want us to know what she was, or why we found her as we did, and curiously, I, at least, do not want to know. She is what women ought to be,' he concluded with sudden pleasure; and slept.

He woke the next morning to find it very late, and stretched out his hand to wake John.

'We've all overslept. Look at the time.'

'Good Lord! Better wake Sharon.'

Sharon lay between them on the floor, which they had ceded her because, oddly enough, it was the widest and most comfortable bed. She seemed profoundly asleep, but at the mention of her name sat up immediately, and rose, almost as though she had not been asleep at all.

The morning routine which, involving the clothing of three people and shaving of two of them, was necessarily a long and complicated business, began. Sharon boiled water, and Clifford, grumbling gently, hoisted himself out of his bunk and repaired with a steaming jug to the cockpit. He put the jug on a seat, lifted the canvas awning, and leaned out. It was absolutely grey and still; a little white mist hung over the canal, and the country stretched out desolate and unkempt on every side with no sign of a living creature. The village, he thought suddenly: John's village: and was possessed of a perilous uncertainty and fear. I am getting worse, he thought, this holiday is doing me no good. I am mad. I imagined that he said we moored by a village wharf. For several seconds he stood gripping the gunwale, and searching desperately for anything, huts, a clump of trees, which could in the darkness have been mistaken for a village. But there was nothing near the boat except tall rank rushes which did not move at all. Then, when his suspense was becoming unbearable, John joined him with another steaming jug of water.

'We shan't get anywhere at this rate,' he began; and then . . . 'Hullo! Where's my village?'

'I was wondering that,' said Clifford. He could almost have wept with relief, and quickly began to shave, deeply ashamed of his private panic.

'Can't understand it,' John was saying. It was no joke, Clifford decided, as he listened to his hearty puzzled ruminations.

At breakfast John continued to speculate upon what he had or had not seen, and Sharon listened intently while she filled the coffee pot and cut bread. Once or twice she met Clifford's eye with a glance of discreet amusement.

'I must be mad, or else the whole place is haunted,' finished John comfortably. These two possibilities seemed to relieve him of any further anxiety in the matter, as he ate a huge breakfast and set about greasing the engine.

'Well,' said Clifford, when he was alone with Sharon. 'What do you make of that?'

'It is easy to be deceived in such matters,' she answered perfunctorily.

'Evidently. Still, John is an unlikely candidate you must admit. Here, I'll help you dry.'

'Oh no. It is what I am here for.'

'Not entirely, I hope.'

'Not entirely.' She smiled and relinquished the cloth.

John eventually announced that they were ready to start. Clifford, who had assumed that they were to recover their journey, was surprised, and a little alarmed, to find John intent upon continuing it. He seemed undeterred by the state of the canal, which, as Clifford immediately pointed out, rendered navigation both arduous and unrewarding. He announced that the harder it was, the more he liked it, adding very firmly that 'anyway we must see what happens.'

'We shan't have time to do anything else.'

'Thought you wanted to explore.'

'I do, but . . . what do you think, Sharon?'

'I think John will have to be a very good navigator to manage that.' She indicated the rush and weed-ridden reach before them. 'Do you think it's possible?'

'Of course it's possible. I'll probably need some help though.'

'I'll help you,' she said.

So on they went.

They made incredibly slow progress. John enjoys showing off his powers to her, thought Clifford, half amused, half exasperated, as he struggled for the fourth time in an hour to scrape weeds off the propeller.

Sharon eventually retired to cook lunch.

'Surprising amount of water here,' John said suddenly.

'Oh?'

'Well, I mean, with all this weed and stuff, you'd expect the canal to have silted up. I'm sure nobody uses it.'

'The whole thing is extraordinary.'

'Is it too late in the year for birds?' asked Clifford later.

'No, I don't think so. Why?'

'I haven't heard one, have you?'

'Haven't noticed, I'm afraid. There's someone anyway. First sign of life.'

An old man stood near the bank watching them. He was dressed in corduroy and wore a straw hat.

'Good morning,' shouted John, as they drew nearer.

He made no reply, but inclined his head slightly. He seemed very old. He was leaning on a scythe, and as they drew almost level with him, he turned away and began slowly cutting rushes. A pile of them lay neatly stacked beside him.

'Where does this canal go? Is there a village further on?' Clifford and John asked simultaneously. He seemed not to hear, and as they chugged steadily past, Clifford was about to suggest that they stop and ask again, when he called after them: 'Three miles up you'll find the village. Three miles up that is,' and turned away to his rushes again.

'Well, now we know something, anyway,' said John.

'We don't even know what the village is called.'

'Soon find out. Only three miles.'

'Three miles!' said Clifford darkly. 'That might mean anything.'

'Do you want to turn back?'

'Oh no, not now. I want to see this village now. My curiosity is thoroughly aroused.'

'Shouldn't think there'll be anything to see. Never been in such a wild spot. Look at it.'

Clifford looked at it. Half wilderness, half marsh, dank and grey and still, with single trees bare of their leaves; clumps of hawthorn that might once have been hedge, sparse and sharp with berries; and, in the distance, hills and an occasional wood: these were all one could see, beyond the lines of rushes which edged the canal winding ahead.

They stopped for a lengthy meal, which Sharon described as lunch and tea together, it being so late; and then, appalled at how little daylight was left, continued.

'We've hardly been any distance at all,' said John forlornly. 'Good thing there were no locks. I shouldn't think they'd have worked if there were.'

'*Much* more than three miles,' he said, about two hours later. Darkness was descending and it was becoming very cold.

'Better stop,' said Clifford.

'Not yet. I'm determined to reach that village.'

'Dinner is ready,' said Sharon sadly. 'It will be cold.'

'Let's stop.'

'You have your meal. I'll call if I want you.'

Sharon looked at them, and Clifford shrugged his shoulders. 'Come on. I will. I'm tired of this.'

They shut the cabin doors. John could hear the pleasant clatter of their meal, and just as he was coming to the end of the decent interval which he felt must elapse before he gave in, they passed under a bridge, the first of the day, and, clutching at any straw, he immediately assumed that it prefaced the village. 'I think we're nearly there,' he called.

Clifford opened the door. 'The village?'

'No, a bridge. Can't be far now.'

'You're mad, John. It's pitch dark.'

'You can see the bridge though.'

'Yes. Why not moor under it?'

'Too late. Can't turn round in this light, and she's not good at reversing. Must be nearly there. You go back, I don't need you.'

Clifford shut the door again. He was beginning to feel irritated with John behaving in this childish manner and showing off to impress Sharon. It was amusing in the morning, but really he was carrying it a bit far. Let him manage the thing himself then. When, a few minutes later, John shouted that they had reached the sought after village, Clifford merely pulled back the little curtain over a cabin window, rubbed the condensation, and remarked that he could see nothing. 'No light at least.'

'He is happy anyhow,' said Sharon peaceably.

'Going to have a look round,' said John, slamming the cabin doors and blowing his nose.

'Surely you'll eat first?'

'If you've left anything. My God it's cold! It's *unnaturally* cold.'

'We won't be held responsible if he dies of exposure will we?' said Clifford.

She looked at him, hesitated a moment, but did not reply, and placed a steaming plate in front of John. She doesn't want us to quarrel, Clifford thought, and with an effort of friendliness he asked: 'What does tonight's village look like?'

'Much the same. Only one or two houses you know. But the old man called it a village.' He seemed uncommunicative; Clifford thought he was sulking. But after eating the meal, he suddenly announced, almost apologetically, 'I don't think I shall walk round. I'm absolutely worn out. You go if you like. I shall start turning in.'

'All right. I'll have a look. You've had a hard day.'

Clifford pulled on a coat and went outside. It was, as John said, incredibly cold and almost overwhelmingly silent. The clouds hung very low over the boat, and mist was rising everywhere from the ground, but he could dimly discern the black huddle of cottages lying on a little slope above the bank against which the boat was moored. He did actually set foot on shore, but his shoe sank immediately into a marshy hole. He withdrew it, and changed his mind. The prospect of groping round those dark and silent houses became suddenly distasteful, and he joined the others with the excuse that it was too cold and that he also was tired.

A little later, he lay half conscious in a kind of restless trance, with John sleeping heavily opposite him. His mind seemed full of foreboding, fear of something unknown and intangible: he thought of them lying in warmth on the cold secret canal with desolate miles of water behind and probably beyond; the old man and the silent houses; John, cut off and asleep, and

Sharon, who lay on the floor beside him. Immediately he was filled with a sudden and most violent desire for her, even to touch her, for her to know that he was awake.

'Sharon,' he whispered; 'Sharon, Sharon,' and stretched down his fingers to her in the dark.

Instantly her hand was in his, each smooth and separate finger warmly clasped. She did not move or speak, but his relief was indescribable and for a long while he lay in an ecstasy of delight and peace, until his mind slipped imperceptibly with her fingers into oblivion.

When he woke he found John absent and Sharon standing over the primus. 'He's outside,' she said.

'Have I overslept again?'

'It is late. I am boiling water for you now.'

'We'd better try and get some supplies this morning.'

'There is no village,' she said, in a matter of fact tone.

'What?'

'John says not. But we have enough food, if you don't mind this queer milk from a tin.'

'No, I don't mind,' he replied, watching her affectionately. 'It doesn't really surprise me,' he added after a moment.

'The village?'

'No village. Yesterday I should have minded awfully. Is that you, do you think?'

'Perhaps.'

'It doesn't surprise you about the village at all, does it? Do you love me?'

She glanced at him quickly, a little shocked, and said quietly: 'Don't you know?' then added: 'It doesn't surprise me.'

John seemed very disturbed. 'I don't like it,' he kept saying as they shaved. 'Can't understand it at all. I could have sworn there were houses last night. You saw them didn't you?'

'Yes.'

'Well, don't you think it's very odd?'

'I do.'

'Everything looks the same as yesterday morning. I don't like it.'

'It's an adventure you must admit.'

'Yes, but I've had enough of it. I suggest we turn back.'

Sharon suddenly appeared, and, seeing her, Clifford knew that he did not want to go back. He remembered her saying: 'Didn't you say you wanted to explore?' She would think him weak-hearted if they turned back all those dreary miles with nothing to show for it. At breakfast, he exerted himself in persuading John to the same opinion. John finally agreed to one more day, but, in turn, extracted a promise that they would then go back whatever happened. Clifford agreed to this, and Sharon for some inexplicable reason laughed at them both. So that eventually they prepared to set off in an atmosphere of general good humour.

Sharon began to fill the water tank with their four-gallon can. It seemed too heavy for her, and John dropped the starter and leapt to her assistance.

She let him take the can and held the funnel for him. Together they watched the rich even stream of water disappear.

'You shouldn't try to do that,' he said. 'You'll hurt yourself.'

'Gipsies do it,' she said.

'I'm awfully sorry about that. You know I am.'

'I should not have minded if you had thought I was a gipsy.'

'I do like you,' he said, not looking at her. 'I do like you. You won't disappear altogether when this is over, will you?'

'You probably won't find I'll disappear for good,' she replied comfortingly.

'Come on,' shouted Clifford.

It's all right for *him* to talk to her, John thought, as he struggled to swing the starter. He just doesn't like me doing it; and he wished, as he had begun often to do, that Clifford was not there.

They had spasmodic engine trouble in the morning, which slowed them down; and the consequent halts, with the difficulty they experienced of mooring anywhere (the banks seemed nothing but marsh), were depressing and cold. Their good spirits evaporated: by lunch-time John was plainly irritable and frightened, and Clifford had begun to hate the grey silent land on either side, with the woods and hills which remained so consistently distant. They both wanted to give it up by then, but John felt bound to stick to his promise, and Clifford was secretly sure that Sharon wished to continue.

While she was preparing another late lunch, they saw a small boy who stood on what once had been the towpath watching them. He was bareheaded, wore corduroy, and had no shoes. He held a long reed, the end of which he chewed as he stared at them.

'Ask him where we are,' said John; and Clifford asked.

He took the reed out of his mouth, but did not reply.

'Where do you live then?' asked Clifford as they drew almost level with him.

'I told you. Three miles up,' he said; and then he gave a sudden little shriek of fear, dropped the reed, and turned to run down the bank the way they had come. Once he looked back, stumbled and fell, picked himself up sobbing, and ran faster. Sharon had appeared with lunch a moment before, and together they listened to his gasping cries growing fainter and fainter, until he had run himself out of their sight.

'What on earth frightened him?' said Clifford.

'I don't know. Unless it was Sharon popping out of the cabin like that.'

'Nonsense. But he was a very frightened little boy. And, I say, do you realize . . .'

'He was a very foolish little boy,' Sharon interrupted. She was angry, Clifford noticed with surprise, really angry, white and trembling, and with a curious expression which he did not like.

'We might have got something out of him,' said John sadly.

'Too late now,' Sharon said. She had quite recovered herself.

They saw no one else. They journeyed on throughout the afternoon; it grew colder, and at the same time more and more airless and still. When the light began to fail, Sharon disappeared as usual to the cabin. The canal became more tortuous, and John asked Clifford to help him with the turns. Clifford complied unwillingly: he did not want to leave Sharon, but as it had been he who had insisted on their continuing, he could hardly refuse. The turns were nerve wracking, as the canal was very narrow and the light grew worse and worse.

'All right if we stop soon?' asked John eventually.

'Stop now if you like.'

'Well, we'll try and find a tree to tie up to. This swamp is awful. Can't think how that child ran.'

'That child . . .' began Clifford anxiously; but John, who had been equally unnerved by the incident, and did not want to think about it, interrupted. 'Is there a tree ahead anywhere?'

'Can't see one. There's a hell of a bend coming though. Almost back on itself. Better slow a bit more.'

'Can't. We're right down as it is.'

They crawled round, clinging to the outside bank, which seemed always to approach them, its rushes to rub against their bows, although the wheel was hard over. John grunted with relief, and they both stared ahead for the next turn.

They were presented with the most terrible spectacle. The canal immediately broadened, until no longer a canal but a sheet, an infinity, of water stretched ahead; oily, silent, and still, as far as the eye could see, with no country edging it, nothing but water to the low grey sky above it. John had almost immediately cut out the engine, and now he tried desperately to start it again, in order to turn round. Clifford instinctively glanced behind them. He saw no canal at all, no inlet, but grasping and close to the stern of the boat, the reeds and rushes of a marshy waste closing in behind them. He stumbled to the cabin doors and pulled them open. It was very neat and tidy in there, but empty. Only one stern door of the cabin was free of its catch, and it flapped irregularly backwards and forwards with their movements in the boat.

There was no sign of Sharon at all.

Rose Macaulay

WHITEWASH

THE sea as it swung gently against the rocks was jade green, like the evening sky. I was reclining on thymy turf, reading *The Story of San Michele*. Six feet down in the sea my aunt was scrambling among broken marble wreckage that had been once an imperial bath. When she surfaced I looked up from Dr Axel Münthe and said, 'It's nice to know what an excellent man Tiberius actually was, after all one was brought up to think of him'.

My aunt coughed up water and turned on her back to float.

'I know nothing of the sort,' she said. 'I would rather believe his contemporaries than these modern whitewashers. And I have the islanders with me, to a man, woman and child.'

'Naturally,' I agreed. 'Timberio is their local industry. If he lost his wickedness, he would have nothing but a few ruined villas and baths and a rock up there by the Faro from which no one was ever thrown. What use would visitors have for a beneficent old gentleman who retired here to flee the corrupt world and commune with his soul? Suetonius and Tacitus and all the legend-makers since are the local Bible. But they are wrong. Timberio has been cleared, and I am delighted that all these villas and baths were used by so saintly an emperor.'

'One after another,' said my aunt, 'they take them from us. Nero. Tiberius. The Borgias. King John. Richard III. Are we to be deprived of all the monsters of the past? Are they all to be of the present? And how long will it be before our contemporary monsters have the whitewash buckets poured over them and emerge saints, or victims of circumstance, more sinned against than sinning? Most of us are more sinning than sinned against; why should monsters be exceptions?'

I made no effort to convert my aunt on this subject. She required monsters, and, so far as I was concerned, could have them.

'I shall go exploring some of the caves,' I said. 'Will you come?'

'Not I,' said my aunt. 'When one thinks what went on in them,' she added primly, as she climbed out of the sea. 'I am going back to the villa. Dinner at nine.'

'I'll be back,' I said.

My aunt draped herself in her scarlet bernous and set off up the steep rock stairway that would conduct her in the end to the villa. I dropped into the warm twilight sea again, and swam round the next jut of rock. Above me the island sloped down to the sea, smelling of pine and thyme and cistus and the stored heat of the August day. Below me lay Roman villas and baths that had slipped long since into the waves and got drowned. I had explored these remains often enough; what I now wanted was a cave. There was one a little further on. I swam into it; it was a deep cave, thrusting far back into the rock. Round it, just above sea level, ran a broad ledge, slippery and green with seaweed. I hoisted myself on to it and walked along it. It was almost dark inside the cave. But, after walking a few yards, I felt a draught on my right, and saw a good-sized round opening in the rock. I remembered tales told by the locals of passages that climbed up from caves to one or another of Timberio's villas. Perhaps this one did so. I entered it, meaning to explore it for a little way. It sloped gently up, and was about the height of my shoulders. But I did not get far; a cold wind suddenly came against me like a hand on my chest, pushing me back. It struck me that I would rather explore that passage by day, and that I was inexplicably shivering, and had better get out of the cave and go home. In a few moments I was back on the slippery ledge; the little waves were lapping against the rock with a sound like whispering voices – or was it sharp, frightened gasps? A frightened crowd, it sounded like; a collection of people scared out of their wits. I slipped down into the water, which had become colder, and swam towards the cave's mouth. Outside was the green evening sky, the green evening sea. At the entrance I felt, oddly, as if a strong tide were running against me; I swam, but made no progress; in fact, I was being pushed back. But there was no tide, and the sea was calm. I struck out harder, and was pushed back further. I began to panic. What current was driving with such force into the cave that I could not swim against it? I remembered nightmare battles with Cornish tides that, swim as I would, carried me out to sea, the landmarks slipping from me in a losing race. I had been rescued by boats. There was no boat now, and I could not get out. I was growing tired; I was not a strong swimmer. Suppose I had to spend the night on that slippery, slimy ledge, among that whispering, frightened chatter? And would the sea rise? The Mediterranean is not quite tideless. I went on struggling; for a moment it seemed to me that I made headway. Then, looking up, I saw a dark shape, floating quietly just outside the cave's mouth; it was just under the surface but for a sharp, sail-shaped fin; it seemed to wait, rolling to and fro, in no hurry, but just waiting. That decided me; I retreated into the cave and climbed on to the ledge. I was shaking so much that I could scarcely make it. If the shark should enter the cave, I would climb into the passage.

I sat on the cold ledge, huddled up, my arms round my knees. It seemed to me that the chattering and whispering of the sea slapping against the rocky wall was louder, quicker, more verbal. The atmosphere in the cave was tense; it was sheer terror. It caught me like a wave, drowning me in cold panic. I have never known fear so intense, such submerging anguish.

Then, above the whispered clamour, rose a soft, jeering voice from the passage behind me. It said, 'Veni, cete, veni'. The next moment the cave mouth darkened; the great white shark drove in with a noise of rushing water. I saw its white belly and its row of terrible teeth. I did not wait; I plunged head first into the passage in the rock.

Then something more than a wind drove against me; it was as if some other strength met mine, pushing me back. I gripped a jut of rock with both hands; my feet were tensed against the side wall of the passage. I looked into the darkness of the corridor that wound ahead; suddenly on it there hung palely, as in phosphorescent light, a head and face I knew: I had seen it on coins, in busts, in reliefs. A handsome, sneering face, its lips curled now in a sensual smile. From them came a rich, pleased chuckling. And from the cave behind me came a snapping of jaws and a thin screaming, and splash after splash, as if things were being dragged down from the ledge into the water. At each splash came the low chuckling.

I was being pushed, but half-heartedly, as if the pusher's attention were concentrated elsewhere; or as if there were no real bodily contact. I held on to my position with hands and feet; I was not really much afraid of losing it, for I was alive, and the pusher had been dead for close on two thousand years, and what physical force can the dead and the living exert over one another? My terror was of the scene behind me; the thin screams, the snapping jaws, the splashing . . . And of the leering phosphorescent face hanging in the dark rock corridor in front of me; and of that enjoying chuckle. I shut my eyes, but could not stop my ears.

I do not know how long the ghastly scene lasted. But before very long I realised that there was silence in the cave, but for a heavy, gorged, wallowing sound. Then the drawling voice said 'Abi, cete, abi hinc'; and the heavy shape seemed to flounder through the water, out of the cave into the sea beyond.

I opened my eyes. The face was gone. I seemed quite alone; the soft slap-slap of water against rock was no longer like whispering voices. I slithered down on to the ledge, staring in horror at the deep green water below me, now silvered by the first long shafts of rising moon. I don't know what I feared to see in it – mangled limbs, ripples running red . . . but there was only green sea water touched with silver. All the same I did not get into it; I followed the ledge round to the cave's mouth, and peered warily out. No dark shape was in sight; no fin. I knew I was alone.

I slipped into the moon-struck sea and swam round the jut of rock to the place where we had bathed among the ruins of the Roman bath. My bathing wrap lay there. Putting it over my shivering body, I was back in the twentieth century. The tension slackened; I lay limply on the rocks and was sick.

What time it was I had no idea. Getting up, I saw *The Story of San Michele* lying open where I had put it down; I picked it up and climbed the path up the hill.

I came in through the open French window; my aunt lay smoking in a long chair.

'So there you are at last,' she said. 'I've kept your dinner for you. Do you know,' she added reflectively, 'I was beginning to fear that Timberio had got you after all.'

'I began to think so too,' I told her. 'And you will be glad to know that Suetonius and Tacitus and the locals are all perfectly right about him, and that Dr Münthe and Norman and the other whitewashers are perfectly wrong; they haven't the faintest idea what they are talking about.'

'No,' my aunt tranquilly agreed. 'Whitewashers never have. Evil does exist, and monsters have always been monsters. Nero, Tiberius, the Borgias, Richard III, John, our contemporary tyrants . . . I believe in them all.'

'Or,' I asked myself presently, when warmed and clothed and fed, 'can I have had some kind of a fit? I shall tell Norman about it to-morrow, and ask what he thinks.'

I met Norman in his favourite piazza café next morning. Though the most patriotic of islanders, he told me that I had been the victim of an erroneous mass mythology. For Timberio had been a most excellent man, kind of heart and temperate of habit.

'Only,' he added, re-filling his three glasses, 'you've hardly begun yet. Timberio, according to the Capraeans, could do much better than that. You must try some of the other caves.'

Elizabeth Taylor

POOR GIRL

MISS Chasty's first pupil was a flirtatious little boy. At seven years, he was alarmingly precocious and sometimes she thought that he despised his childhood, regarding it as a waiting time which he used only as a rehearsal for adult life. He was already more sophisticated than his young governess and disturbed her with his air of dalliance, the mockery with which he set about his lessons, the preposterous conversations he led her into, guiding her skilfully away from work, confusing her with bizarre conjectures and irreverent ideas, so that she would clasp her hands tightly under the plush table-cloth and pray that his father would not choose such a moment to observe her teaching, coming in abruptly as he sometimes did and signalling to her to continue her lesson.

At those times, his son's eyes were especially lively, fixed cruelly upon his governess as he listened, smiling faintly, to her faltering voice, measuring her timidity. He would answer her questions correctly, but significantly, as if he knew that by his aptitude he rescued her from dismissal. There were many governesses waiting employment, he implied – and this was so at the beginning of the century. He underlined her good fortune at having a pupil who could so easily learn, could display the results of her teaching to such advantage for the benefit of the rather sombre, pompous figure seated at the window. When his father, apparently satisfied, had left them without a word, the boy's manner changed. He seemed fatigued and too absent-minded to reply to any more questions.

'Hilary!' she would say sharply. 'Are you attending to me?' Her sharpness and her foolishness amused him, coming as he knew they did from the tension of the last ten minutes.

'Why, my dear girl, of course.'

'You must address me by my name.'

'Certainly, dear Florence.'

'Miss Chasty.'

His lips might shape the words, which he was too weary to say.

Sometimes, when she was correcting his sums, he would come round the table to stand beside her, leaning against her heavily, looking closely at her face, not at his book, breathing steadily down his nose so that tendrils of hair wavered on her neck and against her cheeks. His stillness, his concentration on her and his too heavy leaning, worried her. She felt something experimental in his attitude, as if he were not leaning against her at all, but against someone in the future. 'He is only a baby,' she reminded herself, but she would try to shift from him, feeling a vague distaste. She would blush, as if he were a grown man, and her heart could be heard beating quickly. He was aware of this and would take up the corrected book and move back to his place.

Once he proposed to her and she had the feeling that it was a proposal-rehearsal and that he was making use of her, as an actor might ask her to hear his lines.

'You must go on with your work,' she said.

'I can shade in a map and talk as well.'

'Then talk sensibly.'

'You think I am too young, I daresay; but you could wait for me to grow up. I can do that quickly enough.'

'You are far from grown-up at the moment.'

'You only say these things because you think that governesses ought to. I suppose you don't know *how* governesses go on, because you have never been one until now, and you were too poor to have one of your own when you were young.'

'That is impertinent, Hilary.'

'You once told me that your father couldn't afford one.'

'Which is a different way of putting it.'

'I shouldn't have thought they cost so much.' He had a way of just making a remark, of breathing it so gently that it was scarcely said, and might conveniently be ignored.

He was a dandified little boy. His smooth hair was like a silk cap, combed straight from the crown to a level line above his topaz eyes. His sailor-suits were spotless. The usual boldness changed to an agonised fussiness if his serge sleeve brushed against chalk or if he should slip on the grassy terrace and stain his clothes with green. On their afternoon walks he took no risks and Florence, who had younger brothers, urged him in vain to climb a tree or jump across puddles. At first, she thought him intimidated by his mother or nurse; but soon she realised that his mother entirely indulged him and the nurse had her thoughts all bent upon the new baby: his fussiness was just another part of his grown-upness come too soon.

The house was comfortable, although to Florence rather too sealed-up and overheated after her own damp and draughty home. Her work was not hard and her loneliness only what she had expected. Cut off from the kitchen by her education, she lacked the feuds and camaraderie, gossip and cups of tea, which made life more interesting for the domestic staff. None of the maids – coming to light the lamp at dusk or laying the schoolroom-table for tea – ever presumed beyond a remark or two about the weather.

One late afternoon, she and Hilary returned from their walk and found the lamps already lit. Florence went to her room to tidy herself before tea. When she came down to the schoolroom, Hilary was already there, sitting on the window-seat and staring out over the park as his father did. The room was bright and warm and a maid had put a white cloth over the plush one and was beginning to lay the table.

The air was full of a heavy scent, dry and musky. To Florence, it smelt quite unlike the eau de cologne she sometimes sprinkled on her handkerchief, when she had a headache and she disapproved so much that she returned the maid's greeting coldly and bade Hilary open the window.

'Open the window, dear girl?' he said. 'We shall catch our very deaths.'

'You will do as I ask and remember in future how to address me.'

She was angry with the maid – who now seemed to her an immoral creature – and angry to be humiliated before her.

'But why?' asked Hilary.

'I don't approve of my schoolroom being turned into a scented bower.' She kept her back to the room and was trembling, for she had never rebuked a servant before.

'I approve of it,' Hilary said, sniffing loudly.

'I think it's lovely,' the maid said. 'I noticed it as soon as I opened the door.'

'Is this some joke, Hilary?' Florence asked when the maid had gone.

'No. What?'

'This smell in the room?'

'No. You smell of it most, anyhow.' He put his nose to her sleeve and breathed deeply.

It seemed to Florence that this was so, that her clothes had caught the perfume among their folds. She lifted her palms to her face, then went to the window and leant out into the air as far as she could.

'Shall I pour out the tea, dear girl?'

'Yes, please.'

She took her place at the table abstractedly, and as she drank her tea she stared about the room, frowning. When Hilary's mother looked in, as she often did at this time, Florence stood up in a startled way.

'Good-evening, Mrs Wilson. Hilary, put a chair for your mamma.'

'Don't let me disturb you.'

Mrs Wilson sank into the rocking-chair by the fire and gently tipped to and fro.

'Have you finished your tea, darling boy?' she asked. 'Are you going to read me a story from your book? Oh, there is Lady scratching at the door. Let her in for mamma.'

Hilary opened the door and a balding old pug-dog with blood-shot eyes waddled in.

'Come, Lady! Beautiful one. Come to mistress! What is wrong with her, poor pet lamb?'

The bitch had stopped just inside the room and lifted her head and howled. 'What has frightened her, then? Come, beauty! Coax her with a sponge-cake, Hilary.'

She reached forward to the table to take the dish and doing so noticed Florence's empty tea-cup. On the rim was a crimson smear, like the imprint of a lip. She gave a sponge-finger to Hilary, who tried to quieten the pug, then she leaned back in her chair and studied Florence again as she had studied her when she had engaged her a few weeks earlier. The girl's looks were appropriate enough, appropriate to a clergyman's daughter and a governess. Her square chin looked resolute, her green eyes innocent, her dress was modest and unbecoming. Yet Mrs Wilson could detect an excitability, even feverishness, which she had not noticed before and she wondered if she had mistaken guardedness for innocence and deceit for modesty.

She was reaching this conclusion – rocking back and forth – when she saw Florence's hand stretch out and turn the cup round in its saucer so that the red stain was out of sight.

'What is wrong with Lady?' Hilary asked, for the dog would not be pacified with sponge-fingers, but kept making barking advances further into the room, then growling in retreat.

'Perhaps she is crying at the new moon,' said Florence and she went to the window and drew back the curtain. As she moved, her skirts rustled. 'If she has silk underwear as well!' Mrs Wilson thought. She had clearly heard the sound of taffetas and she imagined the drab, shiny alpaca dress concealing frivolity and wantonness.

'Open the door, Hilary!' she said. 'I will take Lady away. Vernon shall give her a run in the park. I think a quiet read for Hilary and then an early bed-time, Miss Chasty. He looks pale this evening.'

'Yes, Mrs Wilson.' Florence stood respectfully by the table, hiding the cup.

'The hypocrisy!' Mrs Wilson thought and she trembled as she crossed the landing and went downstairs.

She hesitated to tell her husband of her uneasiness, knowing his susceptibilities to women whom his conscience taught him to deplore. Hidden below the apparent urbanity of their married life were old unhappinesses – little acts of treachery and disloyalty which pained her to remember, bruises upon her peace of mind and her pride: letters found, a pretty maid dismissed, an actress who had blackmailed him. As he read the Lesson in church, looking so perfectly upright and honourable a man, she sometimes thought of his escapades; but not with bitterness or cynicism, only with pain at her memories and a whisper of fear about the future. For some time she had been spared those whispers and had hoped that their marriage had at last achieved its calm. To speak of Florence as she must might both arouse his curiosity and revive the past. Nevertheless, she had her duty to her son to fulfil and her own anger to appease and she opened the Library door very determinedly.

'Oliver, I am sorry to interrupt your work, but I must speak to you.'

He put down the *Strand* magazine quite happily, aware that she was not a sarcastic woman.

Oliver and his son were extraordinarily alike. 'As soon as Hilary has grown a moustache we shall not know them apart,' Mrs Wilson often said, and her husband liked this little joke which made him feel more youthful. He did not know that she added a silent prayer – 'O God, please do not let him *be* like him, though.'

'You seem troubled, Louise.' His voice was rich and authoritative. He enjoyed setting to rights her little domestic flurries and waited indulgently to hear of some tradesman's misdemeanour or servant's laziness.

'Yes, I am troubled about Miss Chasty.'

'Little Miss Mouse? I was rather troubled myself. I noticed two spelling-faults in Hilary's botany essay, which she claimed to have corrected. I said nothing before the boy; but I shall acquaint her with it when the opportunity arises.'

'Do you often go to the schoolroom, then?'

'From time to time. I like to be sure that our choice was wise.'

'It was not. It was misguided *and* unwise.'

'All young people seem slip-shod nowadays.'

'She is more than slip-shod. I believe she should go. I think she is quite brazen. Oh yes, I should have laughed at that myself if it had been said to me an hour ago, but I have just come from the schoolroom and it occurs to me that now she has settled down and feels more secure – since you pass over her mistakes – she is beginning to take advantage of your leniency and to show herself in her true colours. I felt a sinister atmosphere up there and I am quite upset and exhausted by it. I went up to hear Hilary's reading. They were finishing tea and the room was full of the most overpowering scent – *her* scent. It was disgusting.'

'Unpleasant?'

'No, not at all. But upsetting.'

'Disturbing?'

She would not look at him or reply, hearing no more indulgence or condescension in his voice, but the quality of warming interest.

'And then I saw her tea-cup and there was a mark on it – a red smear where her lips had touched it. She did not know I saw it and as soon as she noticed it herself she turned it round, away from me. She is an immoral woman and has come into our house to teach our son.'

'I have never noticed a trace of artificiality in her looks. It seemed to me that she was rather colourless.'

'She has been sly. This evening she looked quite different, quite flushed and excitable. I know that she had rouged her lips or painted them, or whatever those women do.' Her eyes filled with tears.

'I shall observe her for a day or two,' Oliver said, trying to keep anticipation from his voice.

'I should like her to go at once.'

'Never act rashly. She is entitled to a quarter's notice unless there is definite blame. We could make ourselves very foolish if you have been mistaken. Oh, I know that you are sure; but it has been known for you to misjudge others. I shall take stock of her and decide if she is suitable. She is still Miss Mouse to me and I cannot think otherwise until I see the evidence with my own eyes.'

'There was something else as well,' Mrs Wilson said wretchedly.

'And what was that?'

'I should rather not say.' She had changed her mind about further accusations. Silk underwear would prove, she guessed, too inflammatory.

'I shall go up ostensibly to mention Hilary's spelling-faults.' He could not go fast enough and stood up at once.

'But Hilary will be in bed.'

'I could not mention the spelling-faults if he were not.'

'Shall I come with you?'

'My dear Louise, why should you? It would look very strange – a deputation about two spelling-faults.'

'Then don't be long, will you? I hope you won't be long.'

He went to the schoolroom, but there was no one there. Hilary's story-book lay closed upon the table and Miss Chasty's sewing was folded neatly. As he was standing there looking about him and sniffing hard, a maid came in with a tray of crockery.

'Has Master Hilary gone to bed?' he asked, feeling rather foolish and confused.

The only scent in the air was a distinct smell – even a haze – of cigarette smoke.

'Yes, sir.'

'And Miss Chasty – where is she?'

'She went to bed, too, sir.'

'Is she unwell?'

'She spoke of a chronic head, sir.'

The maid stacked the cups and saucers in the cupboard and went out. Nothing was wrong with the room apart from the smell of smoke and Mr Wilson went downstairs. His wife was waiting in the hall. She looked up expectantly, in some relief at seeing him so soon.

'Nothing,' he said dramatically. 'She has gone to bed with a headache. No wonder she looked feverish.'

'You noticed the scent.'

'There was none,' he said. 'No trace. Nothing. Just imagination, dear Louise. I thought that it must be so.'

He went to the library and took up his magazine again, but he was too disturbed to read and thought with impatience of the following day.

Florence could not sleep. She had gone to her room, not with a headache but to escape conversations until she had faced her predicament alone. This she was doing, lying on the honeycomb quilt which, since maids do not wait on governesses, had not been turned down.

The schoolroom this evening seemed to have been wreathed about with a strange miasma; the innocent nature of the place polluted in a way which she could not understand or have explained. Something new, it seemed, had entered the room which had not belonged to her or become a part of her – the scent had clung about her clothes; the stained cup was her cup, and her handkerchief with which she had rubbed it clean was still reddened; and, finally, as she had stared in the mirror, trying to re-establish her personality, the affected little laugh which startled her had come from herself. It had driven her from the room.

'I cannot explain the inexplicable,' she thought wearily and began to prepare herself for bed. Home-sickness hit her like a blow on the head. 'Whatever they do to me, I have always my home,' she promised herself. But she could not think who 'they' might be; for no one in this house had threatened her. Mrs Wilson had done no more than irritate her with her commonplace fussing over Hilary and her dog, and Florence was prepared to overcome much more than irritations. Mr Wilson's pomposity, his constant watch on her work, intimidated her, but she knew that all who must earn their living must have fears lest their work should not seem worth the payment. Hilary was easy to manage; she had quickly seen that she could always deflect him from rebelliousness by opening a new subject for conversation; any idea would be a counter-attraction to naughtiness; he wanted her to sharpen his wits upon. 'And is that all that teaching is, or should be?' she had wondered. The servants had been good to her, realising that she would demand nothing of them. She had suffered great loneliness, but had foreseen it as part of her position. Now she felt fear nudging it away. 'I am not lonely any more,' she thought. 'I am not alone any more. And I have lost something.' She said her prayers; then, sitting up in bed, kept the candle alight while she brushed her hair and read the Bible.

'Perhaps I have lost my reason,' she suddenly thought, resting her fingers on her place in the Psalms. She lifted her head and saw her shadow stretch up the powdery, rose-sprinkled wall. 'Now can I keep *that* secret?' she wondered. 'When there is no one to help me to do it? Only those who are watching to see it happen.'

She was not afraid in her bedroom as she had been in the schoolroom, but her perplexed mind found no replies to its questions. She blew out the candle and tried to fall asleep but lay and cried for a long time, and yearned to be at home again and comforted in her mother's arms.

In the morning she met kind enquiries. Nurse was so full of solicitude that Florence felt guilty. 'I came up with a warm drink and put my head round the door but you were in the land of Nod so I drank it myself. I should take a grey powder; or I could mix you a gargle. There are a lot of throats about.'

'I am quite better this morning,' said Florence and she felt calmer as she sat down at the schoolroom-table with Hilary. 'Yet it was all true,' her reason whispered. 'The morning hasn't altered that.'

'You have been crying,' said Hilary. 'Your eyes are red.'

'Sometimes people's eyes are red from other causes – headaches and colds.' She smiled brightly.

'And sometimes from crying, as I said. I should think *usually* from crying.'

'Page fifty-one,' she said, locking her hands together in her lap.

'Very well.' He opened the book, pressed down the pages and lowered his nose to them, breathing the smell of print. 'He is utterly sensuous,' she thought. 'He extracts every pleasure, every sensation, down to the most trivial.'

They seemed imprisoned in the schoolroom, by the silence of the rest of the house and by the rain outside. Her calm began to break up into frustration and she put her hands behind her chair and pressed them against the hot mesh of the fireguard to steady herself. As she did so, she felt a curious derangement of both mind and body; of desire unsettling her once sluggish, peaceful nature, desire horribly defined, though without direction.

'I have soon finished those,' said Hilary, bringing his sums and placing them before her. She glanced at her palms which were criss-crossed deep with crimson where she had pressed them against the fireguard, then she took up her pen and dipped it into the red ink.

'Don't lean against me, Hilary,' she said.

'I love the scent so much.'

It had returned, musky, enveloping, varying as she moved. She ticked the sums quickly, thinking that she would set Hilary more work and escape for a moment to calm herself – change her clothes or cleanse herself in the rain. Hearing Mr Wilson's footsteps along the passage, she knew that her escape was cut off and raised wild-looking eyes as he came in. He mistook panic for passion, thought that by opening the door suddenly he had caught her out and laid bare her secret, her pathetic adoration.

'Good-morning,' he said musically and made his way to the window-seat. 'Don't let me disturb you.' He said this without irony, although he thought: 'So it is that way the wind blows! Poor creature!' He had never found it difficult to imagine that women were in love with him.

'I will hear your verbs,' Florence told Hilary, and opened the French Grammar as if she did not know them herself. Her eyes – from so much crying – were a pale and brilliant green, and as the scent drifted in Oliver's direction and he turned to her, she looked fully at him.

'Ah, the still waters!' he thought and stood up suddenly. '*Ils vont*,' he corrected Hilary and touched his shoulder as he passed. 'Are you attending to Miss Chasty?'

'Is she attending to me?' Hilary murmured. The risk was worth taking, for neither heard. His father appeared to be sleep-walking and Florence deliberately closed her eyes, as if looking down were not enough to blur the outlines of her desire.

'I find it difficult,' Oliver said to his wife, 'to reconcile your remarks about Miss Chasty with the young woman herself. I have just come from the schoolroom and she was engaged in nothing more immoral than teaching French verbs – that not very well, incidentally.'

'But can you *explain* what I have told you?'

'I can't do that,' he said gaily. For who can explain a jealous woman's fancies? he implied.

He began to spend more time in the schoolroom; from surveillance, he said. Miss Chasty, though not outwardly of an amorous nature, was still not what he had at first supposed. A suppressed wantonness hovered beneath her primness. She was the ideal governess in his eyes – irreproachable, yet not unapproachable. As she was so conveniently installed, he could take his time in divining the extent of her willingness; especially as he was growing older and the game was beginning to be worth more than the triumph of winning it. To his wife, he upheld Florence, saw nothing wrong save in her scholarship, which needed to be looked into – the explanation for his more frequent visits to the schoolroom. He laughed teasingly at Louise's fancies.

The schoolroom indeed became a focal point of the house – the stronghold of Mr Wilson's desire and his wife's jealousy.

'We are never alone,' said Hilary. 'Either Papa or Mamma is here. Perhaps they wonder if you are good enough for me.'

'Hilary!' His father had heard the last sentence as he opened the door and the first as he hovered outside listening. 'I doubt if my ears deceived me. You will go to your room while you think of a suitable apology and I think of an ample punishment.'

'Shall I take my history book with me or shall I just waste time?'

'I have indicated how to spend your time.'

'That won't take long enough,' said Hilary beneath his breath as he closed the door.

'Meanwhile, I apologise for him,' said his father. He did not go to his customary place by the window, but came to the hearth-rug where Florence stood behind her chair. 'We have indulged him too much and he has been too much with adults. Have there been other occasions?'

'No, indeed, sir.'

'You find him tractable?'

'Oh, yes.'

'And are you happy in your position?'

'Yes.'

As the dreaded, the now so familiar scent began to wreathe about the room, she stepped back from him and began to speak rapidly, as urgently as if she were dying and must make some explanation while she could. 'Perhaps, after all, Hilary is right and you do wonder about my competence – and if I can give him all he should have. Perhaps a man would teach him more . . .'

She began to feel a curious infraction of the room and of her personality, seemed to lose the true Florence, and the room lightened as if the season had been changed.

'You are mistaken,' he was saying. 'Have I ever given you any hint that we were not satisfied?'

Her timidity had quite dissolved and he was shocked by the sudden boldness of her glance.

'No, no hint,' she said smiling. As she moved, he heard the silken swish of her clothes.

'I should rather give you a hint of how well pleased I am.'

'Then why don't you?' she asked.

She leaned back against the chimney-piece and looped about her fingers a long necklace of glittering green beads. 'Where did these come from?' she wondered. She could not remember ever having seen them before, but she could not pursue her bewilderment, for the necklace felt familiar to her hands, much more familiar than the rest of the room.

'*When* shall I?' he was insisting. 'This evening, perhaps? when Hilary is in bed?'

'Then who is *he*, if Hilary is to be in bed?' she wondered. She glanced at him and smiled again. 'You are extraordinarily alike,' she said. 'You and Hilary.' 'But Hilary is a little boy,' she reminded herself. 'It is silly to confuse the two.'

'We must discuss Hilary's progress,' he said, his voice so burdened with meaning that she began to laugh at him.

'Indeed we must,' she agreed.

'Your necklace is the colour of your eyes.' He took it from her finger and leaned forward, as if to kiss her. Hearing footsteps in the passage she moved sharply aside, the necklace broke and the beads were scattered over the floor.

'Why is Hilary in the garden at this hour?' Mrs Wilson asked. Her husband and the governess were on their knees, gathering up the beads.

'Miss Chasty's necklace broke,' her husband said. She had heard that submissive tone before: his voice lacked authority only when he was caught out in some infidelity.

'I was asking about Hilary. I have just seen him running in the shrubbery without a coat.'

'He was sent to his room for being impertinent to Miss Chasty.'

'Please fetch him at once,' Mrs Wilson told Florence. Her voice always gained in authority what her husband's lacked.

Florence hurried from the room, still holding a handful of beads. She felt badly shaken – as if she had been brought to the edge of some experience which had then retreated beyond her grasp.

'He was told to stay in his room,' Mr Wilson said feebly.

'Why did her beads break?'

'She was fidgeting with them. I think she was nervous. I was making it rather apparent to her that I regarded Hilary's insubordination as proof of too much leniency on her part.'

'I didn't know that she had such a necklace. It is the showiest trash that I have ever seen.'

'We cannot blame her for the cheapness of her trinkets. It is rather pathetic.'

'There is nothing pathetic about her. We will continue this in the morning-room and *they* can continue their lessons, which are, after all, her reason for being here.'

'Oh, they are gone,' said Hilary. His cheeks were pink from the cold outside.

'Why did you not stay in your bedroom as you were told?'

'I had nothing to do. I thought of my apology before I got there. It was: "I am sorry, dear girl, that I spoke too near the point".'

'You could have spent longer and thought of a real apology.'

'Look how long Papa spent and he did not even think of a punishment, which is a much easier thing.'

Several times during the evening Mr Wilson said: 'But you cannot dismiss the girl because her beads break.'

'There have been other things and will be more,' his wife replied.

So that there should not be more that evening, he did not move from the drawing-room where he sat watching her doing her wool-work. For the same reason, Florence left the schoolroom early. She went out and walked rather nervously in the park, feeling remorseful, astonished and upset.

'Did you mend your necklace?' Hilary asked her in the morning.

'I lost the beads.'

'But my poor girl, they must be somewhere.'

She thought: 'There is no reason to suppose that I shall get back what I never had in the first place.'

'Have you got a headache?'

'Yes. Go on with your work, Hilary.'

'Is it from losing the beads?'

'No.'

'Have you a great deal of jewellery I have not seen yet?'

She did not answer and he went on: 'You still have your brooch with your grandmother's plaited hair in it. Was it cut off her head when she was dead?'

'Your *work*, Hilary.'

'I shudder to think of chopping it off a corpse. You could have some of my hair, now, while I am living.' He fingered it with admiration, regarded a sum aloofly and jotted down its answer. 'Could I cut some of yours?' he asked, bringing his book to be corrected. He whistled softly, close to her, and the tendrils of hair round her ears were gently blown about.

'It is ungentlemanly to whistle,' she said.

'My sums are always right. It shows how I can chatter and subtract at the same time. Any governess would be annoyed by that. I suppose your brothers never whistle.'

'Never.'

'Are they to be clergymen like your father?'

'It is what we hope for one of them.'

'I am to be a famous judge. When you read about me, will you say: "And to think I might have been his wife if I had not been so self-willed"?'

'No, but I hope that I shall feel proud that once I taught you.'

'You sound doubtful.'

He took his book back to the table. 'We are having a quiet morning,' he remarked. 'No one has visited us. Poor Miss Chasty, it is a pity about the necklace,' he murmured, as he took up his pencil again.

Evenings were dangerous to her. 'He said he would come,' she told herself, 'and I allowed him to say so. On what compulsion did I?'

Fearfully, she spent her lonely hours out in the dark garden or in her cold and candlelit bedroom. He was under his wife's vigilance and Florence did not know that he dared not leave the drawing-room. But the vigilance relaxed, as it does: his carelessness returned and steady rain and bitter cold drove Florence to warm her chilblains at the schoolroom fire.

Her relationship with Mrs Wilson had changed. A wary hostility took the place of meekness, and when Mrs Wilson came to the schoolroom at tea-times, Florence stood up defiantly and cast a look round the room as if to say: 'Find what you can. There is nothing here.' Mrs Wilson's suspicious ways increased her rebelliousness. 'I have done nothing wrong,' she told herself. But in her bedroom at night: '*I* have done nothing wrong,' she would think.

'They have quite deserted us,' Hilary said from time to time. 'They have realised you are worth your weight in gold, dear girl; or perhaps I made it clear to my father that in this room he is an interloper.'

'Hilary!'

'You want to put yourself in the right in case that door opens suddenly as it has been doing lately. There, you see! Good-evening, Mamma. I was just saying that I have scarcely seen you all day.' He drew forward her chair and held the cushion behind her until she leaned back.

'I have been resting.'

'Are you ill, Mamma?'

'I have a headache.'

'I will stroke it for you, dear lady.'

He stood behind her chair and began to smooth her forehead. 'Or shall I read to you?' he asked, soon tiring of his task. 'Or play the musical-box?'

'No, nothing more, thank you.'

Mrs Wilson looked about her, at the tea-cups, then at Florence. Sometimes it seemed to her that her husband was right and that she was growing fanciful. The innocent appearance of the room lulled her and she closed her eyes for a while, rocking gently in her chair.

'I dozed off,' she said when she awoke. The table was cleared and Florence and Hilary sat playing chess, whispering so that they should not disturb her.

'It made a domestic scene for us,' said Hilary. 'Often Miss Chasty and I feel that we are left too much in solitary bliss.'

The two women smiled and Mrs Wilson shook her head. 'You have too old a head on your shoulders,' she said. 'What will they say of you when you go to school?'

'What shall I say of *them*?' he asked bravely, but he lowered his eyes and kept them lowered. When his mother had gone, he asked Florence: 'Did you go to school?'

'Yes.'

'Were you unhappy there?'

'No. I was homesick at first.'

'If I don't like it, there will be no point in my staying,' he said hurriedly. 'I can learn anywhere and I don't particularly want the corners knocked off, as my father once spoke of it. I shouldn't like to play cricket and all those childish games. Only to do boxing and draw blood,' he added, with sudden bravado. He laughed excitedly and clenched his fists.

'You would never be good at boxing if you lost your temper.'

'I suppose your brothers told you that. They don't sound very manly to me. They would be afraid of a good fight and the sight of blood, I daresay.'

'Yes, I daresay. It is bedtime.'

He was whipped up by the excitement he had created from his fears.

'Chess is a woman's game,' he said and upset the board. He took the cushion from the rocking-chair and kicked it inexpertly across the room. 'I should have thought the door would have opened then,' he said. 'But as my father doesn't appear to send me to my room, I will go there of my own accord. It wouldn't have been a punishment at bedtime in any case. When I am a judge I shall be better at punishments than he is.'

When he had gone, Florence picked up the cushion and the chess-board. 'I am no good at punishments, either,' she thought. She tidied the room, made up the fire, then sat down in the rocking-chair, thinking of all the lonely schoolroom evenings of her future. She bent her head over her needlework – the beaded sachet for her mother's birthday present. When she looked up she thought the lamp was smoking and she went to the table and turned down the wick. Then she noticed that the smoke was wreathing upwards from near the fireplace, forming rings which drifted towards the ceiling and were lost in a haze. She could hear a woman's voice humming softly and the floorboards creaked as if someone were treading up and down the room impatiently.

She felt in herself a sense of burning impatience and anticipation and watching the door opening found herself thinking: 'If it is not he, I cannot bear it.'

He closed the door quietly. 'She has gone to bed,' he said in a lowered voice. 'For days I dared not come. She has watched me at every moment. At last, this evening, she gave way to a headache. Were you expecting me?'

'Yes.'

'And once I called you Miss Mouse! And you are still Miss Mouse when I see you about the garden, or at luncheon.'

'In this room I can be myself. It belongs to us.'

'And not to Hilary as well – ever?' he asked her in amusement.

She gave him a quick and puzzled glance.

'Let no one intrude,' he said hastily. 'It is our room, just as you say.'

She had turned the lamp too low and it began to splutter. 'Firelight is good enough for us,' he said, putting the light out altogether.

When he kissed her, she felt an enormous sense of disappointment, almost as if he were the wrong person embracing her in the dark. His arch masterfulness merely bored her. 'A long wait for so little,' she thought.

He, however, found her entirely seductive. She responded with a sensuous languor, unruffled and at ease like the most perfect hostess.

'Where did you practise this, Miss Mouse?' he asked her. But he did not wait for the reply, fancying that he heard a step on the landing. When his wife opened the door, he was trying desperately to light a taper at the fire. His hand was trembling, and when at last, in the terribly silent room, the flame crept up the spill it simply served to show Florence's disarray which, like a sleep-walker, she had not noticed or put right.

She did not see Hilary again, except as a blurred little figure at the schoolroom window – blurred because of her tear-swollen eyes.

She was driven away in the carriage, although Mr Wilson had suggested the station fly. 'Let us keep her disgrace and her tearfulness to ourselves,' he begged, although he was exhausted by the repetitious burden of his wife's grief.

'*Her* disgrace!'

'My mistake, I have said, was in not taking your accusations about her seriously. I see now that I was in some way bewitched – yes, bewitched is what it was – acting against my judgment; nay, my very nature. I am astonished that anyone so seemingly meek could have cast such a spell upon me.'

Poor Florence turned her head aside as Williams, the coachman, came to fetch her little trunk and the basket-work holdall. Then she put on her cloak, and prepared herself to go downstairs, fearful lest she should meet anyone on the way. Yet her thoughts were even more on her journey's end; for what, she wondered, could she tell her father and how expect him to understand what she could not understand herself?

Her head was bent as she crossed the landing and she hurried past the schoolroom door. At the turn of the staircase she pressed back against the wall to allow someone to pass. She heard laughter and then up the stairs came a young woman and a little girl. The child was clinging to the woman's arm and coaxing her, as sometimes Hilary had tried to coax Florence. 'After lessons,' the woman said firmly, but gaily. She looked ahead, smiling to herself. Her clothes were unlike anything that Florence had ever seen. Later, when she tried to describe them to her mother, she could only remember the shortness of a tunic which scarcely covered the knees, a hat like a helmet drawn down over eyes intensely green and matching the long necklace of glass beads which swung on her flat bosom. As she came up the stairs and drew near to Florence, she was humming softly against the child's pleading; silk rustled against her silken legs and all of the staircase, as Florence quickly descended, was full of fragrance.

In the darkness of the hall a man was watching the two go round the bend of the stairs. The woman must have looked back, for Florence saw him lift his hand in a secretive gesture of understanding.

'It is Hilary, not his father!' she thought. But the figure turned before she could be sure and went into the library.

Outside on the drive Williams was waiting with her luggage stowed away in the carriage. When she had settled herself, she looked up at the schoolroom window and saw Hilary standing there rather forlornly and she could almost imagine him saying: 'My poor dear girl; so you were not good enough for me, after all?'

'When does the new governess arrive?' she asked Williams in a casual voice, which hoped to conceal both pride and grief.

'There's nothing fixed as far as I have heard,' he said.

They drove out into the lane.

'When will it be *her* time?' Florence wondered. 'I am glad that I saw her before I left.'

'We are sorry to see you going, Miss.' He had heard that the maids were sorry, for she had given them no trouble.

'Thank you, Williams.'

As they went on towards the station, she leaned back and looked at the familiar places where she had walked with Hilary. 'I know what I shall tell my father now,' she thought, and she felt peaceful and meek as though beginning to be convalescent after a long illness.

Elizabeth Jenkins

ON NO ACCOUNT, MY LOVE

MY cousin Hero is beautiful but unmindful of the fact. Though her husband has done well in his profession it has needed ceaseless energy on Hero's part to keep up the domestic standard she thinks worthy of him and the children; therefore, capable and high-spirited though she is, she bears the stamp of care. Her beauty is the last thing in her mind, though sometimes when she fixes you with her keen blue eyes, intent on discovering just how misguided you have been so that she may put you right, the loveliness of her face, sharp as a cameo, astonishes even someone who knows her as well as I do.

Decisiveness is one of Hero's leading qualities, and a passionate conviction that she is right: not from any virtue of her own, but because she knows what the right is, and has joined herself to it. In the present degenerate state of society there is a great deal that is wrong, and against everything of the sort Hero is dauntlessly embattled. Her upright carriage, small as she is, and her great eyes filled with stern resolve give her rather the look of being posted on the ramparts. Her affection takes the form of a protective, almost proprietary interest in the ones she loves; she cannot help knowing what is best for them; she only wishes, for their sake, that they could see the facts as clearly as she does.

Her kindness to me is of a critical sort, for I am, though so nearly related, entirely outside the strain of heredity that distinguishes my cousin. I am vague, unpractical, and, as she does not disguise from me, often downright silly in the management of my affairs. At the same time, there are matters into which I fancy that I can see farther than she can.

These characteristics and the chiselled features and blue eyes that go with them, of which Hero is the present embodiment, have appeared in my mother's family for four generations. They missed me, but my mother had them, so had two of her sisters. In all three, the look of blazing moral energy was tinged with a faint terror and desperation, as if they had been called on to sustain some ordeal like that of the Boy on the Burning Deck. It was not open to them to save themselves by failure, and they could see the flames licking up the ground in front of them. In the generation before my mother and her sisters, photographs of my great-aunts showed more faces with the unmistakable stamp of beauty, intensity and care; and behind these again, the *fons et origo* of all this, my great-grandmother. Hers was the mould of the family face and her descendants were startlingly like her; yet there was a great difference between them. Their beautiful faces, in early youth even, were strained and anxious; her expression, though intense, was confident: they were oppressed and she was triumphant.

She was one of those people whose personality makes such a strong impression that it lasts a long while after death. Great-grandmother, with her strictness, her sternness, her domineering will, was an alarming story to us in our childhood though she had died long before we were born. As we grew up, I felt how much I should have disliked and shrunk from her. In Hero, her idea aroused a passionate resentment. Hero used to say, she would just have liked to see her trying it on with *her*. Indeed, she and great-grandmother would have been worthy of each other's steel.

No one knew where she came from; her name was or was said to be Seymour, but she had been adopted by two maiden ladies and if she knew in what circumstances she never said. She was proposed to, at the then late age of twenty-nine, by a gentleman of modest means. We have her written reply in which she barely puts down her thanks for the honour of his regard before she says: 'I must tell you that I have no fortune and no prospect of any.' This letter amused my father for he said that when he proposed to my mother she immediately exclaimed: 'Oh! But I am much older than you think I am.' Our great-grandfather, like my father after him, paid no heed to these disclaimers. Miss Seymour became Mrs Standish and went to live in Derbyshire in a town that was rapidly developing as a health resort. Her husband died early, leaving her with several young children and little else beside the house they lived in. This was one in a crescent on the hillside, at what was then the top of the town. At that time the graceful curve of its façade stood out white against the murky violet of the hills, now the whole hillside has been engulfed in a tide of building development. The expansion was beginning in the 1860s and it gave Mrs Standish the opportunity of supporting her family by a girls' boarding school. She made a really remarkable success of this project; before long she acquired the houses on each side of her own and these considerable premises were filled to overflowing with her young family, her employees and the girls under her care. The whole household was welded together under her vigilant and energetic rule. The domestic conditions were those of almost supernormal cleanliness, neatness, economy and punctuality, at the cost of many a red-armed servant girl crying on the back stairs, and the teaching was carried on with such gusto, the drilling in grammar and dates and tables and maps and principal exports had the stimulus of a round game, but a game slightly nightmarish in quality, a game played with tigers. The school throughout its long life, for it passed from hand to hand, till Magnall's Questions gave way to the Examinations of the Joint Board, preserved intact its original tradition of thoroughness, enthusiasm and clear handwriting. The relentless driving that produced it had, one must suppose, a good effect on the average pupil but it bore hardly on the two extremes; it burdened the dull and in the intelligent and highly strung it induced a morbid conscientiousness. Mrs Standish's own descendants were among the latter. An enlightened policy of child-care would have soothed and kept them back; Mrs Standish goaded them on till their talents were unnaturally burnished and their nervous systems a wreck. As Mama she had been formidable, as Grandmama she was a holy terror, and it was from that phase of her rule that the stories came of her severe discipline, the preposterous tales of what she exacted and what she wouldn't allow, that made such an impression on the rest of us who had never seen her. One of her daughters was in love with a young man who sought her hand. They had met at choir practice but great-grandmother objected to his principles and forbade the match. She knew best, naturally. Our great-aunt developed what was called brain-fever and lay in bed for weeks. It was summer and the day of the school fête when parents came to a great tea-drinking, inspected needlework and listened to songs, recitations and piano pieces afterwards. Downstairs all was gaiety and commotion, white frocks, striped awnings, geraniums and strawberries on a fleet of glass plates. No one could be spared to watch the invalid, except my mother, a child of five, who was left in her aunt's bedroom, perched on a high stool from where she could see the figure in the white bed with a bandage over its eyes, moving its head on the pillow very slightly but all the time. The child was told to come downstairs at once and tell somebody if the patient started to get out of bed. The white curtains were drawn across the sunny window, the walls were in shadow; the dreadful bandage round the head made it look like something on an ancient tomb near to where the little girls sat in church. From far below came up the sounds of the party, too far away to be of any help. The child sat transfixed in an agony of fright lest the terrible figure should begin to rise. My mother said she thought that if that had happened, she would have gone out of her mind with fear.

The story used to fill me with indignation, for my mother communicated her sufferings to me in a way I never forgot, and I laid them, and a great deal of nervous unhappiness, at my great-grandmother's door. My mother, feeling sometimes that she had given an unfair impression, would say in contrite tones: 'She had, I think, a wonderful way of giving pleasure by small things: these dolls that were kept in the drawing-room! They had their own tea-set and a trunk for their extra dresses and hats: we used to be allowed to play with them on special occasions. I have never forgotten the excitement and delight of seeing them put down on the yellow hearthrug.'

'When everything was more or less horrid, I suppose anything that wasn't did seem wonderful,' I suggested. My mother said, it was not *that*, exactly. 'So much of what she did was excellent; it was only . . .' My mother broke off and sighed. 'Only!' cried Hero, sparkling with ire. 'I should think it was, indeed! *Only* that she was an abominable old tyrant who made people's lives a misery!' My mother succeeded thoroughly in making us understand the harsh side of the régime but she could not with all her efforts induce us to see that there had been a part of it that was worth having.

The school after four generations had been honourably wound up; the later phases of its existence had no distinctive interest for me, but whenever I met someone who had had, or heard of, first-hand experience of its early days, there was always brought to light some new detail of my great-grandmother's reign; of hot afternoons when thirsty children were not allowed to go for drinks of water because, said Mrs Standish with inexorable logic, drinking was drinking, and if you did not learn to control a desire for water, where would you be when wine and spirits were within your reach? And of festivals of delicious things, religiously kept: gooseberry pies and cream at Whitsun, hot rolls for breakfast on Sunday mornings and two or three times a term, a Sweet Saturday, when everyone was allowed to choose sweets and order sixpenny-worth of them, and they were brought in to the big schoolroom in great baskets. No doubt the child of today, devouring chocolate and ice cream at all hours, has never had a gastronomic sensation like that produced by a single brandy ball under Mrs Standish's aegis.

Of the three houses occupied by her, one was now a private hotel, one empty and for sale and the third in the possession of some very old friends. They asked me to visit them on my way back from a journey in the north. I was especially pleased to go; I wanted to see with my own eyes the houses of which I had heard so much, and besides this, our friends were in the middle of a very interesting experience. They had newly acquired a cook-housekeeper, a Mrs Garnish, who, it turned out, was a medium and received messages in automatic writing every night. Mrs Garnish went to bed with a pencil and sheets of paper beside her, and in the morning the latter were covered with regular handwriting, a little different from her own. The lines were even but they sometimes went at an angle across the paper and sometimes were written right off it so that the end of a line would be lost. Nonetheless a great body of communication was received, and it was of absorbing interest to our friends, for the greater part of it appeared to come from their own relations who were dead, and some from friends and connections whom they themselves could barely remember except by name.

There was no doubting the good faith of the medium, and whatever might be the explanation of it, they were witnessing a very singular phenomenon. On a few occasions when clairvoyants had read cards for me they had asked me whether I were mediumistic, and when told no, they had said I should develop the faculty later. As they had never read my future with any marked success, and as the development they foretold had showed no signs of taking place, I had almost forgotten it. I remembered it again as I came down from Yorkshire into Derbyshire and leaning in a corner of the railway carriage, gazing at the wonderful landscape as we wound among dales and streams, I felt a stir of excitement, wondering if any messages would come for me during the night that I was under what had once been my great-grandmother's roof.

The crescent no longer stood out against the hills, for buildings had encroached around and far above it, and at close quarters the façade was seen to be cracked and darkened and patched with boards announcing hotels and offices. Inside however was all the space and gracefulness of its period. I walked in through a vestibule with inner doors whose panels of milky glass were scattered with clear glass stars and edged with strips of glass in ruby, amber, emerald, sapphire and violet. There were gothic-pointed windows on each side of the front door and embrasures for statues or plants. I was so much moved by all this that I barely noticed Mrs Garnish as she let me in and yet I knew it was she: short and square with a face of glistening pallor, pince-nez, a quiet smile and the most respectable clothes, ending in stockings of clerical-grey and black strapped shoes.

Our friends with sympathetic kindness had got the key of the empty house from the house agent, for they thought I should be able to imagine the original scene more clearly from empty rooms than from their own, filled with modern comforts. After lunch therefore on a bright afternoon in April, I let myself into the middle of the three houses, the one that had been my great-grandmother's home. The functional nature of the premises and her restricted income by all accounts saved her from the over-furnishing and over-ornamentation of the late Victorian era. Her rooms had been almost as elegantly bare as if she had furnished them in the previous century. The only rich objects in view had been the lofty gilt pier glasses already over the chimney-pieces when she had taken the house. Two of these were still there on the first floor; one was enclosed and separated into three by gilt Ionic columns, the other reared a gilt trophy of musical instruments, from which fringed gold scarves drooped in festoons on each side of the glass. The mirrors themselves were filled with watery gleams and shadows, for they were opposite the great sash windows through whose panes the girls had looked at the roofs of the town below or up at the great marbled expanse of the northern sky. I walked slowly across dusty boards, everything I had ever heard about the rooms coming back to me; I wondered in which of the three drawing-rooms it was that my mother had played with dolls on the yellow rug, where the round table had stood that was covered with a magenta velvet cloth, on which of the chimney-pieces there had been the famous pair of emerald glass baskets. These objects had remained in many minds with a brilliance accentuated by the extent of drab serge and plain drugget around them. I climbed the front staircase till the stairs grew almost as narrow and steep as those of a church tower and found myself in a row of small bedrooms whose sash windows, filled with a pale blaze of sky, were so immediately in front of one on opening the door, one felt about to fall through them. So high up, a strong breeze was rattling the frames. I looked about the empty walls and wondered if this room or one like it had been the scene of my great-aunt's brain fever, but for once the memory did not appal me; it now took on the proportion of a part in a much larger whole. After a long while I let myself out of the house and returned to the next door one through a pair of glass doors identical with those through which I had just emerged. Indoors I saw that it had become dusk, and an electric light was burning in the hall outside the drawing-room door. On a space of wall just beside it, was an enlarged photograph in an oval frame of Mrs Standish taken in advanced years. I had seen similar ones but never one that showed the face so well. The hair drooped smoothly under lace, the features in their symmetry and their sharpness were what I had often seen, but the eyes were sunken and tired; the hands rested on her lap palms upward, the back of one curved in the palm of the other. There was no suggestion of a posed portrait; this was a moment's pause in the day of a busy woman, who had sat still for a minute that someone might take her photograph. As I stood looking at it I felt growing in me, unexpected and unsought, a feeling of sympathy, of admiration, of affection even for my great-grandmother. I saw, for the first time objectively, what a creature of spirit and style she had been, of what buoyancy of intellect. I imagined her *obiter dicta*, so many of which had come down to us, uttered in that voice I knew so well but louder, more resonant, with a twang like that of a harpsichord. Looking at the photograph with its saffron and mulberry gloss, I pored over the expression, calm and positive and a little fatigued, and I remembered all the good things said about her which I had so perversely disregarded: how splendidly capable she was with a child in the throes of croup, how unfailingly she remembered birthdays and would think of special treats for anyone who had been left out, how she had said that to be one of a family was a blessing, and that brothers and sisters must endure anything rather than quarrel. As I stood in the quiet hall, noises in different parts of the house came to my ears, a waft of radio music from behind the drawing-room door, and a sound of saucepans from the regions at the back. I thought with a rising excitement of Mrs Garnish. The idea of being able to get into touch with my great-grandmother gave me a thrill of interest keener than any book or picture had ever evoked in me. I felt sure that some contact was possible, was waiting for me, and as I went into the lighted drawing-room I was so rapt with the thought, I could barely see what was in front of me.

In the course of the evening I told our friends what my hopes were. They were sympathetic but non-committal. Then we dropped this matter and spent an evening full of news and reminiscence. My bedroom was one of the lofty ones, but curtained, carpeted, warmed, with books, bedside lamp and a large soft eiderdown. I gave one glance through the panes before getting to bed. The sky was quite black and the harsh lights from the streets and the noise of traffic and nocturnal shouting deprived the scene of any visual depth or any charm. I suffered a reaction from my previous mood: I felt that everything I cared about was lost and went to my comfortable bed in a prosaic frame of mind.

Next day I was to leave by a train shortly after twelve, and in the course of the morning when we had the breakfast-room to ourselves, my hostess handed me a sheet of paper, saying something on it might refer to me. I left the room with it in my hand but my eagerness would not let me mount the stairs with it and I carried it into the glassed-in vestibule to examine it by one of the gothic windows. It was a sheet from an exercise book, blue-lined. The pencilled writing did not keep to the lines but it was regular and firm and had been crossed, almost at right-angles, by more writing, which made the whole thing difficult to read. The writing parallel with the lines seemed to be about a Colonel Mortimer-Fisher who had had three sons but all were with him now. They were working for those left behind, and sent messages of a hopeful and joyous nature to various groups of initials. My heart sank as I made all this out: I suddenly remembered all I had ever heard of the trite, depressing clichés of spirit communication; here was an example. I felt that even those who had known Colonel Mortimer-Fisher and his sons and held them dear could hardly be stirred by this. In a moment of disappointment and self-contempt I turned the paper round to bring the diagonally written lines straight. Their writing though less black was a good deal larger.

Elizabeth Elizabeth Elizabeth Elizabeth, I read, and the repetition of my name made my heart stop beating. No dangerous for you very dangerous very very dangerous on no account my love.

I stood quite still, I have no idea for how long. Then I crossed the vestibule and the hall, both of them sunny and empty, and made my way, hesitating, to the semi-basement kitchen to say a word and a goodbye to Mrs Garnish. The door stood open and a large clock ticked on the narrow shelf high above what had once been a range, its cavern now occupied by a gas cooker. The light came over a stone wall and slanted through the top row of panes in a broad, clear shaft. A row of green plants stood under it on the deep sill. At the scrubbed white table Mrs Garnish was sitting in a mid-day pause. A bright blue canister was before her, a small brown teapot and a large white cup and saucer. She sat motionless with her eyes closed but her head, instead of being sunk forward as another person's would have been, was upright, even raised a little. Her greenish-pale face glistened. Nothing moved but the jerking hands of the clock.

It came over me that I had no business there, that I had already been told as much. I came upstairs again to objects that looked like cardboard, to mechanical words and automatic actions.

I came back unable to say much to anyone about my visit. Hero, whom I met a couple of days afterwards, was struck by my unusual silence. When she had satisfied herself that I was not sickening for anything, she looked at me anxiously but without saying more. She is now turning over in her mind whether I had better go abroad for a little.

Rosemary Timperley

THE MISTRESS IN BLACK

THE school was deathly quiet and seemed to be deserted. Nervously I approached it from the road, followed a path round the side of the building and came to the main entrance. I tried the door but it was locked, so I rang the bell.

Footsteps approached. The door opened. A tall, pleasant-faced man with a grey moustache stood there.

'Good morning,' I said. 'I'm Miss Anderson. I have an appointment with the Headmistress at ten o'clock.'

'Oh, yes. Come in, Miss. I'm the caretaker.' He stood aside for me to pass and closed the door again. 'If you'll wait here, I'll see if Miss Leonard is ready for you.'

He went along the corridor in front of me, turned to the right and vanished.

With my back to the front door, I looked round the hall. On the wall to my left was a green baize notice-board with a few notices neatly arranged and secured with drawing-pins. I wondered whether that board would still be so tidy when the vacation was over and the children were back. Past the notice-board were swing doors opening on to an empty gymnasium, its equipment idle, its floor shining with polish. The paintwork was fresh and the place looked as if it had just been redecorated. To my right were a number of other doors, closed and mysterious – for everything in an unfamiliar building seems mysterious. And ahead of me, to the left of the corridor and alongside it, was a flight of stairs leading upwards.

My nervousness increased. Interviews always panic me and I really needed this job. Trembling a little, I waited. The silence itself seemed to make a noise in my ears. I listened for the caretaker's returning footsteps.

Suddenly a woman appeared at the top of the stairs and began to descend. She startled me as she had made no sound in her approach, and I was reminded of one of my previous headmistresses whose habit of wearing soft-soled shoes had given her an uncanny ability to turn up silently when she was least expected. This woman on the stairs was pale, dark, very thin, and wearing a black dress unrelieved by any sort of ornament. Unsmiling, she looked at me with beautiful but very unhappy dark eyes.

'Miss Leonard?' I said.

She didn't reply or even pause, merely moved towards the doors of the gymnasium. At the same moment I heard the caretaker's returning footsteps and turned to see him re-enter the corridor.

'This way, dear,' he called. 'Miss Leonard will see you now.'

As I went towards him, I thought I smelt something burning, so hesitated. Again I looked through the glass at the top half of the gymnasium doors. The woman in black was out of sight.

'What's the matter?' The caretaker came up to me. 'Feeling nervous?'

'Yes, I am – but it's not that – I thought I smelt burning.'

He looked at me sharply. 'No, not now,' he said. 'That's all over, and I should know. But I've got a bonfire going in the grounds. Maybe the smoke is blowing this way.'

'That'll be it. Anyway, I can't smell it any more. Was that Miss Leonard I saw a second ago?'

'Where?' he asked.

'On the stairs, then she went into the gymnasium –'

'You're in a proper state of nerves, you are,' he said, as I followed him along the corridor. 'There's no one in the building today except you, me and Miss Leonard, and she's in her office waiting for you. Coming on the staff, are you?'

'I hope so. I've applied for the job of English teacher.'

'Good luck, then,' he said.

We stopped outside a door.

'This is Miss Leonard's room, Miss.' He knocked on the door. A voice called: 'Come in!'

And I went into the Headmistress's room.

Miss Leonard was at her desk, the window behind her. She rose immediately, a plump yet dignified figure with neat white hair and a pink suit which heightened the colour in her cheeks. She was utterly unlike the woman in black.

She smiled. 'Do come right in and sit down, Miss Anderson. I'm glad to see you. It's not easy to find staff at a moment's notice at the end of the autumn term.'

'It's not easy to find a job at this time either,' I said. 'Most schools are fixed up for the whole of the school year.'

'We were too – then suddenly there was a vacancy. Now, you're twenty-five, you have a B.A. degree in English, and two years' teaching experience.' She was looking at my letter of application which lay on her desk.

'That's right, Miss Leonard.'

'You haven't been teaching for the past twelve months. May I ask why?'

'My mother and I went to live in Rome with my sister and her husband, who is Italian. Mother was ill and she wanted to see my sister again before – well, Mother's dead now so I decided to come back to England.'

'And do you know anything about this school?'

'No. I simply answered your advertisement.'

'I'm glad you did.' She picked up a folder of papers and handed it to me. 'In here I've enclosed your timetable for next term and details of syllabus and set books. So you can "do your homework" before you arrive.'

'You mean I've got the job?'

'Yes. Why not?'

'That's marvellous. Thank you.'

We talked for a while then, as she took me back to the main door, she said: 'You'll find the rest of the staff very nice and friendly.'

'I think I've seen one of them already,' I said.

'Really? Which one?'

'I don't know. It was just that she came down the stairs while I was waiting in the hall. She was wearing a black dress.'

Miss Leonard said casually: 'Staff do come back during the vacation sometimes, to collect forgotten property or whatever. Good-bye for the present, Miss Anderson. When you arrive on the first day of term, come to my office and I'll show you the staff room then take you to your first class.'

And the interview was over.

Christmas passed, January began, diligently I studied my folder of information and then, on the night before first day of term, snow fell. My lodgings were a train journey away from the school and on the very morning when I wanted to be punctual, my train stuck. Ice on the points. By the time I reached the school, I was late, and distraught.

Added to this, the school itself looked different under snow. I couldn't even find the path to the main door. I took a wrong path, lost myself wandering round the building, then peered through a classroom window.

Lights were on inside. About thirty-five little girls in white blouses and dark tunics were sitting at their desks and listening to the teacher. That teacher was the dark, thin woman in the black dress whom I had seen before. Fascinated, I stood and gazed. It was like watching a silent play, myself in the outside dark, the actors in the light, playing their parts.

In the front row of the class was a little girl with golden hair falling like bright rain over her shoulders. Next to her was a dark child, her black hair cropped close as a boy's. And next to this one was a child with a mop of red curls.

All the pupils were attentive, but this red-haired child was gazing at the teacher with an expression of adoration. It was touching, yet a little alarming. No human being deserves that much young worship. . . .

I retraced my steps along the wrong path in the snow, found the right one and finally reached the entrance door. It was not locked this time. I let myself in and hurried to Miss Leonard's room.

'Come in!' she called in answer to my knock.

As I went in I blurted out: 'I'm so sorry I'm late. It was my train – the snow –'

'Never mind, Miss Anderson. I guessed as much. I'll take you to the staff room.'

She led me up the stairs from the hall, along a first floor corridor, into a room. It was an ordinary staff room – notice-board, lockers, tables, hard chairs, easy chairs, electric fire. The light was on but the room was empty – at least, I thought it was empty at first, then realized that someone was sitting in one of the chairs. I saw her only out of the corner of my eye, and she was in a chair in the far corner of the room, away from the fire; so although I recognized her as the woman in black, I didn't turn to look at her. If I thought anything, it was just that she had a bit of a nerve to leave her class, which I'd seen her teaching a few minutes ago, and come to sit in the staff room – and now she's been caught out by the entrance of the Headmistress.

Miss Leonard, however, took no notice of her. She said: 'This will be your locker, Miss Anderson. The bell will ring any minute now for the end of first period, then I'll take you to your first class. It's a double-period of English – you'll have seen that from your timetable. Mrs Gage is looking after them at the moment – she's our biology teacher – and she'll be glad to see you as by rights these first two periods should be her free ones. That's why the staff room is empty.'

But the staff room was not empty. There was the woman in black, looking at me seriously, with those beautiful sad dark eyes . . .

Miss Leonard led the way to my first class. The teacher there looked quickly round as we entered. She was a lively, dark, fairly young woman with eagerly bent shoulders and black-rimmed spectacles. She wore a red sweater and brown skirt.

'Here we are, Mrs Gage,' said Miss Leonard. 'Now you'll get your second free period all right.' She faced the class. 'Now, girls, this is Miss Anderson, your new English teacher. Help her as much as you can, won't you?'

And I too stood facing the class. It was the same class which I had seen through the window only fifteen minutes earlier. There was the child with fair hair in the front row, and the dark one next to her – and . . .

No. It was different. The child with curly red hair was not there. Her desk was empty. And, of course, the teacher was different . . .

Miss Leonard and Mrs Gage left the room. I was on my own with this familiar, unfamiliar class. I spent the next forty minutes or so in trying to get to know them, checking on their set books, and so on, then the bell rang for morning break and I returned to the staff room.

The chair where the woman in black had been sitting was empty now but other chairs were occupied. The staff had gathered for elevenses. I heard someone say, above the noise of the many voices: 'How does that damned chair get over into the corner like that? Who puts it there?'

'Night cleaners have strange ways,' said another voice.

'Extraordinary about night cleaners,' said the first. 'They work here for years, and so do we – and which of us are the ghosts? We co-exist, but never meet.'

A woman in an overall came in with a tray bearing a pot of coffee and cups and saucers. Mrs Gage came over to me. 'Coffee, Miss Anderson?'

'Oh – thank you.'

'How do you like it?'

'Black. No sugar.'

'Same here.' She collected coffee for us both.

'Sorry you missed a free period because of me,' I said. 'My train got held up in the snow.'

'That's all right.'

Sipping my coffee, I studied the other women around me.

'Doesn't everyone come here for coffee at break?' I asked Mrs Gage.

'Everyone! It's only our elevenses that keep us going.'

'Then where is – well – one of the teachers? She was taking your class – my class – this morning – I saw her through the window –'

'Not that class,' said Mrs Gage. 'I started with them immediately after morning assembly.'

'But it *was* that class. I recognized some of the girls. And the one with red hair wasn't there.'

Mrs Gage looked at me sympathetically. 'You're all upset over being late, aren't you? And maybe you're upset for other reasons too. I don't blame you. It's not easy to be taking Miss Carey's place.'

'Miss Carey? Who –' But as I tried to ask more, the woman in the overall came to collect our dirty cups and the bell rang for third period. We all went off to our classes.

I still had one more period with the same class I'd taken before – or so I thought, until I reached the room. Then I saw that the teacher's chair was already occupied.

The woman in black sat there.

And the child with red hair was in the third desk in the front row.

'Sorry,' I murmured, withdrew again, and stood in the corridor to re-examine my timetable. Surely I hadn't made a mistake – no – I was right –

this was my class. So I went back. And the teacher's chair was empty now. So was the third desk in the front row . . .

That was when I began to be afraid. So afraid that a sick shiver travelled down my spine, sweat sprang out on my skin, and I needed all my self-control to face the class and give a lesson.

At the end of the lesson, when the bell rang for next period, I asked the class in general: 'Where's the girl who sits there?' I indicated the third desk in the front row.

No one answered. The children became unnaturally quiet and stared at me.

'Well?' I said.

Then the fair-haired child said: 'No one sits there, Miss.' And the dark child next to her added: 'That was Joan's desk.'

'But where is Joan?'

Silence again.

Then Mrs Gage walked in. 'Hello, Miss Anderson. We seem to be playing Box and Cox this morning. Do you know which class to go to for last period?'

'Yes, thank you. I've got my timetable.' I hurried away.

Busyness is the best panacea for fear, and I was very busy getting to know a different class until the bell rang for lunch. Back to the staff room again – and it was full again – and there was Mrs Gage, kindly taking me under her wing.

'Miss Leonard asked me to look after you until you find your way around,' she said. 'The staff dining-room is on the second floor. Would you like to come up with me?'

I was glad of the offer.

The staff, all female, sat at three long tables in the dining-room, and the place was as noisy as a classroom before the teacher arrives! Two overalled women, one of whom I had seen at break, served our meal. Conversation was mostly 'shop' – the besetting sin of female teachers. As the newcomer, I kept quiet, but I looked at those women one by one, trying to identify the woman in black.

She wasn't there.

Unhungry, I did my best with the meat pie and carrots, then when rice pudding and prunes arrived (for teachers have children's diet) I murmured to Mrs Gage: 'Who is the member of staff who wears a black dress?'

She looked round. 'No one, as far as I can see.'

'No – she's not here – but I've seen her.'

'Really? But I think everyone's here today. We do go out for lunch sometimes, but when the weather is like this it's easier to have it on the premises. What was she like?'

'Dark, pale, thin, not very young – with lovely eyes –'

'And wearing a black dress, you said?'

'Yes.'

Mrs Gage gave a small, unamused laugh. 'Sounds like Miss Carey, but you can't possibly have seen her.'

'The one who's left – whose place I've taken –'

'No one could take Joanna's place.'

'Oh – I didn't mean –'

'Miss Anderson, I'm sorry. I didn't mean anything either.' She didn't look at me, but she had stopped eating her prunes.

'Did something bad happen to her?' I asked.

'She tried to burn down the school.'

The words were whispered and the noise of voices around us was so loud that I thought I must have misheard, so I said: 'What?'

'She tried to burn down the school,' Mrs Gage repeated. Others at our table heard her this time. Conversation faded, ceased. Heads turned towards Mrs Gage.

'Don't all look at me like that,' said Mrs Gage. 'I'm only telling Miss Anderson what happened last term. She has a right to know.' Leaving her sweet unfinished, she pushed back her chair with a scraping noise and left the room. I sat petrified. Murmurs of conversation began again, but no one spoke to me, so I pretended to eat a little more, then rose and left.

I found my way back to the staff room.

Mrs Gage, cigarette in hand, was sitting by the electric fire. 'Sorry about that,' she said. 'Until you asked, I presumed you knew. It was in the newspapers.'

'I've been living in Italy. I only came back just before Christmas. Could you tell me what happened, before the others return from lunch?'

'Sure. Have a fag. Rotten first day for you.' She passed me a cigarette and lit it for me.

'This smell of burning,' I said. 'I've noticed it before.'

'It's only our cigarettes, Miss Anderson. And we'd better get them smoked before the rest of the staff come back. Some of them abhor cigarette smoke. These spinsters!'

'I'm one too.'

'Not really. You're still young. So you want to know about Joanna Carey?'

'Of course I do. After all, I've seen her. Did she get the sack, and now she comes back uninvited – or what?'

'My dear child, you can't have seen her. She's dead.'

'Then whom did I see?'

Mrs Gage ignored this question. She said: 'Miss Carey, Joanna, had been a teacher here for twenty years. She was excellent at her job and the kids adored her. Then, about a year ago, she changed.'

'In what way?'

'Not in the way she taught. Her teaching was always brilliant. But in her attitude. After being most understanding and sympathetic with the young, she gradually became more and more cynical, to the point of cruelty. She made it clear to all of us, staff and pupils, that she now hated her job and only went on doing it because she had to earn a living somehow.'

'But why did this happen?'

'Why? Who knows why anything? But in fact I do know more about her than most of the staff. Joanna and I were friends, before she changed. She often visited my husband and me, in the old days. She and I had occasional heart-to-hearts over the washing-up. So I learned something of her private life. She was the mistress of a married man, for about ten years. That *was* her private life. Then he ditched her – decided to "be a good boy" again. When it happened, she told me, and she laughed, and didn't seem to care very much. But it was from that moment that she began to change, grow bitter, disillusioned. The world went stale for her. The salt had lost its savour. She began to take revenge, not against the man, but against everyone else with whom she came into contact. That meant us – staff and kids. She was filled with hate, and hate breeds hate. Even I, who had been her friend, began to avoid her. She was left alone.'

'You said she tried to burn down the school.'

'She did. She failed in that. But while she was trying, she burned herself to death. And one of the children.'

'One of the children? Oh, no!'

'It's true, Miss Anderson. I wouldn't say it if it weren't. I, of all people, once so friendly with Joanna – I'd be the last person to admit it, if it weren't true. But it happened.'

'What exactly did happen?'

'One Friday evening, towards the end of last term, she came back to school. This is what the police found out when they investigated afterwards. Everyone except Mr Brown, the caretaker, had gone. She soaked the base of the long curtains in the gymnasium with paraffin and set fire to them. Imagine the flare-up that would make – all those curtains in that big room. Why she didn't get away afterwards, no one knows. Maybe she fainted. Maybe she deliberately let herself be burned – like that Czech student – you know. People do these things. When they're desperate. Mr Brown saw the flames, sent for the fire service, and after they'd come and put out the fire, her body was found among the ashes of the curtains.'

'And the child? You said –'

'Yes. Little Joan Hanley. A dear little girl with red curly hair. She adored

Joanna. She was found there too, burned to death, among the ashes of the curtains.'

'But how did she come to be there in the first place?'

'Once again, no one knows. She was one of Joanna's worshippers. There were several in the school. Girls' schools are diabolical in this respect. Rather like all-female wards in hospitals. Unnatural passions are aroused. Joan Hanley would have done anything in the world for Joanna Carey. So did Joanna invite the child to the "party"? I don't know. But it looks like it.'

'Didn't the police find out anything about why Joan Hanley was there?'

'They tried. She had told her parents that she was going to the cinema, which she often did on Friday nights. When she didn't come home at her usual time, her parents wondered – and the next thing they knew, the police were on their doorstep, telling them that their daughter had been burned to death at the school. That's all I know, Miss Anderson – all any of us knows. Since it happened, workmen have put the gymnasium to rights, hence all the fresh paint and the pretty new curtains. These tragedies are happening all the time, all over the world – I know that – but when I think of Joanna, in her hatred and bitterness, drawing a child into such a burning – Oh, God !' She put her hands over her face.

The staff room became deathly quiet. Only the two of us there, Mrs Gage and me, crouching over the electric fire, our cigarettes burning down, the silent snow covering the world outside – and God knows why I suddenly looked behind me.

I looked at that chair in the far corner of the room. It was no longer empty. The woman in black sat there. She looked straight at me, with those tragic eyes.

Then the staff room door burst open and the other women poured in, filling the quietness with noise, filling the empty chairs with bodies, talking 'shop' – and I thought: No wonder Joanna Carey took a hate against all this. And yet – to burn a child – along with oneself – No!

'I didn't!' The sound came over, clearly, loudly, as if it filled the world. Yet no one seemed to hear it. It had spoken into my head only.

'I'll prove it,' said the loud voice in my head. 'Come!'

Mrs Gage was leaning back in the chair by the fire. She had lit another cigarette and closed her eyes. She looked tired out, and no wonder. I got up and left the room, that room full of talking women.

I walked, blindly, yet guided, along the unfamiliar corridors. Outside, in the snow, the children were having snowball battles. They were having a lovely lunch-hour! Heaven was outside. Hell was within.

I walked, without knowing why, into the classroom which I had seen through the window, the classroom where I had taught during the second and third periods of the school morning.

I walked up to the third desk in the front row.

I sat down in that desk, as if I were the little girl, Joan Hanley, who had, day after day, sat down in that desk . . .

I opened the desk lid. There was nothing inside.

I looked at the scratchings and carved initials on the top of the desk lid.

I found: 'J.H. LOVES J.C.' And, over it, an unsymmetrical heart pierced by a rather wonky arrow.

But I knew already that J.H. had loved J.C. I had seen the child's face through the window, only this morning – I had seen what did not exist – yet which did exist –

What to do now?

My hand, guided, by God knows whom or what, put its fingers into the empty inkwell-socket. The fingers found a closely folded piece of paper.

I unfolded it, carefully, and read:

'Dear Mum and Dad, I do not love you. I love Miss Carey. Where she goes, I go. I follow her everywhere. Tonight I have followed her to the school. She has gone to the gymnasium. I shall follow her there. Something is going to happen. That is why I am writing. Whatever she does, I shall do too. Because I love her. I must hurry now, to be with her. Funny really – as she does not even know I follow her! I'll put this under my inkwell. I don't expect you'll ever read it, but you never know. Yours sincerely – Your daughter, Joan.'

'I didn't know she was there!' cried that voice in my head, loud with its silence. 'I didn't know she was there!'

'Of course you didn't!' I answered aloud, loudly. 'It's all right! I'll tell them!'

The classroom door opened and Miss Leonard walked in.

'Miss Anderson, what on earth are you doing?'

What on earth was I doing? I was sitting at a dead child's desk, a scrap of paper in my hand, and 'talking to myself'.

'I've found something, Miss Leonard.' I passed her the letter. She read it. 'So that's what happened,' she said. 'Miss Carey didn't take the child there with her at all. The little girl secretly imitated her goddess, even to the point of suicide. Where did you find the letter?'

'In the inkwell-socket. I'm surprised it hasn't been found before, maybe by one of the children.'

'No. I cleared that desk myself, removed the inkwell and didn't think to look underneath it. And the children never touch this desk. I did think of removing it, but that's too much like giving in to superstition. What made you look there, Miss Anderson?'

'She – she led me here – she spoke in my head – I don't understand it – but it happened –'

'You're psychic, aren't you? Did you know that already?'

'Not until I came to this school.'

'You saw her on the day of your interview, didn't you?'

'Yes. On the stairs.'

'I remember. And I fobbed you off with a practical explanation.'

'Did you ever see her, Miss Leonard?'

'No. But Mr Brown did, more than once. And one of the children, last term, after the fire, insisted that Miss Carey wasn't dead as she'd seen her in the corridor. Neither of them was lying. Some individuals see and hear more than others. Have you been very frightened?'

'At first I wasn't, because I thought she was real. Later, I did feel frightened.'

'And now?'

'Now I just feel desperately sorry for her. Her eyes, Miss Leonard. If you could have seen the sadness in her eyes!'

'Mr Brown mentioned that. You may talk to him if you like, but please no talk of ghosts to anyone else.'

'Of course not. Anyway, I think she'll go away now. She'll be free of the place. She's been punished so dreadfully. Maybe ghosts are people in purgatory and we see them around us all the time without realizing that they are ghosts.'

'Maybe *you* do,' said Miss Leonard, smiling a little.

The bell rang for the beginning of afternoon school. A wail of disappointment rose from outside. I looked out of the window, saw the children cease their snowballing and move obediently towards the building.

Only one figure moved away from the building, moved through the oncoming crowd of girls, who took no notice of her at all. She walked farther away, on and on, past the playground, across the snow-covered playing-field. A pale sun was shining and the snow dazzled, accentuating the thin, dark outline of the woman in black. She looked so utterly alone. Then a small figure began to follow her, running quickly and eagerly, and the sun turned the little figure's mop of red curls into a flame shaped like a rose.

The child overtook the woman in black and walked beside her, lightly, dancingly. And the two retreating figures cast no shadows on the snow, and left no footprints.

Norah Lofts

A CURIOUS EXPERIENCE

I ONCE had a curious experience; and those who dismiss it as a silly girl's fancy should think again. I was twenty-three at the time and had been married for two years.

When Greg proposed to me, in an offhand way, I said, 'You know, or you should do, that I am not the domestic type. If you really want little wifie waiting with a casserole in the oven and your slippers warming by the well-swept hearth, you must look elsewhere.'

Greg said that if he had been interested in casseroles and well-warmed slippers, he'd have settled for Amanda. Between me and Amanda, I must confess, it had been as the Duke of Wellington said of Waterloo, 'a damned close run thing.' But I had won; and for two years Greg and I lived a bit of that happily-ever-after stuff. Happy as larks, as they say, though we had no nest. The firm for which he worked was busy 'grooming' him – a nice term for holding the carrot well out of reach at one end and applying stick at the other. Young men with potential must be mobile, must gain experience at all levels, so Greg shuttled about, and I went with him, dragging my portable typewriter, my thick notebook, and a bag of reference books. I had already published one novel, highly praised, savagely criticised, not very profitable.

And then Greg's firm decreed that to complete his grooming, he must spend three months in New York. The wives of the fully groomed are recognised and they may accompany their husbands, expenses paid. But those ungroomed are presumed to be single, foot-loose. I said, 'Darling, we simply can't afford it. I'll find some place and tuck in and finish my book. Three months will just about do it.' I squinted at him; I do squint when I concentrate. I said, 'You go and fall in love with some American floosie and I'll disown you!'

I didn't want him to feel that he must provide for me while we were separated. It had been all right when I tagged about after him – Leeds, Bradford, Glasgow, Edinburgh, Bristol, Norwich. Mostly we had lived in cheap hotels, cheap furnished flats. When we were somewhere where food was provided, we ate what was offered; otherwise I bought things like beefburgers, fish-fingers. Very often my only cooking facility was a frying pan on a gas ring. But I had felt that in a way I earned my keep. For the next three months he would not have even the benefit of my company, and living is expensive in America; so I began to look round for a job. A fairish knowledge of archaeology and ancient history is not the most readily marketable asset and I was quite glad to find part-time employment in a public library in a Suffolk town called Baildon.

There I was also lucky enough to find, not a flat, but a furnished house at an astonishingly low rent – so low indeed that until I saw the place I had the darkest suspicions. The agent made an appointment for me to meet Mrs Willis at the house, 18 Hillcrest Avenue, on the following afternoon.

Hillcrest Avenue was a quiet cul-de-sac within easy walk of the town centre, at the top of what, in Suffolk, passes for a hill; a very slight rise. It consisted mainly of pairs of semi-detached houses, neither ancient nor modern, all very neat and spruce with a small garden in front, a longer one behind. The house had a living-room, a dining-room, kitchen, two fair-sized bedrooms and a tiny one, a bathroom. It was completely furnished and good solid stuff.

'Everything,' Mrs Willis said, pulling open a drawer in the kitchen, 'down to the last egg spoon.' Then, I asked myself, why so cheap? I'd lived in some tatty rooms that called themselves flatlets, and cost double.

She answered my unspoken question.

'I didn't feel justified in asking much because there are so many snags from the tenant's point of view. Insecurity of tenure for one thing. I have to ask for a signed agreement that a week's or at most a fortnight's notice will be accepted. You see, the house belongs to an old aunt of mine. She is very arthritic, quite incapable of looking after herself, and I'm much too far away. And too busy. Personally I don't think she will ever leave the Home where she now is. But she is convinced that she will one day find a housekeeper and be able to come back. It would be unkind to try to make her see sense. Then she began to fret about the house standing empty, so I offered to let it and she quite took to the idea. It's a great nuisance for me. I have to see potential tenants and generally keep an eye on things.' She glanced around. 'It doesn't look too bad, does it? And you needn't worry about the garden. A man comes half a day a week.'

I felt that this could not be a very profitable enterprise.

'How long has your aunt been in this Home?' I asked.

Mrs Willis did mental arithmetic.

'Almost four years,' she said. 'Fortunately she is comfortably off. I reckon that she spends at least three pounds a week, answering advertisements, enclosing stamped addressed envelopes, most of which never come back. But there it is, it's her hobby, the one thing that keeps her alive.'

'What about the gas and electricity?' I asked.

'Oh, well there I did make a stand. It was such a nuisance. Having the stuff cut off and put on again and people going off without paying their bills. So I had meters. They're under the sink. Well, I must be off. I hope you'll be happy here. And don't worry too much about a week's notice. The housekeeper my aunt is looking for went out with the crinoline.'

I moved in later that afternoon, blessing my luck. I decided that the dining-room, at the back and adjoining the kitchen, should be my work- and living-room; one end of the good solid table holding my typewriter and my books, the other my simple haphazard meals. The house had, I now realised, that faintly musty smell that comes from disuse, and I opened all the windows. I had noticed that, despite its nearness to the main shopping centre, this near-suburb had a little shopping precinct of its own. I went down to investigate and found it perfect for my purpose. The general store had a deep freeze and a delicatessen counter. Next door was a laundrette, and beyond it an off-licence and a sub-post-office, both endearingly miniature. A chemist's shop and a hairdresser's completed the semicircle. The housewives in this area were well catered for. And I was one of them. Lucky me . . .

The rot set in when, the June evening glow waning, I got up and switched on the light. As I type I tend to look up and stare straight ahead, and from the place where I had chosen, what I looked at was a sideboard, of the kind called a chiffonier. Somebody – either the last tenant, or perhaps Mrs Willis – had given its flat surface a hasty swipe with a duster. The thing was made, I think, of rosewood and the semicircular swipe had left a richly glowing area edged thickly with grey dust. A similar swipe had been made at the delicately framed mirror which formed its back. For some reason that I cannot explain, what remained, dusty on the rosewood, smeary on the glass, bothered me. I simply could not concentrate. I got up, went into the kitchen, found a rather dirty duster, and did a bit of cleaning up. At the same time I took my coffee cup and the plate from which I had eaten my two sausage rolls into the kitchen. Then I sat down, typed a few lines, and knew that 'the good spirit' had gone from me.

Who said that cogent thing – the complaint of all writers,

What can I do for poesy
Now that the good spirit has gone from me?
What can I do, but useless sit
And over read what I have writ?

Deadly. The thing we all fear. So check. I wasted an hour in a futile chase and then gave up and went to bed.

In the morning I woke quite early and got out of bed with a thought new to me – I don't want to come back to an unmade bed and a littered kitchen. Up to that morning, although I had never enjoyed absolute squalor, I had been a bit slap happy about time; so long as a bed was made before it was occupied, a cup washed before it was used again, I had been content to shuffle along. What had got into me? I left a neatly made bed, a tidy kitchen behind me when I went to the library. It was Saturday, a busy day, my longest day; ten in the morning to three in the afternoon. At about half-past twelve there was a little lull and I had time to say to the Head Librarian, a pleasant, very academic-looking woman, 'Miss Forbes, who wrote that verse beginning, "What can I do for poesy?" It haunts me and I can't trace it.'

She said, 'I never heard it. "Poesy" sounds a bit archaic. Could it be Chaucer?'

Not that it mattered. Just an idle thought . . .

On my way home I bought enough of what is called 'convenience' food to sustain me through the week-end. I'd put in a good session of work. The musty smell inside the house still bothered me and I again opened the windows, this time noticing that they were very dirty. Something impelled me to clean them . . .

When I told Greg that I was not the domestic type I was being – as I always try to be – flatly truthful. I was born and lived until I was eight in Jamaica, where hired help was plentiful. I was sent to school in England, and there we made our beds and took turns with the washing-up. After that, college, digs, marriage, and a nomad life. The only ordinary household of which I had ever been a part was that of my grandmother in school holidays, and she not only wanted no help from me, she had the obsessive idea that unless I was studying I was wasting my time – and my parents' hard-earned money. I had never in my life cleaned a window.

From the sour-smelling cupboard under the sink I chose the least filthy of a number of cloths, washed it, and armed with it and a duster and a bucket of water, set to, starting on the dining-room window. I was awkward and slow. As a matter of fact physical activities have never been my thing; hopeless at gym, a mockery on the hockey field. I'm not built for it; too tall, too loosely put together. It took me most of the morning to clean that one window, largely because smears would shift. When I was inside, they were out, and vice versa. I wasted a lot of time making exits and entrances through the kitchen. But in my way I am thorough and shortly before lunch time that window looked a lot better. So much so indeed that I made resolve to clean all the others. In due course; one a day perhaps.

Instant coffee and some fish-fingers restored me and I sat down to type: but the smell of that kitchen cupboard haunted me. I simply could not concentrate. Work done in such circumstances is never good. So I gave in and went to empty and cleanse that offensive retreat. It was a disgusting job, but I was rewarded by finding in the cupboard's farthest corner a container of something called Clearshine, on which the label promised that it took the labour out of window cleaning. Simply spray on and rub. I put this treasure carefully on one side and carried the rest out to the dustbin which was crammed to the brim, largely, it seemed to me, with cartons and packets of discarded foodstuffs, a half-empty pack of biscuits, an unopened pack containing four currant buns, hard as wood, some mouldy green cheese, some evil-smelling fish, still in the can.

I braced myself and remembered that fire purges.

June is not a month when birds suffer much privation, but I gave them the biscuits and the buns, hoping that some woodpecker might come along to deal with the latter. Then I made a bonfire at the farthest end of the back garden. As I returned to the house the sun shone on the clean window and twinkled at me, encouragingly. I needed encouragement. I was bone weary, far too tired now to face the typewriter.

When Mrs Willis showed me round I had noticed that the sitting-room contained a television set. I'd relax, I thought, as so many thousand do, feet up, in front of the box. But relax I could not. The sofa and the armchairs in this room were covered in a pretty, floral chintz which on closer acquaintance didn't feel or look or even smell right. All through a moderately entertaining programme half my mind was busy with the thought of that laundrette at the foot of the hill and with the thought that tomorrow was Monday, my free day. Few people change books on Mondays; either they have not completed the reading or they are busy with other things. Such as washing at home, or visiting laundrettes . . .

The thing snowballed. I found out, for instance, that every tenant the house had ever had, had used the same few articles of bed linen, those at the front. Further back there were blankets with which the moths had made merry, and linen that had acquired black stripes simply by being in the cupboard for so long, unused. The laundrette saw a lot of me that week. On my free days, Monday and Thursday, I did a 'do-it-yourself' job, on other days I left my bundle on my way to the library, the woman in charge took care of it and I collected it on my way home.

Another ridiculous thing happened, too. In the general store I saw some fresh garden peas. I could just remember how they tasted, cooked with a sprig of mint. I thought – *How silly to buy frozen peas when fresh ones are in season* . . .

I never studied psychology, but I had read enough to know what was wrong with me. Fundamentally, I thought, I did not like, or was not satisfied with, the story on which I should be working. Second novels are notoriously tricky; anyone can write a first novel . . . I'd lost my nerve; 'never glad confident morning again,' or I'd chosen a bad subject, or made a wrong approach, or, God help me, I was one of the one-novel gang. And I was taking refuge from my predicament by pretending to be busy with other things. Not a pleasant thought. In fact a thought to flee from. Scrub the kitchen floor; scrub the larder shelves. That activity brought me a bonus; my right wrist gave way and I had to wear a wide leather strap, a kind of miniature buskin, on it for a fortnight. Perhaps professional typists, or those profoundly inspired, can type with one hand. I could not; I could only do little jobs such as separating meat knives from tablespoons in the baize-lined compartments of the kitchen drawer, and bringing order to the things which hung on hooks on the dresser, and throwing out seven – why seven? – stinking old sweaty socks that somebody had secreted in the cupboard under the stairs.

During this period a sweet girl at the library typed four letters to Greg for me and I made shift to sign them, hoping that he would not think that I had taken to drink or drugs. Her spelling was highly individual.

By the time I could discard the strap I knew what was wrong with my book. It was the approach. It was a first-person story and I had been writing in the third. The 'good spirit' had not abandoned me; it came back now, very powerful. The character 'I' can only relate what he, or she, sees with his own eyes, hears with his own ears. So I needed more than one narrator, and by Heaven I had them, quite suddenly; three of them, three people saying 'I' and with their separate, differing stories making a whole. Wonderful! The kind of thing that makes up for the self-distrust, the loneliness, the frustrations . . . I couldn't wait to get started.

I practically ran home, pausing only to buy a slice of veal-and-ham pie, some eggs, a loaf, and a bit of cheese. This was Wednesday – a clear free day tomorrow. Tomorrow, in my immaculate, sweet-smelling house I should sit down, make a fresh start. Prove myself to be not one of the one-book brigade.

But, even as I put my purchases down on the kitchen table, the gas cooker cried out – What about me? Me first!

I had cleaned it once. Like the rest of the house, under a kind of superficial cleanliness, it had been filthy. It was now not filthy, but a little soiled; pulling off a saucepan left-handedly I had spilt some milk.

All right, I said to it, but that is the last thing in the cleaning line that I shall do here. Using my right hand a little cagily, I cleaned it. Then I went into the dining-room, sat down, made the usual sandwich, top paper, carbon, copy paper. With steady confident fingers I typed. Part I. Chapter I. Oh joy! And then the bell rang. I cursed as I went to the door. Somebody collecting, somebody wanting to know if I had put my name on the electoral roll, somebody wanting to know if Mr A, Mrs B, Miss C still lived here, and if not was there any forwarding address? Hell, I said; blast. I'll tell whoever it is where to look for a subscription, a vote, a bygone tenant. Squinting I opened the door and there was Mrs Willis.

She said, 'Good evening, Mrs Fraser. I'm sorry to disturb you so late.' In fact it was not late but possibly my squinting scowl made her think that she was not exactly welcome. I said, 'Do come in,' and she said, 'Well, just for a minute. I am in a bit of a hurry but I was fairly near and I thought I should come and explain . . . personally. A completely unforeseen thing has happened. My aunt has found a housekeeper.'

What did she expect me to do? Fall flat on my face? Set myself on fire?

I said, 'How nice for her. When do I move?'

We were in the sitting-room with its sparkling window, fresh curtains, crisp, clean chintz. I could see her taking it all in.

'Well,' she said, hesitatingly. 'I *told* her a fortnight. I thought you must have a week's notice and that it would take me at least a week to . . . But you seem to have done it. The place even smells differently. I'm *so* sorry. It does seem a shame.'

A thought struck me.

I said, 'Would you call your aunt a dominant personality, Mrs Willis?'

She gave that a second's consideration. 'Yes, I would. I mean the way she has stuck to this idea about coming home. Most women of her age . . .'

'And was, I mean *is* she house-proud?'

'Oh, very much so. Terribly particular. She'd empty an ash-tray as soon as you'd ground out the stub. You know?'

'I know,' I said; meaning that I knew what had got into me. I'd been for a month possessed.

Mrs Willis said, 'I do hope you don't mind too much. I did want . . .'

'I don't mind a bit,' I said truthfully. I thought – Tomorrow the world! A cheap hotel, a bed-sitter, anonymous and undemanding, a chalet in a holiday camp, a caravan, a tent in the middle of a field.

Mrs Willis touched a chintz cover. She said,

'You must have gone to considerable expense. I think it would be only fair to return, shall we say, a week's rent?'

I thought of the wrong story line, with which, in any other surroundings, I might have bashed on; the bad second novel that can ruin one's career. And of the good, sound, wonderful one that was waiting.

I said, 'That is very kind, Mrs Willis. But in fact I owe the house more than it owes me. Living here has been quite an experience . . .'

Fay Weldon

BREAKAGES

W E *blossom and flourish*
Like leaves on a tree,
And wither and perish
But nought changeth the-e-e – sang David's congregation in its laggardly, quavery voice. Some trick of acoustics made much of what happened in the church audible in the vicarage kitchen, where tonight, as so often, Deidre sat and darned socks and waited for Evensong to end.

The vicarage, added as a late Victorian afterthought, leaned up against the solidity of the Norman church. The house was large, ramshackle, dark and draughty, prey to wet rot, dry rot, woodworm and beetle. Here David and Deidre lived. He was a vicar of the established church; she was his wife. He attended to the spiritual welfare of his parishioners: she presided over the Mothers' Union, the Women's Institute and ran the Amateur Dramatic Society. They had been married for twenty-one years. They had no children, which was a source of acute disappointment to them, and to Deidre's mother, and of mild disappointment to the parish. It is always pleasant, in a small, stable and increasingly elderly community, to watch other people's children grow up, and sad to be deprived of that pleasure.

'Oh no, please,' said Deidre, now, to the Coronation mug on the dresser. It was a rare piece, produced in anticipation of an event which had never occurred, the Coronation of the Duke of Windsor. It was, so far, uncracked and unchipped, and worth some £300, but had just moved to the very edge of its shelf, not smoothly and purposively, but with an uneven rocking motion which made Deidre hope that entreaty might yet calm it, and save it. And indeed, after she spoke, the mug was quiet, and lapsed into the ordinary stillness she had once always associated with inanimate objects.

Immortal, invisible,
God only wise –
In light inaccessible –
Deidre joined in the hymn, singing gently and soothingly, and trying to feel happy, for the happier she felt the fewer breakages there would be and perhaps one day they would stop altogether, and David would never, ever find out;

that, one by one, the ornaments and possessions he most loved and valued were leaping off shelves and shattering, to be secretly mended by Deidre, with such skills as she remembered from the early days, before marriage had interrupted her training in china restoration, and her possible future in the Victoria and Albert museum.

Long ago and far away. Now Deidre darned. David's feet were sensitive to anything other than pure, fine wool. Not for him the tough nylon mixtures that other men wore.

Deidre darned.

The Coronation mug rocked violently.

'Stop it,' said Deidre, warningly. Sometimes to be stern worked better than to plead. The mug stayed where it was. But a fraction further and it would have fallen.

Deidre unpicked the last few stitches. She was in danger of cobbling the darn, and there is nothing more uncomfortable to sensitive skin than a cobbled darn.

'You do it on purpose,' David would complain, not without reason. Deidre's faults were the ones he found most difficult to bear. She was careless, untidy and extravagant. She broke dishes, lost socks, left lids unscrewed, taps running, doors open, saucepans burning: she bought fresh bread when yesterday's at half-price would do. It was her nature, she maintained, and grieved bitterly when her husband implied that it was wilful and that she was doing it to annoy.

The Coronation mug leapt off its shelf, arced through the air and fell and broke in two pieces at Deidre's feet. She put the pieces at the very back of the drawer beneath the sink. There was no time for mending them now. Tomorrow morning would have to do, when David was out parish visiting, in houses freshly dusted and brightened for his arrival. Fortunately, he seldom inspected the sink drawer, as he did the others in the house, looking for dirt and disorder. It smelt, when opened, of dry rot, and reminded him too forcibly of the large sums of money which ought to be spent on the repair of the house. 'We could sell something,' she would sometimes venture, but the prospect upset him. His mother had died when he was four, his father had gone bankrupt when he was eight: relatives had reared him and sent him off to boarding school where he had been sexually and emotionally abused. Possessions were his security.

She understood him, forgave him, loved him and tried not to argue. She had her own problems, with her mother.

She darned his socks. It was a larger pile than usual. Socks kept disappearing, not by the pair, but singly. They always had. David had lately discovered a pillowslip stuffed full of them pushed to the back of the wardrobe. It was his wife's deceit which worried him most, or so he said. Hiding socks! That and the sheer careless waste of it all. Losing socks! So Deidre tried tying the socks together for the wash, and thus, in pairs, the night before, spun and dried, they had neatly lain in the laundry basket. In the morning she had found them in one ugly, monstrous knot, and each sock oddly long, as if stretched and stretched by a hand too angry to know what it was doing. Rinsing had restored them, fortunately, to a proper shape, and now she darned where the ordeal had worn the wool thin.

It was always like this. David's things were attacked, as if the monstrous hand were on her side, yet it was she, Deidre, who had to repair the damage, follow its source as it moved about the house, mending what it broke, wiping tomato purée from the ceiling, toothpaste from the lavatory bowl, replanting David's seedlings, rescrewing lids, closing doors, refolding linen, turning off taps. She scarcely dared leave the house for fear of what might happen in his absence, and this David interpreted as a lack of interest in his parish. Disloyalty, to God and husband. Times were bad between them.

Deidre's finger was bleeding. She must have cut it on the sharp edge of the broken Coronation mug. She opened the table drawer, and took out the first piece of cloth which came to hand, and wrapped the finger. The cold tap started to run, but she ignored it. Blood spread out over the cloth but presently stopped.

The invisible hand swept the dresser shelf, knocking all sorts of treasures sideways but breaking nothing. It had never touched the dresser before, as if awed, as Deidre was, by the ever increasing value of its contents – rare blue and white pieces, frog mugs, barbers' bowls, lustre cups, a debatedly Ming bowl.

It was getting bolder.

David did not give Deidre a housekeeping allowance. She asked for money when she needed it, but David seldom recognised that it was in fact needed. He could not see the necessity of things like washing-up liquid, sugar, toilet rolls, new scourers. Sometimes she stole money from his pocket: once she took a coin out of the offertory on Sunday morning instead of putting a coin in it.

Deceitful, dishonest; Deidre knew the sort of person she was and despised herself for it. A bad wife, a barren wife, and a poor sort of person.

David came home. The house fell quiet, as always, at his approach. Taps stopped running and china rattling. David kissed her on her forehead.

'Deidre,' said David, 'what have you wrapped around your finger?'

Deidre unwrapped the binding and found that it was a fine lace and cotton handkerchief, put in the drawer for mending, which once had belonged to David's grandmother. It was now sodden and bright, bright red.

'I cut my finger,' said Deidre, inadequately and indeed foolishly, for what if he demanded to know what had caused the wound? But he was too busy rinsing and squeezing the handkerchief under the tap to enquire. Deidre put her finger in her mouth and put up with the salt, exciting taste of her own blood.

'It's hopelessly stained,' he mourned. 'Couldn't you just for once have used something you wouldn't spoil? A tissue?'

David did not allow the purchase of tissues. There had been none in his youth: why should they be needed now, in his middle age? 'I'm sorry,' said Deidre. She was always saying she was sorry, and always providing cause for her own remorse.

He took the handkerchief upstairs to the bathroom, in search of soap and a nailbrush. 'What kind of wife are you, Deidre?' he asked as he went, desperate.

What kind, indeed? Married in a Registry Office in the days before David had taken to Holy Orders and a Heavenly Father more reliable than his earthly one. Deidre had suggested that they re-marry in Church, as could be and had been done by others, but David did not want to. Hardly a wife at all.

A barren wife. A fig tree, struck by God's ill-temper. David's God. In the beginning they had shared a God, who was bleak, sensible and kind. But now, increasingly, David had his own jealous and punitive God, whom he wooed with ritual and richness, incense and images, dragging a surprised congregation with him. He changed his vestments three times during services, rang little bells to announce the presence of the Lord, swept up and down aisles, and in general seemed not averse, in Church as at home, to being mistaken for God.

The water pipes shrieked and groaned as David turned on the tap in the bathroom, but that was due to bad plumbing rather than unnatural causes. She surely could not be held responsible for that, too.

When the phenomena – as she thought of it – first started, or rather leapt from the scale of ordinary domestic carelessness to something less explicable and more sinister, she went to the doctor.

'Doctor,' she said, 'do mumps in adolescence make men infertile?' 'It depends,' he said, proving nothing. 'If the gonads are affected it might well. Why?'

No reason had been found for Deidre's infertility. It lay, presumably, like so much else, in her mind. She had had her tubes blown, painfully and unforgettably, to facilitate conception, but it had made no difference. For fifteen years she endured the monthly cycle of hope followed by disappointment, and bore the weight of David's sorrow, as she, his wife, deprived him of his earthly immortality, his children. 'Of course,' he said sadly, 'you are an only child. Only children are often infertile. The sins of the fathers –' David regarded fecundity as a blessing; the sign of a woman in tune with God's universe. He had married Deidre, he vaguely and hurtfully let it be known, on the rebound from a young woman who had gone on to have seven children.

David's fertility remained unquestioned and unexamined. A sperm count would surely have proved nothing. His sperm was plentiful and he had no sexual problems that he was aware of. To ejaculate into a test-tube to prove a point smacked uncomfortably of Onanism.

The matter of the mumps came up during the time of Deidre's menopause, a month or so after her, presumably, last period. David had been in the school sanatorium with mumps: she had heard him saying so to a distraught mother, adding 'Oh, mumps! Nothing in a boy under fourteen. Be thankful he has them now, not later.'

So, he was aware that mumps were dangerous. And Deidre knew well enough that David had lived in the world of school sanatoria after the age of fourteen, not before. Why had he never mentioned it to her? And while she wondered, and pondered, and hesitated to ask, toothpaste began to ooze from tubes, and rose trees were uprooted in the garden, and his seedlings trampled by unseen boots, and his clothes in the wardrobe tumbled in a pile to the ground, and Deidre stole money to buy mending glue, and finally went to the doctor.

'Most men,' said the doctor, 'confuse impotence with infertility and believe that mumps cause the former, not the latter.'

Back to square one. Perhaps he didn't know. 'Why have you *really* come?' asked the doctor, recently back from a course in patient-doctor relations.

Deidre offered him an account of her domestic phenomena, as she had not meant to do. He prescribed valium and asked her to come back in a week. She did.

'Any better? Does the valium help?'

'At least when I see things falling, I don't mind so much.'

'But you still see them falling?'

'Yes.'

'Does your husband see them too?'

'He's never there when they do.'

Now what was any thinking doctor to make of that?

'We could try hormone replacement therapy,' he said.

'No,' said Deidre.

'Then what do you want me to do?'

'If I could only feel angry with my husband,' said Deidre, 'instead of forever understanding and forgiving him, I might get it to stop. As it is; I am releasing too much kinetic energy.'

There were patients waiting. They had migraines, eczema and boils. He gave her more valium, which she did not take.

Deidre, or some expression of Deidre, went home and churned up the lawn and tore the gate off its hinges. The other Deidre raked and smoothed, resuscitated and blamed a perfectly innocent child for the gate. A child. It would have taken a forty-stone giant to twist the hinges so, but no one stopped, fortunately, to think about that. The child went to bed without supper for swinging on the vicar's gate.

The wound on Deidre's finger gaped open in an unpleasant way. She thought she could see the white bone within the bloodless flesh.

Deidre went upstairs to the bathroom, where David washed his wife's blood from his grandmother's hankie. 'David,' said Deidre, 'perhaps I should have a stitch in my finger?'

David had the toothmug in his hand. His jaw was open, his eyes wide with shock. He had somehow smeared toothpaste on his black lapel. 'This mug has been broken and mended. Why was I not told? Did you do it?'

The toothmug dated from the late eighteenth century and was worn, cracked and chipped, but David loved it. It had been one of the first things to go, and Deidre had not mended it with her usual care, thinking, mistakenly, that one more crack among so many would scarcely be noticed.

'I am horrified,' said David.

'Sorry,' said Deidre.

'You always break my things, never your own.'

'I thought that when you got married,' said Deidre, with the carelessness of desperation, for surely now David would start on an inspection of his belongings and all would be discovered, 'things stopped being yours and mine and became ours.'

'Married! You and I have never been married, not in the sight of God, and I thank Him for it.'

There. He had said what had been unsaid for years, but there was no relief in it, for either of them. There came a crash of breaking china from downstairs. David ran down to the kitchen, where the noise came from, but could see no sign of damage. He moved into the living room. Deidre followed dutifully. 'You've shattered my life,' said David. 'We have nothing in common. You have been a burden since the beginning. I wanted a happy, warm, loving house. I wanted children.'

'I suppose,' said Deidre, 'you'll be saying next that my not having children is God's punishment?'

'Yes,' said David.

'Nothing to do with your mumps?'

David was silent, taken aback. Out of the corner of her eye Deidre saw the Ming vase move.

'You are a sadistic person,' said David, eventually. 'Even the pains and humiliations of long ago are not safe from you. You revive them.'

'You knew all the time,' said Deidre. 'You were infertile, not me. You made me take the blame. And it's too late for me now.'

The Ming vase rocked to the edge of the shelf: Deidre moved to push it back, but not quickly enough. It fell and broke.

David cried out in pain and rage. It was as if he himself had broken.

'You did it on purpose,' he wept. 'You hate me.'

Deidre went upstairs and packed her clothes. She would stay with her mother while she planned some kind of new life for herself. She would be happier anywhere in the world but here, sharing a house with a ghost.

David moved through the house, weeping, but for his treasures, not for his wife. He took a wicker basket and in it laid tenderly – as if they were the bodies of children – the many broken and mended vases and bowls and dishes which he found. Sometimes the joins were skilful and bareful detectable to his moving forefinger: sometimes careless. But everything was spoilt. What had been perfect was now second-rate and without value. The finds in junkshops, the gifts from old ladies, the few small nick-nacks which had come to him from his dead mother – his whole past destroyed by his wife's single-minded malice and cunning.

He carried the basket to the kitchen, and sat with his head in his hands.

Deidre left without saying another word. Out of the door, through the broken garden gate, into the night, through the churchyard, for the powers of the dead disturbed her less than the powers of the living, and to the bus station.

David sat. The smell of rot from the sink drawer was powerful enough, presently, to make him lift his head.

The cold tap started to run. A faulty washer, he concluded. He moved to turn it off, but the valve was already closed. 'Deidre!' he called, 'what have you done with the kitchen tap?' He did not know why he spoke, for Deidre was gone.

The whole top of the dresser fell forward on to the ground. Porcelain shattered and earthenware powdered. He could hear the little pings of the Eucharist bell in the Church next door announcing the presence of God.

He thought perhaps there was an earthquake, but the central light hung still and quiet. Upstairs heavy feet bumped to and fro, dragging, wrenching and banging. Outside the window the black trees rocked so fiercely that he thought he would be safer in than out. The gas taps of the cooker were on and he could smell gas, mixed with fumes from the coal fire where Deidre's darning had been piled up and was now smouldering. He closed his eyes.

He was not frightened. He knew that he saw and heard these things, but that they had no substance in the real world. They were a distortion of the facts, as water becomes wine in the communion service and bread becomes the flesh of the Saviour.

When next he opened his eyes the dresser was restored, the socks still lay in the mending basket, the air was quiet.

Sensory delusions, that was all, brought about by shock. But unpleasant, all the same. Deidre's fault. David went upstairs to sleep but could not open the bedroom door. He thought perhaps Deidre had locked it behind her, out of spite. He was tired. He slept in the spare room, peacefully, without the irritant of Deidre's warmth beside him.

In the morning the window cleaner arrived to do the windows which Deidre could not reach. He could not get into the bedroom through the door, so David held the ladder while he got in through the window.

'Funny sort of burglars,' the window cleaner said to the police, later. 'They'd thrown everything about, furniture, clothes, the lot, all upside down and everywhere. The wardrobe was wrong way up and blocking the door. And the carpet! Great heavy thick thing. They'd picked it right off the floor, and wrung it out as if it was a dishcloth, and wedged it between the floor and the ceiling. The Rev and three strong men were all morning trying to untwist it but they couldn't. Now what sort of burglars can do a thing like that? If you ask me –' which they didn't, of course. They wrote the matter down on their files as U.P., or Unexplained Phenomena.

'She was a very strong woman,' said David to his new young lady organist. 'She did all that to my things and then somehow got out by the window. She wanted to frighten me, and make me believe in ghosts. That was the level of her spiritual potential, I'm afraid.'

Later they were to marry, but had no children, which as he was growing older was something of a relief though a disappointment to her, and to the parish.

Elizabeth Walter

DUAL CONTROL

'YOU ought to have stopped.'

'For God's sake, shut up, Freda.'

'Well, you should have. You ought to have made sure she was all right.'

'Of course she's all right.'

'How do you know? You didn't stop to find out, did you?'

'Do you want me to go back? We're late enough as it is, thanks to your fooling about getting ready, but I don't suppose the Bradys'll notice if we're late. I don't suppose they'll notice if we never turn up, though after the way you angled for that invitation . . .'

'That's right, blame it all on me. We could have left half an hour ago if you hadn't been late home from the office.'

'How often do I have to tell you that business isn't a matter of nine to five?'

'No, it's a matter of the Bradys, isn't it? You were keen enough we should get asked. Where were you anyway? Drinking with the boys? Or smooching with some floozie?'

'Please yourself. Either could be correct.'

'If you weren't driving, I'd hit you.'

'Try something unconventional for a change.'

'Why don't you try remembering I'm your wife –'

'Give me a chance to forget it!'

'– and that we're going to a party where you'll be expected to behave.'

'I'll behave all right.'

'To me as well as to other women.'

'You mean you'll let me off the leash?'

'Oh, you don't give a damn about *my* feelings!'

'Look, if it hadn't been for you, I should have stopped tonight.'

'Yes, you'd have given a pretty girl a lift if you'd been on your own. I believe you. The trouble is, she thought you were going to stop.'

'So I was. Then I saw she was very pretty, and – Christ, Freda, you know what you're like. I've only got to be polite to a woman who's younger and prettier than you are – and believe me, there are plenty of them – and you stage one of your scenes.'

'I certainly try to head off the worst of the scandals. Really, Eric, do you think people don't know?'

'If they do, do you think they don't understand why I do it? They've only got to look at you . . . That's right, cry and ruin that fancy make-up. All this because I *didn't* give a pretty girl a lift.'

'But she signalled. You slowed down. She thought you were going to . . .'

'She won't jump to conclusions next time.'

'She may not jump at all. Eric, I think we ought to forget the Bradys. I think we ought to go back.'

'To find Cinderella has been given a lift by Prince Charming and been spirited away to the ball?'

'She was obviously going to a party. Suppose it's to the Bradys' and she's there?'

'Don't worry, she couldn't have seen what we looked like.'

'Could she remember the car?'

'No, she didn't have time.'

'You mean she didn't have time before you hit her.'

'God damn it, Freda, what do you expect me to do when a girl steps in front of the car just as I decide – for your sake – I'm not stopping? It wasn't much more than a shove.'

'It knocked her over.'

'She was off balance. It wouldn't have taken more than a touch.'

'But she fell. I saw her go backwards. And I'm sure there was blood on her head.'

'On a dark road the light's deceptive. You saw a shadow.'

'I wish to God I thought it was.'

'Look here, Freda, pull yourself together. I'm sorry about it, of course, but it would make everything worse to go back and apologise.'

'Then what are you stopping for?'

'So that you can put your face to rights and I can make sure the car isn't damaged.'

'If it is, I suppose you'll go back.'

'You underestimate me, as usual. No, if it is I shall drive gently into that tree. It will give us an excuse for arriving late at the Bradys' and explain the damage away.'

'But the girl may be lying there injured.'

'The road isn't that lonely, you know, and her car had obviously broken down. There'll be plenty of people willing to help a damsel in distress . . . Yes, it's as I thought. The car isn't even scratched. I thought we might have a dent in the wing, but it seems luck is on our side. So now, Freda, old girl, I'll have a nip from that flask you've got in your handbag.'

'I don't know what you mean.'

'Oh yes you do. You're never without it, and it needs a refill pretty often by now.'

'I can't think what's come over you, Eric.'

'Call it delayed shock. Are you going to give it me or do I have to help myself?'

'I can't imagine – Eric, let go! You're hurting!'

'The truth does hurt at times. Do you think I didn't know you had what's called a drinking problem? You needn't pretend with me.'

'It's my money. I can spend it how I choose.'

'Of course, my love. Don't stop reminding me that I'm your pensioner, but thanks anyway for your booze.'

'I didn't mean that. Oh Eric, I get so lonely, you don't know. And even when you're home you don't take any notice of me. I can't bear it. I love you so.'

'Surely you can't have reached the maudlin stage already? What are the Bradys going to think?'

'I don't give a damn about the Bradys. I keep thinking about that girl.'

'Well, I give a damn about the Bradys. They could be important to me. And I'm not going to ruin a good contact because my wife develops sudden scruples.'

'Won't it ruin it if they know you left a girl for dead by the roadside?'

'Maybe, but they won't know.'

'They will. If you don't go back, I'll tell them.'

'That sounds very much like blackmail, and that's a game that two can play.'

'What do you mean?'

'Who was driving the car, Freda?'

'You were.'

'Can you prove that?'

'As much as you can prove that I was.'

'Ah, but it's not as simple as that. Such an accusation would oblige me to tell the police about your drinking. A lot of unpleasant things would come out. I should think manslaughter is the least you'd get away with, and that could get you five years. Because please note that apart from that swig I am stone cold sober, whereas your blood alcohol is perpetually high. In addition, you're in a state of hysteria. Who d'you think would be believed – you or I?'

'You wouldn't do that, Eric. Not to your wife. Not to me.'

'Sooner than I would to anyone, but it won't come to that, will it, my dear?'

'I've a good mind to –'

'Quite, but I should forget it.'

'Eric, don't you love me at all?'

'For God's sake, Freda, not that now, of all times. I married you, didn't I? Ten years ago you were a good-looking thirty —'

'And you were a smart young salesman on the make.'

'So?'

'You needed capital to start your own business.'

'You offered to lend it me. And I've paid you interest.'

'And borrowed more capital.'

'It's a matter of safeguarding what we've got.'

'What we've got. That's rich! You hadn't a penny. Eric, don't start the car like that. You may not be drunk but anyone would think you are, the way you're driving. No wonder you hit that girl. And it wasn't just a shove. I think you've killed her.'

'For God's sake, Freda, shut up!'

'Well, it was a good party, wasn't it?'

'Yes.'

'Moira Brady's a marvellous hostess.'

'Yes.'

'Jack Brady's a lucky man. We ought to ask them back some time, don't you think?'

'Yes.'

'What's got into you? Cat got your tongue? You're a fine companion. We go to a terrific party and all you can say is Yes.'

'I'm thinking about that girl.'

'She was all right, wasn't she? Except for some mud on her dress. Did she say anything about it?'

'She said she'd fallen over.'

'She was speaking the literal truth. Now I hope you're satisfied I didn't hurt her.'

'She certainly looked all right.'

'You can say that again. Life and soul of the party, and obviously popular.'

'You spent enough time with her.'

'Here we go again. Do you have to spend the whole evening watching me?'

'I didn't, but every time I looked, you were with her.'

'She seemed to enjoy my company. Some women do, you know.'

'Don't torment me, Eric. I've got a headache.'

'So have I, as a matter of fact. Shall I open a window?'

'If it isn't too draughty . . . What was the girl's name?'

'Gisela.'

'It suits her, doesn't it? How did she get to the Bradys'?'

'I didn't ask.'

'It's funny, but I never saw her go.'

'I did. She left early because she said something about her car having engine trouble. I suppose someone was giving her a lift.'

'I wonder if her car's still there?'

'It won't be. She'll have got some garage to tow it away.'

'Don't be too sure. They're not so keen on coming out at nights in the country, unless something's blocking the road.'

'I believe you're right. That's it, isn't it – drawn up on the grass verge.'

'Yes. And Eric, that's her. She's hailing us.'

'And this time, I'm really going to stop.'

'What on earth can have happened?'

'It looks like another accident. That's fresh mud on her dress.'

'And fresh blood on her head! Eric, her face is all bloody!'

'It can't be as bad as it looks. She's not unconscious. A little blood can go a very long way. Just keep calm, Freda, and maybe that flask of yours will come in handy. I'll get out and see what's up . . . It's all right, Gisela. You'll be all right. It's me, Eric Andrews. We met at the Bradys' just now. My dear girl, you're in a state. What in God's name happened? Has someone tried to murder you? Here, lean on me . . .'

'Eric, what's the matter? Why have you left her alone? Gisela . . .'

'Christ, Freda, shut that window! And make sure your door's locked.'

'What is it? You look as if you'd seen a ghost.'

'She *is* a ghost . . . Give me that flask . . . That's better.'

'What do you mean – a ghost?'

'There's nothing there when you go up to her. Only a coldness in the air.'

'But that's nonsense. You can't see through her. Look, she's still standing there. She's flesh and blood – blood certainly.'

'Is there blood on my hand?'

'No, but it's shaking.'

'You bet it is. So am I. I tell you, Freda, I put out my hand to touch her – I *did* touch her – at least, I touched where she was standing – but she's got no body to touch.'

'She had a body at the Bradys'.'

'I wonder.'

'Well, you should know. You hung round her all the evening, making a spectacle of yourself.'

'I never touched her.'

'I'll bet it wasn't for want of trying.'

'Now I think of it, nobody touched her. She always seemed to stand a little apart.'

'But she ate and drank.'

'She didn't eat. She said she wasn't hungry. I don't remember seeing a glass in her hand.'

'Rubbish, Eric. I don't believe you. For some reason you don't want to help her. Are you afraid she'll recognise the car?'

'She has recognised it. That's why she's there. We – we must have killed her on the way to the party that time when we nearly stopped.'

'You mean when *you* nearly stopped. When you hit her. Oh God, what are we going to do?'

'Drive on, I think. She can't hurt us.'

'But she could get inside the car.'

'Not if we keep the doors locked.'

'Do you think locked doors can keep her out? Oh God, I wish I'd never come with you. Oh God, get me out of this. I never did anything. I wasn't driving. Oh God, I'm not responsible for what he does.'

'Oh no, you're not responsible for anything, are you, Freda? Does it occur to you that if it hadn't been for your damned jealousy I should have stopped?'

'You've given me cause enough for jealousy since we were married.'

'A man's got to get it somewhere, hasn't he? And you were pretty useless – admit it. You couldn't even produce a child.'

'You're heartless – heartless.'

'And you're spineless. A sponge, that's all you are.'

'I need a drink to keep me going, living with a bastard like you.'

'So we have to wait while you tank up and make ourselves late for the Bradys'. Do you realise, if we'd been earlier we shouldn't have seen that girl?'

'It's my fault again, is it?'

'Every bloody thing's your fault. I could have built up the business a whole lot faster if you'd put yourself out to entertain a bit. If I'd had a wife like Moira Brady, things would be very different from what they are.'

'You mean you'd make money instead of losing it.'

'What do you mean – losing it?'

'I can read a balance sheet, you know. Well, you're not getting any more of my money. "Safeguarding our interests" I don't think! Paying your creditors is more like it.'

'Now look here, Freda, I've had enough of this.'

'So have I. But I'm not walking home so there's no point in stopping.'

'Then try getting this straight for a change –'

'Eric, there's that girl again.'

'What are you talking about? Anyone would think you'd got DTs.'

'Look – she's bending down to speak to you. She's trying to open your door.'

'Christ!'

'Eric, don't start the car like that. Don't drive so furiously. What are you trying to do?'

'I'm trying to outdistance her.'

'But the speed limit . . .'

'Damn the speed limit! What's the good of having a powerful car if you don't use it? . . . That's right. You hit the bottle again.'

'But the way you're driving! You ignored a halt sign. That lorry driver had to cram on his brakes.'

'What the hell! Look round and see if you can see her.'

'She's right behind us, Eric.'

'What, in her car?'

'No, she seems to be floating a little way above the ground. But she's moving fast. I can see her hair streaming out behind her.'

'Well, we're doing seventy-five ourselves.'

'But we can't go on like this for ever. Sooner or later we've got to get out.'

'Sooner or later she's got to get tired of this caper.'

'Where are we? This isn't the way home.'

'Do you want her following us home? I want to lose her. What do you take me for?'

'A bastard who's ruined my life and ended that poor girl's.'

'No one warned me you'd ruin mine. I wish they had. I might have listened. Warnings are only given to the deaf . . . Look again to see if Gisela's still following.'

'She's just behind us. Oh Eric, her eyes are wide and staring. She looks horribly, horribly dead. Do you suppose she'll ever stop following us? Gisela. It's a form of Giselle. Perhaps she's like the girl in the ballet and condemned to drive motorists to death instead of dancers.'

'Your cultural pretensions are impressive. Is your geography as good?'

'What do you mean?'

'I mean where the hell are we? I swear I've never seen this road before. It doesn't look like a road in southern England. More like the North Yorkshire moors, except that even there there's some habitation. Besides, we couldn't have driven that far.'

'There's a signpost at this next crossroads if you'll slow down enough for me to read . . .'

'Well?'

'I don't understand it, Eric. All four arms of the signpost are blank.'

'Vandals painted them out.'

'Vandals! In this desolate, isolated spot? Oh Eric, I don't like this. Suppose we're condemned to go on driving for ever?'

'No, Freda, the petrol would give out.'

'But the gauge has been at nought for ages. Hadn't you noticed?'

'What? So it is. But the car's going like a bird.'

'Couldn't you slow down a bit? I know you didn't for the signpost, but she – she's not so close behind us now . . . Please, Eric, my head's still aching.'

'What do you think I'm trying to do?'

'But we're doing eighty . . . I knew it. We'll have to go on driving till we die.'

'Don't be such an utter bloody fool. I admit we've seen a ghost – something I never believed existed. I admit I've lost control of this damn car and I don't know how she keeps running on no petrol. I also admit I don't know where we are. But for all this there's got to be a rational explanation. Some time-switch in our minds. Some change of state.'

'That's it! Eric, what's the last landmark you can remember?'

'That blanked-out signpost.'

'Not that. I mean the last normal sign.'

'You said there was a halt sign, but I must say I never saw it.'

'You drove right through it, that's why. We shot straight in front of a lorry. I think – oh Eric, I think we're dead.'

'Dead! You must be joking. Better have another drink.'

'I can't. The flask's empty. Besides, the dead don't drink. Or eat. They're like Gisela. You can't touch them. There's nothing there.'

'Where's Gisela now?'

'A long, long way behind us. After all, she's had her revenge.'

'You're hysterical, Freda. You're raving.'

'What do you expect but weeping and wailing? We're in Hell.'

'The religious beliefs of childhood reasserting themselves.'

'Well, what do you think Hell is? Don't hurry, you've got eternity to answer in. But I know what *I* think it is. It's the two of us driving on alone. For ever. Just the two of us, Eric. For evermore.'

Sara Maitland

LADY WITH UNICORN

THE series of five tapestries at Cluny – *La Dame au Licorne* – and the series of six in New York – *The Hunt of the Unicorn* – are completely different, depict different themes, have different purposes and together, united in imagination, against all good sense, form the apogée of a myth whose origins are lost in the magical Orient, and whose meanings are hidden in the core of a religion, which, against the will of its own humble heart, has come to dominate the world. The twin and terrible themes of purity and passion, are woven together too tightly in those tapestries, and we have lost the spell that can separate and so reunite them.

The two series were made at the same time – the fifteenth century – and in the same country – France. But good fortune has dictated that, as the speed of travel has increased, they have moved steadily further apart. It is unusual to see both sets while still so young as to be still permeable by such powerful and ancient myths; it is extraordinarily unlucky to see them both within a single moon-cycle of menarche. And this was Clare's malchance. And the timing was fatal for her: the previous virgin lady of the unicorn, a happy Italian peasant woman who had been able to carry her dangerous destiny safely into the heart of a convent where she had lived with great joy and considerable usefulness for seventy-eight years, had recently died, and the unicorn, bereft of that long sweet simple relationship, one of the happiest it had ever enjoyed, had been impatient. Clare stood a few entranced moments in front of the image of the unicorn and fell in love. And the unicorn responded as it will to that moment of innocence, taking possession of her heart and her soul to meet its own needs, for it is an untamed and ferocious beast.

So when, some years later, she first came to the university with its pale towers and pale poets, people said that Clare reminded them of someone they had seen before, but they could not remember who. Clare knew who, but she did not tell; in fact she did everything she could to disguise the likeness, even trying to cover her curiously high forehead and perfectly hemispheric eyebrows with an unsuccessful fringe, which did not suit her, though she did not care. And though many people found her distance alarming, many others found the same quality both appealing and challenging. They were all very young and still able to speak of sexual conquest as though it were a gift to be bestowed and of those that did not want the gift, even half-packaged and discourteously offered, as victims of a serious but curable malaise.

Clare was clever and well-educated, she had charming manners, that somehow scary beauty, an easy hospitality, a highly literary wit, and a gentle sweetness. Nonetheless, she never seemed quite to belong to and with other people, who found her strange and therefore desirable. They could not know the impossibility of their desire; they could not know that she already had a lover, a secret and dangerous lover. She herself did not know the danger, only the delight.

Throughout her adolescence the unicorn had been a comfort and a haven for her. Quickly she had learned the power of her summoning. She had only to go deep into the forests of her mind, where the trees were tidily ranged and pleached alleys opened up between them. There she could sit, on soft green moss studded with jewel-like flowers, while birds not known to the ornithologists sang around her, and wait. At first the waiting was chancy; but later, and especially once her high, wide-spaced breasts had grown, she could call in her will and the great white unicorn with his long spiralled horn the colour of moonbeams on water and his delicate ankle bones would come, picking his way through the forest to her.

He would come and they would play together. They could escape from the material and trying world to rampage the hills; flirting with the power of storms, riding out the wind and lightning, roaring back to the power of thunder. Better still perhaps, when they were both tired, the unicorn would come where she sat and lay his great fierce head against her heart, tamed in all his terrible strength and purity. He would spread the warm silk of his great mane gently across her stomach and they would be at peace together.

And she learned in that loving to see the world's turning, to know the shaping and growing and meaning of wild things and of the stars themselves. And she could not, being untaught, know that it was dangerous to have a spirit which rose like a fish in a cool pool to the lure of a joyful pink morning and a heart that was inflamed by summer thunder storms.

Gradually, too, she learned the rules of her fierce lover, the bindings to fidelity and secrecy. But she did not, unguided as most young women of our days are, fully understand. She was meant to control the unicorn, command, bend and bind the magic beast to her royal will, but she did not. She allowed herself a dangerous tenderness towards her lover and that was a fatal error. She let him come and go as he pleased, she let him master her imagination, she let him rule her and he grew fiercer and more dangerous still under such improper handling. Chastity is a power not a negation, but nobody told her this. She had no one to help her. The unicorn became not her obedient servant but her Lord and Master, the sole source of her joy, of her interest, of her engagement.

So naturally she seemed strange and distant to her peers. She had friends, but she did not know she needed them. She worked hard, but without passion; and so failed to find a way into those medieval or theological studies that might have helped her to deal with her destiny, or into the more modern areas of psychoanalysis or politics which might have exorcised her haunting.

For virginity may be a moment of chance, but chastity is a harsh virtue and one that must be hunted down the cold, sharp crags of self-knowledge.

And then one day, sitting curled on a floor, drinking a cup of instant coffee in the company of some pleasant people, she heard a voice say with considerable indignation:

'Don't be stupid, of course unicorns can't fly; winged horses fly, unicorns don't.'

She looked up, and those huge round eyes in the pale face met a pair of grey ones, and her whole face lit up with recognition.

He was a lovely youth, William was, and how could he not be enchanted by a glance so radiantly welcoming? He could hardly have interpreted her look correctly, particularly as he had little knowledge and less concern about the habits of mythological beasts and had been merely jibing at a friend. He saw an astonishingly lovely woman greeting him with an entrancing smile. She, poor fool, saw a Man who Understood.

He walked her back to her digs chatting of mutual friends, nineteenth-century politics and holiday plans. And once she laughed and swept her hair back off her face with her forearm. He looked at her and said, 'I know who you look like; you look like the wonderful lady in that unicorn tapestry.'

And she blushed, rosy and sweet on her pale face; not with shame but with delight. He had recognised her and she was safe. But he was baffled. He did not understand the blush and so joked, 'Fair Lady, may I be your unicorn and lay my head against your virgin breast.'

At that she looked scared, like a little child, and he was ashamed of himself. He saw and misinterpreted her vulnerability, with only such arrogance as is unsurprising.

'I'm sorry,' he said gently, 'I'd rather be your "parfait, gentil knight", to serve and to obey.'

And in her careful innocence she believed him.

She believed because she wanted to believe; because she was lonely; because the magical tyranny of the unicorn was too much for her, so young. And he, well, he was a nice boy, gentle, ordinary, untouched by magic white or black, and responding mainly to the welcome in her, to her greeting of him as her soul-mate. Should she have told him? If she had he would not have understood. Her error was not in her silence but in her conviction that he did not need telling, that he already knew, whereas all he knew was that unicorns do not fly, and that she had an almost perfectly oval face which resembled a tapestry that his mother, a deft if slightly tasteless needlewoman, had once copied. Her face spoke to him not of strangeness, but of his mother sitting of an evening plunk-plunking her needle in and out of a stretched canvas. A homely image, but hardly one sufficiently powerful to protect a young man in this dangerous situation.

So they fell in love. Of a sort. A sort which even fifty years before would have been safe and pleasant for them both. But times change: new forces have been raised against unicorns and chastity. He knew she loved him. He assumed therefore that she desired him. His ignorance was no more abysmal than hers. She assumed he knew the rules of her strange game. They were both wrong.

And as winter came upon them and made her long solitary walks in woods and fields less inviting, made cosy and companionable evenings more inevitable, the tension inside her grew. She felt very frightened and very excited.

And soon William kissed her. In a moment of abstraction, perhaps, she responded. And she learned something that she had not known before: desire. Just a moment, for a second longer than ever before she clung to another human being, her lips asking as well as accepting, and her solitude for a passing instant evaporated.

She left him later to go home, and as she walked down the damp streets, she saw in front of her the unicorn picking its way across the street, its rump haughty towards her and he did not turn his head, vanishing into the jewel-bright forest just ahead and to the left of them, apparently without noticing her. And just for an instant, unexpectedly sudden, she felt a flash of irritation against her ancient friend. How dare he treat her with such contempt, how dare he treat the Lady so? She would not, she would not stoop to charm him back, to seduce and to cajole. She tasted the clean, sweet, distant flavour of William's toothpaste in her mouth and turned away from the forest with resolution. She had spoiled the animal, she had been too kind, too indulgent.

But later in the night she woke confused, and mounting a little dappled pony of dreams she rode off into the wood seeking her own pleasure. The grass was soft as always and scattered with tiny scarlet and white flowers. She sat down under her tree and waited. She knew, she could hear the unicorn in the wood, searching for something that he could not find; he was wandering somewhere in the dark trees behind her, sniffing the air anxiously and pawing the ground with his hooves. She knew he was looking for her and did not understand his difficulty. Slowly she pulled her sweatshirt over her head, thinking that her bare breasts would help him, although he had never needed such assistance before; she noticed almost amazed that her nipples were hard and tight. She sat there, naked from the waist up and called to him, but when he turned his head he did not seem to see her. He paced over her stretched out legs and disappeared into the woods beyond. She sat there for a while overwhelmed by desolation and aware that the tightness in her nipples was now caused solely by the bitter cold. There was nothing she could do. The unicorn had deserted her.

Her heart was broken. She was betrayed. And she was furious. She thought at once of William, her knight, her huntsman, whose duty it was to break down the thicket of her long sleep with the magic power of his sword. Who should recapture her milk-white unicorn and lead it into the King's palace of the real world for her, tamed and broken. She sat up on the bed in her midnight room and wanted him out of a terrible and vengeful desolation. Then she remembered, with overwhelming relief and with a stubbornness born too late, that she lived not in some mystical forest but in the real world of a university town and that she had indeed arranged to see him the next day. They were going to a party together. She curled up to sleep, embracing the memory of his gentle kisses with pleasure.

The next day came, suddenly sharply colder and with a heavy yellow smell in the air. She knew that it would snow, but all through the morning it did not snow. By the afternoon there was a wind that shook the very insides of her, but still it did not snow. Clare waited in mounting tension; by the late afternoon when the dark descended she felt she could wait no longer and she went outside into the evening. From the street she could see the pools of golden light made by the windows, each one sheltering warm people while the wind assaulted her. The unicorn loved such weather but she would not summon him to her, angry and hurt at his betrayal of the day before. All day she had fasted; she did not want to eat; the inside of her mouth was waiting too and there was an edge to her stomach, hard and real. It was silly to be so excited about a party, she told herself, and went and ran a bath. The noise of the taps was immensely reassuring, shutting out the howling outside. She lay warm and luxuriant and watched her stomach muscles quiver on the very surface of the water: she commanded them to relax and in the steamy heat they gradually did. But when she came to get dressed she found that her hands were trembling, awkward and clumsy, and she sat on her bed and tried to breathe smoothly.

Despite the waiting, when she went out she was overwhelmed: the whole world was changed, the darkness had deepened but only so that it could exhibit each white flake of snow more perfectly. It was snowing, not gently but horizontally, and the ice-hard flakes were driven down on the wind, unwilling, unable to settle. And their passionate restlessness met hers and caught her up in their mania so, driven herself, she leapt out from the shelter of her doorway and threw herself into the storm.

It was too much; she felt as though all her clothes would be stripped off her and she would be blown white and frail, another snowflake, into the void of the night. When she tried to run, as much in fear as in excitement, she started to slip and panic. Another wild gust inside her coat turned her terror into a kind of exultant madness and she battered her way up the road. The snow which was white against the black sky turned golden in the floating pools of the street lamps and then white again, as they flew out untouched. The snow on her face plated her hair back from her forehead and the cold began to snarl against her inner flesh. She went on, sometimes with the snow as implacable enemy determined to defeat her, and sometimes together with it, she a part of the storm and a body for the wind to play with. And the storm was the mane of the unicorn lashing her skin; the snow flakes were the turning of his lovely ankle bones and the wind the long sinews of his body, and she took his wildness for approval and was full of a fierce and crazy joy.

At length the wind blew her up against William's front door and she rang the bell. It was answered by someone from the ground-floor flat, but she did not notice. The wind carried her up the stairs and into his room; his warmth came out of it to meet her coldness. William looked up from his book and saw the amazing beauty of the wind and the storm and the snow on her high white forehead. He got up and came towards her.

'I didn't hear the bell,' he said, and his warm lips on her icy face released the storm inside her.

And they were together. Together on the rug in front of the small gas fire. He burning with her lovely coldness, she melted by his rising warmth. He knew somewhere out of his own experience that this was not right; not for her, not for him, but the passion of her wanting was stronger – breaking a thousand years of chastity in one wild storm of desire, and there was no place for tenderness in the desert place of her new need. She took him and mastered him and the fire melted the snow on her and turned her whiteness into rose and they lay together on the damp rug passionately.

In the hospital she did not speak. She did not have the energy. She wanted to explain, but the habit of silence was too ancient. It was important to explain, but there were no words.

The unicorn had come upon her unexpectedly even as she lay in William's arms, and in her happiness she had been glad to see him. She wanted to have her ancient friend and childhood playmate share this with her too. But the unicorn did not share. He had come to her with a wild and dangerous rush and her first joy had been broken by the glance of one eye which was red rimmed and stood away from the whiteness of his coat. There was to be no gentleness, and she had felt the slashing of his hooves, falling down on her from his great reared height. She had felt the crashing weight of his knees against her chest and her rib cage had been too frail and bird-like. She knew the authority of his fury; and she could not blame him, because she, who had loved him and accepted his love for so long, had been unfaithful to her high calling. He had trampled her and run her through, deep into her belly with his long horn, now rust-stained with her guts; and he had picked her up with his teeth biting deep across her shoulder and tossed her over onto her stomach and had held her there and penetrated into her and his breath, hotter and harsher than anything she had ever known or dreamed of, burned into her neck and she smelled the scorching of her own hair and there was vomit in her mouth and shit on her legs and no escape from the hardness of him. And the mud and grit of the trampled forest floor was in her eyes, her nostrils, her tongue, and the hardness of his hooves hammered into her pinned legs, and the hotness of him had been deep deep inside her, pounding and plunging at the heart of her in a rhythm she could not, did not, resist. Plunging in and down, and there was no possible escape, because of the mud and sick in her mouth and the terror on William's face as she had been shaken by the great monster; and there was no love, no love, but only the everlasting thrusting until there was no part of her gut unmoved by the unicorn. Without love but in anger, not delight but punishment, and she could have no appeal, no defence, no hope against him, because she, who had known the terms of his sweet loving, had been unfaithful. She had sinned and he owed her nothing but his fury, but rape and foulness and finality.

And when he had done with her he went away. He disappeared into the woods for ever and there would be no recall. For eternity now he would be as lost and lonely as she, for ever. Neither of them were virgins now, and the ancient charm was broken. It was her fault, she had been unfaithful, her fault, her sin.

And she wanted to explain and knew it was impossible, and in despair she would turn her face to the wall, away from all the caring, anxious eyes. She never saw the way they widened in shock at the sight of her wounded back: the huge, straight toothmarks in her shoulder, the deep round wounds, like stabs, in her white buttocks and the huge bruises across her arms and thighs, like extended semi-circles and digging deep into her flesh at the top of the curve.

Lisa St Aubin de Terán

DIAMOND JIM

THEY call it Tarlojee, that grey stretch of land that fans out from the Esequebo, and it's got a strange history buried under every rock and tree. It's a stony place, and where the fields have been cleared and the sugar grows and flowers with its grey fluff, the piles of stones make little hills like shrines in places. No wonder, then, that people forget the past when there's so much of it and all heaped up like that. So, who came and when, and whether they were Dutch or Scots or Portuguese, and whether they were good or bad, or stayed or died, nobody really cares or knows on Tarlojee.

The sun is too hot there to go filling your head with tales. It's enough to remember where the shifting sands lie along the river, and where the snakes are worst, and which of the many paths and tracks through the estate are safe. Everyone knows that the lands belong to the Hintzens, and they know they always have; and they can't help knowing that the Hintzens are mean and hard. And then, everyone knows about Diamond Jim and old man Hintzen's daughter, Miss Caroline.

That Caroline was wild, so they say. She didn't seem to have that boiled water and steel filings for blood that Germans often do, especially the old ones who've been out pushing back the jungle for so many years they forget to be properly human. She didn't even have the soft blood of the other rich folks, with their mixing of Spanish and Dutch. I've heard say that her mother somehow put the eye of the hurricane in her little girl's eye, and dead-hour sun in her blood and a goatskin drum in her heart. Not even New Amsterdam on a Saturday night was wild like her. She could make a bean stew into a banquet by laughing over it. I think the reason why those two lovers didn't get caught at first was because they were so wild no one could even imagine what they were getting up to. The last person to know about it on the whole of Tarlojee was old man Hintzen himself, and that was because he didn't know what imagination was, let alone possess any. So Miss Caroline and Diamond Jim spread two years of harvest of diamond seed over the fields and in the sheds, and, for all I know, in some of those empty rooms along the top of the big house where nobody ever goes.

It seems the good Lord didn't want to waste that fine seed, and Miss Caroline started growing big under the red sash round her middle.

Things like that will happen anywhere, and there's always trouble when it happens to rich folk. People like Diamond Jim though, they liked the style of him, the way he'd sit and hum under the guava tree with that diamond pin as big as a child's eye, fixing the bandanna round his neck. He had rum for everyone, real rum and not even dregs. And he had city stuff in his pockets. There were a lot of black men working in the fields, a lot of black men going home dusty and grey – with dirt. There were some brown men too, all the shades of the earth: red, brown, grey; and I suppose we all looked much the same with our trousers cut from the same bolt of cloth and tied round with lengths of the same string. There were ways of being different, mind you, in the shades of a bandanna round your neck, or the tilt of a fibre hat, or even the cut of your shirt. But when it came to who had what, we were all poor and we all had a lot of mouths to feed, and we used to joke that the cane hairs that stuck in our backs were the iron filings old man Hintzen had for spit because he talked so rough. Which made it only natural that we should all admire Diamond Jim. He wasn't just black, he shone. I swear his skin shone like the rings on his fingers and the great stone at his throat. And, when he smiled, he looked like he could swallow up the whole of Tarlojee in that smile. The kids used to say he could take anything and spit it out as diamonds.

I don't know why we called him Jim, because his name, I believe, was Walter. I don't know either, who his family were. He must have been somebody's son, and if they were about they would surely have claimed him when he came striding home with all his money and his confidence. Some say he must have seen Miss Caroline somewhere in town and followed her to Tarlojee and that was why he was there. But nobody knew for sure. The fact is he came and stayed, and, when he started messing with Miss Caroline, everyone just waited and held their breath for the deal that they liked that Diamond Jim for, and the dread they all had of old man Hintzen. Miss Caroline had so much charm, it was a weight for her to carry it about. It was as though she was born knowing what was to happen to her. All her high spirits seemed bottled up, and when she laughed it came out like an explosion of locked-away things. She used to say she liked the feel of the sun on the back of her neck. People who work with cane can't understand a thing like that. And she liked to lie in the grass and sit on the prickly cane leaves, and she never had any fear of snakes. That's all I know about her as a girl, just how strange she was and fanciful for the outdoors and full of life and laughter. She must have really loved to be alive to have lived on those twenty years in the tower, with nothing to see but the cracks of light through her boarded window and the walls cracking as the years went by.

I've heard talk of people dying of laughter, and I think that's just what killed that mismatched pair. When Caroline Hintzen laughed it unsettled everything from the Big House down to the river. It even made old men shudder and hold themselves, and the little kids were scared. It had a strange effect. The sound of it carried far and wide like the crashing of boulders along the river bed of a flood. She was said to look like an angel and to laugh like a witch.

I don't know, and I don't expect I ever shall, who did bewitch the other out in the orchard under the noses of the whole world, and Tarlojee was a world in those days. Whoever it was who began that crazy love affair, it soon reached such a pitch that it was just burning up worse than a cane fire with a following wind. There wasn't anyone left who didn't know about it. If they'd have run away, who knows how far they would have got. Maybe they knew that not all the diamonds that Jim owned or even all the diamonds left in the hills could save that white girl and her big black lover. Maybe they could have made a dash into the Dutch countryside and hid out there, but black is black and Diamond Jim wasn't exactly inconspicuous anywhere. Then, maybe they thought they were invisible, protected somehow by the Lord himself in their great love from the vengeance of a man so cold he didn't even know that love existed.

It seems the lovers lasted longer than anyone dared hope for, because of Hintzen's stubborn negation of the thing. While, every night as the sun sank into the river and the stars signalled across the fields, Miss Caroline's frenzied laughter was like a flare to some and a map reference to others. No matter where they went, the whole work force of Tarlojee, and even her sisters, knew where they were tumbling because of that manic braying that she did. There were times during the day, with no respect for the sun or the dead hours and no sense of a Sunday or rest, when the same thing would rise from field or hut as their lovemaking gathered pace.

Why, every day those two fools could have been caught. But it seems that time was suspended over Tarlojee while Miss Caroline nearly cloyed in the sweetness of her feelings for big Jim, while he sat of an evening and hummed with his back up against the grey bark of a guava tree, staring up at the stars with his eyes half closed, passing messages, it seemed, from his big diamond up into the sky. Whatever it was he learned from that, it seemed to keep him there and vulnerable, for all the months when he could have fled, alone or with the girl, and saved his life. He must have known that Hintzen would kill him when he knew. He must have known that, but didn't seem to care. Perhaps that's what the stars were telling him, that long after Hintzen died and his dust was spread, he, Diamond Jim, would still be sitting under his favourite tree, still humming his old tunes.

The rains came first, and they didn't look like the heaven-sent rain of other years because the storms kept coming down red. Then it must have been July when the bats died one night and everywhere around the house their thin furry bodies made a stretched grey layer like a carpet of tiny hidden bones. Later, it must have been in September, the yucca crop failed and the cane itself was slow to grow. That was when it became apparent that Miss Caroline was growing in its stead. Some girls get pregnant and they can conceal the thing for months on end, but Miss Caroline wasn't just big, she was massive.

There were some good people out on Tarlojee around her, and some of them worked hard to cover up her tracks. But she herself seemed to have set her face against her fate and not to care, because she flaunted her great belly as though she was the proudest mother-to-be. And that went on until her father locked her up. I don't believe a mother would have let the old man drive her mad like he did. Maybe no mother could have saved poor Jim, but any one with a heart could have helped Miss Caroline. It was her misfortune to be orphaned of any kindness in that house.

On that first night, Miss Caroline was locked up in the liquor room. It was always cold in there, windowless, with just a grid and a heavy-bolted door. For a working man, that would be paradise, not punishment; but for the girl in love, used to a soft bed and company, it must have been hard. People said she called all through the night. Called and called, they said, with her great high voice winding through the cane and over the ridges.

Diamond Jim could have run away then, but he didn't. Instead, he stayed out all night long with his bright eyes glazed over, looking at the sky and humming fit to bust like a vibrating engine. Even the cicadas and the tree frogs stopped eventually and there was just the wailing from inside the big house and that one chord buzzing in Big Jim's throat. That was how he calmed her down. So the sun rose over the crest of the high fields, the ones that hillocked up beyond the dykes, with only the throbbing of Jim's voice to beckon it out of its sleep. He made the sun rise for him that day, willed it to set his stones in its gold because his own sun was going to set over Tarlojee before the day was out.

Eight o'clock saw the children passing by, scuttling past Jim as he sat waiting. They held the billycans close to their chests and looked away, giggling shyly, and then looked back at the black giant they'd heard was going to die. They regrouped behind him, dawdling on the dust track, disappointed. He'd looked the same. He'd even smiled. Condemned men shouldn't smile. Dying was a serious matter.

People knew that Hintzen would never settle for a shooting. He'd want a proper lynching. So the work force dwindled to the old and the boys that day, with a few women standing in for their men. All the strong ones stayed away drunk or feigning sickness, or just plain sick at the thought of helping to string up their hero. They couldn't do it. Well, Hintzen never had trusted his men, he hadn't counted on them before and he didn't count on them then. He sent away to New Amsterdam in the night, and four big mulattos rode into the forecourt that morning, with hats and spurs and their eyes red with greed and rum.

Diamond Jim watched them coming and he didn't stir. That was when the mystery happened. Those four mulattos swore that when they rode by, Jim's diamonds glistened and sparkled in the sun. But just moments later, when they went to get him, all his diamonds had gone. Now, no one passed by to take them, and the ground around him was dug and scratched and sieved and dug and no diamonds were ever found there . . . The mulattos said they thought Jim had hid the stones in his clothes, but after he died they stripped him bare and shredded the cloth. Nothing.

Before Jim died, Miss Caroline started calling again. But this time it wasn't just sounds and moans, it was straight words:

'Jim, don't ever leave me, Jim, Jim . . .'

Then he stood up and his big voice gathered that was rarely heard except to sing, and he called back to her, 'Caro, honey, I ain't going nowhere.'

The man never spoke again, as such. I don't really know what happened next. Some say they cast the rope around his neck and hanged him but he wouldn't die, so those four riders shot him through. Some say they had to shoot him to get the noose on him at all. One thing's for sure, though, the diamonds never were found. All down the years, vandals have been turning over Jim's bones to see if he swallowed those diamonds, but no good ever came of it, and no stones were ever found.

And no good ever came from hanging Jim. Before the year was out, the four mulattos who did it were jinxed, and they drank themselves to their ruin, haunted, they said, by the big smile on his face. And Hintzen? Even Hintzen wished he'd waited with his hanging, because four months later, when Miss Caroline gave birth to a huge grey baby girl, he wanted to kill Jim all over again and there was nothing left of him to hurt. Being a Christian, he couldn't destroy the child, but he took her away one night and returned a week later without her. That's what the towns were like, they'd swallow up the living and the dead. The baby must have been two weeks old then, and already turned as black as the man who made her.

After the baby went, Hintzen shifted his daughter into the stone tower, and that was when Miss Caroline started some serious calling. It seemed that she'd got the idea that all she had to do was cry out hard enough and Big Jim would answer her. Well, Miss Caroline stayed in that tower for twenty years calling out across the cane fields for the man she loved. She never gave up in all that time trying to summon him back to her. It must have been about a year later that her tired, sad voice cracked and turned into bouts of crazy laughter.

Her call had come to be a part of Tarlojee, like the animal call of the bush, and the keening of circling birds. It carried through the lanes between the sugar, and it settled in the daubed mud on the huts. People seemed to stir it in with their bean stew and corn. The dregs of her wailing sat with the pineapple rinds and fermented in pitchers of water. Jim's name was everywhere.

A lot happens in a lifetime, and things get forgotten. Details blur and disappear, and facts merge until only a few events stand out. Sometimes they're not events at all, just passing images, and sometimes they're so powerful they stop your blood from running for a while. That was how the laughter sounded after a year of tears. To hear Miss Caroline braying again chilled all of Tarlojee to the bone. It was her mating call, and, I suppose, it was all part of what held Jim to her because the night she started rattling her wild laugh about, Diamond Jim came back. He had his diamonds on again – the rings and the big one at his throat that communed with the stars. He sat all night under his guava tree and he hummed, a loud throbbing hum, and although no one touched him – because no one dared – he was there, smiling like he could, as though he knew something special, with his big teeth shining out and almost competing with the eye-diamond, the diamond that started it all, and gave him his name, and made him a myth.

A lot of nights have passed since then, and a lot of years, and Miss Caroline has been dead now for a long time, but Big Jim still sits out sometimes, waiting, and he still hums. And, although he's never done any of us any harm, there's no one goes down to the ruins of the Big House on a full moon. The kids nowadays laugh about him too, but there's not one of them eats guavas on Tarlojee or ever hums like a lost tune finding its way out of the sugar cane.

Angela Carter

✿

ASHPUTTLE: OR, THE MOTHER'S GHOST

A BURNED child lived in the ashes. No, not really burned – more charred, a little bit charred, like a stick half-burned and picked off the fire; she looked like charcoal and ashes because she lived in the ashes since her mother died and the hot ashes burned her, so she was scabbed and scarred. The burned child lived on the hearth, covered in ashes, as if she was still mourning.

After her mother died and was buried, her father forgot the mother and forgot the child and married the woman who used to rake the ashes, and that was why the child lived in the unraked ashes and there was nobody to brush her hair, so it stuck out like a mat, nor to wipe the dirt off her scabbed face and she had no heart to do it for herself, but she raked the ashes and slept beside the little cat and got the burned bits from the bottom of the pot to eat, scraping them out, squatting on the floor, by herself in front of the fire, not as if she were human, because she was still mourning.

Her mother was dead and buried but still felt perfect, exquisite pain of love when she looked up through the earth and saw the burned child covered in ashes.

'Milk the cow, burned child, and bring back all the milk,' said the stepmother, who used to rake the ashes and milk the cow before, but now the burned child did all that.

The ghost of the mother went into the cow.

'Drink some milk and grow fat,' said the mother's ghost.

The burned child pulled on the udder and drank enough milk before she took the bucket back and nobody saw and time passed and she grew fat, she grew breasts, she grew up.

There was a man the stepmother wanted and she asked him into the kitchen to give him his dinner, but she let the burned child cook it, although the stepmother did all the cooking before. After the burned child cooked the dinner the stepmother sent her off to milk the cow.

'I want that man for myself,' said the burned child to the cow.

The cow let down more milk, and more, and more, enough for the girl to have a drink and wash her face and wash her hands. When she washed her face, she washed the scabs off and now she was not burned at all, but the cow was empty.

'You must give your own milk, next time,' said the ghost of the mother inside the cow. 'You've milked me dry.'

The little cat came by. The ghost of the mother went into the cat.

'Your hair wants doing,' said the cat. 'Lie down.'

The little cat unpicked her raggy lugs with its clever paws until the burned child's hair hung down nicely, but it had been so snagged and tangled that the cat's claws were all pulled out before it was finished.

'Comb your own hair, next time,' said the cat. 'You've taken my strength away, I can't do it again.'

The burned child was clean and combed but stark naked. There was a bird sitting in the apple tree. The ghost of the mother left the cat and went into the bird. The bird struck its own breast with its beak. Blood poured down onto the burned child under the tree. It ran over her shoulders and covered her front and covered her back. She shouted out when it ran down her legs. When the bird had no more blood, the burned child got a red silk dress.

'Bleed your own dress, next time,' said the bird. 'I'm through with all that.'

The burned child went into the kitchen to show herself to the man. She was not burned any more, but lovely. The man left off looking at the stepmother and looked at the girl.

'Come home with me and let your stepmother stay and rake the ashes,' he said to her and off they went. He gave her a house and money. She did all right for herself.

'Now I can go to sleep,' said the ghost of the mother. 'Now everything is all right.'

NOTES ON THE AUTHORS

Lady Cynthia Asquith (1887-1960) was a pioneer editor of anthologies between the wars, notably *The Ghost Book* (1926), *Shudders* (1929) and *When Churchyards Yawn* (1931); and occasionally wrote ghost stories of her own which were collected as *This Mortal Coil* (US, 1947), revised as *What Dreams May Come* (GB, 1951). 'The Follower' was originally broadcast on BBC Radio in 1934, one of a series bearing the title 'Nightmares' (other contributors included Marjorie Bowen, Noel Streatfield, and Algernon Blackwood), later published in the anthology *My Grimmest Nightmare* (1935).

Enid Bagnold (1889-1981) is best known for her novel *National Velvet* (1935) and successful plays such as *The Chalk Garden* (1955). Her other novels include *The Happy Foreigner* (1920), *The Squire* (1938) and *The Loved and Envied* (1951). She served as a nurse during the First World War, but displeased the hospital authorities by basing her *Diary Without Dates* (1917) upon her V.A.D. experiences. 'The Amorous Ghost' was written in 1926.

Phyllis Bottome (1884-1963) had a distinguished career as a novelist, lasting for sixty years. Born in Kent, she spent many years abroad, in America and on the continent, but always considered England her home. Her novel *The Mortal Storm* (1937) received much praise and attention for its anti-Nazi theme, and her political expertise made her spokeswoman for the Ministry of Information during the Second World War. 'The Waiting-Room' originally appeared in *Strange Fruit* (1928).

Elizabeth Bowen (1899-1973) is one of the finest writers to come out of Ireland in the past hundred years, her best-known novels being *The Death of the Heart* (1938) and *The Heat of the Day* (1949). Among her varied collections of short stories (*Encounters* (1923), *The Cat Jumps* (1934), *The Demon Lover* (1945) from which 'The Happy Autumn Fields' is taken, and others) are some of the best weird and supernatural tales ever written. Several were inspired by the Second World War and most of them use uncanny elements indirectly to explore human reactions to fear.

'Marjorie Bowen' (1886-1952) was one of the pseudonyms of Mrs Gabrielle Margaret Vere Campbell Long. A sensitive child, hating her mother's bohemian life, she studied art before beginning a career as a historical novelist, children's author and short-story writer, with over 150 books to her name. The miniature stories included in this volume originally appeared as the headpiece and tailpiece in her collection

Dark Ann and other stories in 1927. The cream of her ghostly and weird short stories can be found in *The Last Bouquet* (1933) and *The Bishop of Hell* (1949).

Dorothy Kathleen Broster (1877-1950) was highly regarded as a leading historical novelist. At St Hilda's, Oxford, she took full honours in History, before women were admitted for degrees. When she returned after the First World War, she was in the first group of women to receive a BA and MA. Much admired for her accuracy as well as dramatic power, she is said to have consulted eighty works before embarking on *The Flight of the Heron* (1925). Her best supernatural fiction appeared in the rare collection *Couching at the Door* (1942), from which 'Juggernaut' is taken. The title story of this volume concerned a poet whose evil past haunts him in the form of a malignant feather boa constrictor.

Angela Carter (1940-), is one of the most inventive and original writers of fiction today. Amongst her novels are *The Magic Toyshop* (1967), *Heroes and Villains* (1969), *The Passion of New Eve* (1977) and *Nights at the Circus* (1985). Her short stories, which include *Fireworks* (1974), *The Bloody Chamber* (1979) and this new story 'Ashputtle', frequently draw on – and radically transform – traditional fairytales.

'E. M. Delafield' (1890-1943), an Anglicised simplification of her maiden name (Edmée Elizabeth Monica de la Pasture) was the daughter of the novelist Mrs Henry de la Pasture. Primarily known for the extremely funny *Provincial Lady* series, she wrote many other novels including *Thank Heaven Fasting* (1932), *Messalina of the Suburbs* (1923) (suggested by the Thompson-Bywaters murder case) and *The Way Things Are* (1927). She was also a local magistrate and bastion of the Women's Institute. Like *Diary of a Provincial Lady* (1930), 'Sophy Mason Comes Back' first appeared in the magazine *Time and Tide* in 1930.

Henrietta Dorothy Everett (1851-1923) was a popular novelist of the late Victorian and Edwardian era with many titles to her credit, including *A Bride Elect* (1896), *Miss Caroline* (1904), *Cousin Hugh* (1910), *Grey Countess* (1913) and *Malevola* (1914). Some of these appeared under a pseudonym, 'Theo Douglas'. She is best remembered today for her collection of ghost and horror stories, *The Death Mask* (1920), now a very rare book.

Stella Gibbons (1902-) achieved instant fame with her first novel, *Cold Comfort Farm* (1932), a witty parody of the Mary Webb/Sheila Kaye Smith school of regional fiction. Many other novels and short stories have followed since. This unusual and memorable tale is taken from her collection *Roaring Tower and other short stories* (1937).

Ellen Glasgow (1874-1945) enjoyed the distinction of being, along with Edith Wharton and Willa Cather, one of America's three foremost women novelists of her time. Her studies of Southern life include *The Deliverance* (1904), *Virginia* (1913), *Barren Ground* (1925), *The Sheltered Life* (1932) and *Vein of Iron* (1935). She also wrote comedies such as *They Stooped to Folly* (1929) and her autobiography, *The Woman Within* (1954), perhaps the most unforgettable self-portrait of an artist in American letters. She was a woman of advanced views, and an active supporter of women's suffrage. Her best short tales were published in 1923 in *The Shadowy Third & other stories*, now a very scarce book.

Hester Gorst (1887-), whose great-aunt was the celebrated Victorian author Mrs Gaskell, has been writing stories for nearly sixty years. Besides a few novels written under her maiden name (Hester Holland), Mrs Gorst contributed excellent tales of the supernatural to anthologies in the thirties, including *Horrors*, published by Philip Allan in 1933, in which 'The Doll's House' was included. Her best-known story, 'The Scream', was filmed in 1953 with Douglas Fairbanks Jnr and Constance Cummings. Mrs Gorst is also an artist and a retrospective of her work was recently shown in London.

Winifred Holtby (1898-1935), director of *Time and Tide* in the 1920s, and author of *South Riding* (1936), wrote several other novels of high merit and originality, among them *Poor Caroline* (1931), *Mandoa! Mandoa!* (1933), and *The Land of Green Ginger* (1927). Her best short stories, including 'The Voice of God', can be found in *Truth is Not Sober* (1934), and also *Pavements of Anderby* (1937). A campaigning feminist and an expert on international affairs, she was commemorated by her friend Vera Brittain in *Testament of Friendship* (1940).

Elizabeth Jane Howard (1923-) is best known for her novels *The Beautiful Visit* (1950), *The Long View* (1956) and *The Sea Change* (1959). From 1947 to 1950, she was Secretary of the Inland Waterways Association, and the memorable tale 'Three Miles Up', one of the finest ghost stories since the war, was written at that time. It first appeared in the collection *We Are For the Dark: Six Ghost Stories* (1951: containing three stories by her, and three by Robert Aickman).

Elizabeth Jenkins is especially noted for her biographies of *Lady Caroline Lamb* (1932), *Jane Austen* (1938), *Elizabeth the Great* (1958), and *Ten Fascinating Women* (1955); and her bestselling novel *The Tortoise and the Hare* (1954). She was awarded the OBE in 1981. 'On No Account, My Love' originally appeared in *The Third Ghost Book* (1955).

Pamela Hansford Johnson (1912-81), who married the writer C. P. Snow in 1950, was a distinguished critic and novelist for over forty-five years. Her first novel, *This Bed My Centre*, was published in 1935, and her talent for comedy is clear in the 'Dorothy Martin' novels, such as *The Unspeakable Skipton* (1959). She also wrote some very fine ghost stories, among them 'Ghost of Honour', 'Sloane Square', and the story reprinted here, 'The Empty Schoolroom', from *The Uncertain Element* (1950).

'Marjory E. Lambe' was one of several pseudonyms used by Gladys Gordon Trenery (1885-1938), a leading practitioner of the ghost story between the wars. This story first appeared in *Hutchinson's Mystery-Story Magazine* in March 1924, and was soon reprinted in the US under another pseudonym, 'G. G. Pendarves'. Although she wrote many occult and ghost stories, unfortunately they were never reprinted in book form and remain only in long-forgotten magazines on both sides of the Atlantic.

Margery Lawrence (1889-1969) was a devout believer in the supernatural, who wrote a fascinating book on the occult *Ferry Over Jordan* (1944) as well as over sixty ghost stories (several based on reported incidents) to her credit. Among her many novels, the best-known was *The Madonna of Seven Moons* (1931), made into a film starring Phyllis Calvert. The story reprinted here is taken from her very scarce book *Nights of the Round Table* (1926), in which twelve members of a club relate 'strange tales'.

Norah Lofts (1904-83) was a very successful novelist with 'an obsession about houses' and a fondness for ghost stories. 'Any ghost story finds in me a ready customer,' she said, 'though I prefer something less concrete than ladies in grey draperies and gentlemen in buff coats.' For her, the essence of a good ghost story, like the essence of the horror story, should lie in what lurks unseen behind the ordinary, often pleasant façade. 'A Curious Experience' appeared in *Woman's Journal* in 1971 and in her collection of twelve ghost stories, *Hauntings: Is There Anybody There?* (1975).

Rose Macaulay (1881-1958), satirical novelist and superb travel writer, won both popularity and critical respect with novels like *Told by an Idiot* (1923), *Crewe Train* (1926), *They Were Defeated* (1932), *The World My Wilderness* (1950) and *The Towers of Trebizond* (1956). In the year of her death, she was awarded the DBE. 'Whitewash' was written for Cynthia Asquith's *Second Ghost Book* in 1952.

Sara Maitland (1950-) won the Somerset Maugham Award in 1979 for her first novel, *Daughter of Jerusalem*. She has published a collection of short stories, *Telling Tales* (1983), another novel, *Virgin Territory* (1984), and a study of the music-hall artist and male impersonator, *Vesta Tilley* (1986). She lives in a Gothic vicarage in East London, and this is her first ghost story.

Flora MacDonald Mayor (1872-1932) is now attracting a steadily increasing number of admirers after years of neglect. Her important theme of the woman alone occurs in all three of her novels, *The Third Miss Symons* (1913), *The Rector's Daughter* (1924), and *The Squire's Daughter* (1929). Also long ignored, and worthy of revival, are her short stories – many with uncanny and ghostly elements – which were published posthumously in *The Room Opposite* (1935).

Edith Nesbit (1858-1924), the writer of such celebrated children's books as *The Railway Children* (1906), *The Magic City* (1910), *The Treasure Seekers* (1899) and *The Enchanted Castle* (1907), was a woman of enormous energy. In the years following her marriage to Hubert Bland she wrote, painted, recited poetry to earn money for the household, and became an active socialist, and a founder member of the Fabian Society. She broke from convention by wearing her hair short, smoking, and dressing in unfashionably loose and flowing clothes. Her fine supernatural tales appeared in leading magazines and the best including 'The Violet Car' were collected in *Fear* (1910). The story reprinted here is one of the earliest in the genre to feature a car.

Edith Olivier (1879-1948), wrote several fine novels between the wars including *The Love Child* (1927), *As Far as Jane's Grandmother's* (1929), and *Dwarf's Blood* (1931). Among her later non-fiction works are *Country Moods and Tenses* (1941), and *Four Victorian Ladies of Wiltshire* (1945). She wrote excellent ghost stories in the 1930s, among them 'Dead Men's Bones', 'The Caretaker's Story', and 'The Night Nurse's Story'. She was Mayor of Wilton (her birthplace in Wiltshire) from 1938 to 1941.

Eleanor Scott wrote five novels in the late 1920s and early 1930s including *War Among Ladies* (1928) and *Puss in the Corner* (1934) and two bestsellers on *Adventurous Women* (1933) and *Heroic Women* (1939). One reviewer of *Puss in the Corner* described her as 'a witty and discerning observer of female character, and more especially of the reactions of women to one another'. Little is known of her life and she is now chiefly remembered for her collection of brilliant supernatural tales, *Randalls Round* (1929), from which 'Will Ye No' Come Back Again?' is taken. She claimed that most of the ghost stories in her book had their origin in dreams.

May Sinclair (1863-1946), philosopher, biographer, novelist and short story writer, was a keen supporter of women's suffrage and an early devotee of psychoanalysis. She began her long writing career with *Nakiketas and other Poems* (under the name 'Julian Sinclair') in 1886. In her novels, which have been compared to those of Gissing, like *The Divine Fire* (1904) and *Three Sisters* (1914), she displayed considerable understanding of the lives of men and women in cramped and difficult circumstances, while in *May Olivier* (1919) and *Life and Death of Harriet Frean* (1922) she was one of the pioneers of the 'stream of consciousness' technique. Her collection, *Uncanny Stories* (1923), with illustrations by Jean de Bosschere, is now a collectors' item.

Elizabeth Taylor (1912-75), among the most admired and important of British post-war writers, has been extensively reprinted by Virago: *Palladian* (1946), *A View of the Harbour* (1949), *A Game of Hide and Seek* (1951), *The Sleeping Beauty* (1953), *Angel* (1957), *The Blush* (1958), *In a Summer Season* (1961), *The Soul of Kindness* (1964), *The Wedding Group* (1968), *Mrs Palfrey at the Claremont* (1971), and *The Devastating Boys* (1972), are all currently available as Virago Modern Classics. 'Poor Girl' originally appeared in *The Third Ghost Book* (1955).

Lisa St Aubin de Terán (1953-), novelist and poet, lived for seven years in the Venezuelan Andes. Winner of the Somerset Maugham Award for her first novel, *Keepers of the House* (1982), and the John Llewellyn Rees Prize for her second, *The Slow Train to Milan* (1983), she has published three further novels, *The Tiger* (1984), *The Bay of Silence* (1986) and *Black Idol* (1987). Much of her fiction, including the story published here for the first time, is rooted in her South American experience, combining powerful narrative with a strong sense of the fabulous.

Rosemary Timperley (1920-), the novelist, is Britain's finest living regular creator of ghost stories, and one of the most prolific. She has written well over a hundred short stories since her first, 'Christmas Meeting', appeared in *The Second Ghost Book* in 1952. Although her highly respected tales have been published in innumerable anthologies, they have sadly never been collected together in book form. The majority of her stories feature ghosts of the gentle and non-horrific variety. 'The Mistress in Black' is taken from *The Fifth Ghost Book* (1969).

Elizabeth Walter ranks among the finest British post-war writers to have specialised mainly in the art of the ghost story, and is now one of the most widely respected practitioners of the genre. Her collections of uncanny tales include: *Showfall* (1965), *The Sin Eater* (1967), *Davy Jones's Tale* (1971), *Come and Get Me* (1973) and an American assembly of her work, *In the Mist, and other uncanny encounters* (1979). 'Dual Control' is taken from *Dead Woman* (1975).

Mary Webb (1881-1927), born Mary Gladys Meredith, is best known for her passionate novels of rural Shropshire life such as *Precious Bane* (1924) and *Gone to Earth* (1917). Her style has a lyrical quality which owes much to her Welsh and Celtic ancestry. The sense of overhanging doom, combined with her love of nature, has often invited comparison with Thomas Hardy. The short story reprinted here was her last, and was first published in the year of her death.

Fay Weldon (1933-), novelist, playwright and television script-writer, is the author of superbly comic/ pathetic novels of female frustration from *The Fat Woman's Joke* (1967) to *Praxis* (1978) and *Life and Loves of A She-Devil* (1984), which also reveals her talent for the fantastic. 'Breakages' is taken from the anthology, *The Midnight Ghost Book* (1978).

Amy Catherine Robbins (1872-1927) was a versatile artist and writer, chiefly remembered now as the wife of H. G. Wells (whom she married in 1895). After her premature death, Wells collected twenty-one of her stories and poems into *The Book of Catherine Wells* (1928) from which 'The Ghost' is taken. In his touching introduction, Wells wrote: 'The personality of Catherine Wells predominates. In all these pieces you will find her brooding tenderness, her sense of invincible fatality, her exquisite appreciation of slight and lovely weakness and that predisposition towards a haunting, dreamland fantasy of fear which the courage and steadfastness of her substantial life repudiated altogether. Never I think in the work of any other writer has mood so predominated over action.'

Edith Wharton (1862-1937) spent her early years in New York, but for most of her adult life she lived in Europe, mainly in France. One of the leading women writers of her generation, she was a close personal friend of Henry James. Her novels include *The Valley of Decision* (1902), *The House of Mirth* (1905), *The Fruit of the Tree* (1907), *The Reef* (1912) and *The Age of Innocence* (1920). The ghosts in her cerebral short stories are often projections of men's mental obsessions. One of the finest examples, 'The Eyes', is taken from *Tales of Men and Ghosts* (1910).

THE VIRAGO BOOK OF VICTORIAN GHOST STORIES
Edited by Richard Dalby
Introduction by Jennifer Uglow

'Arching from an early pastiche by Charlotte Brontë to a turn-of-the-century tale by Willa Cather, this is a collection that is marvellous in more ways than one. With illuminating flair, Richard Dalby's collection of twenty stories shows off the ghost story in its heyday' – *Sunday Times*

'A must for anyone who enjoys being thrilled and disturbed by the people who arguably know how to do it best' – *Time Out*

'*The Virago Book of Victorian Ghost Stories* . . . pulls us back over the rim of years into a spooky yet reassuring past. The stories are fascinating' – *Observer*

The Virago Book of Victorian Ghost Stories stretches back in time to the sublime terrors of the nineteenth century: here are Charlotte Brontë, Elizabeth Gaskell, Mary Braddon, Amelia Edwards, Rhoda Broughton, Mrs Henry Wood, Vernon Lee, Violet Hunt, Gertrude Atherton, Willa Cather, and many others. A magnificent collection of some twenty tales, *The Virago Book of Victorian Ghost Stories* is both an important addition to literary history and a thrilling, chilling read.

REVENGE
Edited by Kate Saunders

'There are fates more terrible than death; weapons more keen than poniards, more noiseless than pistols. Women use such, and work out a subtler vengeance than men can conceive' – Louisa May Alcott

The stories in this collection show revenge in all its forms – from bloody, impulsive acts of violence, to the subtlest turning of the tables. Revenge is the deepest form of justice, and goes beyond any man-made law. Sometimes, not even death can stand in its way.

Including such past mistresses as Elizabeth Gaskell, Mary Braddon, and Winifred Holtby, and the cream of contemporary writers – among others Muriel Spark, Ruth Rendell, Shena Mackay, Emma Tennant, Alice Walker and Ellen Gilchrist – there are also new stories from Mary Flanagan, Candia McWilliam, Lucy Ellmann, Kate Saunders, Lisa St Aubin de Terán and Maureen Freely. All demonstrate that revenge, tragic or melodramatic, horrifying or hilarious, is *always* sweet.

THE VIRAGO BOOK OF FAIRY TALES

Edited by Angela Carter

Illustrations by Corinna Sargood

Once upon a time fairy tales weren't meant just for children, and neither is *The Virago Book of Fairy Tales*. This stunning collection contains lyrical tales, bloody tales, hilariously funny and ripely bawdy stories from countries around the world. And no drippy princesses or soppy fairies. Instead girls, women and crones, wise as serpents, gentle as doves and occasionally daft as brushes.

ANGELA CARTER has long had a passion for fairy tales. This collection reflects to the full her distinctive tastes and expertise in the area. One of Britain's most original writers, she is highly acclaimed for her novels, short stories and journalism. She has translated the fairy stories of Charles Perrault and adapted two of her works for film, the much praised *The Company of Wolves* and *The Magic Toyshop*.